Pamela is an award-winning author for both adults and children. She has a Doctorate of Creative Arts from the University of Technology, Sydney, where she has also lectured in creative writing. Under the name Pamela Freeman she wrote the historical novel *The Black Dress*, which won the NSW Premier's History Prize for 2006 and is now in its third edition. Pamela is also well known for her fantasy novels for adults, published by Orbit worldwide, the Castings Trilogy and her Aurealis Award–winning novel *Ember and Ash*. Pamela lives in Sydney with her husband and their son, and teaches at the Australian Writers' Centre. Her acclaimed novel *The Soldier's Wife* was published by Piatkus in 2015, followed by *The War Bride* in 2016 and *A Letter from Italy* in 2017. *The Desert Nurse* is her thirty-fourth book.

To find out more about the true story behind the book and to sign up to Pamela's newsletter, visit:

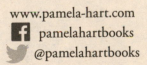

www.pamela-hart.com

pamelahartbooks

@pamelahartbooks

PAMELA
HART

The Desert Nurse

piatkus

PIATKUS

First published in Australia and New Zealand in 2018 by Hachette Australia
An imprint of Hachette Australia Pty Limited
First published in Great Britain in 2018 by Piatkus
This paperback edition published in 2019 by Piatkus

A CIP catalogue record for this book is available from the British Library.

ISBN 978-0-349-41714-1

Text design by Bookhouse, Sydney
Typeset by Bookhouse, Sydney

Printed and bound in Great Britain by Clays Ltd, Elcograf S.p.A.

Papers used by Piatkus are from well-managed forests
and other responsible sources.

Piatkus
An imprint of
Little, Brown Book Group
Carmelite House
50 Victoria Embankment
London EC4Y 0DZ

An Hachette UK Company
www.hachette.co.uk

www.littlebrown.co.uk

For Vicki, never-failing

CHAPTER 1

29 OCTOBER 1911

She's 21 today, 21 today
She's got the key of the door

'What on Earth?'

Laughing, Evelyn went to the parlour door. Harry was banging away on the piano, the morning light coming through the lace curtains to light up his blond hair:

Never been 21 before
And Pa says she can do as she likes
So shout, Hip Hip Hooray!
She's a jolly good fellow
21 today.

He finished with a loud if not exactly tuneful arpeggio and sprang up to hug her.

'Happy birthday, old girl!'

She hugged him back. It was so kind of Harry to have
come back from university for the weekend of her birthday.
A long trip in a rattling train and nothing entertaining to
do at the end of it. How many nineteen-year-old boys would
have done that? But in the years since their mother's death
they had drawn close.

'Thank you, dear,' she said. He produced a small package
from his pocket with a flourish.

'Not much,' he shrugged.

She undid the package – professionally wrapped, by the look
of it; Harry had never done up anything so neatly in his life.

A pair of surgical scissors, with her initials on the hilt.

'Oh, Harry!' She hugged him again, tears threatening to
fall, grateful beyond words for his unspoken support.

'That'll do, that'll do,' he said, backing away. 'By Jove, if
I'd known it would turn you into a watering pot I'd never
have given it to you!'

But when she smiled at him, he smiled back, and for a
moment it was as though they had never been parted.

'What's all this noise on a Sunday?' Their father glared
at them from the doorway, but his expression softened when
he saw Evelyn. 'Happy birthday, my dear,' he said. He, too,
produced a small box – but this was a jeweller's box, unwrapped.

'Thank you, Father.' She reached up to kiss his cheek,
and opened the box with a real sense of excitement. Would
it be the key of the door? Or, better yet, a safe deposit key
from the bank!

A pearl brooch. How . . . conventional.

'It was your mother's,' he said, and cleared his throat as
though moved. She bit her lip at her momentary disappointment,

and smiled at him. After all, she could afford to be generous. Today was the day of her liberation.

'It's very lovely,' she said, and pinned it onto her shoulder.

'Well, let's have breakfast,' her father said, with an air of someone who had brushed through a difficult situation better than he had expected.

She walked into the dining room happier than she had been for years. Finally of age. Finally able to follow her own path, instead of obediently following his. This was the day she shook off his rule over her once and for all. To return to the goals she'd laid out for herself when she was fourteen.

After her mother's long illness and death, she had expected to return to school – was prepared, even, to be put in the year below due to her absence, although she had been keeping up her studies as well as she could.

'No,' her father had said at the dinner table. 'I need you here now, to run the house and look after Harry.'

Harry, then twelve, who was going back to boarding school in Sydney the next week, had looked surprised, as well he might. Their housekeeper spoiled him day and night.

'But –'

'I've made my decision, Evelyn.' That was that.

'That's not fair, Father!' she broke out. She had never spoken against him before, not once.

He stood up, enraged beyond reason, and pointed to the door.

'To your room, miss!' he hissed. 'You'll not gainsay me in front of your brother.'

And later, he'd switched her on her legs fourteen times. One for each year of her life. He had a strong arm.

Her anger didn't go away, but she controlled it. What other choice did she have? A parent was allowed – encouraged, even! – to punish their children, and certainly to decide about their schooling.

She had gone on studying alone for another few months, because there was nothing else she could do. Until her father declared that, while Harry was at school, she was underemployed and could help him in his practice.

It wasn't until much later that she realised his motives were twofold: to save money on a practice nurse and to prevent her from studying. The work was interesting, though. Fascinating, really, and just confirmed her desire to be a doctor. And, as a doctor, her father was faultless. Not only competent and up-to-date, but also gentle; a side of him she had never experienced came out when he was dealing with patients. Soft, compassionate, almost tender. Whenever she was most angry with him, she would see him with his patients and lose that anger completely. Although a resentment that *she* had never been treated so gently still grated, underneath it all.

And he was happy – even eager – to discuss medicine with her. On their buggy rides around the district for his house calls, on their horseback rides into wilder country, he would tell her about the latest medical journal, the most recent treatments. They enjoyed those conversations, both of them.

So at eighteen, when she had broached the subject of going to university, she'd expected him to agree immediately. But she'd learnt her lesson about public discussions, and asked him in his office when he was particularly pleased with her handling of a small child who had come to have his broken arm set.

He laughed.

'What would you study? Needlework?'

'Medicine, of course.'

He looked at her as though he'd never seen her before. But surely he'd known? She'd talked about it often enough, in the days before her mother had died.

'No.' That was all.

'But I've been keeping up with my studies, Father. I might have to study hard for a few weeks – perhaps not accompany you on your rounds for a while – but I'm confident I could pass the matriculation test.'

'No.'

'Father –'

'Women doctors are anathema. It's morally wrong to have women give orders to men. And beyond that, women don't have the mental capacity. They can't possibly make reasoned decisions about patient care. Their emotions get in the way. I am completely opposed to female medicos.'

He spoke as if to a small child. As if she were a natural, unable to grasp even the simplest concept. Resentment burned through her.

'I've been helping you capably enough!'

'Of course!' He smiled, jovially. 'With proper direction, a woman can be most helpful in medicine. As a nurse.' The good humour went out of his eyes. 'Anything else is impossible. I will not pay for you to study at university, Evelyn. Put it out of your mind.'

'I have an inheritance from my mother,' she said numbly.

'Yes. As your trustee, I pay your pin money out of it. When you reach the age of reason, it will be given to you. Or if you marry, your mother's will provides that it go into the care of your husband. I very much hope you *will* marry and have children. That's the best way you can serve your country and your family.'

At eighteen, the 'age of reason' seemed a long way off; the three years until she was twenty-one had stretched bleakly ahead of her. But, she told herself, she could continue to learn from her father in those three years, and come into medicine knowing a great deal more than the other students.

And now the three years were up. She could sit the matriculation examinations in mid-November, and start university the following February. Her blood fizzed in her veins as she thought champagne might, imagining the lectures, the companionship of other students, the *freedom* of intellectual discoveries.

'I've written to the University of Sydney,' she said, standing at the sideboard, putting bacon and toast on her plate. With light steps, she carried it to the table and sat opposite her father, the place of the lady of the household. 'They have agreed I can sit the matric next month. I thought I might be able to stay with Aunt Johanna.'

'Why would you sit that examination?' her father asked, slicing the top off his boiled egg.

She blinked at him.

'You know why. I'm going to enrol in medicine.'

'And how are you going to pay the fees?' He was quite bland. Harry looked quickly from his face to hers, and then gazed resolutely at his plate.

This wasn't how she had imagined this conversation. She had expected him to be annoyed, dismissive, but not this.

'From my inheritance. I'm of age now. You said . . .'

'I said, "When you reach the age of reason." The age of reason in a woman is thirty. You can't possibly think I would hand over control of your dowry to you *now*.' His face was grave, but his eyes revealed a secret enjoyment. He had misled her deliberately.

She wanted to shout at him, to yell and scream and throw things. The desire to simply slap his face welled up in her, hot and volcanic. She pushed it down. That would reinforce his ideas about her unfitness for medicine, and she wouldn't give him the satisfaction.

Pushing back her chair, she walked out of the room, her legs shaking. She wouldn't sit there and watch him gloating over her powerlessness.

In her room, she sat on the side of her bed, heart racing, stomach churning. Rage shook her until she felt her rib cage might break under the strain.

Thirty. Nine years away. She could not live in this house for nine more years.

She could walk out. She *should* walk out. But then – where would she go? Her abdomen cramped with worry and frustration.

It was Sunday, the long quiet of a Protestant Sabbath ahead of her. Church was in half an hour.

No. Not today. She couldn't sit in a pew next to her father and pretend to feel Christian love. It would choke her. Today she needed respite.

She changed into her riding clothes and slipped down the back stairs, out through the kitchen (with an apple in her pocket) and into the stables.

Leaving Barney had been the one dark spot on her plans for the future. He was a plain, ordinary bay Australian stockhorse, and that meant he was clever and kind and untiring. He greeted her with a whicker and a soft nose in her ear. She gave him the apple and saddled him up while he ate it.

'Come on, lad, let's get out of here.'

Riding on Sunday for pleasure wasn't exactly frowned on, but it was best not to flaunt it in front of the conservative country matrons parading to church. She went down the lane, past the back of weatherboard houses and stable blocks, to where the small township petered out into market gardens which stretched down to the river, the wide, placid-seeming Manning, curving around the mangroves, shining with the reflected blue of the open sky.

It felt wrong that it should be such a beautiful day. Why couldn't she have storms and thunder, like in *Wuthering Heights*?

There was only one place to go when she felt like this.

•

Once free of the town and on the river path, she gave Barney his head and he cantered for a while until the hard baked track began to hurt his hooves and he dropped back to a walk.

The bracken was high and the last of the wattle blazed gold against the scrub. Taree was timber country, but near the town the forests had been felled decades ago, replaced with mixed farming: some sheep, wheat still green and purple in the fields, and a couple of dairy farms which serviced the local townships. Hereford steers being fattened for market stared at her over a wire fence.

Her mother had been a squatter's daughter, and was buried in the private cemetery on her family's old land, a half-hour's easy ride. It was down near the river, removed from the main house, so she could visit without having to keep company with the new owners.

She dismounted and tied Barney to a branch loosely enough to let him lip at the grass edging each tree trunk.

Not only her mother lay in this shady grove of river gums. Two younger sisters and a brother were there, all dead before they were two, as so many children were. There was still so far to go in medical science. Saving the newborns, the babies dead of fever, the mothers who bled out or suffered puerperal fever . . .

She sat by her mother's grave and picked the weeds from it, talking as she went.

'I don't know how you bore living with him!' A dandelion, a clover, some native grass. 'I don't know what to do . . .' Abruptly, grief overwhelmed her, tears rising, throat catching, a pain below her heart pressuring her . . . not just grief for her mother, although that raw ache was always present. But something sharper, less natural: grief for the father she might have had but didn't, a father who would support her, be proud of her, steady her and keep her on course to achieve her goals. It wasn't *fair*! Why *couldn't* she be a doctor? It was her money, for God's sake!

'How could you have let him talk you into putting *thirty* down as the age?' She thumped the grass over the grave in righteous anger, tears running down her cheeks. 'Didn't you trust me?'

But she knew the answer. Her mother had been a compliant woman; loving, gentle, generous, the perfect mother – but never able or willing to stand up to her husband. Evelyn knew, deep down, that she hadn't *wanted* to defy him. That something in her mother had liked his masterfulness. She had once said, 'He's a proper man,' with a deep, almost lascivious satisfaction. Evelyn had been thirteen, and uncomfortable with that declaration without knowing why; now she understood what might have been underneath that satisfaction, and was still uncomfortable, and angry.

Her mother should have stood up for her daughter, if not for herself.

But there was nothing she could do. A will was binding. She felt rage building in her, but there was no way to let it out which would do any good. The unfairness of the world wasn't something she could change – not right here and now. Her father's disdain for women wasn't going to affect how the law buttressed his rights. Society was against women, pushing them down. Even though Australian women had the vote, it hadn't changed anything. Men were still in charge. Fathers and husbands and judges and parliamentarians. She lay on the rough grass and looked up at the gum leaves, feeling a deep thrumming of anger in her solar plexus, as though her body wanted to pounce on something – someone – and hit and hit and hit. Once she got her inheritance, *no one* was ever going to have control of her again.

She had no formal qualifications in nursing, although she'd been active in that role now for several years. If she left home, her pin money would be stopped – oh, he was petty enough for that, certainly. She would have to earn her own living – and the best she could hope for was as a nurse's assistant, on pitiful money, living in servants' quarters of some hospital. A drudge.

She didn't hate her father enough to live like that. She wasn't such a fool.

Qualifications. Nursing qualifications would get her out of this house and into a respectable profession – a profession in which she could continue to learn medicine until she came into her inheritance. It looked like a long cold future, but it was the best she had access to. University was so expensive that there was no possibility she could afford it without her mother's money. Harry was going to university at her father's expense. Of course.

In Taree, nursing qualifications meant the Manning District Hospital, the only teaching hospital in the area. Her father, for some arcane reason she didn't understand, rarely used it, preferring the smaller private hospitals. Which meant she might be able to train there undetected. Or, at least, take her exams there.

Only one way to find out.

•

The next morning, once surgery hours were over and her father had retired to his smoking room with the newspaper, she went to the Manning District Hospital and talked to Dr Chapman, who was the assistant director and had control over the nursing staff.

He was energetic and charming, a favourite of the local ladies, and a friend of her father's in a professionally distant way.

'What can I do for you, Miss Northey?' he asked, with a spark of admiration in his eyes for her – she had worn a smartly cut suit and fashionable hat to give her confidence. 'Please, sit down.'

She sat on his visitor's chair, her purse clutched on her knees. The office was in a corner of the ground floor of the hospital, and strong spring sun streamed through the window. A wisteria vine was in full bloom outside, and the perfume filled the room.

'I want to get my nursing qualifications, Doctor. I was hoping I could take the exams here, at the hospital. In confidence.'

He looked at her silently.

'I won't lie for you, Miss Northey,' he said, stirring restlessly, tapping a pencil on his blotter.

'I wouldn't ask you to, Doctor.' A pause, while he looked out the window, his mouth pursed, considering who knew what ramifications of her request. 'I just want to have my experience recognised,' she added.

'Yes. Yes, I can see that.' He put the pencil down and leant forward. 'But there's a bit more to it than exams. We'll need you to take some shifts in the operating theatre, and demonstrate certain skills on the ward . . .'

'I'd like that,' she said. Oh, yes, she'd like that! To work with others, to learn from other doctors and nurses. It was like a window opening.

'We're short-handed at the moment. Perhaps I can ask your father to lend you to us for some weekend shifts.'

Her father would love to play the beneficent doctor, helping out the local community – with *her* time. It was shaming that Dr Chapman knew him so well.

Their eyes met. His were blue, sympathetic and under-standing. She swallowed down a lump in her throat.

'Thank you, Doctor. That would be wonderful.'

'You can probably take your first- and second-year exams together,' he added cheerfully. 'Have you been studying anatomy? Here –' He reached behind her and grabbed a book from the shelves behind his desk. '*Gray's Anatomy*. That's what you need. I'm sure your father has a copy.'

'Yes,' she said, 'but I think I'd better get my own.'

He grinned at her. 'Borrow this one until it arrives. You'll have to order it from Sydney.' He paused, and looked out the window again. 'Have them deliver it here.'

Tears pricked her eyes. He was so understanding. So truly the gentleman, to not put into words the difficulties she faced.

'Thank you, Dr Chapman,' she said. She'd never meant anything more in her life. He smiled at her.

'Not at all,' he said. 'We need competent nurses.'

6 AUGUST 1914

'There!' Her father ripped the certificate in two and threw the pieces on the floor. 'So much for that.'

He smiled at Evelyn with unpleasant satisfaction and a lingering rage. She drew in a breath. She had to stay calm. But no matter how old she got, her father's anger always called up an answering fear in her. Which was ridiculous. There was nothing he could do to her anymore.

Still, it took an effort to answer him.

'Dr Chapman gave me two certificates,' she said, hoping he didn't hear the slight tremor in her voice. 'In case you tore up that one.'

That brought him up with a jolt. He didn't like the idea of Dr Chapman judging him so accurately, nor of her being prepared for his actions.

'There's nothing you can do, Father,' she said. She went to the window and opened it, ignoring the cold of the metal catch against her fingers. 'Listen.'

Their house was on the main street of Taree; a typical country town street, usually drowsy and quiet in mid-afternoon. But today the town was alive and buzzing. People, men and women alike, crowded the footpaths, talking avidly, and sulkies and carts were stopped in mid-street as their drivers leant down to chat to passers-by. A newspaper boy was doing a roaring trade, shouting, 'War! Britain at war with Germany!'

Evelyn faced her father.

'I'm enlisting as a nurse, Father.'

'I forbid it!' His face was mottled with rage, his hands gripping the back of his chair, knuckles white.

'I'm nearly twenty-four and now,' she gestured to the pieces of certificate on the carpet, 'I'm fully qualified *and* I've been registered by the Australasian Trained Nurses' Association. There's nothing you can do.'

Her father smoothed his sparse hair back and stared at her as if he'd never seen her. She realised with a small shock that he was staring her in the eyes; she'd known he wasn't a tall man, but now they were the same height. 'You're needed *here*,' he insisted.

'You'll have to find someone else to do your dressings for you.' Her voice was firm at last. Her father barely glanced out the window, and turned back, sneering.

'This is a fool's errand. They're saying it will be over by Christmas, and then what will you do?' His voice was bitter.

'Get a job in Sydney as a private nurse,' she said swiftly, and had the satisfaction of seeing his brows twitch together. The front door banged and Harry rushed in, bringing winter air with him in a gust.

'Have you heard the news? It's good, isn't it? We'll show those German blighters. I'm off to Sydney to enlist!' He grinned at them both, and she felt her heart twist. She was enlisting as a nurse because she knew that the victims of battle would need all the help they could get. To think of Harry being one of them was piercingly hard. He was a solicitor newly minted, about to take up a position with the local solicitor's office. He would be safe behind a desk.

Still, if anyone could come through unscathed, it was Harry. Tall and long-limbed, strong as an ox, he'd never even had the normal illnesses of childhood. She couldn't remember the last time he'd been ill. And he was a crack shot and rider.

'Did you see what *The Sydney Morning Herald* says?' he went on, as if not noticing their silence. He read from the paper crushed in his fist. '"For good or ill, we are engaged with the Mother Country in fighting for liberty and peace." That's the spirit, eh?'

'Nonsense!' her father said, ignoring her. Where her announcement of enlisting had brought nothing but wrath from him, Harry's had brought fear to his eyes. 'They can't need lawyers in the Army.'

'I'm a reservist with the Light Horse, Dad, you know that.' He beamed, genuinely excited. 'What a lark! Off to Europe to fight old Fritz! I've got to get my kit together.' He ran up to his bedroom, taking the stairs two at a time. Evelyn and her father stared at one another, united at least in their worry for him.

'Wouldn't you want a nurse available if he's injured?' she asked. Perhaps that was cruel, but it was the truth. The Army was going to need every possible nurse before this war was over, even if it did only last until Christmas.

'I forbid it,' he said quietly.

She bit her lower lip to stop herself saying words she would regret – saying, 'Yes, Father. Whatever you say, Father.' The habit of obeying him – of fearing him – was so strong, but she was an adult now.

'I'll pack and leave on the late train,' she said, speaking as she turned away and went out the door. 'Rebecca Quinn will put me up in Sydney until they need me to embark.'

'If you leave this house, don't think you can come back.'

Alone in the world with only her own meagre resources. It was a daunting image; women had a hard enough time of it when they had a family at their back. She'd be completely dependent on her own income, with nowhere to retreat to if she were sick, or out of work or otherwise in trouble. What father would do that to his own daughter?

She paused in the doorway, her back to him. Anger burned out fear. But for her mother's sake, for her memory, she wouldn't, couldn't, tell him what she thought. After a split-second's stillness, she went on, moving up the stairs as quickly as she could, so she could get to her room before she began to cry.

CHAPTER 2

Rebecca Quinn was delighted to put her up, and to take her to the enlistment office.

'I'm so glad to see you out of that dreary little town, Lynnie,' she said, briskly weaving her sulky through the Sydney traffic. 'And to get your nursing qualifications behind your father's back, too! Well done.'

Rebecca was a journalist, and the daughter of a prominent women's rights campaigner. They had met playing hockey against one another in their schooldays. Her blonde-haired sophistication always made Evelyn feel like a red-headed frump, but although they had never been close friends she had known she could rely on Rebecca's support.

'He had no right to stop you being a doctor in the first place,' Rebecca continued.

'Well, he had the legal right,' Evelyn said, half-amused and half-comforted by her partisanship. 'My inheritance from my mother is held in trust until I'm thirty, and he's the trustee.'

'Until you're thirty or you get *married*,' Rebecca said darkly, as if she herself hadn't married her Jack only six months before.

'Well, that's not going to happen,' Evelyn said firmly. No. If she married, her money would come under her husband's control, automatically. She would never again put herself in the position of having her life controlled by someone else. Anyone else.

They followed a line of carriages up a hill, beside a long sandstone wall. The gate which was eventually revealed was staffed by soldiers. A crowd of men had gathered outside.

'There you are,' Rebecca said. 'Victoria Barracks. Ask for the Army Service Corps' Drill Hall. Enlistments opened at ten o'clock, and it's only 10.30 now, so you should have plenty of time.'

Evelyn laughed. 'How do you *know* all this?'

'It's my job to know!' Rebecca laughed too. 'Speaking of which, I have a ladies' charity auction to get to by eleven. You'll be faster walking from here anyhow.'

'Thank you, Bec. I'll see you back at your flat . . .' Evelyn hesitated, suddenly unsure. 'At least, I *suppose* I will. I'll send you word, anyway.'

Rebecca smiled at her. 'What an adventure! I half wish I could come with you.'

Evelyn climbed down, reassured. She wished she had a soupçon of Rebecca's charm. Particularly now, when she'd be facing strangers. Although she hoped that charm wasn't the main qualification the Army was looking for.

The walk up to the gate wasn't long, but she had to make her way through the crowd of men, all wanting to get in, presumably to enlist.

She had been in crowds of men before, naturally. Train stations, town fairs. But she realised, as she eeled her way through, that not a single one of these men was paying her any attention. Not one was giving her the eye, or assessing her looks. No one whistled or catcalled. They were so concentrated on getting in through that green gate that it was like she'd been turned into a man.

It was curiously fortifying. They were all here together for the same purpose: to fight for King and Country. No matter if she thought this war could have been avoided. No matter if Serbia had been stupid, or Russia overly aggressive. Germany had invaded Belgium, and that meant war for all Belgium's allies, including Britain. And when Britain, the Mother Country, went to war, so did Australia.

She had come as far as she could; now she just had to wait for the line to inch forward.

Forty minutes later, she said to the long-suffering sergeant at the gate, 'I'm here to enlist for the nursing service.'

'Good-oh,' he said. 'We need all the nurses we can get. Go along there to the hospital office, and they'll give you your medical straightaway. We've got a rush on for nurses.'

The hospital was to the right of the gate, a lovely old sandstone building, as they all seemed to be in the enormous quadrangle. There was a short line of young women, mostly in nurses' uniforms, at the front door, and she joined them, thankful beyond measure for the extra certificate Dr Chapman had given her, and for the letter of accreditation from the Nurses' Association. She wished she'd thought to wear her own uniform.

The other girls were welcoming.

'What a lark!' one of them, a vivacious brunette with spectacles, said, reminding Evelyn vividly of Harry. He would be here in a few days, once he'd served out his notice at his job in Taree.

'We'll have some fun,' another girl agreed.

'You've got a strange idea of fun,' an older woman said. 'I was in the Boer War, and I can tell you, it's not much fun when the boys are brought in bleeding.'

They fell to silence then, going in one by one as a voice within called out 'Next!'

Evelyn reached the head of the queue about twenty minutes later.

'Next!' A matron sat behind a desk in the hall, flanked by a sergeant and a civilian clerk.

Evelyn had her papers ready, and put them on the desk in front of the matron. They were quickly checked by all three, then the clerk copied her details down.

'You've just qualified?' the matron asked.

'I've just received my certification, but I've been acting as my father's practice nurse since I was sixteen,' she said. 'A country doctor. I've seen a lot of different kinds of patients.'

'Theatre experience?'

'Yes. At the Manning District Hospital.'

'Any emergency experience? Wound treatment?'

'We're a timber town,' Evelyn said. 'There have been accidents. With saws, and milling equipment.' She tried not to think of the last one, a little girl crushed by a log falling off a timber dray. She cleared her throat and went on. 'And fishermen. Gaff hooks, filleting knives . . .' Trailing off, she waited for pronouncement. It didn't sound very impressive to her.

The matron looked her over, and finally smiled. 'Good. We like an all-rounder.' She nodded to the clerk, who gave Evelyn a form. She was directed to a smaller desk in a side room to fill it out.

She sat and looked at it. An actual enlistment form. Or, as the heading suggested, an 'Attestation Paper for Enlistment of Persons Abroad'. A shiver ran over her. What was she getting herself into? The older nurse's comment came back with full force. *Not much fun when the boys are brought in bleeding.* Her imagination filled with images of wounds and blood and pain, and she shuddered.

She didn't have to do this.

But Harry, and all the thousands of boys like Harry, where would they be if there were no one to staunch that blood and alleviate that pain, to help the doctors to treat those wounds? Dead, that's where they'd be.

She printed her name at the top of the paper with a firm hand.

Evelyn Joy Northey.

For better or worse, she was in this thing, and she would see it through.

After handing in her form, she was directed to the medical officer. She expected an Army doctor, but the man waiting for her was in a civilian suit – or, rather, in his shirtsleeves and waistcoat, stethoscope around his neck.

Although tall, he was lean and elegant rather than burly, and as he moved towards her, to shake her hand, she saw that he had a slight limp; a halt on his right leg. His face showed, to her nurse's eyes, the traces of old pain. But his features were good, and his hazel eyes were alight with an intelligence that seemed to scorn her compassion. He smiled gaily at her.

'They've had to draft in a few of us civilians to help out today, Miss Northey,' he said. 'I hope you don't mind. I'm William Brent.'

A lovely speaking voice, but with a hint of an Australian drawl underneath it, as though he'd had to learn to speak well at some time. She blushed a little, ashamed of herself. A doctor would hardly be from the lower classes. Besides, his suit was well tailored, and his shoes were excellent.

'Of course not,' she said. A nurse acting as a clerk had her papers, and took down information as the doctor inspected her: height, weight, teeth.

'Do you wear glasses? No? Good. We've just had to knock someone back on those grounds, and my! she was disappointed!'

Evelyn wondered if it had been the brunette who had thought war would be a lark.

'No false teeth? Good.'

He prodded and poked, took her temperature, all the standard elements of a physical examination. It was decidedly odd. She had never been examined by a stranger before. Her father had been her physician.

She was conscious of his dark hair as he bent to listen to her lungs through the stethoscope; without pomade, it had a fresh, natural smell of soap, and was slightly curly. Easier to think about the way it sprang from his scalp than to think about his hand tapping just below her breast.

She swallowed, trying hard to be calm. She had worked with doctors at Manning District Hospital before, sometimes in close proximity. This was no different. But she had known those men pretty much all her life. They were family friends. To be so close to a stranger, and an attractive one at that . . .

well, she'd better get used to it. She'd be working with all kinds of men soon.

'Wonderful!' he said, straightening up. 'No problems there. Welcome to the Army, Sister Northey.'

Warmth went through her and she smiled brilliantly at him. 'Doctor' was her eventual goal, and had been since she was a little girl, but 'Sister' was an honourable stop along the way.

'Thank you,' she said. 'Thank you very much.'

•

'Next!' William eased himself into a chair for a moment's respite. Standing all day was playing havoc with his hip.

A short, weedy man in his forties, in a clerk's cheap suit and waistcoat came in. What were they thinking, even letting him through the door? He'd have to have a word with the sergeant at the gate. This man was clearly unsuitable.

He stood up, his leg dragging a little, and came forward but didn't reach to take the forms the man held out to him.

'How old are you?' he asked.

The man shuffled his feet. 'Thirty-five,' he declared.

'Sir –'

'I just want to do my bit!' His tone was desperate, and made William equal parts angry and pitying.

'I know,' he said. 'But you're under regulation height and chest measurements, *and* you're too old!'

'I know I can't *fight*,' the chap said. 'But I'm a good clerk. I figured I could do some backroom job.'

'Not how it works, I'm afraid.' No. Otherwise *he'd* have enlisted weeks ago.

The man cast a shrewd glance at William's leg. 'You'd know, I reckon.'

'Yes.'

'Can't you fudge it, just the once? I'd work my arse off, I would!'

'I know. I wish I could. Really. But you wouldn't make it through basic training.'

Resignation bowed the man's shoulders and he half-turned away. 'At least you're doing your bit here,' he said bitterly.

'Everyone at home'll have to do their bit before this is over.' So he told himself.

A snort was the only reply as the man walked out the door and slammed it behind him.

William flinched at the sound and a line of hot electricity ran down his hip and leg. 'Damn it to hell!' He would close up for the day – they'd run an hour late as it was. The private on duty stuck his head in the door.

'All right, sir?'

'Yes. We'll finish up now. Send the rest home.'

'Righto.'

'Jenkins – give them all a number to mark their place in the line so they don't have to queue up again tomorrow.'

'Good thinking, Doc!'

He packed his bag and walked out through the throng as Jenkins was giving out slips of paper. There was less complaining from the queue than he had expected. Perhaps being given a guaranteed place was placating them; or perhaps the men just accepted that a war was a difficult thing to organise.

He came out the gate of Victoria Barracks onto Oxford Street and groaned. The traffic was bad and there wasn't a cab in sight. A small mob of men were still clustered around the gatehouse, the sergeant there loudly declaiming, 'All off for today, gents! Come back tomorrow, ten ack emma.'

Even the trams weren't moving. He'd have to walk. He'd rather lie on the footpath and roll down the hill to Sydney Hospital. Chuckling, he wondered if he could actually do that, if it were physically possible. Perhaps he should try it some quiet Sunday morning.

As he walked down, trying with all his strength not to limp, because he knew it just reinforced the weakness in his muscles, a group of women on the corner – respectable women, waiting for the omnibus – regarded him with disdain.

'You'd think a tall young man like that would join up!' one said loudly.

'Shameful!'

'Terrible.'

'Coward.'

The last word was hissed by a dark-haired matron, only a few years older than him. It hit him like a blow. He wanted to shout at her: 'I'd go in a minute if they'd take me!' But what would be the good of that?

He tipped his hat to them. 'Ladies.' They were flustered, avoiding his gaze, and he walked on with some sense of satisfaction, but it soon left him.

He wasn't sure he could take much more of being out of things.

•

He was rostered on for a night shift at the Mission House and despite his weariness, he went. As a volunteer, he could have opted out, but he couldn't let Dr O'Reilly down. The first woman medical student ever to be employed by Sydney Hospital, she was in private practice now and untiring in her efforts to help the less fortunate.

She was leaving the surgery, in the front office of the big house, as he got there. 'Will!' she said with pleasure. 'Excellent. Didn't think you'd make it after being on your feet all day.' Dr O'Reilly was nothing if not blunt, and never pretended not to notice his disability. He found it comforting, although he wasn't sure why. She was a pretty, strong-willed woman who was also a lady, and the combination was unstoppable.

'I hope it's a quiet night,' he said ruefully.

'Should be. Tuesdays are normally quiet. Wednesdays are worse, though I've never understood why.'

'It's because they drink their winnings from the Wednesday race meetings,' he said absently, 'and then they fight.'

'Or beat up their wives,' she said grimly.

He nodded just as grimly.

'We might have to recruit,' she said. 'I'm thinking of heading to France.'

He was startled. 'France? But they're not taking women doctors.'

She grinned at him, her weary face shining a little under the light. 'They may not be taking them officially yet,' she said. 'But I'll bet a pound to a penny that if a qualified doctor turns up in the middle of things, they'll be welcome. They can't possibly have enough.'

She clapped him on the back. 'So if any of your friends at Sydney Hospital are inclined to join us in our good works here . . . Ask around.'

'I will,' he said.

He set himself up in the surgery and dealt with the steady stream of women coming in. Mostly small things: a boil that needed lancing, a talk about how to avoid pregnancy with an overburdened mother of seven (and what could he tell her when no two doctors could agree on when in her cycle a woman was fertile, and her husband refused to wear a condom?), a prostitute with the clap, a young woman with a split lip and bruising all down her side.

'You need to leave him,' he said.

'And live on what?' she asked. 'I've got a kiddie. Who's going to look after her if I'm in work?'

'In that case, slip him some laudanum when he gets aggressive. In his tea. The chemist will tell you how much.' It was unethical. Totally unethical. But after only a couple of weeks' work here, he had decided that the safety of women and children was more important than some heavy-handed man's right to know what was in his tea.

'Now that's an idea!' Laudanum wasn't even expensive, and could be bought from any pharmacy. Opium dissolved in alcohol, it could be depended on to soothe anyone into lassitude.

'Not too much, though, or too often, or else he'll turn into an opium addict, and you'll be even worse off!'

As she left, far more cheerful, he reflected that working here was a privilege – how many men got to know the reality of women's lives? It had turned him into a supporter of women's rights, which had pleased his mother and bemused his father.

Dr O'Reilly had opened his eyes, too, to what women could do. Off to France.

He wondered if she were right; would they take any qualified doctor in the heat of battle? Or would she have to return with her tail between her legs?

He couldn't imagine that, somehow. She would start her own hospital if she had to!

Was an able-bodied woman more or less acceptable to the powers that be than a crippled man? Was it six of one, half a dozen of the other? Or was able-bodiedness the winner?

The thought tugged at him all through the shift.

•

Mid-morning the next day, the endless stream of men threw up a tall tow-headed boy of no more than fifteen, who had lied manfully all the way through the enlistment process. One Miles Dougherty, puffed up with his success so far.

William looked at him with benign eyes.

'Sonny, you may have fooled the sergeant, but you haven't fooled me. Off you go!'

'*Please*, doctor. My brothers are both going. It'll be such a lark!'

'Not for you, Miles. And your parents will be glad of you.'

'Not them! They signed my papers and all. They're patriots!' He was proud of his parents, but William wanted to kick them. What were they thinking of, sending a baby off to face the guns? This war mania could go too far.

'No,' he said. He took the red pen and slashed two big lines across the boy's enlistment papers, writing UNDERAGE between the lines. 'Come back when you're eighteen,' he said, handing the papers to the boy.

'You – you *rotter*,' Miles said, red with disdain and disappointment. 'Just because *you're* a cripple, you don't want anyone else to have any fun!'

He almost ran out of the room, shouldering aside the men waiting in the doorway.

The man at the head of the queue, an older man of thirty or more, came forward, smiling placatingly.

'Don't take any notice of him, Doc,' he said. 'You're doing your bit.'

The comforting words pierced him in a way the boy's contempt hadn't. They had a 'there, there' feel about them which reduced him to a child. Not a man.

He dealt with the recruit briskly and competently, but the tone of the man's voice seemed to etch into his insides, corrosive and painful.

He couldn't take this. Couldn't spend this war sending other men to fight. He might not be able to be on the front lines, but by God! Dr O'Reilly was right. When they needed doctors – and they would – they might not care where they came from.

At the end of the shift, he found the lieutenant in charge of recruitment and despatch.

'Where are this lot going to end up?' he asked.

The lieutenant pushed his cap back on his head and scratched the very short hair behind his ear. There was a white line showing the level of his previous haircut. Not in the Army long, then. Indeed, he seemed almost a boy himself; probably straight out of the university cadets.

'Well, they say they're going to France, but who knows? Odds are they'll end up in Egypt. Something's got to happen there.'

Egypt.

William's spirits rose. He had been dreading the French winters, knowing how cold incapacitated him, but Egypt! Warm and sunny and perfectly suited to him. And perhaps the British officials there would be less wedded to Army orders when it came to finding doctors . . .

He felt on the edge of a great adventure. Taking a step into the unknown. His life had been so careful up until now; it was time to take a risk.

'Where can I find the commander?' he asked. 'I'm afraid I have to resign from doing the medicals.'

CHAPTER 3

14 JANUARY 1915

She had thought Victoria Barracks was grand, but Heliopolis Palace was – a palace!

Its façade was a huge, sweeping outward curve; a great almost semi-circle of columns which soared several stories into enormous brick Moorish arches, the whole fronted by a matching terrace overlooking a sharp drop-off to the hotel grounds. Army tents were already being erected on the sandy lawns. It looked . . . expensive; and as though it were built to celebrate the greatness of Arabic culture. Which was odd, considering it had been built by Belgians. But whatever the architect's inspiration, Heliopolis Palace took your breath away.

It was high noon; suddenly, from all around them, came the cries of the muezzin, calling the faithful to prayer. She had heard it before, from the docks at Port Said and Alexandria, but now it surrounded her, the unfamiliar language and the drawn-out notes sounding like some strange lament.

The voyage already felt months in the past, and Australia so far back that it was hard to bring to mind. Here and now were so *real*, and yet so fantastical. She and a group of other nurses – already friends after the long voyage – stood and stared.

The hotel was new. Almost brand new; the Army driver who'd dropped them here had said it had only been built in 1910, as a casino, and was fully up-to-date. Even the servants' quarters, apparently, had bathrooms with running water.

Bliss.

'For the greater good,' the matron said, as if it were a prayer, and led them into the foyer of what was to be their hospital. Men – Egyptian men, in white trousers and tunics and red fezzes – were moving furniture out, a stream of them bringing tables and chairs and bedsteads and washstands down the wide stairs and through to some back area.

'The owners are moving all the good furniture away,' Matron said. 'Wise of them. Go up this staircase and someone will direct you to your rooms.'

It was a splendid place: octagonal columns and arches everywhere, vaulted ceilings and rooms divided by intricate woven screens, and all the walls painted in deep, rich colours. It felt very . . . foreign. She was here, in foreign parts, in *Egypt*. Even the air smelt different, of sand and spices.

But some things remained the same. The higher they went up the staircase, the less ornate the rooms became. Their rooms, of course, were on the top floor.

Evelyn would bet that they were the housemaids' quarters, but she hadn't expected better.

•

'Third on the right,' the subaltern with the clipboard said.

Evelyn counted off the doors and went in without knocking. A girl was already there; startled, she dropped the pair of cotton knickers she'd been folding.

'Sorry,' Evelyn said. 'I'm Evelyn Northey. I think we're roommates.'

Flushing a little, the girl picked up the knickers and stuffed them in the top drawer of a chest which stood against the left-hand wall. She was a couple of years younger than Evelyn, but taller, full-bodied and dimpled, with dusky hair and dark eyes. Pretty rather than beautiful, but with a generous mouth and an air of gentle femininity which Evelyn thought men would find very attractive.

'Hannah Page.' Hannah smiled and held out her hand and they shook briskly. 'I just arrived on the *Kyarra*. I'm from Hobart.'

'Taree, in New South Wales. I came on the *Nestor*.' Evelyn plonked her suitcase on the bed to the right and looked around. Even in these servants' quarters, Heliopolis Palace outdid anything she'd ever seen. The walls were half-panelled in dark wood, and above wallpapered in a charming flower pattern. Even the window frames were carved. 'Looks like there's a lot to do.'

'Oh, we've been planning for weeks on the ship,' Hannah said confidently. 'Matron says that we'll be opening in ten days.'

Evelyn looked out her window and was brought up short by the sight of an amusement park – Luna Park, the sign said, just like in Melbourne! But there were no crowds, no music, no lights, and all the rides were stationary. Silenced by war, as this casino had been emptied of gamblers to make room for the results of the biggest gamble of all, using human lives for stakes. It was a forlorn sight, the merry-go-round horses standing still, the rollercoaster cars sitting dead in their tracks, the tall tower with a spiral slide around the outside looking weirdly ominous. On the other hand, she thought prosaically, lights and screams of excitement wouldn't keep her awake at night.

To the side of Luna Park, the new suburb of Heliopolis. Flat roofs and blindingly white walls, sharp shadows and minarets curving against a cloudless sky.

•

That afternoon, only an hour later, a bell sounded which drew them all to what had been the old dining room. The furniture had all been removed and was being replaced with iron bedsteads. This hospital would have 450 of them.

Matron was a youngish woman, perhaps thirty-five, and slim almost to thinness. She had a narrow, eager face which was full of enthusiasm as she gave her orders. Her blue eyes were afire with excitement and determination.

'We are going to show the British Command that an Australian hospital can be just as good as an English one – better! Which means that everything will be run to order, and no shilly-shallying! What we do here is every bit as important as the soldiers' work. Every man we save is another man to fight the enemy!'

They nodded and smiled. What else could they do? But Evelyn did feel the stirring of a kind of patriotism in her chest. The British would probably look down on the 'colonials'. It was up to them to show that Australian nursing was as good as any in the world.

'You each have your supplies.'

Again, they nodded, most touching the chatelaine they wore at their waists. The tin cases held forceps, probes, scissors, pins, spatulas, thermometers. They'd been required to provide their own equipment; she hoped that wasn't a sign of privation to come.

Matron became very serious indeed. Her face tightened with purpose, and her pale blue eyes fixed on each of them in turn. 'This posting will be unlike any other you've had. It's not just that you'll be dealing with the effects of war – you'll be nursing fit young men, and *only* fit young men. To speak frankly, you'll be a temptation to them, and they'll be a temptation to *you*. Keep your mind on your job. Any nurse who looks like she's husband-hunting will be packed back to Australia on the first ship. Do I make myself clear?'

'Yes, Matron,' they murmured.

'Off you go to the staff dining room, then. We'll have afternoon tea and then start setting up the wards.'

At afternoon tea, they introduced themselves. A fine collection of young women: Mabel, Connie, Alice, Annie, Hannah and herself were at one table, some older women at another.

'Husband-hunting!' Mabel laughed as she poured the tea. 'No fear.' She was a strong, down-to-earth girl with a broad Australian accent.

'Don't you want to get married?' Alice asked. Alice was fine-boned and pretty, with a determined chin. She spoke like a lady.

''Course I do,' Mabel replied heartily. She was a determined sort – had got herself to Egypt and enlisted at Heliopolis. 'But with these fellas in uniform? Not on your life! You don't know where they come from or what they're like. I'm not buying a pig in a poke, that's for sure.'

They all laughed. Connie grimaced. 'Girls, I'm making a prediction. We won't have time to think about romance once this show gets going.' Connie was a snapper – shrewd intelligence showed in her eyes and her speech was crisp. 'We have to set this place up so it runs like clockwork, or else we'll be chasing our own tails once the wounded come in. Marriage can wait.'

'I'll say,' Evelyn muttered.

Hannah teased her. 'But how *long* are you prepared to wait?'

'Forever,' she declared. These women would be her colleagues. They might as well know the worst (and the best) about her right from the start. 'I'm planning to study medicine after the war. You can't marry and be a doctor – not as a woman.'

That silenced them, but Alice and Connie nodded. 'All right then,' Connie said with decision. 'We're all agreed. No romances until after the war.'

'Let's hope it doesn't last too long, then,' Hannah said wistfully. 'I want to have my kiddies before I get too old!'

It was easy to imagine Hannah with a brood of children at her knee. A pang went through Evelyn's heart; but children and doctoring didn't mix if you were female.

•

They were told to call the Palace 1AGH, for 1st Australian General Hospital, the Army designation, but in her own mind Evelyn couldn't help thinking of it as Heliopolis. Such a grand word suited the grandeur of the building.

There were few doctors visible at Heliopolis Palace as they went about organising the hospital, and sometimes they had to guess at what the doctors would prefer, especially in the operating theatre which she had helped Alice (an experienced theatre sister) set up in a luxurious set of rooms known as the King of Belgium's suite – because he really had stayed there!

Evelyn was pretty sure that the King of Belgium would be more than happy for soldiers to use his rooms, since it was the invasion of Belgium which had started this whole conflict.

She loved the operating theatre: its precision, its cleanliness, its sense of promise of lives to be saved. Originally she had imagined herself as a country doctor like her father, but for the first time she wondered about surgery. She'd never heard of a woman surgeon, but that was no reason not to try. Still, plenty of time to make up her mind about a speciality – no doubt she'd get a lot of experience in these rooms before the war was done.

•

Two days after they arrived, a new Commanding Officer was appointed to the hospital. They lined up to meet him as he arrived in a spiffing motor, complete with adjutant to jump out and open the door for him.

At first, Evelyn thought her eyes weren't focusing right; he seemed strangely hard to see in the bright Egyptian sun as he descended from the car, straightened his major's cap, and came forward to greet Matron.

Then she realised that he was coloured. Dark skin, although not black like an Aboriginal. Brown. An Indian, or an Egyptian, perhaps? But . . . but he was wearing a British Army uniform, and he was taller than the Egyptian men she had seen, and broader across the shoulders. A big man, muscled more like a soldier than a doctor.

'Matron McPherson,' he said, holding out his hand. 'I'm Major Fanous. Or call me Doctor, perhaps. That might be easier for everyone.'

His voice was pure Oxford. The contrast between skin tone and voice made one of the nurses giggle, and Matron hesitated before she took the proffered hand. They were all shocked. It wasn't so much that she was prejudiced, Evelyn told herself. She didn't hold with racialism. But she was profoundly surprised that the British Army had put a brown-skinned man in charge of *anything*. Perhaps hospitals didn't count.

As Matron turned to walk with the doctor up the stairs to the main ward, Evelyn saw her surreptitiously wipe her hand on her apron. The hand she'd touched Dr Fanous with.

Oh, dear. That didn't bode well.

•

The big rooms of the hotel were turned into wards: the ballroom, the dining room, billiards room, even the foyer.

The suites were set up as 'special' wards: infectious diseases, fever, the VD ward.

'Not that you girls will be having anything to do with the patients in *there*,' Matron said with stark disapproval. 'The Army has, quite properly, decided that those patients only need the male orderlies.'

Evelyn couldn't say she was sorry about that. Venereal diseases were both unpleasant and, and . . . well, disgusting, if everything she'd heard was true. They'd only had one lecture about VD in her training. That had been quite enough. Her father had always kept her well away from VD cases.

They didn't have to wait long for their first patients. The foyer ward – general nursing – was half full by the time they'd finished making the beds, all the dysentery and measles cases from shipboard merely reporting to their Army post and then being redirected to the hospital. They were glad of the bedpans and more than glad that Heliopolis had actual flushing toilets for the ambulatory.

The speed of it all was astonishing. With unlimited manpower and Sister Eddison having coached them all on Army procedures on the voyage over, they moved at a breakneck pace and barely drew breath until, a few days later, there they were: a hospital.

Measles and influenza cases in the special wards, dysentery and general cases in the foyer. They had the usual accidents and incidents, and the unusual: a man whose foot had been broken when a camel stamped on him, a youngster who'd tried to climb the biggest pyramid, and who had been dragged off by the camel drivers and given a thorough bashing. The camel drivers made their living giving tourists rides around the monuments, but Evelyn thought their outrage had been real, not mercenary. It wasn't *right* to climb the Pyramids which were, after all, graveyards.

She tended the boy efficiently, though. He was so young. Barely old enough to have enlisted, even with his father's consent.

'How old are you really?' she asked as she rubbed arnica into the worst of the bruising on his back. He stiffened, and then shrugged.

'Sixteen.'

'Your parents must have been mad to let you come!'

'Haven't got any.' He twisted around on the table they used for massages and grinned at her. 'I'm a poor orphan. Bin on the streets, tell ya the truth. At least in the Army you get fed.'

'How did you –'

'Forged the signatures. Not hard, really.' And he grinned at her as though completely without fear. None of them seemed to be worried about the future. The nurses were, imagining these strong young bodies brought back bleeding and wounded, but the boys themselves were cock-a-hoop, itching for a fight.

•

Dr Fanous was clever. And organised. And determined. Evelyn liked him, but as soon as he arrived, the pace of work picked up markedly – and they'd thought they'd been working hard already. More wards were created. More bandages prepared. More dressing packs made – far more than they were using on a daily basis. The girls on the day shift gave a couple of hours after they had finished their shift, to make them up.

'Doctor, what are we preparing for?' Evelyn asked him after he'd pronounced their stack of sterile dressings far too small.

He looked at her, assessing her as she'd seen other doctors assess their staff at Manning District. 'I wish I could tell you, Sister Northey,' he said. 'But the war has barely started. When it does . . . we'll be wishing we had made twice as many of these.'

Hannah and Annie looked properly solemn. Connie Keys pressed her lips together, determined. Evelyn nodded. 'Then we'd better make three times as many. Things always go worse than you expect.'

Dr Fanous threw his head back and laughed, like a boy instead of a man in his forties. The women couldn't help but smile. Then Matron appeared at the doorway and both laughter and smiles were cut off. Matron had an odd look on her face; Evelyn wondered if she had been standing outside in the passageway, listening.

'Dr Fanous?' Matron said. 'There's a message from the camp commander.'

'I'll be right there, Matron. Now, young ladies, more dressings!'

'Yes, Doctor,' they murmured, and watched as he and Matron left together.

'Well, I don't care if he's brown as a bay horse,' Vivian Smith said. She was a Yorkshire girl, and outspoken. 'He could put his shoes under my bed any day!'

'Viv, don't!' they all said, and laughed, but none of them disagreed. Evelyn thought it over, afterwards, while she was having her bath. She didn't find Dr Fanous as attractive as the others obviously did. He was too . . . too *big*. Too brawny. Unexpectedly, she remembered that young doctor who had given her clearance to enlist. Now *he* was just right; tall and lean and elegant, except for the limp.

CHAPTER 4

MARCH 1915

Port Said, the last port before the Suez Canal, was disgustingly dirty and full of beggars, but William was glad to be there.

He had been held up in Colombo – one of the ship's crew had developed yellow fever, and they had been held in quarantine for five weeks. A horrible confinement, in a ship which baked in the tropical heat. His cabin had been so hot that he'd joined a number of other men sleeping on deck in deckchairs, but his leg reacted badly to the angle of the chairs and he'd been in constant pain.

The only relief had been swimming – they were allowed to climb down a rope ladder and swim as long as they didn't touch any other craft or swim to land.

In the water, he was elated by the freedom it always gave him.

The best times of his childhood had been spent in the Parramatta River, jumping off the bridge and swimming to Little Coogee, a sandy beach on a bend of the river. In the water, he was the physical equal of any of the other boys, making up for his bad leg with powerful shoulders and a strong crawl stroke.

The Indian Ocean was warmer than the river, and he floated with little effort, able to swim for hours. He climbed the ladder back to the ship each day with regret.

His first sight of Africa: unimpressive. The constant barrage of beggars wore him down, and the shops were so dirty he couldn't bear to go into any of them. Feeling rather poor-spirited, William went back on board with nothing to show for his trip ashore but dusty trousers and a week-old British newspaper.

The men pored over the war news in the dining room together. Most of them were older, British businessmen making their way back home, but there were a couple of Australian and British officers on their way to new postings.

'They're keeping the Australians and New Zealanders in Egypt, looks like,' Captain Hoskings, another Australian doctor, said. 'To keep the Canal open, I suppose. We can't afford to lose that.'

The Suez Canal was British property. Connecting the Mediterranean to the Red Sea and thus, effectively, the eastern half of the planet, it was a vital link for both trade and military transport. Now that the Ottoman Empire, as Turkey called itself, was joined with Germany as an ally, the Canal was at risk from Turkish troops. It made sense to stop the Australians halfway on their journey to Europe, rather than send British troops out.

William had a sense that the military order might not be so fiercely applied in an outpost like Egypt. Particularly by the Australians, who, he was pleased to admit, weren't the best at taking orders from the British. He grinned, and Hoskings clapped him on the back.

'Looks like a pretty little stoush starting up, eh?'

'Yes,' William said. 'And I suspect they'll need doctors.'

Hoskings laughed. 'Oh yes, they will,' he agreed.

They stood side by side, looking at the map, until William's leg began to ache. He rubbed it surreptitiously.

'How'd you do that?' Hoskings asked, professional curiosity in his voice. 'An accident?'

'Poliomyelitis, when I was eight,' William answered. Why shouldn't he answer? It wasn't anything to be ashamed of.

'Damn. Wish we had something that could stop diseases like that. Something like the smallpox vaccine.'

'Yes,' William said, heartfelt. That was what he wanted to do at Edinburgh University. Study the science of vaccination, try to come up with a solution to the terrible childhood diseases which took so many young lives, and ruined so many more.

'I guess all that work will have to wait until this bally war's over,' Hoskings said. 'We'll all be concentrating on other things for the duration.'

'They say it won't last long.'

Hoskings laughed bitterly. 'I'm career Army,' he said. 'They always say that, and they're always wrong.'

•

Alexandria was a marvel – a beautiful, European-looking city which reflected the long French influence on Egypt.

Along with Captain Hoskings, William presented himself to the British Command HQ – Hoskings to pick up any telegrams which might have come for him, and he to offer his help in the war hospitals.

The officer in charge, a mere captain who looked barely old enough to shave, looked at him with amazement.

'You've come from Sydney?'

'Yes. I thought you could do with more doctors.'

The young man cast an anguished look at William's leg; his limp had been quite clear as he'd walked across the room, of course.

'Yes, well, jolly good and all that, but really, old chap, if you're not – er – fit for the Army, I don't see how we can place you . . .' William became aware that the captain was suffering extreme embarrassment. His pale English skin, barely touched yet by the Egyptian sun, was reddening.

'I see,' William said, his own tone becoming very posh, his face settling into a familiar, deceptively calm expression while his heart sped up and his palms sweated with shame. 'Well, in that case, perhaps you could steer me to a civilian hospital.'

The captain looked around imploringly for help, and a sergeant, an older man with quick intelligent eyes, came up and whispered in his ear.

'Ah, yes,' the captain said with relief. 'Excellent idea, Davis. Lady de Walden has established a convalescent hospital. Convalescent Hospital No. 6. She's the Lieutenant-Colonel's wife, don't you know. It's not, strictly speaking, one of ours, but we're sending our boys there when they're not quite ready for the field.' He rapidly wrote down an address in execrable handwriting and passed it over to William, then overtly looked beyond to the next person in the queue. Hoskings.

Hoskings shook William's hand and wished him luck. William was pretty sure he'd replied with all that was right because Hoskings' expression didn't lose its heartiness, but he had no idea what he'd said.

Why did he let himself in for these impossible, embarrassing situations? He should have written from Colombo and asked to be assigned a position, instead of waiting until he was here. But he'd thought that the powers that be would brush off a letter; today's little scene had confirmed that. A polite refusal by letter would have hurt less. How many times would he set himself up to be knocked down? Why let others point out, over and over again, just how far from the ideal of masculinity he stood?

His mother had been worried about this; telling his parents he was leaving for the war had been hard, but particularly hard for her, who still tended to treat him like he was ten years old.

'Don't worry,' he'd said, kissing her cheek. 'They won't let me anywhere near the front line.'

She'd grabbed at his hand and held it tightly. 'They'll be lucky to have you. But –' She looked miserable. She always tried to ignore his disability, until he overworked himself or did something stupid. 'Take care of yourself. Don't try to do more than everyone else – you're prone to that, Will. You try to prove that you're fit by outdoing everyone, and you pay for it in the end.'

He'd just hugged her, and his father had shaken his hand with deep feeling, and he'd walked out the door.

He *wasn't* fit. Why pretend he was? Unfit for everything. For war, for marriage, for a normal life. But he could still serve. If not on the battlefield, then in a hospital, even a convalescent hospital.

At least he had a lead on a possible job. If he could decipher the handwriting.

CHAPTER 5

The hospital staff went to the Pyramids properly as a Sunday treat, all the nurses who were off duty. Evelyn rode on a camel (so uncomfortable!) and touched the Sphinx, astonished at its baleful beauty.

She and Mabel stood at its base, looking up at the jagged, eroded edges of the Pyramids. The actual *Pyramids*!

Her hand was still stretched behind her, on the warm stone of the Sphinx, and she felt light as air, truly happy. She almost didn't recognise the sensation. Here she was, in Egypt, doing a job that was worthwhile, with friends her own age (how she had missed her schoolfriends!) and the high blue desert sky arching above her.

She had known the Pyramids were big, but . . . they were made to dwarf human ambition, she thought. Intended to make us feel small and unimportant.

'Makes you feel rather temporary, doesn't it?' Mabel asked.

'Just remember,' Evelyn said, 'the men who made them are dead and long turned to dust, and so is the empire they ruled. And here we are, alive.'

Mabel laughed. 'Trust you not to be cowed, Lynnie. It's that red hair of yours! The legendary Highlander spirit.'

Evelyn laughed. 'It'd take more than a pile of bricks to cow me.' But in her heart she was impressed. Not by the dead Pharaohs who had ordered the building, but by the hundreds, probably thousands of people who had built with nothing but basic tools. *That* was the extraordinary thing, what human beings could accomplish if they worked together.

She took a deep breath and let it out, then tucked both her hands into her jacket pockets. It was early spring here, after all, and the air was crisp.

Then Matron went by, atop a camel she clearly couldn't control, and they both ran after her, following the camel driver, who was swearing some round oaths in Arabic. Evelyn laughed as she ran. Harry had been right – this *was* a lark!

But underneath that thought was the truth that, in wartime, jollity was temporary. All the more reason to enjoy themselves now.

When they got back, she added a bright and cheerful description of their outing to her weekly letter to Harry. She had written regularly since the day she had left home, but now she was settled at Heliopolis he had a return address to reply to, and she was hoping to hear from him soon. Hesitating, she poised her fountain pen over another piece of notepaper. She had written to her father once, from Sydney, giving Rebecca's address, but there had been no reply. She would try once more, and never again. If he didn't want to be in contact, that was his choice, and bedamned to him.

Dear Father, she began, *today we visited the Pyramids . . .*

•

A horse-drawn cab took William to the outskirts of Alexandria, on the shoreline of the Mediterranean. It was a clear, warm day; not too hot. Palm trees swayed just as they had in his imagination when he was reading Robert Louis Stevenson. But the sea was a different colour to the Pacific, and the waves were barely ripples. You couldn't have surf-shot on one, as he had done at Bondi so many times as an undergraduate.

He cheered up a little; if he worked here, he would be able to sea-bathe frequently.

Convalescent Hospital No. 6 was a fair way out of the city – a big Victorian house with a Romanesque porch big enough to shelter several stretchers, and substantial gardens around. Lady de Walden herself came out to greet him. A small woman, trim and handsome, with auburn hair wound into a bun around her head, she greeted William cordially.

'A doctor, you say?' she asked. She had a lilting voice with a peculiarly pleasant timbre. He'd expected a middle-aged stiff-upper-lip lady, but she was younger than he was, he thought, in her mid-twenties, and vivaciously engaging. 'How wonderful! We have Mustafa, you know, the mayor of Alexandria, two afternoons a week but we could certainly do with a doctor in residence!' She led the way into an impressive entrance hall and signalled for an Egyptian servant to take his bag. He smiled his thanks at the man, who looked startled at being noticed. 'Welcome to Maison Karam, as it used to be called,' Lady de Walden went on. 'Come, I'll show you your room.'

His room was palatial – at least, he thought so, but 'you must call me Margherita, and I shall call you William' didn't agree.

'Oh, it's a hovel, really, but we must make sacrifices, mustn't we?'

William looked around the spacious, well-lit, comfortably furnished room and smiled at her.

'I'd be happy to sacrifice myself here any day,' he said. She trilled a laugh, but he caught her giving him a searching look; she was by no means a silly woman, despite her mannerisms.

She gave him some time to settle in, and then sent the servant to escort him around the wards. The man was quiet and respectful – too much so for William's Australian tastes. Even in the best restaurants and hotels in Sydney you didn't get this kind of subservience.

'What's your name?' he asked as they negotiated the long stairs down – he always found it harder going down than climbing up.

'Tewfik, sir. The lady has assigned me to be your . . .' he hesitated. 'Batman was the word she used, but I don't know the meaning?'

'A batman is an officer's servant. A valet, really.'

'Ah,' Tewfik said, nodding. 'Excellent, then, sir.'

He seemed happy enough – perhaps the work would be lighter than general duties.

As they went through the wards and the single rooms where the rare infectious cases were kept, William thought about this servant thing. It was odd – in a hospital, he was more than happy for orderlies and nurses and junior doctors to call him 'sir' and jump when he said to. But he'd always felt a little uncomfortable around waiters and house servants. They'd never had any when he was growing up, of course, although his mother had had a woman come in to do the heavy laundry on Mondays. But that was a neighbour who'd needed a bit of a helping hand because her husband drank his wages. There was no subservience there. He laughed inwardly at the thought of Aunty Carol bowing down to anyone! She gave even her husband the hard side of her tongue, though she couldn't stop his bingeing.

It was just a class thing, of course. Margherita sailed past servants as though they didn't exist. Perhaps they didn't, to her. Perhaps they only became real during the moments they did something for her. An odd way to live.

The wards were under the stewardship of a young woman with dark brown hair pulled back in a no-nonsense bun.

He had thought her a nurse, but she was dressed far better than any nurse ever was, and spoke to him with that upper-class accent which could cut glass, with a faint Scottish burr behind it.

'Kitty Stewart-Murray,' she introduced herself. 'Technically Lady Katherine, but we don't stand on ceremony around here. I help Margherita de Walden run this place.'

He didn't know what to say. His mind couldn't take in all these British titles and flatly refused to call her anything at all.

'Pleased to meet you,' was all he could manage. Being back on a ward should have made his feet hit the ground and steadied him, but the odd nature of the ward – a large ornately decorated room he suspected might have been a ballroom in Maison Karam's past – and the odd sight of a room full of men in blue and white striped pyjamas, had unsettled him.

He was thankful for Kitty's clear competence; it would make his job much easier.

'We keep them in the blue and whites so the local brothel knows they're ours and sends them back.'

She articulated this brightly and loudly, and a couple of big Maori-looking lads ducked their heads in embarrassment. William grinned. So, not as innocent as a lady might be expected to be, he thought. Fair enough.

'Now,' she said, 'have a look at this boy's bottom for me, will you?'

•

'I'm off to the bazaar for Matron,' Gertie Gardener said, popping her head into the ward. 'Need anything, Lynnie?'

Groaning Gertie always seemed to be the one whom Matron sent to the bazaar for whatever they had run out of. She was prone to looking pale and faint, and 'needing a break'.

'Oh, yes,' Hannah said. She unpinned her little coin purse from under her apron and gave Gertie some money. 'Get me some lollies with that, will you?'

'Hooray!' a man in a nearby bed said.

'That's enough out of you,' Evelyn scolded him, but she unpinned her own purse and handed Gertie a few shillings. 'A couple of packs of cards, Gertie, thanks. And the rest in lollies.'

'Lemon drops tonight!' the same wag called out. Hannah rounded on him.

'None for you if you don't quieten down. There are sick men here!'

'That's right, Rogers,' a laconic voice from across the ward said. 'Us delicate flowers need our rest!'

Gertie shook her head. 'I don't know why you keep spending your money on these no-hopers. They get paid, don't they?'

'Well, yes,' Evelyn said, 'but they can't access their money until they go back to camp. It's a flaw in the system. A few lollies won't break the bank.'

But still, she worried that her savings weren't getting on as fast as she'd have liked. She needed to save – but how could she be so mean as to begrudge these poor sick boys a lolly or two? Besides, she was sure it helped them recover, no matter what Captain Malouf, the doctor on this ward, said. He kept the dysentery patients on a diet of very light gruel and strongly disapproved of any other additions, even tea. That was one order the nurses all ignored. You couldn't ask your patients to go without *tea*. Sometimes she thought they would all have got better faster if they'd been fed cheese and meat – wouldn't it make sense to give them foods known to stop up the bowel if eaten in excess? She wondered if anyone had done any research on it.

'Lemon drops, if they have them,' she said to Gertie. 'And peppermints.'

'We love you, Sister!' a man called out.

'You can show how much you love me by helping Gartley to the toilet,' she called back. 'And drink something, for God's sake!'

Hannah laughed at her and she grinned back. Thank God there was no need to be too proper around Australian soldiers! After years of biting her tongue with her father, this new freedom to say what she was thinking was exhilarating. As long as she didn't make the mistake of trying it with Matron.

The hospital was already half full, and the men hadn't even been into action yet – it was all dysentery and malaria cases, with the occasional inflamed appendix. Evelyn wondered how they would cope if a real wave of casualties hit them. Perhaps she'd give some extra time to making dressing packs.

•

Over the next few weeks, Margherita and Kitty did their best to make William feel at home, including showing him the best place to swim nearby. He took to swimming every morning, before breakfast, as he had back in Sydney and, before that, in the Parramatta River near home. The swims kept him fit and took the strain off his leg, and the walk back along the shore, under the date palms, was always the time he moved most freely.

It was an exotic setting, but the work itself was – well, boring. These were convalescents. After some days of checking temperatures and taking out stitches, when the greatest medical challenge was bed sores, he wondered if this had been worth leaving home for.

He was at his best in an operating theatre, where his hands and his mind working together were all that mattered. He missed those periods of fierce concentration. In those moments he forgot he had a body at all; his leg was irrelevant, no matter how much it hurt. Doing ward rounds here gave him no chance to forget that.

Almost the end of April already. After breakfast, he went to Margherita's office and tapped on the door. She welcomed him warmly and he sat at her desk and explained his intention.

'Ye-es,' she said. 'I can see why you might want to . . .' Sighing, she reached for her notepaper. 'I'll write a note of introduction to the Colonel at the 1st British Hospital in Cairo. He's a friend of my husband's.'

'Thank you,' he said. This was the way the British did things, he thought. They simply *knew* people. Too bad for the ordinary folk who knew no one.

•

He had thought it would be easy enough to pack a bag and catch a cab to Alexandria station, but the roads were clogged with carts and lorries and cars, and ambulances everywhere.

'What's going on?' he asked the cab driver, but the man didn't speak English and merely spread his hands and shook his head.

It took them half an hour to get close enough to the station that he could walk.

He grabbed his doctor's bag and his cane (Margherita would send his luggage on once he knew where he would be stationed) and headed towards the trains.

Even before he rounded a corner and saw the station concourse, he could smell the blood and the rank, unmistakable stench of a gut wound. The platform was filled with stretchers, with men using a branch or a stick for a crutch, with men with bandaged arms leading men with bandages around their eyes. A train was drawn up and stretcher-bearers were ferrying the wounded onto the train.

The attack on the Dardanelles. Everyone had been waiting for it. And this was the result. The *scale* of it was staggering. The carnage was so great it made him sick to his stomach. For a moment, he hesitated. Where to start?

A subaltern with a clipboard and his arm in a sling stood nearby, watching helplessly, tears running down his face.

'I'm a doctor,' William said. 'Where am I most needed?'

Relief spread across the subbie's face and he pointed to the end car. 'We're putting the worst ones in there. Thank God you've come!'

William moved as quickly as he could to the carriage, stopping here and there to examine a man who seemed particularly bad. He pulled a tourniquet tighter and told the soldier's mate, who was watching him, to loosen it every fifteen minutes. He moved a vomiting man onto his side lest he choke. He gave a shot of morphine – thank God he'd brought the ampoules instead of the tablets! – to a man screaming with pain.

It was surprisingly quiet, apart from that and the normal hissing steam noises of a train. The men were too exhausted to groan or cry out. But a few mumbled, 'Mum, Mummy . . .' and his heart bled for them.

There were other figures moving amongst the wounded, in uniform, labelled as doctors by their bags. So he could move to the carriage without feeling he'd abandoned all these men.

The carriage with the worst cases had a nurse there. She looked exhausted too, and almost sobbed when she saw his doctor's bag.

'Oh, Doctor, here, this one, I can't stop the bleeding.'

The man was a Maori, a New Zealander, a sturdy fellow whose naturally dark complexion had turned pale and greenish. It was a stomach wound but there was no smell of corruption, so the bullet had missed his bowels. William set to work as best he could in the unsanitary conditions, while the nurse kept watch over her other patients.

'Get as much water into them as you can,' William said over his shoulder, readying suture silk. His hands were shaking.

'Yes, Doctor.' The automatic response gave him courage. He threaded his needle and set to work.

A white woman poked her head in the carriage door. 'All right in here? Good. I'll take the next carriage. Dr Agnes Bennett.'

'William Brent,' he said automatically. He knew Agnes Bennett. She'd worked at the Mission House in Darlinghurst when he'd been a medical student.

'Will! Didn't recognise you without your white coat on. Good show.' She disappeared. He took a breath and concentrated on his stitching,. feeling far more confident they'd be able to manage it. With Agnes Bennett here, the odds had turned in their favour.

CHAPTER 6

'Incoming casualties!' Matron called. 'All staff to the rear of the hospital! The train from Alexandria will be here in ten minutes!'

It was here. The war had arrived. Evelyn took in a deep breath and sprang to her assigned duty, gathering as many wheelchairs as she could find and organising them into a long line near the back door, leaving space for stretcher-bearers to get past.

The train drew up right behind the palace, long white carriages, with the Egyptian star and crescent painted on each.

The orderlies moved forward, followed by the nurses. Evelyn was assigned to the middle carriage.

'Sort them according to urgency,' Dr Fanous had said. 'Worst first. Get *them* into the ambulances and then deal with the rest.'

It had sounded simple, but looking at the ground by the train, which was being covered – literally *covered* with stretchers and wounded men, Evelyn was paralysed. What to do first? They *all* looked so bad; and smelt bad, too, of mud and blood and excrement. Every man there was covered with a pall of yellow dust and grime; red-rimmed eyes gazed into nothingness, or implored her for help. They were in rags, only barely covered, and those mostly bloodstained. So many. Too many. But they lay in silence; all she could hear was the ambulant patients' footfalls, shuffling over the white gravel towards the palace.

Those with simple wounds, any who had the use of their legs, were being directed to the big back door of the palace, where stores were usually delivered, and sorted there into lines for dressings, beds, food and water.

She shook herself and began with the stretchers closest to the entrance, taking her big first-aid kit from stretcher to stretcher. A broken leg; painful but not life-threatening. An arm wound; ditto. She spoke words of reassurance to each man, and moved on, ignoring their pleas.

'Sister! Sister!' someone shouted. An orderly, his face white, holding someone down – no, the patient wasn't struggling, so he must be pressing on a wound. She hopped and scrambled her way through the throng.

'It's an artery!' the orderly said. The soldier was unconscious, and the big artery in his inner thigh was spurting through a field dressing. That was very bad.

'Hold it a moment more.'

In her chatelaine, she had catheter tubing. It would make a serviceable tourniquet. She fished it out and tied it above the wound, pulling it cruelly tight. The bleeding slowed, but didn't quite stop. She couldn't sit like this when so many men needed her help, but she couldn't leave this man without repairing the artery, and that was a job she wasn't qualified for – wasn't even a job which *could* be done by one person.

There were no doctors of their own here – all the Heliopolis doctors were prepping for surgery. These men were supposed to have been stabilised on the hospital ship, to be ready for transport, but clearly that hadn't happened. Too many of them, not enough staff or time. She was rocked by the number of casualties. Far above the numbers Dr Fanous had predicted. They weren't going to have enough dressing packs.

She realised that she wasn't thinking clearly. Her head seemed muddled. *Shock*, a professional part of her said, but why should she be in shock? Overwhelmed, more like it, by the number of wounded and the sheer size of the task they faced.

The bleeding began to increase. She did what she could: packed the wound with lint, which turned red immediately. She was going to have to try something radical, or this man – she looked at him for the first time – this dark-haired, brown-skinned man would die. But she couldn't think what.

'Right!' a voice said behind her. A man knelt on the other side of the stretcher. 'We'd better get that sewn up.' His voice, his manner, unmistakably declared him a doctor. 'What have you got in there? Can you sterilise the wound?'

'Yes, Doctor,' she murmured automatically. He had his own bag. As she used the lint in the wound to clear out any fragments and pulled out the disinfectant, he got himself into surgical gloves and found a suturing needle and thread. They came out of sterile packs, thank God. He handed her a pair of surgical gloves and she pulled them on over the blood.

And suddenly, just like that, she could *think* again. She knew her job, and knew how to help him do his. She'd done this exact procedure before, helping her father save a logger whose saw had broken and cut him.

The feeling, of being returned to who she was, was so exhilarating that she smiled. The doctor assumed she was smiling at him.

'Sister Northey, isn't it?' he asked, smiling back even while concentrating on suturing the artery together.

'Dr Brent!' He was the one who had given her the Army physical at Victoria Barracks. What on Earth was he doing here? Surely they hadn't let him into the Army? No, he was in civvies.

'The one and only,' he said. His face was intent, his hazel eyes sharp with intelligence and purpose. She felt a wave of thankfulness. Even one more doctor – one more *competent* doctor – would make a world of difference.

She concentrated on blotting up the seeping blood so he could see to suture, and checked the patient's lower leg. It was cold. 'We're going to have to let the tourniquet off pretty soon,' she said.

'A few more minutes, and we might save both the man and the leg,' he muttered.

So she shut up and blotted, and tried to ignore the moans and whispered pleading from the wounded men around her.

As he finished, another shout went up for a doctor from further down the platform. Dr Brent looked up, but a female voice answered, 'Coming, sonny!' and he grinned.

'That's Dr Agnes Bennett,' he said, tying off the last suture and holding the thread for her to cut. 'She arrived at Alexandria and took over. Wonderful woman. I worked with her in Sydney.'

'A woman doctor?' Evelyn looked down the platform, but she couldn't see this wonder of the ages. It gave her a warmth inside, though, to know there was at least one woman who was doctoring the wounded – and a spurt of anger. If her father hadn't been so recalcitrant, *she* might have been doctoring too. She wouldn't have had to wait until someone else came to save this man.

'Right!' Dr Brent stood up, a little stiffly. 'They can close him up at the hospital, do a thorough disinfection. Thank you, Sister.'

'Thank *you*, Doctor.'

Then they were off in opposite directions. She found orderlies to take the leg wound to the ambulance and began her job of sorting the saveable from the dead or merely hurt.

There were quite a few dead.

In the rush, all they could do was place them to the side for later collection; the living had more use of their stretchers than they. But she made sure to close their eyes tenderly, and to say a swift prayer over each.

After an hour or so, one of the ambulance drivers, George, gave her a message.

'Back to base, Sister, they need you in the operating theatre.'

Looking around, she realised that she had worked her way right to the back of the train, a long way from the palace. It would be quickest to hop in the nearest ambulance. She ran and scrambled in just as it started off.

Dr Brent was there, caring for a neck wound which threatened to burst its stitches. The soldier on the other stretcher was unconscious. He had a leg half blown off; she could smell the gangrene which meant the man would lose the rest of the leg in order to save his life.

They sat on the fold-down seats opposite each other, so she finally got a good look at him. Yes, it was Dr Brent.

'So you just – came?' she asked him.

He shrugged. 'Couldn't keep me out of it. I figured they might need more doctors than they thought.' He gestured to the train tracks behind them as the ambulance raced towards the casualties door. 'Seems like I was right. And if they're letting women doctors help, I reckon they'll take a cripple like me.'

'You're not a cripple,' she said without thinking, then blushed. It wasn't her place to comment on him.

'Well, not entirely,' he agreed with admirable equanimity. 'I can be useful.'

The ride to the hospital was short, a welcome break, and then it was a rush to the operating theatre, where the cases were backed up right down the corridor.

Evelyn looked out the window. As far back as she could see, the white ambulances were lined up, full of more wounded. The scale of the situation put lead in her stomach. How could they ever manage?

'Matron, we have another doctor!' Evelyn shouted down to where Matron and two nurses were prepping the next two cases.

Relief went over Matron's face, and then it was calm again. 'We'll need another operating theatre. Scrub down the table in the mess,' she said. 'And you, you get some better lights in there for the doctor.' The orderlies she'd nodded to said, 'Yessir!' and ran.

Evelyn ran too.

It took her, two VAD nurses and four orderlies, working as fast as she'd ever worked in her life, to prepare the makeshift operating theatre.

The trolleys were ready, at least, with their sterilised instruments and dressing packs.

Dr Fanous had sent out a cry for help, and an Egyptian anaesthetist had come in. Dr Brent, the anaesthetist and she became the central team for this theatre, with orderlies their backup, coming in to scrub the table between cases.

The first case was a bowel repair from a bullet wound; straightforward in some ways, but tricky in that her job – to keep the contents of the bowel from contaminating the abdominal cavity – was pernickety and easy to get wrong. For the first time, she blessed her father's insistence on perfect hygiene and strict hospital procedure, no matter where they were working, in his rooms or in the patient's home. At least here she knew what she was doing. And she realised that perhaps she was one of the few nurses who had assisted at operations in settings which weren't hospital-perfect.

After the first operation, she noticed Dr Brent rubbing his leg. The mess table wasn't as tall as a normal operating table, and he had been on his feet all day.

'George, get a stool for Dr Brent, and Walter, see if you can find a taller table, or a way to chock up these legs safely to make this one taller.'

The Egyptian doctor looked askance at her, as though a woman giving orders in this circumstance was intolerable, but Dr Brent smiled at her.

'That's very thoughtful of you, Sister.'

He was the first man she'd ever met who didn't protest, 'No, I'm fine.' His injury, whatever it was, must have forced that upon him. Poor man.

They brought a big flat packing crate to put the table on. She could feel the relief in her own back now she didn't have to bend over to the patient. The tall stool Dr Brent used between patients; he hitched his hip onto it and just rested his leg. It helped – she could see that.

'Wish I'd thought of this years ago, Sister,' he said, and grinned at her. She couldn't help smiling, although it was completely inappropriate. As operation followed operation, they had moved into a quiet, competent teamwork. He gave few instructions, relying on her to see what was needed, but didn't reprimand her if she didn't see immediately. Just told her quietly what he wanted.

Outside the room, she could hear the rush and shouts and occasional screams of an emergency being dealt with; here, while working at breakneck pace, Dr Brent created an illusion of calm and steady industry.

Matron came and insisted they all eat and drink. But there was no other time to rest. The sky paled outside and slid into darkness, and the lights the orderlies had set up seemed brighter in comparison to the growing dusk.

They had been at it for, what, six hours or so? And still they came, stretcher after stretcher, shrapnel wounds and gunshot wounds and bayonet wounds, broken ankles which had to be set and pinned, and, worst of all, amputations.

The man she'd travelled with in the ambulance was their first of those. The infection had spread so far they had to take the leg well above the knee, which reduced the man's chances. But without it, he would be dead in a couple of days. Once it got going, gangrene would spread rapidly and take over every body system until death occurred.

It took two hours. 'We have to go faster than that,' Dr Brent said, and gave orders about preparing the amputation cases in the corridor. Simple things that the VADs could do, which would save precious minutes on the table.

One boy, surely no more than eighteen, came in raving, begging them not to take his arm, crying hysterically.

'I'm a *pianist*,' he said, over and over again.

'What's your name, lad?' she asked him.

'John.'

'John, you can be a dead pianist, or a live man looking for a new profession.' He looked her in the eyes, and she could see that part of him would rather be dead, so she added, 'And you're a soldier now, laddie, so you have to take orders.'

Resignation filled his face and he turned it away from her. They could save him, she thought, but he probably wouldn't make it, and she was angry with him for giving up.

'Don't you *dare* lie down and die!' she said. 'Think of the people who love you. You fight to stay alive for their sake.'

He looked back at her, his eyelashes wet with tears.

'All right, Sister,' he whispered brokenly. 'I'll fight.'

'If you've *quite* finished, Sister,' the Egyptian anaesthetist said in purely British tones.

'Let's go,' Dr Brent said, but he nodded at her as though he approved.

•

Every decision seemed to take forever. Her arms and legs were heavy with fatigue. How long since she had slept? Two days? Three?

The rush of casualties had slowed by a degree. It was a flood now, rather than a deluge. But it was a flood they couldn't stem, or cope with except in the most basic of ways. A bed, a doctor's check, pain medication, X-rays where needed and operations when the theatre became available. The operating theatres were still going twenty-four hours a day. She had worked for two days straight, and then Matron had come to tell them that she was insisting on sleep, and that another doctor had been found to continue. The worst cases, the most life-threatening, were still being dealt with or sent off to other hospitals. There were others, scores of others, which had to be looked at in the morning.

Evelyn's feet were on fire and her back felt as though it had burning wires inside it. She stretched, uncaring of protocol.

Dr Brent's limp was very pronounced.

'Where are you staying, Doctor?' Matron asked.

'I have no idea,' he said. 'I arrived on the train with the wounded and came straight here.'

'Quite right,' she said. 'I have a bed made up for you in the doctors' quarters.'

A very tired-looking George came to show him the way. Before he left, Dr Brent turned to her and smiled. Such a sweet, open smile.

'Thank you, Sister. That was quite a day's work we put in.'

She ducked her head in acknowledgement, suddenly shy.

As he and Matron walked off, she heard him say, 'Can I have Sister Northey as my permanent theatre sister? She's very good,' and felt a weary remnant of pride wave within her.

Bed. Before she fell down right here in the corridor and slept on the floor.

As she went up the back stairs to her room she realised that the night staff was still working furiously, getting men bathed and fed and dressed, checking temperatures and pulses, changing dressings . . . and this was only the beginning. What would happen tomorrow?

That foreboding pushed her into having a bath before she flopped onto her bed. She might not have time in the morning.

She would have no time to study if this kept up. Perhaps she should take notes on the operations. Keep an aide-memoire for later, when she had time to go over things and relate what she had seen in theatre to her anatomy lessons. Yes. Her eyes closed without her willing it. Yes. She was learning so much, she should take notes.

•

The train which arrived the next morning had far more stretcher cases than walking wounded.

Connie Keys was in charge of the nurses while Matron got the operating theatre in the King of Belgium's suite fully staffed.

'Sister Northey,' Connie said, 'Matron has assigned you to the second operating theatre.'

Dr Brent was there, waiting, and a different anaesthetist, a British officer with a huge handlebar moustache.

'Sister Northey!' Dr Brent said. 'Excellent. Send the first one in.'

And it began again.

After every operation, while the orderlies changed the linen on the table, she took out her notebook and scratched a few words in pencil – just enough to jog her memory of the important things she'd learned. And she learned something, every time. How tendons were attached to knees, the line a muscle took under the shoulder, the best way to clamp off a big blood vessel . . .

Matron made her switch with another nurse after six hours, and eat, but there was no rest. In the mess hall, every nurse there was making dressing packs between mouthfuls.

Evelyn picked up the rhythm. It was a relief to sit down, but she worried about Dr Brent, until she saw him come in and grab a sandwich.

'Sit down for a while!' she told him, only realising after she'd said it how scolding her voice was.

'Yes ma'am,' he said. He slid into the seat beside her and sighed a little as he settled his hip.

She wondered if aspirin made any difference to his pain. Probably not much.

•

The ticket office at Luna Park was set up as a theatre, so the pace should have eased. But the casualties kept coming, and she was put on night duty, with one of the Australian Army doctors, Dr Goldstein. A nice enough man, but without Dr Brent's air of calm competence.

At the morning meeting to give out Daily Orders, Matron said, 'We've received, on average, three hundred casualties a day for the last three weeks, and I'd like to commend everyone on their hard work and professionalism.'

The numbers struck them dumb. Of course, they hadn't kept all of those patients here. Some had been sent to other hospitals, and those who had minor wounds, or simple dehydration, were sent back to camp with orders to present themselves to the dressing tents each morning for a check-up. But still. Three hundred a day. And how many of them had died?

She, Mabel and Alice Kitchin, a new girl, hurried off to the dressing tent after the meeting. They had been granted an 'easy day' after their weeks of theatre duty.

The dressing tent was hot, as usual, and within minutes she had sand in her shoe, grating uncomfortably. The 'easy day' had started after only three hours' sleep, and they had dressed fifty men's wounds by noon, the three of them working like navvies in the sweltering tent. She could feel a deep vibrating tiredness in her body, threatening a collapse if she didn't get to sit down soon. And eat something. Maybe it was hunger instead of fatigue which was making her woozy.

But the line was almost gone. Now there were only a couple left. A dark-skinned digger with a leg wound on the upper thigh, and a big Light Horse trooper with an ulcerated bullet crease on his leg which Mabel was seeing to while Alice piled the old bandages into the washing bag.

The dark-skinned man was the artery repair which she and Dr Brent had done next to the train on the first day of casualties. It gave her a moment of deep satisfaction to see him up and around. He didn't recognise her, having been unconscious the whole time of the repair, and she wouldn't draw attention to herself by telling the story. It was enough that he was getting better. And she realised, listening to his Aussie accent, that he must be Aboriginal, rather than the Indian or Gurkha she had first thought him.

'Yerse, I'm a Kamilaroi man myself,' the digger said to her, answering her question. 'Long way from my country, here.'

'I think we all get a bit homesick,' she agreed, smoothing down the lint pad over the worst of his wound.

'Better than being on the Mission, though,' he said cheerfully. 'A few of us joined up, see the world, have a lark.'

He reminded her of Harry – probably wasn't much older, and just as full of fun.

'Got a smoke on you?' he asked.

Evelyn grinned at him. 'No, but I'll give you a lolly once we're through. No smoking in the tents.'

'Fair enough.'

As she concentrated on tying the bandage flat, she could hear Mabel speaking to the trooper. That was Mabel's 'calm down please' voice, and it meant the patient was being stroppy.

'Don't worry. This is nothing but a scratch,' Mabel said soothingly. 'We'll have you back on the front line in no time.'

A crash and bellow of 'NOOOOO!'

Evelyn whipped around, instinctively standing in front of her patient. The trooper, all six foot four of him, had lurched to his feet and was screaming.

He grabbed a dressing tray and hit out with it, scissors and antiseptic flying. He caught Mabel on the shoulder, sending her stumbling back. Alice shrieked and ran. Evelyn stepped forward. Her knees were shaking, but the patient's safety was her responsibility.

'It's all right,' she said. He turned to look at her, anger and fear and desperation in his eyes.

'I'm *not going back*,' he snarled. 'I'm *wounded*. I did my bit.' He raised the tray as if to strike her and she braced for it.

Behind her, the digger was talking, 'Come on, mate, come on, it's not the sister's fault, eh, can't hit a woman, mate,' but the trooper didn't listen. He grabbed a scalpel from Evelyn's tray and held it like a dagger, and the dressing tray like a shield, eyes wild.

Mabel and the digger froze, and Alice whimpered.

'What's all this then?' Dr Brent's voice, inappropriately cheery, and he was suddenly standing in front of her, insinuating himself between her and the trooper. 'What's the problem here?' He was almost as tall as the soldier, and he looked him straight in the eyes.

'They're gonna send me back,' the big man growled, still glaring at Mabel and Evelyn.

'Nonsense!' Dr Brent said. 'Sister, what have you been telling this man? I'm the doctor, and I say you're going home.'

The trooper faltered, the tray dropping a little. 'Home?' His voice cracked like a boy's.

'Yes, of course, home. You can go on the next hospital ship,' Dr Brent said, still artificially bright. 'I'm the doctor, and I say so.'

The trooper began to weep. Great, racking sobs shook him and he sank to his knees, grasping Dr Brent's legs and bowing his head against his thigh, one big hand digging in tight. Evelyn saw pain flash across Dr Brent's face and started forward, taking the scalpel out of the trooper's hand. He dropped the tray and kept crying, saying, 'Home, home, home,' over and over again.

'Come on now,' she said gently. 'Come on, up you get.' But he was too far gone and they had to wait, standing there, until he'd cried himself out and was a limp, exhausted heap. It took three orderlies to get him on his feet and guide him out of the tent.

'Shell shock ward,' Dr Brent said, rubbing his own thigh, the leg that dragged a little when he walked. 'Treat him gently. He's had all he can take.'

'So have you,' Evelyn said. 'Sit up here and let me do that.'

'No need,' he said, moving to pick up the tray briskly and somehow managing to hide his limp. 'I'm fine.'

He wasn't, but what could she say? That the white pain lines around his mouth gave him away? She wouldn't drag a man down that way.

'Thank you. For saving us.' It was true. He'd rushed in without a thought and saved them all. And done it with compassion instead of force. Any other doctor would have ordered the man to stand down, and that might have led to disaster. She said so, and then wished she hadn't because he looked rueful.

'A lack of Army training can be an asset, you think?' he asked ruefully.

'It was this time.' He drew in the corners of his mouth, as though unconvinced. She paused, not sure what else to say.

'Sister Northey!' Mabel called. Evelyn turned to the next task with gratitude. All the bandages and instruments on the tray the trooper had flung around needed to be gathered and re-sterilised. But as she stooped and picked them up, she was aware of the flap of the tent being lifted, and when he left, the tent felt empty.

CHAPTER 7

'Ten minutes,' Dr Fanous said, looking at his watch. 'We can afford ten minutes to plan our shifts, before the next train arrives.'

He led William and Agnes Bennett into his office; behind them came the anaesthetists, and another doctor, an Australian Army captain whose name William hadn't caught.

Fanous's unit clerk was there already, at a small desk set to the side. There weren't enough chairs. Agnes took one as a matter of right, and Fanous waved William to the other. He tried not to limp as he moved into it, but after the hours he'd spent on his feet, it was a losing battle.

'The news from the Dardanelles is not good, gentlemen,' Dr Fanous said. William bit back a smile. Fanous was pretending Agnes was a man, apparently. She'd find that funny, so he'd better not meet her eyes. 'We can expect a steady stream of casualties for some time.'

A heavy silence fell. Then Fanous took a breath. 'Dr Bennett, Dr Brent . . . I appreciate that you are not Army, but if we're to deal with this crisis, we need you to stay. Are you willing to work under Army discipline?'

'As long as I get paid the same as Dr Malouf here,' Agnes said. Malouf! That was his name. An upright, not to say stiff, man with a big moustache.

'*Captain* Malouf!' the clerk piped up.

'A captain's pay will do just fine,' Agnes said. She put her blunt, capable hands down flat on her knees. The men in the room were flummoxed, as men so often were around Agnes Bennett. A woman asking for equal pay! William said nothing. She could handle these boys with one hand tied behind her. 'And the same for Dr Brent, of course,' she added.

He smiled at Fanous. 'I'm not sure I'm worth the same pay as Dr Bennett,' he said gently. Fanous blinked.

''Course you are, Will! You're a fine doctor.' Agnes turned to include Malouf and the others in the conversation. 'Susan O'Reilly speaks very highly of him. He's a good surgeon and an excellent physician.' She nodded with finality at the clerk. 'Put him down on captain's pay too.'

The clerk looked at Fanous while the others stared at William. He nodded back to them with a half-smile; polite but noncommittal. Fanous sighed.

'Yes. All right. Organise that, will you, Ridge?'

'Yessir.'

'You'd better stay here in the hospital, too.'

William sighed with relief. He hadn't been looking forward to finding digs in Cairo. A captain's pay was probably less than he had been getting at Sydney Hospital, but with room and board thrown in, it was a good deal more.

'Twenty-four-hour on-call, gentlemen, for the foreseeable future.' Fanous's face was grim. 'Let's try to keep down the body count, eh?'

'Every man we save is one more returned to the battlefield,' Malouf said. 'We know our duty.'

'I'll settle for saving lives,' William said. Malouf glared at him, but Agnes nodded and Fanous half-smiled.

'I don't think it's appropriate that Dr Bennett be on the same floor as the rest of us,' Malouf continued, still glaring.

'What? Why not?' Fanous looked puzzled, but Agnes laughed.

'For the *proprieties*,' she said. 'As if I'm going to flit in and out of your bedrooms! Hah! Don't flatter yourself, Malouf!'

Malouf's face went purple with embarrassment and rage.

'I think we can trust each other to that extent, Captain,' Fanous said quellingly. 'And Dr Bennett – perhaps just a *little* decorum?'

She grinned at him as she levered herself out of the chair. Even Agnes, indomitable Agnes, was showing her fatigue.

'All right, Major. I'll be a lady.' She went to the door and then looked back, her face full of mischief. '*If* I can remember how.' The door shut behind her and William laughed.

Malouf turned on him. 'Can't you keep that woman under control?' he hissed.

'Me? You've got me confused with someone else, Captain. I'm just a doctor, not a superman.'

In turn, he pushed himself upright, stifling a yawn. Only two hours sleep last night, and he was feeling it. Fanous tossed him a small packet. Aspirin. 'Keep that hip under control,' he said. 'We need you.'

'Yes, sir,' William said, half-embarrassed and half-gratified.

He limped to the door, wishing he'd brought his cane. Before he reached it, the door swept open. An orderly poked his head in.

'Train's coming!'

All of them ran out, William limping in their wake, towards more death and pain and, possibly, the saving of lives. Horrible. But the place in the world where he was most useful.

CHAPTER 8

That week, she was rotated back to ward duty.

Theatre was easy by comparison. Yes, you had to concentrate, but you could concentrate on one thing at a time. The wards were chaos – or, rather, controlled chaos where each sister juggled a dozen things at once.

Space was the main problem. When she'd arrived at Heliopolis, she'd thought the palace enormous, so huge that they would never fill it up. But the first day's casualties had done that, and now they were scrabbling for every inch of floor. Because she'd just come off theatre duty, she was placed in the surgical ward, in the old ballroom. A double height area with a balcony all around, wood-panelled and with a glorious parquet floor which was being destroyed by the scraping of iron bedstead legs, it was bursting.

The handover was illuminating. She and Hannah and Connie Keys were on together, and the sister-in-charge from the last shift pulled out a clipboard with a fan of paperwork to show them.

'When they're well, they get themselves back to camp. We don't have many of those, though. If they're ready to convalesce, they go by train to Alexandria, or sometimes to another hospital in Cairo – back to their own. If a New Zealander got caught up with our men and treated here, as soon as he can be moved he's sent to the New Zealand Army Hospital. The boys do better among their own.'

They nodded like marionettes, because they all knew it was true. When a man heard the accent of home, he relaxed, as though he was sure he'd get treated right. And that helped recovery.

'The dead are taken to the ice house until burial, which happens quickly, so get them out quick as you can. It upsets the others to have a corpse lying around.'

Hannah sighed. She was so soft-hearted, Evelyn wondered how she coped with the realities of nursing.

'Don't worry, we don't get too many of them either. Mostly what we've got,' she raised her voice, 'is a bunch of whingers and whiners.'

There was laughter from the men and a chorus of, 'That's right, Sister,' and 'You tell 'em, Sister!'

The sister-in-charge smiled and handed the clipboard to Connie. 'Keys, you're in charge. Dressings first, then breakfast. And watch yourselves. We got a bunch of the 4th Light Horse in last night, and they're cheeky buggers.'

Harry's unit! Evelyn had been working so hard that she'd barely had time to worry about Harry, but it hit her now. She found herself wondering which of the unkempt heads in the ward belonged to Light Horsemen, and had to restrain herself from rushing wildly from bed to bed, asking if Harry was all right.

But the list on Connie's clipboard didn't have Harry's name on it. She took a deep breath and let it out. She had to concentrate on her work.

Their shift started at six, so they had been woken by the cries of the muezzins and now the sharp morning light was cutting through the shutters and striping the beds with bands of gold.

While Hannah began making breakfast gruel in a dixie over a camping stove, Connie and Evelyn, with two orderlies each, busied themselves with checking the dressings and redoing any that needed it. It was a huge job. Evelyn now understood why every spare moment was spent making dressing packs. The orderlies here were two older men, very sure of themselves, and inclined to patronise the nurses as not being 'regular Army'.

The doctor arrived halfway through the dressing round, in uniform. A captain. Captain Malouf. Regular Army. Evelyn hadn't had anything to do with him, but he had the reputation of being very spit and polish.

One of the orderlies, seeing him, shouted, 'TEN-HUT!' and the men struggled out of bed to stand to attention. How ridiculous!

'Get back into bed!' she ordered a man with a gut wound who was struggling to rise. He risked all his stitches bursting by getting up like that. She put her hand on his shoulder and pushed him down.

'Sister! Army discipline has to be maintained!' Malouf said sternly, as though she were an idiot.

She knew who the idiot was. She opened her mouth but before she could say anything, Hannah had rushed up to the doctor, fluttering her eyelashes.

'Oh, Doctor, these men are too sick to stand up. Surely you don't want them to strain their stitches?' Her voice was so soft and reasonable, and her gaze up at him so troubled, that the doctor muttered, 'All right, I suppose . . .'

Hannah immediately turned to the men with a beaming smile, 'All right boys, you can all hop back into bed!' The men let out a cheer; most of them fell back onto their sheets, exhausted even by the brief time on their feet. Evelyn laughed at the doctor's expression. He stalked past her muttering about 'barbaric Australians'. Wasn't he Australian himself?

Connie and Hannah and Evelyn shared looks brimful of laughter with the men around them, but the orderlies weren't impressed.

'We're supposed to keep proper military discipline here, miss,' one of them, Clive, said.

Evelyn smiled at him. 'I'm sure the boys won't forget their discipline while they're healing, Corporal, but just think of this as their home – they're on leave, in a way, while they're here.'

As she and Hannah followed the doctor on his rounds, taking down his orders about each of the men, Evelyn resolved not to underestimate Hannah again.

One of the wounded was Linus Yates, Rebecca Quinn's brother. Evelyn felt a quick spurt of alarm, but his good colour and ability to sit up showed he hadn't been badly wounded. On the contrary, he was keen to get back to the front despite the bullet wound on his lower arm which still showed proud and weeping. He waved at her over the doctor's head as

Captain Malouf bent to examine his wound; they had met in her schooldays, when she had visited Rebecca in the holidays.

'At least one more day here,' the doctor told him, 'and then a week in camp with daily dressings before you get the all-clear. You might even get some leave.'

'But I'm *fine*,' Linus insisted.

Hannah put a hand to his forehead. 'Temp's up still,' she said.

'It was only a crease.' He pulled her hand down and kissed the palm. 'Please, wonderful Sister, glorious Sister, tell the nice doctor I'm fine.'

Hannah snatched her hand back and narrowed her eyes at him, although she was smiling. They were all smiling – even the orderlies. Linus was, as the last sister had said, a cheeky bugger.

'At *least* one more day here,' Hannah said firmly. 'You heard the doctor.'

Linus sighed dramatically. 'Well, don't blame me if they lose the peninsula because I'm not there. Harry can't hold it alone, no matter how fit he is!' He winked at Evelyn.

Evelyn bit back a laugh. He was joking, of course, but like so many of these young men he was thirsting for action – and to thirst for action while knowing firsthand what it was like was real bravery. It was nice of him to reassure her about Harry, too.

'Now,' the doctor said, moving on to the next patient, 'what have we here?'

As she followed him, out of the corner of her eye Evelyn saw Linus say something else to Hannah quietly – and this time she blushed, as she hadn't blushed when he kissed her hand. But she moved away smartly. Good girl. Their pact not to become romantically involved was just good sense. Loving one of these boys was an invitation to grief.

The doctor's round showed her how badly off some of the men were. Amputation cases were the worst for the men, but medically the gut wounds were the most worrisome. She took down instructions regarding pain relief very carefully; and after the doctor left that was her first priority. These boys were in so much pain, and bore it so stoically. Morphine was a blessing.

From there, the day descended into a scramble: to get the dressings done and then make enough dressing packs to replace the ones they'd used, to get the men fed their breakfast, when half of them couldn't hold a spoon, to take the hourly observations which were crucial to ensuring the newly operated upons' good health, to begin to get lunch ready – and at that point it became surreal, because women began to arrive to help. Mostly British expats, in elegant hats and gorgeous stoles, but also some Egyptian women, equally well dressed and followed by their maids. They wafted in on clouds of perfume and good will, nodding graciously to the nurses.

Evelyn was dumbfounded. She'd had no idea this was going on. From baskets and bags the women took fruit, sweetmeats, newspapers and even, in one case, a cream bun.

'I'm not sure he should be having that,' Evelyn said to the woman, but the man in question had a leg wound, and there was no real reason he shouldn't, so she turned a blind eye. These women were so generous – with their time, as well as their food. They sat and talked quietly, or played cards with the wounded, or read them their letters from home.

She grabbed a quick moment to ask Linus more about Harry. He grinned at her with brotherly affection. 'When I got winged, Harry said to me, "Get into Lynnie's ward, she'll look after you."'

'And . . . he's well?'

'Was when I left,' Linus said cheerfully. 'Born to be hanged, that lad.'

So that was all right. She fought not to imagine Harry at Anzac. That way lay endless anxiety.

'Don't leave for the front without me giving you a letter for him.'

'Right you are.'

'Sister!' one of the men called, and she moved away from Linus Yates, giving a slight wave as farewell.

The patients tried their best, but sometimes, especially as the morphine wore off, they would moan, or call out. That was part of nursing, too, and an important part, to go to those in pain and comfort them. Evelyn didn't begrudge the moments spent whispering reassurance to a frightened teenager, or to holding the hand of a man racked with pain. But it did cut into the other work.

The shift was almost over before she realised that she hadn't had anything to eat except a cup of tea and a mouthful of the men's soup that Hannah had heated over their camp stove in the scullery.

She really hadn't expected that nurses would be cooking lunch – *cooking*, for heaven's sake. Or at least heating up; the kitchens sent up soup to be heated and served.

Nothing was like a normal hospital, including shift changes. Ten minutes before they were due to go off duty, a new batch of casualties arrived. Some had been treated on the hospital ship, and they came straight to the ward and had to be bathed, clothed, fed and given pain relief, so both shifts were needed.

Evelyn was so tired that her eyes kept closing on their own, even while she was standing up. She daren't sit down. She would fall asleep in seconds. The dust from the desert seemed to have got under her eyelids. Every time she blinked it gritted.

She and Hannah left the ward at eight o'clock, having been on duty for fourteen hours. They were looking after four or five times as many patients as in a normal hospital ward, and every day there were more. Evelyn dragged herself up the huge curving stairs with their intricate carving and couldn't muster a single drop of appreciation. Except for the Red Cross women. Without the stores sent to them by the Red Cross in Australia and Britain, those men would have no clean pyjamas or socks, no slippers, no shaving tackle, no notepaper or pens. Angels, she thought wearily as she undressed and fell into bed. Angels with armbands.

Hannah turned off the light. In the darkness, unbelievably, her voice was bright. 'That Lieutenant Yates is nice, isn't he?'

'Don't you go falling for a man in uniform, Hannah Page. They just go off and get themselves killed.'

'Don't say that!' she protested. 'Anyway, I'm not falling for him. He just makes me laugh.'

'Uh-huh . . .'

•

On their last afternoon on the surgical ward, Lieutenant Yates was finally marked 'Release to camp'. His fever had been up and down unpredictably, and although he'd kept begging to be discharged, no one had listened to him.

As he finally dressed and got to his feet, Hannah and Evelyn moved in to strip the bed ready for the patient waiting on a stretcher in the corridor. In his new uniform, cleaned and pressed, he looked both handsome and rather dashing, particularly with his arm in a sling.

He hesitated and spoke softly. 'Sister Page . . .' Hannah straightened up, an armful of sheets forming a decent barrier between them. He passed her a piece of paper. 'My Army postal direction. If you were inclined to write a note now and then . . .'

Hannah bit her lip. She usually looked, Evelyn thought, like the perfect nurse, but her soft brown eyes weren't so professional now.

'If I have time,' she said, brisk and businesslike. And then ruined it by blushing.

He put his cap on and raised it politely to her. 'I'll look forward to hearing from you, Sister.'

Whistling jauntily, he joined two other men who had been discharged and they went out to the waiting buggy, which would take them back to camp.

Evelyn and Hannah continued to make up the three beds. As soon as they did one, the orderlies whisked a new patient onto it.

'So,' Evelyn said as she stuffed the dirty sheets into the hamper at the side of the ward. 'Letters, eh?'

'Oh, don't be like that. He's a nice man, and it won't do any harm.'

Evelyn smiled at her teasingly, but Hannah's face was serious. 'Who knows what will face them? We've seen the results. If a letter or two makes it easier . . . well, that's just my patriotic duty.'

'And the fact that it's Lieutenant Yates is just a coincidence?'

Hannah tilted her nose into the air and looked down it in an unconscious imitation of Matron.

'As a matter of fact, I'm already writing to a couple of younger lads. Like a sister. So there.'

Evelyn raised a hand in defeat, but she couldn't help but think that the 'couple of younger lads' probably hadn't made Hannah blush.

•

Two weeks on the ward and then, thankfully, back to the operating theatre. Dr Brent had asked for her again, Matron said halfway through a shift, and she could start at the Luna Park theatre the next day. 'But we don't want to get him too set in his ways, do we Sister, so encourage him to work with other nurses, eh? I'm putting Mabel Walker on as assistant so you can train her up to the way he likes things.' She paused. 'It's very good of him to come here and help, of course.'

Her tone implied there was something not quite right about that. Evelyn bristled a little.

'He's very patriotic,' she said.

'Mmm. Well, we're *all* patriotic.'

Of course, it was true. Unlike the British Army, the Australian Expeditionary Force was made up entirely of regular Army and volunteers. Every single member of their Force had chosen to be there. As had every single one of the nurses and orderlies.

Working at the operating theatre in Luna Park had an odd rhythm to it, and not only because she had drawn night duty. Every evening, drivers George and Hartley picked up the shift's worth of nurses and orderlies and took them to their posts. They went in the back gates, first to the merry-go-round, which had been cleared of its horses, so that the beds of the ward formed a circle on the carousel base. Only the almost recovered were sent there, as the heat and wind could be fierce.

Then the hall of mirrors. Then the haunted house.

Then to the ice rink – a huge echoing space which had been filled in with wooden flooring and which held more than four hundred beds. That was a general ward. Most of them were ambulatory, although malaria and dysentery kept some in bed.

She and Mabel were last off this evening, along with their orderlies, Grosvenor and Stewart. The orderlies were usually called by their last names, although the ambulance drivers weren't. She would never get the hang of all the subtle distinctions Army traditions imposed.

Then the work began. The operating theatres went twenty-four hours a day, which meant their job was to seamlessly take over from the day shift and ensure that nothing stopped the steady flow of stretchers in and out of theatre – as well as acting as theatre sisters and assisting at each operation. The orderlies brought the patients in and, afterwards, took them off to the haunted house, which was the post-op ward.

The men had been X-rayed, when needed, before they came over, so one of her jobs was to get the X-ray films and hold them up to the light for the doctor. The images – so strangely blurred, so elusive in meaning – nonetheless had immense power. To see inside a human body: that was a great gift for a surgeon. But when she held up the films, and saw the bright white shapes which meant shrapnel embedded in the living tissue, it made her shudder. She controlled it so no one saw, but it was something she never got used to.

The first op this evening was a shrapnel case. She held up the film for Dr Brent. Sure enough, bright white spots on the X-ray showed up all down the patient's leg and through his buttocks. She went cold, imagining the moment when that metal had torn its way through blood and bone, ripping flesh apart with casual evil.

'Well, this chappie's not going to be sitting down happily any time soon, eh, Sister?' Dr Brent joked, then changed his tone as he looked at her. 'Are you all right, Sister?' he asked quietly.

She shook herself. Fancy letting herself get spooked by a simple X-ray.

'Yes, of course, Doctor. I'm fine.' No one but Dr Brent had ever noticed her reaction; was it getting worse, or was he just very observant? For the first time, she doubted her suitability to be a doctor. If she fell to pieces at an X-ray . . . how could she help her patients if she couldn't control her emotions?

She couldn't think about it now.

'Bring him in, Grosvenor,' she ordered, and they got to work.

CHAPTER 9

William knew he was a competent surgeon, and the last few weeks had honed his skills, but around midnight a man was carried in who was more wound than flesh. And the wounds were red with incipient infection.

'How is he still alive?' Sister Northey wondered aloud as she held up the X-rays for him to peer at.

It was a good question. This bloke had been blasted with shrapnel which had almost cut him to pieces, but in addition to that, he'd caught a sniper's bullet across his shoulders – he'd clearly been standing sideways as it hit, because it had gone through one shoulder, angled down to scrape along a rib, and been deflected backwards. Now it sat lodged against his spine.

Sister Northey was reading the notes which had come on the gurney with the patient.

'He has no feeling below T2,' she said.

The second thoracic vertebra. Well, that made it easier, in a way – he wouldn't have to worry about causing damage to the spinal nerves. Unless it was the pressure of the bullet which was causing the damage.

'It's in very deep,' Sister Northey said.

'Summon the diving bell, Sister,' he said, 'we're going down and under.'

She smiled involuntarily. She always did, no matter how bad or silly his joke was. An admirable thing in a woman, to laugh at your jokes.

They took out the surface shrapnel on the front first, so they could clean and stitch those wounds before they turned the man over onto his face. His limbs, sure enough, had that deadweight feel about them which showed they weren't under his control – even unconscious, the body didn't feel quite so heavy. Fixing the surface wounds was supposed to be safer for the patient, but it worried him that it meant a much longer anaesthetic. With his T2 injured, who knew how his heart was?

William prayed as he made the incision near the spine. It was an awkward angle to go in at, and he might make things worse. Sister Northey was there, steady as always, intelligent eyes noting his needs and supplying them even before he asked. A good nurse was a treasure. The other girl, Mabel Walker, was pretty good, too, but she didn't have Evelyn's quickness of perception. That level of intelligence was rare. He lived most of his life with people who were less intelligent than he was; to find one who matched him was a surprise present.

As he went in with probe and forceps, everything else dropped away: the lingering heat under the old tin roof, the sounds of men's nightmares from the ice rink, carrying this far on the still night air, the tram trundling along the main road in front of the hospital, the churring of a nightjar and the bark of a dog, the pain in his leg . . . even the clinking of instruments in the hiss of the sterilising water faded, until all he could hear was his own breath and heartbeat, and the small sounds his patient made.

These were the moments when he came fully alive, when his hands and his mind worked together to help someone. He came at the bullet from the side, instead of the more obvious dorsal route. It just seemed less likely to cause more damage.

'Blood pressure dropping,' Sister Walker said.

'We're losing him, Will,' the anaesthetist, Dick Kennington, warned.

A quick in and out was the only way. Almost there. Evelyn blotted and held closed the blood vessel nearby with her fingertips; no time for a clamp. He slid the probe in and touched the bullet, jockeyed the forceps into position, and pulled.

He held up the bullet in triumph, but a small sound from Evelyn made him look down. She had let go of the small blood vessel she had been clamping, but the blood was simply seeping into the wound instead of spurting, as it had been.

Failure hit him like a truck. He'd been so *close* to pulling it off. Anger swept through him. If he'd only been a bit *faster*!

'No pulse,' Sister Walker said.

Dick Kennington pulled off the chloroform pad he had been holding over the man's mouth. 'Maybe it's just as well,' he said. 'Hell of a life, no movement below the neck. They don't last long anyway.'

'Pneumonia,' Sister Walker said. 'They're so prone to pneumonia, the paralysed.'

The word swept him back in time, to when he had been paralysed as a small child. Polio had caught him in an iron fist, and for weeks he had only been able to turn his head and sip at a straw, or scramble his fingers on the counterpane. If someone had asked him, then, 'Would you want to live or die if you had to live like this?' he would have chosen life, still. A life of the mind, which was all he could have had, was better than death.

Evelyn reached out and closed the man's eyes, an unnecessary gesture as his eyes were already shut. But the movement had the feeling of a prayer.

'Orderly!' Dick called. 'Note the time of death as 12.14 a.m. Bring the next one in.'

Because there was no time to pause, no time to mourn. Another poor soul was out in the corridor, waiting for his turn.

William pulled off his gloves, threw them forcefully into the bin to be re-sterilised, then went to wash in the scullery. Sister Northey followed him.

'You did all you could,' she said, as they shared the basin and scrubbed at their hands as though they could scrub away the guilt he felt as well as the blood.

'Yes,' he said on a sigh. Her eyes were full of compassion – for him? For herself? For the patient? All three, he thought, and everyone else as well. 'Thank you, Sister.' It was a formal acknowledgement, but heartfelt.

She smiled: a mere pressing of the lips together, a smile full of pain. 'It was a good technique. If that had been the only wound, you would have had no trouble.'

'If-onlys don't help much when you write the letter to the parents,' he said. God, he sounded like a whining schoolboy.

'I'll do that, if you'd like me to. It might be better. I can tell them how hard you tried, and you can't really do that.'

'Thank you, Sister. I'd appreciate that.'

She smiled at him reassuringly, those green eyes shadowed with fatigue, and went out.

What a night! What a fool he was.

•

She got up even earlier than normal – mid-afternoon, the quietest time of the hospital day, unless casualties arrived, and the silence downstairs suggested they hadn't – yet. Hannah was still asleep, so she went to the extraordinary sitting room which had been put aside for the nurses. They had left the original furniture in this room: a big comfortable sofa and two overstuffed armchairs covered in gathered floral chintz, and two enormous carved and pierced wooden screens, inlaid with ivory. The kind of screens one imagined in the *Arabian Nights*, when the sultan is spying on his wife. Even the wall plasterwork was ornate, and the mantelpiece a mastery of carved marble. Evelyn strongly suspected it had been the housekeeper's room, and therefore not considered important enough to empty, but if the housekeeper had lived like this, how on Earth had the guests been treated!

She set herself up on a rattan table in the corner to write the letter to the patient's parents. His commanding officer would write one, too, when the company clerk sent the man's personal effects back to his family.

But when she got his details from the effects Grosvenor had given her, she realised it was his wife she had to write to. He had seemed so young! Too young to have a wife. But there it was in his pay-book, clear as day. Twenty-two and had a wife.

How did you tell a woman her husband was probably better off dead? Particularly when, deep down, you didn't believe it? Surely *nothing* was that bad. The man, Private Wrightson, could have still spoken to the ones he loved, laughed with them, maybe even, if Dr Brent had been right, recovered some feeling. But he would no doubt have been a financial burden, even though he'd have had an Army pension. Oh, what did she know! But she wouldn't write about all that. All she could say was: *Your husband passed away peacefully and without pain.* That was true enough. *His wounds were extensive, and it was possible that he would have been paralysed from the neck down even had the operation to remove the bullet been successful.* No, she couldn't write that. The operation *had* been successful. If he hadn't had the other wounds . . .

She started again with a new sheet of paper. *Your husband passed away peacefully and without pain. The doctors worked for some time, but he . . .* What would his wife understand? She couldn't use medical jargon . . . *but he had lost too much blood, and could not be revived.* Yes, that was better. Simple. *My deepest condolences, yours sincerely, Sr Evelyn Northey.*

Maybe she could make it better.

She worked over it for more than an hour; a precious hour of silence and simple focus. It was the first quiet moment she'd had in weeks. A shame it had to be spent this way. At that thought, some deep emotion rose up in her, and she began to weep. She sat, huddled over the small table in the corner, and shook with silent tears. Hot, scalding, *scolding* tears, as though her body were taking her to task for something. She couldn't stop. She didn't even know why she was crying, except that it had all seemed too much, suddenly. She pushed the letter aside, to keep it dry, and put her head down on the table, hiding her face in her folded arms. And cried.

A long time passed before she stopped.

She took a breath. Another, deeper one. Raised her head.

Well.

She mopped at her eyes and went to the bathroom nearby to splash cold water on her face. That was the worst of being a redhead: skin so pale that any redness around the eyes made you look half-dead.

There. She would do now. She looked at herself in the mirror and smiled wryly. She looked like something the cat had dragged in, but that was the good thing about a nurse's uniform – patients saw the veil, not you.

It was always hard to lose a patient. Thank God she was a woman, and able to give in to tears. She wondered how Dr Brent was feeling.

CHAPTER 10

William leant back on the stool with relief. His leg was full of hot wires, burning and painful, and his hip . . . best not to even think about that. He hoped he wasn't doing permanent damage, but what could he do? He'd caught a few hours' sleep five operations ago, but the parade of casualties just kept coming.

He couldn't say, 'My leg hurts, I have to stop,' when a mere boy was lying in front of him with half *his* leg blown off.

Wearily he hoisted himself off the stool – thank God for Sister Northey who had insisted on it! – and went to scrub up and receive a new gown, cap and mask. He wondered when they were going to run out. He mentioned it to the sister on duty.

'Don't worry,' she said. 'Matron has a local crew of launderers working night and day, washing and ironing dry.'

Competence, he thought, was a wonderful thing.

'What's the next one?'

The sister – a nice young thing, with black hair and eyes which were still bright even at this hour – held up the X-ray.

'Not a bad one,' she said. 'Just a bullet wound in the leg. We're bringing him in now because the wound is near the femoral artery and Dr Bennett was afraid the bullet might shift and nick the artery.'

He briefly was sent back to the moment he'd met Sister Northey again, when he'd sewn up that femoral artery near the train. He blinked. Dr Bennett was right. Better not to risk that.

'Bring him in,' he said, slipping on new gloves.

•

He had to lie down, or he would fall down. Dr Fanous had come and relieved him in the operating theatre, saying brusquely, 'Go and sleep, Brent.'

Finding his way back to his bedroom had been trickier than he'd thought; this damn palace was enormous. As he finally made his way up the last staircase, he let himself lean on the railing for support and hop-stepped along, pulling himself up by the banister. His cane was almost useless when his leg was this bad.

'Dr Brent! Are you all right?' Sister Northey came up from behind him, her quick steps seeming to mock his lameness. But her face, as he turned to meet her, was full of concern, without a trace of pity.

'I'm fine. Just paying for being on my feet too long.'

He waited for her to say that he should have been more careful; that he should have stopped sooner; that he should be less than he knew he could be. But she nodded.

'I know. Matron's just ordered me to bed after – three days, I think? We're all walking ghosts.'

Unobtrusively, she offered him her arm to lean on.

It would be rude, not to mention stupid, to refuse.

'I'm on the next floor up,' he said.

'Yes. Doctors get better rooms than nurses. I'm in the servants' quarters in the attics.' Her face was full of mischief, not complaint, and he smiled back at her. The turned-down gas mantles gave a soft blue light, which bleached out her face and made the small bit of hair revealed by her veil seem dark. He preferred it red.

They settled into a pattern which got him up the stairs far more quickly than he could have managed alone. Despite his weariness, he was aware of her warmth, the soft curve of her breast near his arm, her breaths coming a little faster as they climbed. She was beautiful. In the night, in the day, in sunlight or by gaslight, she was beautiful. Intelligent, purposeful, kind. Very kind.

Out of his reach like a star.

They reached the corridor which led to his room and he detached himself firmly.

'Thank you, Sister,' he said. 'I can manage from here.'

'If you say so, Doctor.' She glanced up at him and he realised that, although she gave the impression of height because of the way she held herself, she was only about five foot five. His lips were level with her forehead. 'Sleep well.'

She headed off up the stairs, tactfully not watching him struggle down the corridor.

Out of his reach.

He made it into his room and stripped off his sweaty clothes. Did he have the energy to sponge himself down? Those sheets looked so clean, he couldn't bring himself to sully them. The washstand water was cool, but that was pleasant on a warm night like this. He sponged himself, and afterwards, sitting on the side of the bed, forced himself to massage his accursed leg. He'd be sorry tomorrow if he didn't. The muscles would lock up and he'd be lucky if he could stand at all.

Those battered young men would need him tomorrow. And the next day. So he dug his fingers into the tense, scarred muscle and worked it until it relaxed a little. There were times he hated this leg with a visceral loathing. If he were whole . . .

But he wasn't. And it would only get worse with age. He knew that. *This* was his time to contribute to society, because later he might well be bedridden, or reduced to stumbling around on crutches, or being in a wheelchair.

No normal life for him.

No red-headed, green-eyed Sister Northey. How could he ever ask a woman to marry him, knowing she was marrying a cripple who would deteriorate into being nothing but a burden?

Despite his weariness, it took a while for him to sleep.

CHAPTER 11

Today Dr Bennett was operating. It was thrilling. Really thrilling, Evelyn thought, to stand next to a woman surgeon and assist her. A promise of what the future might hold.

It was hot in the ticket office. They could open the doors and windows only between operations, in case dust or flies got into the open wound. And the flies! She'd always thought Australian flies were bad, but these Egyptian ones were worse. Smaller and darker and often with a bite.

'What do we have here?' Dr Bennett asked. Evelyn held the X-rays up to the light. A long, thin shard of something – not shrapnel, more like a sheet metal fragment from the actual shell – embedded in the soldier's left thigh. The wound was puffy with pus, but there was no smell of gangrene, and the infection was localised.

'Easy one to start with,' Dr Bennett pronounced. She patted the young man on the shoulder with a reassuring hand. 'Don't worry, sonny, we'll have that out of you in no time.'

The soldier smiled weakly at her. 'When's the doctor get here?' he asked.

Dr Bennett rolled her eyes, and Evelyn stepped in. 'Dr Bennett is an excellent doctor,' she admonished him.

'A *sheila*! No fear, I'm not having a sheila cut me up!' He struggled to sit up and the orderlies rushed forward and pushed him down.

'Don't worry,' Dr Bennett said, 'I'll leave your balls intact.'

She nodded to the anaesthetist, a rather dour Welshman called Lewis, and he began to administer the chloroform, dripping it into a mask covered by a single layer of gauze held above the patient's mouth and nose.

'Count backwards, boyo,' he said, slowly dripping.

'But . . .'

'You'll be fine,' Evelyn said. 'Just relax.'

A minute or so later, Dr Lewis lowered the mask to the patient's relaxed face, and a couple of minutes after that, he put on the ether mask and nodded to Dr Bennett to start.

As she had said, it was a routine, quick extraction and clean-up, but somehow it felt important to Evelyn, perhaps because of the man's objections. They'd show him!

After the patient was sewn up and taken off to recover in the quiet ward, Dr Lewis pulled off his gloves and said, quietly and ferociously, 'I'll not be working with a woman with a foul mouth, *Doctor*,' and walked out.

'What on Earth?' Dr Bennett said.

'How *dare* he!' Evelyn said.

The orderlies looked at each other and shuffled their feet.

'Very religious man, Dr Lewis,' Matthews volunteered. 'Methodist.'

'But – what did I say?' Dr Bennett looked honestly astonished.

Matthews gazed imploringly at Evelyn, and she realised what it must have been.

'Because you talked about the patient's testicles, I think, Doctor,' she said, not sure if she should laugh or be angry.

They exchanged a long look of exasperation with male sensitivity.

'Is there anyone else who can deliver anaesthetics?' Dr Bennett demanded. 'We have patients queued up out there!'

'I can,' Evelyn said, very quietly. 'Or rather, I have, for my father. When he had to operate at a patient's house.'

'Excellent! Matthews, go and get another theatre nurse for me. Northey, scrub up for the next patient and get the gear ready. You can use my stethoscope.'

'Yes, Doctor.' What had she done? Had she overreached herself? But she *had* given anaesthetic before, many times. Why shouldn't she do it now? Her gut was buzzing with nerves and excitement. To work, almost as equals, with Dr Bennett! It was like a dream.

The first patient was a slight man, a bit older than normal, with an unfortunate smoker's cough which was going to make sedating him more difficult. She would have to watch him carefully, and be sparing with the ether, because it could irritate the breathing passages and make him cough, which might be disastrous in the middle of an operation.

A long one, too. Multiple shrapnel wounds, several sites, some quite deep.

'Come along,' she said with authority. 'Just lie back and count, and it'll all be over before you know it.' At least this one did as he was told, and didn't seem to object to lady doctors. 'Close your eyes,' she said gently. 'That makes it easier.'

Obediently, silently, he closed his eyes, but his whole body was tense with terror; sweat on his brow, his fists clenched by his sides, his breaths coming short.

'It's all right,' she soothed. 'You'll be fine.' A drop of chloroform on the gauze, and then another, the drug spreading out over the gauze, the heavy fumes seeping downwards, to his panting mouth. 'Breathe deeply,' she said. As the fumes hit, he gradually relaxed. She waited until the small muscles at the side of his eyes let go, and then placed the mask firmly on his mouth and nose. She mustn't press too hard or he would have a rash from the drug around the sensitive skin there. Not the liquid but the fumes did the job.

She even remembered to keep her own face well back so she wasn't affected.

The next two hours were the hardest she had spent since she arrived. Not that the work was difficult – but her fear that she would get something wrong and cause the death of the patient, or have him wake up and feel the full pain of the surgeon's scalpel, kept her tense and hyper-sensitive to any change in the patient's breathing or pulse. She barely took the stethoscope off her ears.

When Dr Bennett pulled down her mask and said, 'That's it, take him away,' she felt the most profound relief of her life.

She pulled down her own mask and sighed.

'You did well,' Dr Bennett said. 'You'll be fine. Walk around a bit. Loosen yourself up before the next one.'

Connie Keys had taken over as theatre nurse.

'Teach me that,' she said quietly to Evelyn as they scrubbed for the next patient.

'Absolutely,' Evelyn said. 'Just don't tell Matron.'

They grinned at each other and then went back to work.

•

The last case was tricky. A shot through the side had punctured the man's lung. It had been patched up hurriedly on the hospital ship, and the lung reinflated, but X-rays showed that part of the bullet was still lodged in the outside surface of the lung. The fragment would have to be removed without reopening the earlier wound.

He came in unconscious, which was bad for Evelyn – it was much harder to judge the patient's level of sedation if they were already unconscious. At least she didn't have to put up with the heavy-handed jokes about women doctors which the last two patients had made before bravely (in their estimation) putting their lives in her care.

If he was unconscious, did she need the chloroform? She decided to move straight to the ether; it was a stronger drug and she'd have to keep a close eye on his pulse and respiration. So far, so like all the others.

But she got a syringe of ephedrine ready, just in case, and was vigilant in taking his blood pressure.

It was a difficult operation, not helped by the intense heat. Connie called an extra nurse in to assist by mopping the sweat from Dr Bennett's forehead. They were all sweating freely, hair sticking to their scalps, hands slippery inside the hot gloves.

'All right, there's the bullet . . . Damn!' Dr Bennett grabbed lint and began to pack the wound. 'We've got a bleeder. The bullet was blocking it . . .'

A terrible burbling, whistling sound, as the hole in the patient's lung let out air and blood.

Evelyn blocked it out, and the sounds of Dr Bennett and Connie diving in to fix it. The patient's colour was changing, moving to grey, and his inner eyelids were too pale. Blood pressure was down. Breathing shaky. She pulled the mask off his face and took up the syringe, her hands shaking slightly. If she were wrong, it would kill the man, but if she did nothing, he was likely to die anyway.

'Dr Bennett. Blood pressure dropping, respiration going down. Ampoule of ephedrine? Yes?'

'Yes!' Dr Bennett said.

She found a vein and pushed in the syringe, feeling both relieved and a little guilty that she had had to ask for reassurance that she was doing the right thing. Then she prayed, and held the mask, waiting.

'Good. Now, let me get a clamp on you ... there ... all right. We can sew him up now.'

'Wait a moment,' she ordered. 'Let him get steady again.'

They waited as the patient's breathing grew deeper and his colour improved. Evelyn replaced the mask.

'All right,' she said. It was only after Dr Bennett had returned to work that she realised how much authority she had pulled to herself on behalf of the patient. Well, Dr Bennett hadn't seemed to mind. She hoped.

•

The stars were bright as they moved out onto the concourse in front of the rollercoaster, which raised its curved skeleton black against the midnight-blue sky. As anaesthetist today, she would be on the first ambulance out, leaving the orderlies and a couple of nurses to clean up. A small reward for the hardest day's work she'd ever done.

Dr Bennett took a deep breath and let it out again. Evelyn knew she had to be tired, but she didn't show it. She was so strong: mentally as well as physically. She never seemed to have a down day; her intelligence and vigour never diminished.

'That was some smart work you did on that last anaesthetic,' Dr Bennett said, meditatively. 'Have you ever thought of becoming a doctor?'

Evelyn's heart seemed to swell and her breath caught. To have Dr Bennett, of all people, think of her that way!

'Yes,' she said. 'I'm planning on going to university after the war – or when I'm thirty.'

'Why thirty?' Dr Bennett's voice was amused.

'Because that's when my inheritance from my mother comes out of trust.' Normally she would have been embarrassed to admit her financial straits, but Dr Bennett, she was sure, would understand.

'Who's your trustee?'

'My father.' Evelyn paused. 'He's a doctor, but he doesn't approve of women doctors.'

Dr Bennett gave a short, sharp laugh. 'Oh, one of those.' She stretched her arms up and brought them down, then leant against one of the lampposts and regarded Evelyn from its pool of light. 'Never let them tell you what you can do. Just do it.'

'I will.'

'You know the biggest obstacle in the road of women doctors? Love.'

Evelyn laughed. 'Love?'

'They start off all fired up and planning to practise and have a professional life. But then they meet some man and go off to have babies. They tell themselves that they can hire nannies and go back to work, but somehow it doesn't work out like that. The husbands talk them out of it – or flat out forbid it.'

Her voice held a deep anger, as though she had seen someone close to her go through it.

'I'm not intending to marry,' Evelyn told her. It was good to be able to say it out loud, to someone who would understand. 'I'll never have someone else take control of my life. *Never.*'

She would be like Dr Bennett – look at what she'd achieved because she had nothing to tie her down. How many lives she had saved . . .

'No,' Evelyn repeated, 'I'll never marry.'

'Good girl,' Dr Bennett said, straightening as they heard the drone of the ambulance coming to take them back to the palace. 'You stick to that and you'll be all right.'

The ambulance was George's car and he greeted them amiably as they climbed in. 'Nice night for it, ladies. Off to bed we go!'

'Thanks, George,' Dr Bennett said.

They sat on the fold-down seats at opposite ends of the ambulance. Dr Bennett's face was shadowed, with light flickering across it as they passed more lampposts.

'You should go to Edinburgh,' she said. 'Best in the world. And they're used to women there. Completely different attitude from Sydney University. I know. I went to both.'

'Edinburgh . . .' It had never occurred to Evelyn that she might study abroad. But why not? It would cost no more, apart from the cost of travelling to Scotland. And she had always wanted to travel . . . Back in Taree, going to Sydney had seemed like a huge adventure, but after Egypt it would be very tame to just go home like a good girl.

Excitement fountained in her. Edinburgh! One of the great universities. And, no doubt, having a degree from there instead of from a colonial institution would make things easier for her when it came time to find her own practice, or to apply for a residency in a hospital.

'That's a wonderful idea,' she said.

Dr Bennett sniffed, but it sounded approving. 'Keep in touch,' she said. 'When you head off for there, drop me a line and I'll send you some letters of introduction. You're just the kind of girl we need in the profession.'

The world seemed to open up before her. Scotland, introductions from the illustrious Dr Bennett, travel and study and accomplishment of her greatest goal . . . The only barrier was the war. She sighed.

'After this is all over.'

'Yes,' Dr Bennett said. 'But I think we'll be waiting a while for that.' Her face, in a sudden splash of light, was sombre, her strong nose casting a sharp shadow over her cheek which moved and vanished as the darkness came back. She looked out the side of the ambulance to the silent houses opposite the palace. 'There'll be a lot more death before this war is satisfied.'

George turned into the palace gates as Evelyn chewed that over. She'd felt that herself, before now: that the war was a hungry animal which fed and fed and delighted in death. It was hard *not* to feel it; otherwise, the futility and destruction was simply man's fault, and who could live under the terrible burden of knowing that?

'I've tried not to hate the Germans,' Dr Bennett said. 'But I can't help but hate the kind of greed which kicked all this off. If they'd only stayed out of Belgium . . .' Sighing, she hoisted herself to her feet as the ambulance came around to the servants' entrance – the nurses' entrance. 'Not much use, if-onlys,' she scolded herself.

'But hard to resist, sometimes,' Evelyn added, and Dr Bennett, clambering down to stand under the entrance light, sent her an amused, approving smile.

'Yes. So many things are hard to resist, but resist them we must,' she said, and went into the hospital.

Evelyn picked up her suitcase and climbed down herself. ''Night, George,' she said. 'Thanks.'

'Any time, Sister.'

He let the clutch out gently so that the car slid away almost silently. For a moment, Evelyn stood, looking out at the darkness, hearing, as if for the first time, the wind in the palm tree fronds, rustling and whispering. The air smelt of desert and cinnamon; somewhere, an early baker was at work. She was overtaken by a sense of unreality. It seemed impossible that she should be here, so far from home; that she had saved a man's life by her skill only an hour earlier; that this was *Egypt*, the land of Bible stories and pyramids. Moses himself might have stood right where she was standing. How could that be possible for a girl from the bush?

And she might go further still. Edinburgh.

Dr Northey, with a degree from Edinburgh. She could be that person.

She *would* be. No husband would stop her, no children demand her attention. Nothing was more important. When she went upstairs, she made notes on the operations she had helped with, for the first time in ages, despite her drooping eyelids.

•

The next day, she wrote to Edinburgh University, asking about their entrance examination and enrolment process. She would be ready when the time came, although she was worried that her Latin might not be up to scratch.

She had brought her Latin, anatomy and mathematics books with her, but there had been almost no time to look at them. That would have to change.

In the meantime, she was doing long shifts at the operating theatre and then falling into bed, only to get up and do it all over again the next day.

Two weeks on theatre duty, two weeks on wards. That was the roster Matron had set up, 'Because *all* of you girls need to be trained in theatre, no matter what the doctors say!'

Evelyn found ward duty more draining, especially the palliative ward, where the patients were known to be on the verge of death. They were kept away from other patients – it upset the men when someone died on their ward – and given painkillers where necessary, but there was no treatment except aspirin, cold baths and ice for their fevers.

Dying men, and men in unendurable pain, call for their mother. Night after night, the calls of 'Mum . . . Mam . . . Mummy . . . Mama . . .' All you could do was hold their hand and whisper gently to them.

Hannah was wonderful at it. She *became* their mother, in some way known only to her, and they quietened and held her hand next to their cheeks and died in peace.

Evelyn hated it. She hated not being able to *do* anything.

'You are doing something. The most important thing you can do,' Hannah said softly, one night after Evelyn had lost a patient. 'You're giving them a good death, surrounded by love.'

'But how can you love them? You don't know them!'

Hannah looked at her searchingly, an odd smile on her lips. 'How can you *not*, Lynnie? They're dying, and they need us.'

She was an infinitely better person, Evelyn thought. Loving and kind and gentle and compassionate. Her own heart was torn apart by these young boys' deaths, but it railed against them, sure that *something* could have been done to prevent them. If she'd been a man, it might have pushed her into politics, to stop this war and any like it, but women's rights were a long way from being influential in that arena.

A man called out, 'No, Mum!', his voice high and shrill with pain, and Hannah went to him immediately, taking his hand and talking quietly until he settled.

She would try to be more like Hannah. To sit acceptingly and help these poor boys over the threshold gently, without fear.

But when it came time for her to go back to the operating theatre, she was glad from the bottom of her heart.

•

Every day blurred into the next. Some moments stood out in her memory: the Egyptian servants singing in the kitchens, a joyful sound just after a 20th Battalion man had died of pneumonia. She had been shaken by longing for an end to all the death, for a return to the happiness that the song promised.

The light coming through the big windows in the entrance hall, falling like benedictions on the beds full of men made restless by the sun.

Being out in the forecourt of Luna Park on a warm late spring day, trying to get the bed bugs out of the woven bed frames they used in the wards by pouring boiling water over the frames, only to have the bugs scurry out across the ground towards them, the nurses, laughing and shrieking, dancing a flamenco to squash them as they came.

The turn of Dr Brent's head as he listened to a patient's heart through his stethoscope. No, she shouldn't remember that.

Matron had authorised them to go into summer uniform – light cotton frocks covered by the standard white apron. It was a great relief; sometimes Evelyn thought that the Egyptian sun was worse than the Australian.

Hannah felt the heat even more. 'It's being from Tasmania,' she said, fanning herself with a piece of the interminable Army paperwork. 'It never gets this hot there.'

The doctors, too, had 'gone tropical', as Dr Brent put it. White linen suits were the norm, except for poor Dr Fanous who, as an Army major, had to wear uniform.

Matron was most solicitous of him. Although rainy days in this season were rare, when they did come the wards immediately turned into steam baths, hard for everyone, but particularly dangerous for the fever cases.

On one of those days, Evelyn was on duty in the fever ward when Dr Fanous did his rounds, looking most uncomfortable in his uniform, complete with tie neatly done up. Captain Malouf, the other Army doctor, had loosened his tie and shed his jacket by nine o'clock, but not Major Fanous.

Matron came in halfway through the rounds with a glass of iced water.

'Here, Doctor,' she said, almost shyly. 'You must keep cool.'

He tried to laugh, 'These uniforms are a trial, eh, lads?' but as he took the glass Matron looked up and for a swift moment their gazes locked. Then Matron looked down and away, her colour heightened, and Dr Fanous took a long drink of the iced water.

PAMELA HART

Alice Ross-King, who was sister-in-charge of that ward, raised her eyebrows at Evelyn. She shrugged.

'Where do you want the ice, Sister?' one of the orderlies asked her, and they were back into the constant effort to keep the men cool.

But she wondered, nonetheless, all through the shift, what that quick, intense glance had held.

'Sister!' cried out one of the men, and she went to him. 'Sister, I'm freezing my nuts off!'

One of the orderlies, instead of packing the ice to either side of the man, had simply dumped a load on top of him including, yes, his genitals.

Trying not to laugh, she pushed the offending ice off into the oilskin tubes on either side which kept the ice from dripping onto the floor.

'All right for you sheilas to laugh at a chap,' the man grumbled, sweat beaded on his forehead. 'I coulda lost my family jewels!'

'Oh, stop your grousing,' Alice said, grinning at him. 'Better that than dying.'

'Only a sheila'd say that,' the man in the next bed said. He was in the latter stages of a bout of malaria, and was sitting up in bed watching everything.

'You think too much about sheilas,' said Alice and those men in the ward who were up to understanding laughed.

Dr Malouf stormed in.

'This is not a vaudeville hall!' he snapped. 'Sisters, you will maintain a proper distance from your patients! I want no immorality, of deed *or* word, on my ward.'

'Yes, Doctor,' Alice said, but her eyes flashed with resentment.

It was odd, Evelyn reflected. Captain Malouf was of Lebanese descent, from Melbourne, she had learned, a light olive-skinned man with sharp brown eyes who drove the nurses hard and was over-alert for any sign of 'immorality'. He appeared to ignore the fact that the men spoke of him as 'the wog doctor', as though his sense of self-importance inoculated him against caring about the opinions of others. He was contemptuous of the British command and openly condemned the Egyptian servants as heathens, refusing to speak to them in Arabic although he knew the language.

Dr Fanous, on the other hand, while equally good at ignoring prejudice, was self-deprecating in any arena but medicine. There, he was decisive and commanding. But out of the ward, he seemed to want to fade into the background – which of course he couldn't do, if only because he was so good-looking.

No wonder Matron preferred him.

•

Next day, one of their most faithful Cairo visitors, Mrs Barton, came in with her grandson, a sturdy little boy who had just been put into short skirts. Of course they couldn't let the kiddie near the fever cases, but he toddled around the surgical ward, grasping onto the bed frames and tottering from one bed to another, crowing with laughter, to calls of encouragement from the men.

'That's it, kiddie!' a young man who had lost an arm said to him, his face alight. 'Keep going! Good boy!'

Evelyn said to Mrs Barton, 'Thank you so much for bringing him. That's the first sign of life we've seen from Cartwright since the operation.'

Mrs Barton smiled fondly at the little fellow. 'There's nothing like a child to remind you that life goes on.'

Her daughter had died in childbirth, Evelyn had heard. 'You're lucky to have each other,' she said.

'Exactly!' Mrs Barton turned to her eagerly. 'That's exactly right. Some of my friends say I should get a nanny, but I couldn't bear it. As long as Neville is with me I don't have to think about Flora.'

'What's going on here?' Matron's voice came from the doorway. She looked as stern as Evelyn had ever seen her, and who could blame her? The noise had almost lifted the roof. Dr Fanous appeared behind her.

Then Matron saw the little boy, and her face, her whole body, changed in a moment. She swept down on him and picked him up, throwing him up in the air until he giggled, and then cuddled him.

'It's very good of you to bring him, Mrs Barton,' she said, 'but I think the men may have been excited enough for one day.'

'Of course,' Mrs Barton said.

They turned and Evelyn followed them to the door. Dr Fanous, standing in the doorway, was looking at Matron with his heart in his eyes, as though she was his wife and holding his own child. It was, Evelyn thought, one of the most beautiful expressions she'd ever seen on a human face.

Matron saw him and flushed, handing the kiddie back to Mrs Barton abruptly.

'I'm afraid I have too much to do to stay and play,' she said, brushing past Dr Fanous as though he weren't there.

He turned to look after her, and there was something about the slump of his shoulders which was eloquent of despair. He moved in the other direction without turning around or excusing himself. Unheard of – his manners were faultless normally.

'Well!' Mrs Barton said. Her tone was breathy with pleasure. What a nugget of scandal that scene must have given her. Evelyn was impelled to intervene. She couldn't bear to think that Dr Fanous and Matron would be for the tea-table gossips.

'Dr Fanous is very fond of children,' she said. She had found out this much from the orderlies, who knew everything. 'He was married, previously, and his wife and son died of malaria. His little boy would have been about the same age as your Neville.'

Mrs Barton clutched the kiddie tighter. 'Oh, how terrible,' she said. 'So he was looking at the baby?'

'Oh, yes,' Evelyn said, lying without compunction. 'Who else would he be looking at?' She laughed a little. 'You didn't think *Matron* . . .' She laughed again.

Mrs Barton was disappointed, but carried it off. 'Of course, I would never imagine that Matron would be involved with a *native*,' she said airily. 'Impossible!'

Evelyn found she had no reply to that which wouldn't start the gossips up again, so she kept silent.

When she went back to the ward, Cartwright was sitting up for the first time. He smiled at her. 'That was as good as a tonic,' he said. 'He reminded me of my little brother. I guess he'd be running around by now and in shorts instead of skirts.'

'You'll see him soon,' she said.

Cartwright's face clouded, and then he took a deep breath in and looked up at her with resolve in his eyes. 'Always a silver lining,' he said. 'At least I get to go home now.'

She patted his shoulder. 'That's the spirit.' What paltry encouragement it seemed to her! But what else could she say?

'At least you didn't lose your right arm'? Not when there were two other men in this ward who had done just that. Keep their eyes on the future, that was the ticket.

'Say hello to Sydney Harbour for me,' she said.

'My oath, won't it be grand to sail in there!' Cartwright said, and around him a murmur of agreement went up.

'Melbourne for me!' said one man.

'Hobart!'

'I'm heading for back o' Bourke,' an older man said. He had lost an ear and had a long scar across the side of his head, up into his hair. 'Where they never expect you to take your hat off!'

Laughter filled the ward, and she slipped back to the scullery to heat up their lunchtime soup.

God bless them, she thought. Bless each and every one of them.

CHAPTER 12

Hannah was unaccountably happy.

'What's going on?' Evelyn demanded as they were getting ready for bed.

'Lieutenant Yates is being kept at camp to help with some logistics problem, or something. I didn't really understand.'

'A-hah!'

'Oh, you. Not that we have time, either of us, to, to associate.'

'But at least he's not getting shot at?'

'Exactly.' Hannah dimpled and slid into bed, looking rather like a schoolgirl, with a long dark plait on either side.

'Don't get serious about him,' Evelyn said, turning off the light and following suit. They lay in the warm darkness, listening to the sounds from Luna Park – the voices of the men on the carousel drifted up to them, cut across occasionally with a command from one of the nurses on duty there.

'I think I am serious,' Hannah said. 'Wouldn't he be a wonderful father!'

'Oh, Hannah. Really?'

'Well, wouldn't he?'

'I suppose he would.' Yes. Linus would be a good father. 'He's a lawyer, back home. Would you want to be a lawyer's wife? I don't think he'd like you nursing.'

'As if I'd want to, if I had a home of my own and a family!' Hannah was so emphatic it was surprising.

'You wouldn't mind not being independent?' To live off someone else's earnings . . . at least in her father's house she had known she was paying her way with her work, even if he hadn't actually paid her.

'Independent! How can a mother be independent? Someone has to raise the children. That's work that's just as important as nursing.'

It was. But that was the crux of it, wasn't it? Someone has to raise the children.

'I guess that's another good reason for me not to get married,' she said.

'I don't understand that,' Hannah confessed. She rolled to look at Evelyn; there was enough light from the moon to show the concerned expression on her face. 'Don't you *want* children?'

A pang of sheer envy went through Evelyn. To have children, to hold her own baby, to cuddle a warm little body . . . she thought of those men, time after time, calling for their mothers as they died . . . was there a more important role in the world? Anyone could doctor, but only women could have children . . .

'I do,' she admitted. 'But it's all the rest of it. Being under your husband's control. Having no say in your own life or your own money.'

'A good marriage isn't like that.' Hannah spoke gently, as she would have to a feverish patient.

'How can a doctor raise her children herself?' Evelyn countered. 'I could give birth to half a dozen children as a wife – but I could save a hundred lives as a doctor.'

Hannah sighed. 'I couldn't do it,' she said. 'It was one of the reasons I became a nurse – my mother had six kiddies but only raised two. The other four died of measles, and convulsions, and chest infections. I thought, if I were a nurse, I'd know what to do, and perhaps I could raise *all* my children to adulthood.'

'I hope you do,' Evelyn said, meaning it. Then she smiled. 'Have a couple extra for me, eh? I'll be godmother!'

Laughing, they settled to sleep.

•

It was just as well that it was her shift in the operating theatre at Luna Park. She couldn't have borne the repetition of the ward.

Dr Brent was operating.

They went through the list quickly. These were mostly bullet or shrapnel extractions, which X-rays made relatively straightforward.

Dr Lewis, the Welsh anaesthetist, approved of Dr Brent and made life much easier for all of them by whipping the mask on as soon as the patient was on the table, with no more than a, 'Relax, boyo,' to the patient.

Then a large man was carried in, writhing in pain.

Dr Fanous came with him, carrying case notes which he held out for Dr Brent and Dr Lewis to read.

'Twisted bowel, I think, don't you?' Dr Fanous said, and both men nodded. 'He's been given morphine, but it's not helping much. And there's nothing on the X-ray. You'll just have to go in and take a look.'

The man groaned and then gasped in pain.

'Right, then, boyo, let's get you to sleep,' Dr Lewis said.

Dr Brent bent over the patient and looked him in the eye. 'It'll be all right, son,' he said, although the man was clearly older than he was. But it was the right thing to say. The patient relaxed enough to take a big breath in, and that was enough for the anaesthetic to start working.

Evelyn had never assisted at a bowel operation that didn't involve a wound. Bowel wounds were the most likely to kill, at least of the ones that made it this far, because of the almost certain infection which followed any perforation of the bowel.

'The key,' Dr Brent said, 'is not to nick the bowel.'

'Yes, Doctor,' she answered.

A few minutes later, when the patient was fully under, he examined the abdomen, palpating and pushing.

'Hm. Best guess is the small intestine. A volvulus.' Evelyn racked her brain to remember what that meant. 'A twist,' Dr Brent added. 'Let's have a look.'

A few moments later they were looking at the small intestine, which was indeed twisted in a strange way. Dr Brent stared at it from all angles, and then let out a breath.

'Sister Walker,' he said, 'take over from Sister Northey, would you? I'll need two sets of hands to manage this.' Mabel came up and Evelyn moved up to make room for her, handing over the clamps that were keeping blood from flowing into the open incision. 'Now you see, Sister,' Dr Brent went on, 'that there's an obstruction which has distended the bowel above it and caused a twist.'

'Yes, Doctor.' The strange, purple and red shape was like a puzzle made out of sausages, but she could see what he meant.

'Now, in a normal setting we might have a go at simply excising that segment of the bowel. But this man's been under great stress and I'm not sure his system is up to the fight against any infection. So we're going to try to get it untangled without having to cut. But be careful. This part of the bowel is quite fragile, and it's already under torsion, so it might tear.'

'Yes, Doctor.' The next five minutes were the most concentrated of her life. Dr Brent indicated what he wanted with a nod or a single word, and she complied, supporting the rest of the bowel while he delicately undid the twist.

It was the oddest feeling, to hold a living part of a human being in her hands. Quite different from clamping off a blood vessel, or even pinching one shut, as she'd had to do in emergencies. Far more personal. She was alert to the slippery movement of the intestine and stopped it moving out onto the patient's skin as it reacted to Dr Brent's manipulation. He nodded to her in thanks and then laid the bowel back into position. Finally, he palpated the mass inside where it had twisted to make sure it could be passed, breaking it up into pieces.

'Right,' he said. 'Neither of us is sterile anymore, Sister, so we'll have to scrub again to close up.'

They did so. He closed, with both Mabel and Evelyn assisting, and even Dr Lewis grunted a 'good job' to her afterwards.

It was the last operation of the day, and it left her with a strange feeling. When she had assisted Dr Bennett it had been exhilarating, although scary. Assisting Dr Brent had been completely different, as though his confidence in her had dispelled all her own doubts. She had merely concentrated on the problem at hand, and felt a great sense of satisfaction when they were successful.

As they all waited for the ambulance to come and pick them up, she wondered again: Perhaps she should seriously consider being a surgeon instead of a physician.

At the same moment, Dr Brent asked: 'Why aren't you a doctor instead of a nurse?'

That question. They were in virtually the same place where Dr Bennett had asked her almost the same thing.

She gave him the same answer, and watched him digest it, his face under the gas lamp pale and clear.

He turned to her, shaking his head. 'What a fool your father is.'

She smiled. 'That's one word for it.'

'So when you're thirty.'

'Or earlier. I'm saving what I can, so perhaps I can go a year earlier. Dr Bennett thinks I should go to Edinburgh.' She grimaced. 'If I can get through the entrance exam. I try to study, but there's so little time . . .'

'If you'd like a hand . . . I could tutor you . . .' His voice was hesitant, as though he weren't offering the most valuable help she could have. For a moment, she wondered if that was at all wise. But he was looking at her with calm friendliness, and it was too good an opportunity to miss.

'That would be wonderful!'

He smiled at her. It was a singularly sweet smile.

As good as his word, Dr Brent got her to bring her Latin books down to the dining room after dinner, and they spent a half hour going over the sections he said she would need in the entrance examination. Until he yawned, making her yawn, and they both laughed and headed for bed.

Climbing the staircase side by side, he said, 'Any night you have enough energy, I'm happy to help.'

'You're very kind,' she said. 'But surely you have other things to do . . .'

'Don't make me admit how miserable a creature I am, that I don't,' he said, laughing at her with his eyes. Her heart clenched a little. He had such lovely eyes.

'I won't, then. But I will thank you for the help.'

'I'm at your service, Evelyn.' Then he flinched as he realised what he'd said.

She flicked him a glance and then stared straight ahead, suddenly shy. Abruptly aware of his long, lean body next to hers.

'Goodnight, Doctor,' she said as they reached his floor and he turned off.

'Goodnight, Sister,' he answered.

She needed help with her Latin; she'd been ashamed by how much she'd forgotten. Part of her, though, wondered if sitting so close, side by side, night after night, would be good for her peace of mind.

●

'He called you *Evelyn*?' Hannah breathed, all agog as they got ready for bed.

'I didn't know where to look,' Evelyn replied. 'I mean, he really shouldn't have, but he *is* the doctor . . . what was I supposed to have said?'

Hannah braided her dark hair and grinned. 'Oh, how about, "and thank *you*, sweet William".'

Evelyn picked up a slipper and threw it at her.

'You should have seen his face,' she said, sitting down and taking her own hair out of its bun. The red strands were cool from the night air; they fell across her thigh like a breeze. 'He realised what he'd done. I think he was afraid I'd slap his face!' She began to brush her hair. It felt wrong, somehow, to be discussing William with Hannah. Time to get off that subject. 'Maybe I should cut this off. Short hair would be a lot simpler.'

'Don't you *dare!* You have beautiful hair.'

Evelyn made a face at her. 'Red. Carrots. Ginger.'

'Titian,' Hannah retorted. 'Exotic. Alluring. Like a Rossetti painting.'

'Hmmm . . .' If truth be told, Evelyn thought, she loved her hair colour for its pure aesthetic qualities. The shimmering colours, the depth and fieriness of it . . . but it did make people think of you in a particular way. One of the things she most liked about being a nurse was having her hair in a veil. Her eyebrows were naturally a little darker, and since she'd started wearing the veil, hardly anyone had made remarks like, 'I'll bet you've got a temper, eh?' or 'You'd be hot at hand, I'll bet.' Or worse, from men in the street.

Dr Brent had never made any comments of any kind, although the first time she had met him her hair had been uncovered.

She had tried to ignore the shiver that went through her when he said her name. So naturally, too, as though that was how he thought of her. Perhaps he *did* think of her that way. And was that good or bad?

'I'm never getting married,' she said aloud, 'so it doesn't matter how alluring I am. No allurement for me.'

Hannah slid down into bed and pulled the covers up. 'That's what you say to *me*. But what would you say to sweet William?'

This time, Evelyn threw the brush at her.

CHAPTER 13

Letters from Australia came irregularly, depending on shipping and the censor. It irritated William beyond measure that some faceless clerk would read everything he wrote to his parents and friends back home, and it was somehow worse that his own mother's letters were opened unapologetically. The red stamp 'Passed by Censor' on the resealed envelopes was an insult.

He knew the martial necessity. But it irked him, nonetheless.

On one Thursday morning sometime in June – he'd lost count of the days when he had worked in theatre for ten hours and followed that up by two hours on the wards – a bundle of letters came. Several were from old friends; he put those aside when he saw his mother's handwriting on an envelope.

Dear Will,
Hoping this finds you well and fit and that you aren't doing too much and overtaxing yourself.

You know I had to say that, but I expect you'll suit yourself, as you always have, and good luck to you.

The news from the Dardanelles seems bad. Sandy Marshall has been killed, and so has Bill Boyd.

Sandy and Billy were boys he'd gone to school with. Bill was a larrikin, good-hearted and wild. Sandy was an evil little sod who had bullied him mercilessly until Will had grown tall enough to be a difficult target. It felt wrong that they'd come to the same end, on the same foreign soil. Bill deserved better than to share a grave with the likes of Sandy Marshall.

The library is doing good business, and I'm laying in more novels — westerns and romances are very popular. I daresay people want a break from the hardness of day-to-day life right now. Your father's business —

She had always referred to his father's SP activities that way. 'That's for your father's business' when a blackboard was delivered and set up in the 'middle room' — a bedroom which his father had taken over for an office. 'Don't bother your father, he's caught up with his business' on racedays.

Your father's business has slowed. Only to be expected, really, with so many men away. At least the races are still happening, although there's talk of bringing the industry under government control. You can imagine what the Jockey Club thinks about that!

The Australian Jockey Club was misnamed — it was made up, not of jockeys, but of owners and racecourse officials. Full of powerful men with even more powerful connections, it wouldn't take kindly to government interference.

But we're doing all right, so don't worry about us. Dad has picked up a bit of extra work at the greengrocer's. Write soon,

Love
Mum and Dad

The greengrocer's! They must really be in trouble. In all his childhood, his father had never had to take another job. How should he handle this? His mother hated taking help; so did his father. He supposed he did, too, but he'd been forced into it because of the polio. But he couldn't let his dad slave away at the greengrocer's when he could so easily help.

He had been saving solidly ever since coming to Heliopolis. To go to Edinburgh and enrol as a postgraduate student he would need a considerable sum of money. Perhaps £500 to see him through. He was paid 22s 6d a day – his Army colleagues had 3s 6d of that reserved for after the war. The Army did that for all who had enlisted, so that they would not be dumped back on the streets when peace came, penniless. It was a good idea, but since he was saving hard anyway, he hadn't followed that example. Of his £7 18s and tuppence, he saved £6 a week. At least.

Living at the hospital, with full room and board, and where the orderlies, servants and clerical staff treated him as though he were Army, he wanted for nothing.

The only things he spent money on were shaving needs, vails for the servants and the daily newspaper – not that he'd had time to read it often. But he let the men in the ward have it, so it didn't go to waste.

He'd need two years, at this rate, to save enough for Edinburgh. He'd have to buy clothes at some point, for one thing. And his fare was another cost. He prayed God this bloody war wouldn't keep on for that long. But that was the great thing about medicine – he could get a job anywhere. He'd be able to find that money somehow, someday, war or not.

But his parents . . . they had very little put away, and that was because of him. If they'd saved the money they'd spent on his education, they'd have a nice little nest egg to tide them over these bad times. But they had spent everything they had to get him through university. Now it was his turn.

After breakfast the next day, he went to the hospital clerk, who organised pays, and arranged to have his parents receive £4 a week. That was an average wage for a skilled worker – it would keep a roof over their heads and bridge the gap until the war was over and betting picked up. He would just have to go without new clothes and everything else.

'While I'm thinking about it,' he told the clerk, 'can you cancel my newspaper delivery? I never get the chance to read it anyway.'

'Will do,' the clerk said.

It wasn't much – the *Egyptian Gazette* was only a penny a day, but that was 30 shillings over a year, and that might be a week's rent in Edinburgh.

Pitiful. He could look at some of the other doctors – Wheatland, say, or Mayo – and see that natural assurance that being comfortably off gave most doctors. Doctors who had comfortably-off parents behind them. Class wasn't as strong in Australia as in Britain, but it was still there.

As though that thought had called her up, Sister Northey came into the clerk's office with a sheaf of papers.

'Doctor,' she greeted him in that lovely, upper-class voice. Low and round in tone, it was like music. She handed the papers to the clerk.

'There you are, John,' she said. 'Pharmacy reports.' The man positively glowed as he took the paperwork and smiled shyly at her.

'Sister Northey,' William said. 'Are you on theatre today?'

He so hoped she was. Not only because she was efficient, but because somehow, when she was around, he was calmer and more focused. A better surgeon.

'Yes, Doctor,' she said. She tilted her head to look at him, her green eyes showing how tired she was after a never-ending procession of theatre days.

'Once more unto the breach,' he murmured, and a flash of humour lit her face.

'For Harry, England and St George,' she agreed.

What a wonderful girl she was.

A doctor's daughter, though, and no doubt expected to marry into a well-off family. Not that it should worry him. Every step reminded him of why he wasn't fit to marry.

As they turned to walk out, a shaft of pain went up his leg and crashed into his hip. He controlled himself, as he always did, so that it didn't show on his face. Time for some more aspirin, but there was a limit to how many he could take without ruining both his stomach and his liver.

Just enough to get him through the theatre session. He had to work while he was still able – who knew how long his leg would allow him to do so? Count your blessings, my boy, he told himself. You can do good work right here and now, and that's all that counts.

After the session, he was limping badly as he went to wash.

Sister Northey stared at him accusingly as they dried their hands.

'You're doing too much. Up on the table and I'll massage that leg.'

He eyed her quizzically but got up on the table obediently. 'I'm not taking my pants off, Sister,' he said. He *had* to keep it light. He couldn't reveal the depth of his embarrassment.

She blushed. The red sweep up her face, her pale skin making it fully visible. William bit his lip, half-laughing and half-contrite. He hadn't meant to embarrass *her*.

'Sorry,' he said.

'You don't look sorry,' she said, attacking the leg with a little more energy than she needed. He winced, and she softened her hands.

The tight, corded muscles loosened under her massage. He was abruptly aware of her scent, of sweat and soap and balsam – of femaleness; remembering the first time they had been physically close, when he had examined her at Victoria Barracks. He kept his eyes on the far wall, keeping his desire under control.

She stepped back. 'That ought to keep you,' she said. 'But you should put a hot pack on it before you go to bed.'

'Thank you, Sister,' he said. He slid off the bed, which brought him close to her again. For a moment, the background bustle of the hospital fell away and all he could hear was her breathing. Then she stepped back and it was normal again.

But he thought he would never forget the particular nature of her touch, and that night he dreamed of her and woke in the small hours, damning himself for a fool.

CHAPTER 14

Two weeks on theatre, two weeks on wards.

Linus breezed into the ward just as they were handing over to the next shift on their first ward day, she and Hannah back together again. There were still five new patients to find beds for, but he ignored Hannah's faint comments about, 'We should stay to help . . .'

Dr Brent was finishing up checking the amputated leg of a young Light Horseman. Linus greeted the man with a quick salute and a grin, but Evelyn noticed he turned away quickly, uncomfortable with the amputation, as so many men were. Perhaps he could imagine it happening to him too easily – horses rolling on their riders and crushing their leg was a common cause of amputation.

'Doc, help me out!' Linus said. 'These girls need a break. They haven't been out of this building for weeks.'

'Not true,' Evelyn said. 'We go to the amusement park all the time. Just for fun.'

Dr Brent laughed. 'I think he's right, ladies. A break would do you good.'

'And you,' Linus said. 'Mate, you look like something the cat dragged in.'

He did look tired. Evelyn worried about him; it seemed to her that he overtaxed his strength on almost a daily basis. Surely it would catch up to him eventually.

'The four of us,' Hannah said, with a swift sideways glance at Evelyn. 'That will be quite nice.'

It reminded them all that, despite the physicality of the work they did, they were still judged by society's rules, especially the women. In public, they had to pretend to no more knowledge of the world than a debutante. It was ridiculous.

Four was safer than two, or even three.

How she managed to be cajoled into it, she didn't know. For Hannah, maybe, who clearly wanted this time with Linus. And Linus was hard to resist once he got his lawyerly arguments going.

'You are *owed* this time, ladies! You have patriotically given up your time off during the crisis, but the crisis is over!'

That was true, and it wasn't. Wounded still came in every day from the Gallipoli peninsula, but not in the waves they first had. They were able to keep the numbers of patients pretty consistent, discharging about the same number they took in. No more stumbling over stretchers in the corridors – but the ice rink ward was still full.

Time off. She tried to remember the last time she'd been out, and couldn't.

'All right,' she said, and smiled. 'If there's four of us.' She had no ambition to play gooseberry.

Dr Brent smiled back at her.

'We'll just get our capes,' Hannah said.

Which was code for: we'll go back to our rooms and make ourselves look prettier.

They raced up the stairs like a pair of children, laughing, and jostled for position at the mirror as they redid their hair. Evelyn bound hers loosely on top of her head in a modified pompadour; Hannah pulled hers back and up in a Regency bun with side curls.

She looked lovely, and her straight little nose and rosebud lips were enhanced.

'Do I look all right? I wish I had some rouge.'

'You're very pretty,' Evelyn told her. 'You don't need rouge. Beautiful.'

Their eyes met in the mirror.

'Be careful,' Evelyn said. 'Don't fall too fast.'

Hannah took a deep breath in and let it out. 'Too late, I'm afraid.'

They snatched up their capes and ran down the stairs again. The men were waiting at the bottom, in a strange parody of escorts waiting for their dance partners.

Linus offered Hannah his left arm to walk out on, but Dr Brent hesitated. It was totally against orders for them to walk arm in arm on hospital grounds. Evelyn smiled at him.

'Let's go,' she said, moving off.

As they went through the front doors onto the street, she and Hannah gasped and stood stock-still.

All along the street, from house to house, on trees, hung on the sides of telegraph poles, were lanterns.

Not simple rectangular white lanterns. These were crazy shapes made out of stained glass. Wonderful colours: gold and orange and a bright, bright blue, green and yellow and even purple. The brass they were framed from shone brightly, and they laid their patchwork crazy quilt over the road and footpaths and over the cars and trams as they made their way along the street.

She'd never seen anything so beautiful.

'It's Ramadan,' Linus said, enjoying their delight.

Ramadan. There had been something about that in Daily Orders a couple of days ago. A Moslem festival. Something about not overtaxing Moslem servants because they couldn't eat or drink during the hours of daylight.

Hannah sighed audibly. 'It's so beautiful.'

'I wonder if they're along the Nile, too,' Dr Brent said.

'Let's find out!' Linus cried. He grabbed Hannah's hand and ran for the tram which was just stopping opposite the hospital.

Evelyn turned with concern to Dr Brent, but he was moving off smartly. So they ran and hobbled together, scrambling on board the tram and collapsing, breathless and laughing, into a seat facing the others.

The tram conductor didn't approve of them, but when he saw Hannah and Evelyn in their veils and capes, some of the condemnation left his face, and he sold them tickets quite equably.

'They seem to approve of nurses, the natives,' Linus said.

'They approve of women wearing veils and long sleeves,' Dr Brent said softly. 'They approve of modesty.' It sounded as though he did too.

'Do you?' Evelyn asked. It came out as a challenge, which she hadn't intended.

'I think if we are guests in a country with certain customs, that we shouldn't go out of our way to abuse those customs,' he said courteously.

Their gaze met and held. In the soft evening light of the tram, his dark hair and hazel eyes made him seem mysterious. Almost a stranger. As they went along, the bright colours from the lanterns slid over his cheek and hair, turning him into a harlequin, but not into a figure of fun. More Feste than clown.

'And if you're going to interrogate me,' he said with a quirk of his lips, 'you'd better call me William.'

She liked the humour in his eyes, the crinkle of lines around them, the beautiful tone of his voice. It was probably a mistake, with them working so closely together, but she'd been calling him William in her thoughts for weeks. 'Evelyn,' she said.

'About time you two got on first-name terms,' Linus said, effectively spoiling the moment. 'Time to get to know each other. I, Linus Lawrence Yates, am the son of Amelia Yates.'

Evelyn knew that, of course, but the others didn't. Amelia Yates was one of Australia's best-known women's rights advocates. A formidable woman who had been at the forefront of the fight for women's suffrage during Federation. It was like being told your friend was one of the Pankhursts.

'Good God man!' Dr Brent – William – said. 'She had *sons*?'

'More to the point, he's the brother of a good friend of mine,' Evelyn said. 'And she says, sir, that you aren't writing often enough!'

Linus buried his head in his hands.

'Oh, Lord. I go to the ends of the Earth, but can I get away from the bossy women in my family? No – now they have henchmen!'

'Hench*women*,' Evelyn said. They all laughed at his mock dismay, and Hannah smiled at Evelyn. With a pang, Evelyn realised that the fact she knew Linus's family, and knew them well, had shifted what might have been brief wartime flirting into a possible courtship. Linus wasn't just a soldier – he was a man who had had his bona fides certified; a potential husband.

'What about you, Doc?' Linus asked. 'Do you have a disreputable mother?'

'No,' William said, smiling. 'I have a disreputable father.'

'Give, give,' Linus begged.

'My dad's an SP bookie.'

Linus crowed with delight, while the two women were taken aback. SP bookies were a fact of life in every town, but gambling outside the racecourse was illegal, so they were never members of society. And certainly they were unlikely to have sons who were doctors.

'Tell us more.'

'My parents run a lending library in Parramatta,' he explained. 'And a lending library is a very good place to run a tote from, because you have people coming and going all day, and they pay in small amounts, so there's nothing suspicious about holding a till. It's a great cover for an SP.'

He glanced at Evelyn and she realised that he was nervous. That he was afraid she would show him the cold shoulder. To be honest, if she'd known all this right from the start, she might have. She could just imagine what her mother would have said about it. But how could she care who his parents were? He had proved himself over and over again to be truly a gentleman.

'*Please* tell me he ran a two-up game,' Linus said.

'Every Saturday afternoon, behind the church.'

'Behind the *church*?'

'The Catholic church. They don't censure gambling. In fact, the parish priest used to come out and throw a few.' He fell silent for a moment, lost in memory, then looked up, his face alight with mischief. 'I used to be the cockatoo.'

'What's a cockatoo?' Hannah asked.

'A lookout,' Evelyn answered. 'Usually a small boy, who whistles or cooees if he sees a policeman coming.'

'I can whistle,' William said. 'Very loudly.'

Somehow, the conversation had gone from shocking to funny, and they all laughed. When they'd calmed down, William said quietly to her, 'That's how I could afford to study medicine. I became a doctor off the back of illegal earnings.' His voice held a question, and she had to answer it. She kept her voice light.

'It's good that something worthwhile has come out of all that debauchery.' But she smiled at him with her eyes, and he relaxed back into his seat.

They arrived at the last stop, in the middle of Cairo proper, not far from the river, soon afterwards.

Evelyn wondered if William would need help getting down from the tram, but he was surprisingly lithe and athletic, swinging himself down easily. He had left his cane at home for once – in fact, she realised he rarely used it except in getting from hospital to theatre and up those ruddy stairs.

They found a restaurant – all the restaurants were wide open, doing a thriving trade, with great buffets of Egyptian food spread out, and big family parties digging in enthusiastically. If they hadn't eaten since sunrise, which was early at this time of year, full summer, they must be starving.

They ate a great deal of strange-tasting food. Garlic abounded, and she wondered what she would smell like the next day. But it was all delicious, especially the honey-soaked pastries which finished the meal.

Afterwards, they wandered down through old cobbled streets, past the flat-roofed houses and the still-open stores, to the wide river.

There were boats out, hung with lanterns, and the houses on the riverbank, the docks and wharves, all had lanterns, so that the river was alive with light, an elusive rainbow which changed with the wind and the current. Above, the stars were bright, the Milky Way clear above them. A patch of water lilies clung to the edge of the river, and gave out a sweet, citrusy scent, though their blooms were closed up tight.

They leant on a stone wall at the river's edge and contemplated the scene.

'Lanterns on the Nile,' Hannah said dreamily. 'It sounds like the name of a song.'

Linus immediately started singing, to the tune of 'A Bird in a Gilded Cage'.

> *They were only the lanterns on the Nile*
> *A beautiful sight to see,*
> *They look so happy and free from care*
> *And they are! Now night can be ...*

'That's just silly,' Hannah said, pushing him. He pulled her back towards him until they were almost in an embrace, and they stood, staring into each other's eyes. Evelyn and William glanced at each other. Propriety said they should break up this tête-à-tête. Friendship said otherwise, so they walked gradually away, down the river and out onto a long dock where dinghies – well, not exactly dinghies, but the Egyptian equivalent – were tied up.

'He's a good lad,' William said. 'A gentleman. He won't hurt her.'

'Not deliberately,' she agreed. 'But if she falls in love with him and he gets killed . . .'

They both sighed, and turned outwards to stare at the graceful boats, going by full of revellers – but without the raucous tone such revels would have on Sydney Harbour, because there was no alcohol drunk by Mussulmans.

'They come to us,' William said softly, 'and we do our best. But every time we fail, we condemn a family, a wife, a sweetheart to the most terrible grief.'

She turned to him and put her hand on his arm. 'You can't think like that. Think the other way: every time we succeed we prevent that terrible grief.'

They were close; she could feel the warmth of his flesh under his jacket sleeve. His breath touched her cheek. For a long moment, they stood there, looking closely at each other, breathing in the same quickening rhythm, alive and aware of each other. His mouth was close to hers.

A family boat went past quite close, coming in to dock not far downriver.

The lights from their lanterns slid across William's face, and she moved back, as though she had been paralysed and was released from it. No. No falling in love for her. No getting close to any man, even someone as nice as William Brent. No feeling this fluster of attraction and arousal. No, no, and no again.

'Shall we go play propriety?' he asked.

They could see, walking back, that Hannah was locked in Linus's arms, being thoroughly kissed. They scuffed their feet and talked in loud voices, and by the time they rejoined them, both Hannah and Linus looked reasonably proper, although there was a flush on Hannah's cheeks that even the night couldn't hide.

'Time to go home,' William said. As they walked back to the tram, he offered Evelyn his arm. It would be rude to refuse. She laid her hand lightly in the crook of his elbow, but let it go as soon as they got to the tram stop, and moved aside, not looking at him. She had to protect him as well as herself. It would be awful if he got the wrong idea about her. But she was aware of him, standing behind her, as though the warmth of his body was reaching across the space between them. No. She mustn't think that way, not ever.

•

Each night, she and Hannah went out to look at the lanterns on the street before going to bed; she was sorry when Ramadan ended and the nights became drab and ordinary again.

On the final night of their ward stint, Linus and William took them out again to a restaurant nearby.

'My last night of freedom!' Linus said, stretching back after the meal was over.

Hannah went very still.

'You're going back?'

'Tomorrow. I got my orders this afternoon. Back on the front line.' He smiled at Evelyn. 'So if you have any letters for Harry, give them to me.'

'Oh, yes!' she said. She was conscious of Hannah sitting there, still and pale. The impulse to shield her by making conversation was overwhelming. 'William, you have your bag with you – do you have any notepaper? A pen?'

'I have a pencil,' he said, bending to look through his bag, which he had had with him when Linus had suddenly appeared and whisked them off. 'But no paper.'

'Use a menu,' Linus advised. His manner was insouciant, but there were white lines around his mouth and eyes, and he and Hannah were holding hands under the table. 'We can pay for it.'

'Yes. Good idea.'

The menu was a scrabbly thing, torn and stained, but she grabbed it and wrote briefly and with much feeling. It was a far more personal message than she would have written if she'd had time to think, and perhaps that was a good thing. She underlined, 'BE CAREFUL' three times.

'Come back to the hospital with us and I'll give you some Red Cross socks and goodies to take with you.'

'Excellent!' Linus said. 'I'm down on socks myself. You can't get decent ones here – my feet are too big for the local version!'

Hannah said nothing, and they didn't press her, but talked around and over her for the last few minutes of the meal.

'I'll just go ahead and get that package organised for you,' Evelyn said as they left the restaurant, the light from its arched doorway on the roadway looking like an illustration from a Gothic tale, betokening danger.

Which was ridiculous.

'I'll help,' William said.

They walked quickly across the road and down to the palace, not looking back.

'Give them as much time as they can have,' William said.

'Yes. Oh, it's *awful*!'

Tears in her eyes blinded her; she stumbled and William held her up by her elbow, and then took her arm.

'Yes,' he said. 'A terrible thing.'

It didn't take long, back at the palace, to put together particularly nice parcels for both Linus and Harry. Why not? What they didn't use they'd share. Evelyn and William wrapped them in brown paper, and made sure to put in notebooks and pencils, which Linus had told them were highly prized in the trenches.

Then they went out, slowly, to find the others.

They were down at the gate, embracing. Not kissing, but standing there, Hannah's head on Linus's shoulder, their arms wrapped around each other. Linus rested his cheek against her hair. The sight cut at Evelyn's heart, it was so beautiful and so tragic. An emblem of this terrible war.

They handed over the parcels and said goodbye, Evelyn kissing Linus on the cheek with a 'Give this to Harry for me' which made him laugh and say, 'I will too!'

She and William walked back to the side entrance which the nurses used, and waited.

'You go up, Will,' Evelyn said. 'It'll be easier on her if it's just me.'

'Very well. Are you all right?' His hand touched her cheek as lightly as Linus's kiss. She didn't want to think about that question. Fear gripped her bowels whenever she thought of Harry over there, in the madness of the front.

'As well as I can be,' she said honestly. His hand gripped hers for a moment and then he left, quickly, as Hannah approached them, her steps dragging.

Evelyn said nothing, just took her arm and walked slowly with her up the stairs. At the door to their room she said, 'Do you want to be alone?' but Hannah clutched at her hand.

'Oh, no! Don't leave me by myself!'

'Shh, shhh, it's all right, I'm here.'

They went through the door and sat on Hannah's bed. She began to cry like a child, big hiccuping sobs that shook her whole body. Evelyn held her and rocked her and said nothing, because what was there to say? Hannah loved him and he might die. It wasn't even unusual. All over the world, there were women crying, and men too, because the people they loved – husbands, fiancés, sons, brothers, friends – were fighting and might die. On both sides of the war: German, Turkish, English, French, Belgian, New Zealander, Australian, even Russian . . . all those beloved men might die.

Harry had thought the war an adventure, but she had held the hands of too many men as they took their last breath. It was an abomination, and she hated it with a deep fervour. Which accomplished nothing. If only all women had the vote, all over the world! Then they might be able to stop these old men sending young men to die.

But she wouldn't hold her breath for it; the women's vote hadn't stopped Australia joining in the war.

CHAPTER 15

'Dr Brent!' Matron called him as he left the dining room after breakfast. 'Could I have a minute?'

'Yes, Matron.'

He followed her to her office, where she turned to face him, her hands clenched at her waist. Whatever she had to say, she wasn't happy about it. He prepared himself for bad news. Was there a telegram from home?

'Dr Brent . . . it's come to my attention that you are . . . spending a good deal of time in the company of Sister Northey.'

Taken aback, he could only stare at her. Sister Northey? Then he realised the implications and anger reared up. How dare this old cat cast aspersions at Evelyn!

'I can assure you, Matron, that all I am doing is helping Sister Northey with her studies.'

'Sister Northey is a fully qualified nursing sister. What can she possibly be studying that would need your help?'

'Latin.'

That surprised her, he saw with satisfaction.

'Why on Earth –'

Evelyn's plans weren't his to share.

'I wouldn't be so presumptuous as to ask her,' he said, giving his best impersonation of an affronted don. 'But if a young person wants to improve herself, naturally I'm happy to help.' He hoped Evelyn would forgive his demotion of her to 'young person'. Matron did not look quite reassured, so he steeled himself. 'Look at me, Matron. Do you really think that a young lady like Sister Northey would be interested in a cripple like me?'

And that, of course, ended the conversation. Because no, Matron didn't think that. Couldn't think that. Because it was so bloody unlikely as to be unbelievable.

'It's very good of you to give up your time, Doctor. Make sure Sister Northey doesn't take advantage of your kindness.'

Her ready acquiescence and relief was like a knife in his side.

•

He would have to tell her. William looked at himself in the mirror of the men's bathroom and said sternly to his reflection: 'You have to tell her.'

In a few moments, he would go out to the dining room, and sit down with Evelyn to help her with her Latin.

Bloody Matron. As if he could! As if Evelyn would ever look at him that way.

But he had to tell her that marriage wasn't on the table. Before she heard any gossip, or before she began to wonder, herself, about his motives.

He didn't flatter himself that she'd be disappointed. But it felt – well, like he was a wrong 'un, not to tell her.

'Out you go, Sonny Jim,' he said to himself. 'Bite on the bullet.'

•

She was waiting for him, her veil laid aside as she bent her head over her textbook. The lights had been turned off in the rest of the dining room: she sat in a circle of light, and there was a nimbus around her head, like a halo. Which was going just one step too far. He grinned. Many things she might be, but she certainly wasn't a saint. Too much strength of will for that.

He slid into the seat next to her and she smiled at him. Like being kicked in the stomach. He smiled back and hesitated.

'Er . . .'

She looked enquiringly at him, her head cocked like an inquisitive bird. Like a linnet. That was a much better name for her than either Evelyn or Lynnie. Linnet.

Oh, for God's sake, spit it out, man!

'Matron was suspicious of us,' he said, self-deprecating as he could be. 'But I reassured her that there was nothing shady going on.'

'I bet Dr Malouf put her up to it,' she said. 'He was watching us the other day.'

'Mmm, yes, very likely.' He sounded like an idiot. Deep breath and just say it. 'But that reminded me that there's something I've been wanting to explain to you.' She looked at her textbook and back at him. 'No, no, not the Latin. This is a little . . . delicate.'

A mischievous smile lit up her eyes. 'You're pregnant!' she said.

He laughed. 'Not that kind of delicate!' She had broken the ice, and he could bless her for it. 'It's about us.'

Her face stilled, assuming that expression of intelligent repose he loved – *liked* – so much.

'I just wanted to make you aware that, um . . . my polio experience . . .'

'Yes?' Now her eyes were full of compassion, warm as a fire on a cold night. They certainly warmed him.

'It's left me with permanent wastage of the muscles of my right leg, as you know, and with some hip disease as well.'

She nodded.

'The likelihood, for someone paralysed as I was as a child, is that as I grow older my condition will deteriorate.' Almost to the worst part.

'That's not definite.' She picked up a pencil and doodled on her notepad, her face away from him.

'No. But it's likely enough that . . . that I can't take the chance of marrying. I wouldn't want to be a burden to my wife and family, or land them with a cripple who needed to be supported. So I'll never marry.' There. That was telling it plain and straight.

He tensed. He wasn't sure what her reaction would be: pity, surprise, indignation that he'd even thought she might be interested in him that way . . .

Her head came up and she was smiling.

'Oh, that makes things *so* much easier!'

Bugger me, he thought. Maybe she hadn't heard him? But she went on.

'You know I want to be a doctor – so I've decided I'll never marry, either. It's just not possible for a woman to have a career as a medico *and* a family. Besides,' her mouth took on an obstinate shape he'd never seen on her before, 'I'll *never* give anyone control over my life, the way a husband can control his

151

wife.' She sat up and beamed at him. 'So that's all right then! Oh, I'm so glad you said something. I didn't like to mention it myself . . .' She patted his hand, as though he were an old lady. 'Now we can be friends, and not worry about all the other nonsense.'

'Yes,' he said. 'We can be friends.'

It was purely ridiculous to feel let down. Conceited and vain and like a popinjay to want her to have been disappointed.

Had he imagined that warmth in her eyes? Or did she look like that at anyone she felt sorry for?

'It's these declensions I'm having trouble with,' Evelyn said. 'Here, you see?'

'Ah, I see. You've got the dative plural instead of the genitive plural. There's a better way to remember that . . .'

They worked solidly for an hour, and the whole time he had to resist the urge to take her by the shoulders and kiss her and see if *then* she'd be glad he wouldn't marry.

At least he had the grace to be ashamed of it.

•

After the tutoring session, Evelyn went back to her room, clutching her books to her chest. Her steps dragged. It was ridiculous to feel disappointed. She'd been so *pleased* that she hadn't had to bring up and dismiss the idea of marriage between them – but after that first surge of relief had died away, she had felt unreasonably flat.

Irrationally sad.

Sad for William, certainly. She was *choosing* to remain single; but he was, in a way, being forced into it. It had been clear that it was only his disability which kept him from marriage.

Why did that make her feel better for herself when it should make her sorry for him? Was she so shallow that she *wanted* a man to fall in love with her even if she couldn't marry him? How selfish and uncaring she would be! Of course she wasn't that puerile! It was merely a natural – *something*.

But no mental gymnastics could obscure the truth; she was attracted to him far beyond anything she had felt before. She must be careful about that.

Just because she intended to stay single didn't mean her heart couldn't be broken.

CHAPTER 16

An influx of casualties put an end to their tutoring sessions; there just wasn't enough time in the day. Evelyn missed them; but perhaps it was for the best, if they were causing gossip.

Matron started sending nurses up to Alexandria to accompany the trains full of wounded back to the hospital. It wasn't a popular duty, but they did keep casualties down a little by having the triage done on the train itself, so that the nurses could direct the stretcher-bearers which patient to take to where as soon as they arrived – and often, the treatment the nurses gave on that journey stopped a man from dying, especially from dehydration.

And the casualties kept coming. They went back to the twelve-hour days – sometimes fourteen, or sixteen. They all became bad-tempered and grumpy with fatigue.

William did better than most, Evelyn thought, but even he snapped at Matron, 'I don't *care* if you have to train your nurses. While we're working at this pace I want Sister Northey as my theatre nurse. In the time it takes to train a new one, a man could die!'

Every day, Evelyn was afraid that she would see Harry on a stretcher carried in to the theatre or, worse, get the dreaded telegram with news of his death.

A couple of weeks after Linus left, Evelyn received a letter from Harry, on paper she recognised as being from the notebook she had sent him.

He started with a few light-hearted words thanking her for looking after Linus and describing a funny scene where Linus had come up and kissed him on the cheek in front of the whole squad, . . . *and then the ruddy chap explains 'Oh, that was from your sister, Harry!' How the men roared. I haven't heard the last of that yet. Every time I walk past a dugout someone makes a kissing sound behind my back!*

But then he became serious.

I've made you the beneficiary in my will, which is lodged with the Battalion, he had written. *And put you in as next of kin. I can be sure you'll tell the old man if I go West. I couldn't be sure he'd tell you. He's still pretty sore about you enlisting. Have you written to him lately? Maybe you should drop him a line. Love AND kisses, Harry.*

Drop him a line?

Hah.

She had written to her father when she arrived in Egypt, telling him her address at Heliopolis Palace. Nothing. There had been more than enough time for a reply to have come. She had written for his birthday in March, making sure she left enough time for the letter to get to him by the day. No reply.

She'd be damned if she wrote again.

She prayed, though, that the next time she contacted him it would not be because Harry had been wounded or killed.

Oh God, let that not happen.

•

The high casualty rate meant that they often had to siphon off new arrivals to other hospitals, so there were nights when the ambulances were late or didn't arrive at all at the end of her shift at Luna Park.

On the twelfth night in a row they'd worked back until ten, the ambulance simply failed to arrive.

Fed up with waiting for George or Hartley to come, Dr Lewis, Lil Mackenzie (a nurse newly arrived from Australia) and two orderlies decided to walk back. William clearly couldn't do the long walk, so Evelyn stayed with him, the two of them leaning back on the low wall next to the ticket office. The nights were turning a little cooler, but it was still warm enough that she flicked her cape back from her shoulders.

A couple of times, William turned to her as though to ask her something, but stopped himself.

'Out with it,' she said, half-laughing. He was so easy to read; transparently honest and good.

'This marriage thing,' he said at last. She stopped smiling. What was he about? 'I understand you not wanting someone else to have control over your financial freedom. But a good lawyer could draw up a marriage settlement which could protect you from that.'

Oh. That.

'No,' she said. 'My mother's will is quite clear on that.'

'But the *right* man could settle the same amount on you. Give it back to you.'

'*If* he chose to. But it would be *his* decision.'

'If he was a man you could trust, though . . .'

She turned away from him and drew her cape back over her shoulders, hugging herself. This wasn't something she'd ever imagined discussing, but it was *William*, who would understand if anyone could. It helped that she knew he wasn't trying to change her mind; merely to understand.

'My father . . .' No, that wasn't the beginning. She cast her mind back, unwillingly, to her teens. 'My mother developed cancer when I was fourteen. I was taken away from school to help nurse her. That was my father's idea.' It sounded simple. Nothing like those chaotic, grief-stricken days which had seemed so impossible to bear. At her back, she felt William's warmth, close to her. But he didn't touch her. 'Mama . . . she never recovered. She died not quite a year later. Emaciated. Taken off by a fever, in the end. She was so weak . . .'

She moved away again, a little, concentrating on the tracery of the rollercoaster against the starlit sky.

'After she was . . . gone, I thought I would go back to school. But my father refused. He said I should help him in the practice. I had no choice. My mother had left me an inheritance, but he was my trustee. He had total control. He still does, until I'm thirty or I'm married, whichever comes first.'

'So you became a nurse . . .'

'In secret. Dr Chapman at the Manning District Hospital helped me. I need some way of supporting myself until I'm thirty, and at least with nursing I'm learning more and more about medicine. My father forbade me to enlist. He won't even pay me my pin money. All I can do is wait.'

He wasn't looking at her. He gazed down the road to the carousel, where dim lights moved, as the nurses took their lanterns on rounds.

'Or you could marry,' he said.

'The day I marry, my inheritance becomes my husband's property,' she said flatly. 'I will *never* put myself in that position again. I will *never* let someone else have control over me.'

She could hear the certainty in her own voice; a kind of absolutism which she suspected wasn't very attractive. Would he be repulsed by it?

William was looking at the ground, as though the story had been too heavy for him. She felt a spurt of annoyance. What did *he* have to worry about? No judge would ever take *his* money away and give it to his spouse.

He looked up at her. 'This is wrong,' he said. 'The law is wrong. It must be changed.'

Some tight knot in her abdomen loosened, a little.

'Yes,' she said.

'And doctors should be leading that campaign. God knows, I've seen enough battered women coming through the Mission . . . if they could control their own finances, they'd have a much better chance of getting away . . .' He fell silent. Sighed. 'After the war, I suppose . . .' He shrugged and smiled wryly at her, but then frowned. 'Not all men are like your father, Evelyn.'

'My mother loved him.' Evelyn pushed her cape back again, suddenly too warm. 'And he was encouraging enough of me as a young girl. It was only after she died . . . It was like she had kept all the meanness in him, all the tyranny, in check, and once she was gone it came out in full force. So how can you tell? How can I trust someone enough, having seen the change in him?'

That was the deepest fear; that no man – *no one* – was trustworthy. That her own instincts about people couldn't be relied upon. At least, not to the level of betting her life and her happiness on it.

He nodded, and put an arm around her shoulder in a companionable hug. 'I shouldn't be trying to talk you out of this, should I? It means we can be friends, without either of us worrying about the slippery slope to matrimony.'

She laughed a little, and turned into him, resting her head on his shoulder. 'Friends,' she agreed. The starch of her veil rustled against his coat. Yes, that was a companionable sound.

'But you *deserve* someone you can trust, Linnet,' he said, his mouth against her temple, breath warm on her skin. 'Someone honourable and good and intelligent. Someone fit and strong . . .' A little bitterness had crept into his voice, and she put her fingers against his lips, wanting to stop the pain she heard there.

'Don't.' His mouth was warm, soft, human under her fingertips. She tilted her head to look up at him, astonished by the rush of desire that ran through her at the touch. Their eyes met. And then his mouth was on hers, his hand on her cheek, cradling her head, his body pressed against hers.

She wanted him. More than she had known. She felt it happen; her body softened and curved into him, her mouth opened under his, she slid her hand around into his hair and pulled him closer, closer, tighter. He tasted like nothing she'd ever had before. Like sex, she thought vaguely. He tasted like sex.

As if at a signal, they both pulled back, breathing hard, staring at each other.

She should say something. Laugh it off. He touched her cheek, an expression of wonder on his face. They were still so close, she could raise her mouth to his with just a thought. Nothing was real but his face in the darkness, and the warmth of his hand. His voice was shaken.

'So . . . where in all this not marrying does passion fit?'

It was harder than ever to breathe, because he was right. This was passion, pure and simple. And good.

'I don't know,' she whispered.

A squeal of brakes cut them apart cleanly, both turning away as the headlights from an ambulance swept over them. She hoped desperately that her veil was on straight. Trying to straighten it now would open the gossip floodgates.

'Here we are!' George's voice floated out of the darkness. 'Sorry I'm a bit late. Had a problem with the spark plugs.'

'No worries,' William said, sounding remarkably calm. Was it her imagination that there was still a slight tremor in his voice? 'Sister Northey?'

He helped her up into the seat by the driver and went to the back of the ambulance himself. Yes, she thought. Better for us to be separate right now. That was a mistake, that kiss. A wonderful mistake. It couldn't happen again. Not ever.

'Good night?' George asked.

With some difficulty, she dredged up the memories of the surgical session they had just finished.

'Not bad,' she said. 'Mostly small wounds, shrapnel, that kind of thing. No amputations, thank God.'

'Amen and hallelujah,' George said.

That seemed as fitting a comment as any to end the night on.

But as she remembered William's voice calling her 'Linnet', her whole body warmed with something deeper than passion.

•

He should be sleeping, but he couldn't settle. William stared out his bedroom window, making out the silent coils of the rollercoaster, and the simpler silhouette of the Ferris wheel.

What a bastard that father of hers was! He'd like to say a few words to him. Or, better yet, perform an orchidectomy on him! A man like that didn't deserve balls.

No wonder his Linnet didn't trust men. Couldn't trust men.

He moved back and forth restlessly. How he would like to teach her to trust him! To show her that a man could be true, and kind, and honourable.

If he taught her that, would his reward be for her to marry another man?

And that kiss. A fine way to get her to trust, to grab her and kiss her without even asking! But memory swept over him and he knew that he was wrong to blame himself entirely. She had come to meet him on equal terms; kiss for kiss, passion for passion. He might be relatively inexperienced with women, but that had been unmistakable. The feeling of her hand in his hair, pulling him closer . . . he shivered with desire and opened the window, needing the night air to cool him down.

To seduce a young lady was the act of a cad. A blackguard. Or, as his father would say, 'A bloody mongrel.'

Was it seduction if she wanted it as much as you?

If marriage wasn't an option?

He hadn't been celibate, although his few encounters had been with 'experienced' women; not prostitutes, but women who had no pretensions to ladylike behaviour and were happy to share a night of pleasure. Those times had been enjoyable, but had left him merely physically sated. They hadn't touched his essential loneliness in any way, except to make him feel it more strongly.

It would be different with Linnet.

So different.

He went and had a cold bath, but it didn't help as much as it should have. By the time he managed to sleep, the sky was rose and gold, and the sun was slipping above the horizon.

CHAPTER 17

1 JANUARY 1916

'I'm sending you to Mustafa Camp,' Dr Malouf said. 'Where perhaps you won't be distracted by affairs of the heart.'

What? He glared at her disapprovingly. He was talking about William, she realised. A cold sick feeling gathered in her abdomen.

'There are relationships which are just not tolerated in the Army, Sister,' he added.

She said nothing, just looked at him. The sick feeling turned to anger. How dare he? He shifted, uncomfortable under her gaze, but he didn't soften.

'Immediately, if you please, Sister Northey. There's a train at two you can take.'

'Yes, Doctor,' she said automatically, and turned on her heel without another word, heading for her room

Embarrassment flared as soon as she left him. For him to have *noticed*, they must have been . . . obvious. It had been hard not to look at William; when he was in the room, any room, she found herself following his movements. And he would look up, and meet her eyes, and the muscles around his eyes and mouth would soften. She would feel a quick hot surge of emotion.

And Malouf had noticed. She wanted to sink into the floor and disappear.

Mustafa Camp was in Alexandria, the place where casualties from the Dardanelles were brought now, to be triaged and treated before they were allocated a bed in a Cairo hospital or sent home on a hospital ship. Now the retreat had happened, this lot of casualties would be Mustafa's last.

On the train to Alexandria with Lil Mackenzie, the other nurse sent off to this duty, she looked out the window at the date palms and grazing goats and told herself that it was good. Separation from William would let her gather her strength. Because although Malouf was a scandal-mongering old woman, he was right. There could be no real relationship between her and William.

She just had to drill that into her head until her body believed it.

•

'Why hasn't this man had his wounds properly tended to?' Evelyn demanded.

The stretcher-bearers shrugged.

'Put him down over here.'

The soldier in front of her, a tall fair-haired man, was lying on his face, his back and right shoulder roughly covered with field bandages. She couldn't believe that no one on the ship had fixed this. He definitely wasn't well enough to go on the train to Cairo with the other, ambulant, patients.

The orderlies wanted her to sign off on the transfer, so she wiped her hands on her apron and pencilled her initials onto the form. Private James Hawkins – now he was here, the battalion clerk would send a telegram to his people back home.

Disinfectant. Gloves. As she used water to soak the bandages so she could pick them off, she saw that Lil was doing the same to a man on another bed in the tent, but on the man's left side. Both caught by the same shell, probably, and then bundled off during the evacuation with no proper medical attention.

Her anger on their behalf was tempered by thankfulness. These were the last. The very last wounded from the Dardanelles. That horror was over.

After eight months of hell, the Allies had pulled out of the Dardanelles – with nothing to show for it, except dead and crippled men. Thousands of deaths, for nothing. They were calling it a complete defeat.

She was just glad she would be closing no more dead men's eyes; at least, not from Anzac or Suvla.

The water chilled quickly; temperatures were in the fifties and nothing stayed warm for long in the hospital tent which was all that Mustafa Camp had in the way of medical care. Blood had stuck the bandages tightly to Hawkins' skin, and as she eased the main field dressing off it pulled pus and flesh with it. Hawkins groaned and raised his head, trying awkwardly to look around him.

'It's all right, James,' she said. 'You're in hospital. Just lie down and rest and we'll get this taken care of quick smart.'

'Jimmy,' he breathed, and became unconscious again. That wasn't a good sign. His temperature was a bit high, and the wounds were infected. The sort of infection that might kill him. But she couldn't smell gangrene.

Well, bedamned to that. She wasn't going to lose the last wounded man from the Dardenelles.

She worked steadily, trying to get as much done as possible before he roused again. She picked out the pieces she could, jagged buttons of metal, shards and pellets of lead, most the same size but some clearly ricocheted fragments of bullets.

Cleaning out the wounds took some time. Some of them needed stitching, but there was still shrapnel in many of them, some of it buried deep. He would need an operation to get those out, and she couldn't sew up even the smallest wound without checking if there were pieces of metal beneath the flesh.

Mustafa Camp didn't have an X-ray machine. He needed to be transferred to Cairo, and she'd have to go with him – there was no way to keep him safe except by constant nursing.

'This bloke needs an X-ray,' Lil Mackenzie announced, straightening up.

'So does mine.' They looked at each other, and shrugged. 'Back to Heliopolis, I guess,' Evelyn said. 'O'Malley,' she called to the chief orderly, 'we have to take these men to Cairo for X-rays. Find out when the next train is, will you? And if there isn't one, organise an ambulance.'

She set to finishing the cleaning, disinfecting and bandaging of the remaining wounds. Hawkins' back looked like a patchwork quilt by the end of it, a crazy quilt with different-sized patches.

He stirred and moaned several times, and his temperature and pulse were worrying; she bathed him in cool water, but it was so cold as the afternoon drew to a close that she worried he would catch a chill if she did more. He took some beef tea, though, which was encouraging.

'No train until morning,' O'Malley announced. 'I've teed up an ambulance.'

They got the camp commander to sign off on the transfer and then took the two men to the ambulance.

'Oh wonderful,' Lil groused when they saw it – it was the type which had roll-up curtains of isinglass on each side; more comfortable in the heat of summer but in this chill wind . . .

Evelyn commandeered extra blankets from the hospital tent. For a moment, she just looked at it. Neat as they always left things, but empty. No more wounded. For now. Tears pricked her eyes, remembering all who had died or been mutilated. For what? Nothing. They'd gained nothing. Anger burned through her; generals were murderers, every single one of them.

But she had two soldiers who might yet be casualties, if she didn't do her job.

•

The trip from Alexandria, in daylight, took just over three hours. At night, with the road damaged by the big Army trucks which used it daily, it was slower. Bumpy, cold and uncomfortable. It gave her too much time to think. William. The memory of his mouth on hers, his heart beating strongly against her hands.

That had been so *stupid*! Her mind and her body were at war with each other. Every time she thought of him every inch of skin on her tingled. Ridiculous. Frightening. She'd always been able to control her own reactions before. Well, really, she'd never *had* this kind of reaction. Never longed for anyone. Never felt her nerves fire with excitement at a touch. If he touched her again, she'd spin out of control.

A part of her thought that was an excellent idea. But she couldn't risk pregnancy; and more than that, she didn't want to hurt him. Because no matter how much her body yearned for him, she wasn't going to marry, and neither was he. So anything they started was doomed from the outset.

Hawkins moaned, and she was recalled to the present. Yes, keeping her mind on the present was the best possible distraction from William. She sponged Hawkins' face and hands.

As they went on, his skin began to redden at the edge of his dressing. Infection. She wished she had maggots on hand, to eat away the diseased flesh and leave the clean behind.

'Is your boy feverish?' she asked Lil.

'A bit. Not too bad.'

They sat on small fold-down seats between the stretchers, Evelyn facing backward, Lil forward because there was more headroom there, and Lil was far taller than she, a long beanpole of a woman. The men had been placed in opposite directions, so they could both sit at their patients' head.

'Come on, Arthur,' Lil said, 'have a drink.' Her patient sipped tea through a straw; like Hawkins, Arthur Freeman lay on his stomach.

Thermoses of beef tea and others of water, some dry biscuits and dates were all they had. It was a good sign that Freeman could drink. She had trouble getting fluid into Hawkins. She couldn't dribble it down his throat the way they usually did because he was face down.

'Suck on the straw, Jimmy,' she urged him, and he finally took a small drink.

'Ruby?' he asked, his eyes vague.

'Ruby's his missus,' Freeman volunteered sleepily.

'You've got to drink this for Ruby,' Evelyn said. Hawkins took another sip.

The ambulance went over a pothole with a thump, and Freeman let out an oath. 'Sorry Sister,' he said, shamefaced.

'We've heard worse,' Lil said. 'You just try to rest.'

Four hours it took them to get to the hospital, and by the last half hour Evelyn was seriously worried about Hawkins, who hadn't fully regained consciousness. She suspected a head wound or, failing that, some other complication. He shouldn't be this tired. His wounds didn't look to be any worse than Freeman's.

She rushed him into X-ray first, and then with the still-wet films to the King of Belgium's theatre.

William was on duty. As he saw her, his eyes warmed; she could see what Malouf must have seen, an involuntary reaction. She took a breath and forced herself back to her task.

'He's failing,' she said. 'We've got to get the shrapnel out and have him sewn up so he can rest comfortably.'

'From Anzac?' he asked, immediately all business.

'Yes. The last ones, he and his mate.' They looked at each other, and she knew they were seeing the same memories; weeks of constant, grinding work, nights and nights of listening to men scream and cry; the graves stretching out in the cemeteries with their plain white crosses. For nothing.

'At least it's over,' William said. 'At least the poor buggers got out.'

She'd never heard him sound so Australian.

'Let's go,' he said. 'Scrub up.'

They moved into action, as they so often had together, with the team. Now that there were so few cases coming in, the anaesthetist was available, and she could be simply the theatre nurse, working by William's side. An orderly held the X-rays up to the light as Will probed each wound, finding and withdrawing each small fragment. He was painstaking and astonishingly accurate as he cut through tissue to find the hidden shards.

The final wound, smaller than some others but very deep, had already partly closed. They examined the X-rays together. This fragment was deep in Hawkins' chest, near the aorta. There was no way to get it out. Other fragments were too near the lungs, or behind important blood vessels, or were so small that the body would be able to deal with them itself.

'That's it,' Will said. 'We can't do any more. I'll close him up.'

With Lil assisting, they went through the same procedure with Arthur Freeman.

And then it was up to the nurses.

•

Over the past two weeks the wards had begun emptying, as the casualties stopped coming in and men recovered or were transferred to the rehabilitation facility at Alexandria.

The post-surgical ward was only just full, not overflowing, and there was ample space to walk between the beds.

But the moans and the nightmares were the same.

Evelyn couldn't help taking a special interest in Hawkins and Freeman. Both had come through their operations all right, but she didn't like the look of Hawkins' shoulder, and both had the chills which were often the first signs of a bad fever, possibly even pneumonia.

Most feverish soldiers cried out for their mothers, but Hawkins always, always called for his Ruby. Even now, when his mouth could barely form words and he was emaciated from dehydration, Evelyn could still hear a faint whisper, pleading, 'Ruby . . .'

It was make or break, tonight. His poor battered body couldn't take another day of fever. His heart would give out, or he'd go into convulsions, and die.

Evelyn gave him cool water sponge baths every half hour, and spooned water into him continually. It was too cold to pack him with ice. He'd get frostbite.

Towards the darkest part of the night, around three, when souls were most likely to slip away, the fever grew worse.

Hawkins was restless, tossing and turning, pulling his mouth away when she tried to spoon water in. William came by to check on him.

'Only nursing will save him now, Sister,' he said sombrely after feeling Hawkins' pulse. 'Or prayer.'

They sat on either side of the bed, waiting. It wouldn't be long, one way or another. Hawkins took long rasping breaths. Not the death rattle, not yet. Prayer. Well, if she could. It had been a long time since she'd prayed properly. She bent her head and began, 'Our Father, who art in heaven . . .'

As though that were a signal, Hawkins turned his head and stared past her – not at her. 'Ruby,' he whispered, and his voice was glad, his eyes bright with tears. 'My girl.'

Then his head flopped back.

Evelyn sat for a long moment. So. She'd failed. Her gut felt as though she were turning to stone from the inside out. As though the hard, bitter rock was filling her, climbing towards her tight throat and burning eyes. She met William's gaze with shared despair.

Then William leant forward, putting his ear to Hawkins' mouth, fumbling for his pulse.

'He's breathing.'

And as they watched, he began to sweat.

The fever had broken. He lay like one stunned, but his temperature was coming down, and he had lost those terrible rasping breaths. He would live, now, with proper care.

William came around the bed to her, and she turned her face into his side and wept in gratitude. Somehow, Hawkins had become symbolic to her – someone she had to pull out of danger. Not only because he was one of the last out of the Dardanelles, but because of the way it had all happened – her and Lil recognising the need for X-rays, the trip from Alexandria, the operation, the subsequent infection – all of it was so typical of a nurse's duty in this war. Without her, without all the other nurses, he would have died, no matter how brilliantly William had operated.

'This one's a notch on your belt, Linnet,' William murmured, his hand on her head both a caress and a way of keeping her steady.

Yes. Hawkins was a nursing triumph. It made her vow that, if she did ever become a doctor, she wouldn't forget how much of successful medicine was out of her hands.

She drew in a deep breath and pulled away from him, then wiped her face with a handkerchief he gave her. How weak she was, how unprofessional! She could feel her face flame with embarrassment, but William's hand came down on her shoulder.

'You've earned a good cry,' he said. She looked up at him, startled, and in the low lamplight she saw his gaze was full of – something. Appreciation, admiration. No, she couldn't lie to herself. Shouldn't lie to herself. His face was full of love.

Careless of who saw, she turned her face against his hand. He slid his palm to cradle her cheek and she rested there for a moment. Then one of the men in the other beds let out a nightmare shriek, and they both jumped and hastened back to their duties.

•

The next day, Hawkins was very weak but back to his right mind. He grinned shakily at her.

'Heard I have to thank you, Sister, for pulling me through,' he said.

'We were a bit worried about you, Jimmy,' she said.

'Ah, no need to worry about *me*,' he said. 'My girl was right there by my side. I couldn't let her down and die.'

She was startled, and showed it. Surely he didn't mean *her*?

He apologised quickly. 'Sorry, sorry, Sister. Not you. My wife.' His voice gentled. 'Ruby. Last night . . . she was there, right with me. In the Valley of the Shadow. She saw me through.'

He believed it. It was clear that he believed it, and some of the other men were nodding, or looking wistful, as though they'd like to have a wife of their own.

Evelyn forced a smile. 'Just as long as someone was,' she said. 'Now, have some sweet tea.'

•

That night, as she bathed and got into her nightgown, the scene returned to her – and memories of the night before, when Hawkins had suddenly murmured '*Ruby!*' as though surprised and delighted.

Was it possible? Stranger things had happened. For a moment, as she tied off her night-time braid with a piece of ribbon, she felt a sharp envy spear through her. To be so close, to love so much – and to marry. To have the certainty of continuing that love. Could that possibly be worth giving up all independence, all control of your life? She wondered what Hawkins' Ruby thought about marriage, and if she would tell the same story of last night.

Her thoughts went inevitably to William. His face, so full of love. His voice, calling her 'Linnet'. Her stomach cramped with desire; not only to touch him, but with a further, ridiculous image of having his child.

Impossible. To become what she wanted to be, she had to make sacrifices. She *knew* that. Children were impossible for a female doctor. An *unmarried* female doctor.

That was just the way it was.

And already, people were gossiping about where the hospital would be sent next, now that they weren't needed for Dardanelles' victims. Wounded, she reminded herself. She mustn't say 'victims' to anyone else, no matter what she felt about that disastrous campaign.

Connie Keys had already left, on a hospital ship back to Australia. Others would go soon, to Australia or France. Perhaps the whole hospital would pack up and move.

She and William might be separated, quite soon.

Could she bear that?

She dreamed that night of baby hands being pulled away from her by a grinning Death, and woke feeling annoyed with the whole world.

CHAPTER 18

FEBRUARY 1916

Dr Fanous called a meeting of all nurses. The operating theatres were closed for the afternoon (what a luxury!) and even those on ward duty were told to leave the dwindling number of patients to the orderlies.

He stood on a chair in the dining room and Matron stood next to the chair, with the nurses gathered in front of them. It was astonishing to see how many of them there were; Evelyn had never seen the whole nursing staff together before – of course not. What a wonderful group of women.

'Well, ladies, it's as we suspected. The 1st Australian General Hospital is to be transferred to France.'

Exclamations and comments murmured around the room. Dr Fanous let them die down.

'We'll begin transferring our patients to other hospitals and convalescent homes over the next week. It will take us a few weeks to get everything packed and ready to go. Luna Park, as an auxiliary hospital, will stay open for a few months, in case of emergencies. Any of the men who won't be fit for duty within a month will be going back to Australia on the *Nestor*, and we will be sending some of you with them. The rest will be coming to France – where, I have to warn you, conditions are unlikely to be palatial.'

A polite laugh followed. He smiled warmly, transformed into the lovely good-natured man Evelyn had always known was there. 'I'd like to say that you have all, each and every one of you, delivered a quality of service and care to our patients that I am very proud of. It's been an honour serving with you here and I'm very glad that we will be continuing to serve together.'

Applause. He got down from the chair and helped Matron up.

'I'll be putting up schedules in the nurses' sitting room by this afternoon. That will assign duties to you for the pack-up. When we leave this place, we leave not a scrap behind except the actual beds. Do I make myself clear?'

'Yes Matron,' they choroused. It was like being back at school, in assembly, but the suppressed excitement all around her was intense.

She wasn't sure how she felt. France. On the one hand, *France* – a place of story and images, of romance and fashion. On the other, *France* – the Front, where the fighting was the heaviest and, if newspaper reports were to be believed, the most useless. Casualties as bad as Gallipoli; conditions even worse, particularly in winter.

And France would have no Dr William Brent.

She had loved it here, she realised. The high desert sky, the camaraderie of the men, and William, always William, kind and encouraging and, yes, handsome, laughing, wry and intelligent and *interesting*. It was ridiculous to feel tears prick her eyes. This was war. She would go where she was sent. That was what she'd enlisted for. To be sent where she was needed.

They went back to the wards in a state of general excitement – most of the women were happy to be moving on, especially to Europe. As Mabel said to her while they were feeding the men lunch, 'It's not like I'd ever have been able to get there any other way. It's a great opportunity. Why, we might even get to see London!'

Immediately her mind's eye filled with all those images of London which she had seen over the years. Big Ben. London Bridge. Piccadilly Circus. And more, in France. The Eiffel Tower. Versailles. The Champs-Élysées. The Elysian Fields, that meant – Heaven. She could practise her French, get it back up to fluency. She used to be good at French, in school. Madame had said so, anyway. Now she'd get a chance to try it out.

Finally, excitement surged through her.

'*Mais oui*,' she said to Mabel. '*Nous irons à Versailles!*'

Mabel looked at her with a dropped jaw.

'You speak French?'

'*Oui, je le parle un peu.*'

'That's *wonderful*. I'll stick with you, mate.'

It would be wonderful. And terrible. And scary and horrible and bloody. But they'd dealt with that before and they'd deal with it again.

Hannah came to the door of the ward and beckoned her. Evelyn handed the soup bowl she was holding to Mabel, apologised to the man she'd been feeding, and went to her.

'I've had a death,' Hannah said. 'And the orderlies are all with Dr Fanous. Help me get him out. You know the men don't like a corpse in the ward.'

Fortunately, the dead man was slight. And not too young. It was worse when they were young. They made short work of getting him onto a stretcher and out to the mortuary — a room set aside for the dead, with tables to lay them on. Empty but for this one man. That, more than anything, made Evelyn realise that 1AGH really was more use elsewhere.

'He was a New Zealander,' Hannah said, 'so we'll have to send his personal effects to them.'

They returned to the ward where Hannah was immediately called to help an amputee whose scab had started to bleed. Evelyn went through the dead man's things, collecting everything that was his and leaving anything that the hospital had given him. Wallet, notebook, shoes, the rags of a uniform which should be thrown out and fumigated, but she'd cut the buttons off for the family. In the mortuary was a small table with brown paper and string, so she could make a parcel of the man's belongings to send to the New Zealand Army company clerk. He would get the family's address from the man's pay-book, which he had kept in his wallet. Yes, here it was . . . along with a French letter, a condom. Better not send that back. She slipped it into her pocket. The nurses often gave them to patients who were being discharged, even though it was completely against orders. It was against orders for the men to frequent the brothels, but they did, and none of the nurses wanted them back a week later in the VD ward.

She put the parcel at the dead man's feet, and said a prayer for him.

Possibly the last time she'd have to do that in Egypt.

That was an odd feeling.

That afternoon, the list of duties went up in the nurses' sitting room.

'I'm staying in Cairo!' Lil said. 'At the 3rd AGH.' She looked like she wasn't sure if she were happy or not.

'Oh God,' Alice Kitchin moaned. 'I've got to pack up the sheets! But France after that.'

'Consider yourself lucky,' someone else said. 'I've got bedpans!'

The crowd of them jostled to see what the next few weeks would bring them.

'The *Nestor*!' a disgusted voice – was that Mabel? No, someone else. 'They're sending me *home*.'

'Oh, bad luck!' Lil said.

'I wish *I* were going home,' Minnie Walters said.

'Maybe we can swap!' The two women went out together, arm in arm, heading for Matron.

Hannah had eeled her way to the front and laughed. 'I've got the theatre. That's not too bad.'

'Look for me,' Evelyn called to her.

There was a silence, then Hannah wriggled her way out of the crowd.

'They're sending you on the *Nestor*,' she said. Her eyes were concerned, and a bit teary.

Australia. Going back to Australia.

Oh, bugger.

'It might not be forever,' Hannah ventured. 'Perhaps they'll ship you right out again.'

'Perhaps.' All she could think was: separated from William for nothing. It wasn't like she was needed in Australia. There were tons of nurses there!

'What about you?' she asked. 'Packing up theatre, and then what?'

Hannah smiled widely. 'I'm to stay here, to help close up Luna Park. Technically it's an auxiliary unit. And then I go to the 14th, the new place!'

She was *pleased*? Oh, of course she was. Linus was here. Better to be somewhere he could get to on leave. Lucky girl. And they'd heard the 14th was to be established somewhere in Cairo, later in the year. So Hannah was all right.

Evelyn sighed. Should she talk to Matron about her posting? Volunteer to pack up Luna Park, like Hannah?

But as she neared the door, Minnie and the other girl – it was Annie Sanderson – came back, downcast.

'Matron said that the postings aren't under her control. Orders from up above about who goes where,' Minnie said. 'No changes, no arguments.'

So that was that.

Matron appeared on their heels, looking more flustered than Evelyn had ever seen her.

'Ladies! I've just heard that the *Nestor* is sailing tomorrow morning! We have to get all the ambulant cases packed and ready to go, and the stretcher cases too. Everything else gets put aside for now!'

It was a long day. The men were so excited about going home, it was hard to get them to concentrate to pack their things, to complete their paperwork, to get them shipshape – new pyjamas for most of them, and new kit. At least they didn't have to eke out the Red Cross supplies anymore. They could use them up – the British Red Cross would surely top up their stores.

Jimmy Hawkins was the most excited of the lot.

'He can't wait to see his missus again,' Arthur Freeman, his mate, put in.

'She's worth getting excited about,' Jimmy said, grinning. 'Here.' He showed her a photo – a wedding photo of the two of them, the girl dark-haired and, yes, beautiful. More than just pretty. Evelyn hoped she had a heart to match; Hawkins was going to need a lot of care and kindness. That right shoulder wound of his would limit his ability to work for quite a while.

Finally, the day was done and the nurses who were to go off to the *Nestor* the next morning released from duty.

Evelyn hadn't seen William all day – he had been on duty in the operating theatre in Luna Park, but he'd be back by now. No need for twelve, fourteen-hour days anymore. He'd be in his room. The thought of leaving him was sharp and painful. Ridiculous. What had they shared? A communion of the mind in the theatre, a few tutoring sessions, a single kiss . . . but she couldn't just leave him.

She *couldn't*.

Was it vanity that made her drag her veil off before she went upstairs? Or just a desire to be herself, not 'Sister'. There was an ache under her heart she'd never felt before, but she didn't want to think about what it might mean.

Will had been on duty all day, and when he opened his door to her light knock she could see the tiredness in the long lines of his face. But as he saw her, the tiredness disappeared, replaced by that smile he seemed to give to no one else.

'Evelyn!'

'I've been posted to the *Nestor*,' she said in a rush. 'We leave tomorrow morning, at six.'

The light in his eyes went out, in a blink. He half-raised a hand to her face, and then let it fall. His lips pulled back, as though he were stopping himself from speaking, but she could see what her news had meant to him, and that gave her resolution.

'Will you let me in?' She put her hand over his where it held the doorknob. He looked at her searchingly, still in silence, and then drew her inside, shutting the door behind her.

They moved into an embrace as if they'd practised this dance all their lives. Her head on his shoulder, his mouth against her hair, both pressing close, and closer, as if to hold on forever.

And then, at the same moment, they moved, mouth seeking mouth, and they kissed.

She tasted salt; she was crying. His lips were hungry, and she wound her arms around his neck, hand on his head, and pulled him into her as fiercely as she could. One night. Perhaps they'd never meet again.

The winds of war blew strongly, and the people, the small, unimportant people, scattered before them. Who knew where they would be whisked off to? Her to Sydney, him perhaps to France, with the hospital.

If they were different people, if marriage had been possible, if they didn't have to worry about her getting pregnant . . . they might have fallen on the bed together in a glad frenzy.

She kissed him with desperation and regret, and drew back.

'Come,' he said, drawing her down to sit on the bed, but perching on the edge so it was clear that he wasn't asking her to lie down.

She sat next to him, and they looked at each other.

'We can't risk –'

'I wish we could –'

They spoke at the same time, and fell silent together. William grimaced. 'I'll be restrained, I promise, but . . . I really need to lie down.'

He was holding his leg; oh, how selfish of her not to have noticed.

'Of course!' She helped him back to sit with his shoulders against the bedhead and his legs stretched out in front of him, and began to massage his thigh.

'Evelyn, don't.' His face was pained, but with embarrassment, not physical hurt. He pulled her to sit beside him. 'Don't. Just sit with me. Tell me – tell me anything, anything about you. I feel as though I barely know you, and yet . . .'

She slipped out of her shoes, and helped him off with his, and then curled up next to him.

He kissed her again, gently, his hand sliding along her jaw and into her hair. He pulled out the pins from her hair, and she let it fall, felt him gather it up in one hand. He buried his face in it, a gesture so full of love and desire that her heart caught, seemed to stutter, and then to beat more strongly. She touched his head with gentle, unsteady fingers, and he looked down at her, eyes dark with pain and desire.

How could she leave him?

She buried the question, and kissed him again, and again, and again.

A little while later he pulled back, and removed his hand from her breast. 'We can't . . .' he sighed.

He was right. If only she'd been prepared! If only she'd kept that French letter from the dead New Zealander, instead of handing it over to a boy being discharged. Then they might have . . . She stopped her thoughts going that way. It would only make her frustration worse. And perhaps it was a blessing

PAMELA HART

that they had to restrain themselves. It would be hard enough to leave him as it was. If they'd made love . . . She shivered at the thought.

'Will you stay in Sydney?' he asked, holding her close and warm against his chest.

'I'll go where I'm sent, I suppose,' she said. 'Don't think we have much choice in the matter.'

'I do,' he said quietly. 'I could come back to Australia with you. Work in the repat hospital there.'

Her heart leaped, but she took the hand that was tangled in her hair and kissed it. 'And if I'm sent to France? And then to Palestine? Or to Melbourne?'

He had no answer.

'You can't follow me all around the world,' she said gently. 'We're not married, and we're not going to be married, so . . .'

'No.'

Will rubbed his leg with his free hand, and then pulled the hand back, as if he didn't want to draw her attention to it. Idiot. She knew what that leg was like – she'd just touched it.

The leg wasn't that bad. Some muscle wastage which was no doubt what caused his limp. A narrow calf, the tendons standing out sharply. The foot turned just a few degrees inwards. She thought of the amputated limbs she'd had to dispose of.

'That's a perfectly good leg,' she said, her tone sharp.

His face dissolved into the laughter which she was beginning to realise was his true self. Wise, self-mocking laughter, full of love.

'Yes, Sister!' he said.

'Quite right,' she said, but her heart was separating into tiny fragments in her chest, as though it were cracked porcelain

184

finally giving way. Her fingers dug into his arms. 'Kiss me again,' she said. He stroked a strand of her hair, bright gold in the gaslight, back from her face, impossibly tender.

'Linnet . . .' he said, his voice rough with desire.

Where Will was concerned, it seemed, her practicality had limits, and they were well past them. She pressed against him fully, not caring anymore. Pregnancy was only a slim chance, surely? He held his hands off her, as though allowing her an escape route. As though she would change her mind if she thought about it for a moment.

She stopped his mouth with a kiss. 'Love me,' she said. 'This night may be all we have.'

He groaned against her lips and gripped her hair with both strong hands, rolling her over, pulling her head back, looking down on her. And then, deliberately, he moved off her.

'No.'

It felt as though the breath was punched out of her. She had *felt* how much he wanted her, his desire pressed against her.

'I can't, Linnet. I care about you too much to let you risk your whole future for one night with me.'

He was shaking with repressed desire. Shaking with need; and yet he had controlled it, for her sake. Her eyes filled with tears — to care about her so much! — and she wanted to hit him at the same time. She was shaking too. They sat side by side, just breathing.

'Talk to me then,' she said eventually. 'Talk to me about your life, your family, everything.'

Gingerly, he leant back against the bedhead, shifting a pillow into place to support her as she did the same.

'Once upon a time?' he asked, a thread of laughter back in his voice.

'Yes,' she said. 'Just that.'

She took his hand, warm and rough against hers, and he squeezed her fingers.

'All right. Once upon a time there was a boy called Will . . .'

CHAPTER 19

After so many nights on duty, she was attuned to dawn, and the light would begin to grey soon. Will was asleep. She slid from the bed and used her hanky dipped into his washstand jug to wash her face clear of the traces of tears. She could have a bath before she dressed to go to the ship.

Her clothes felt stiff and heavy against her skin; any touch which wasn't his seemed like an intrusion. She used his small comb to untangle her hair and rebraid it. She had to get down on her knees to find her hairpins, and when she came up again he was awake, sitting up, his eyes full of farewell and regret.

He smiled at her, mouth twisting with a wry acceptance of their situation.

'We'll know better next time,' she said, breathless. 'We'll be prepared.'

His eyes darkened with renewed desire; he nodded and put a hand up to her. 'I have to go,' she said, but she sat on the edge of the bed and kissed him gently.

'Wherever you are, I'll pray for you,' he said, as though it had been torn out of him. 'For God's sake, take care of yourself.'

Not once had she ever heard him mention God, or prayer. She blinked back sharp, sudden tears.

'You take care of yourself, too.'

'If not before, then after the war, in Edinburgh,' he said, his eyes bright with tears of his own.

'The first intake after the war,' she agreed. 'I'll see you there, if not before.' She kissed him again, quick and hard, and almost ran for the door.

She slipped out of his room as stealthily as she could, veil in one hand, shoes in the other, ready to put on once she'd crept up the staircase to the nurses' level. The building was in the pre-dawn hush, when even the weak screams of the men's nightmares had died away, and there was only the low moaning of the dying, which didn't make it up this high.

She paused, hand on the doorknob after she had slid the door closed. Her last night here. It wasn't only William she was leaving. The other girls would be going to France; the orderlies, too, all the complex paraphernalia of a big hospital packed up and sent off like a boy scouts' camp. The magnificent building would, she supposed, go back to being a hotel, although who would stay here was anyone's guess.

It had a particular scent, this building, which on this floor overlay even the hospital smells of disinfectant and urine. A spicy, fragrant scent; it called up the desert, and Egypt, the Egypt she had imagined as a child, exotic and mysterious and alluring. Her eyes were pricked with tears; she would miss it all, more than she had thought. William was the sharpest pain, but there were so many others . . . Hannah, and Linus, and Connie and Alice and Mabel and Lil. The comradeship, the thrill of saving a life. That feeling of freedom in being where no one from home knew her, which was inextricably wound up with the high sky and wild winds of the desert, and the exotic rainbow lights of the Ramadan lanterns. Sydney would seem very tame in comparison.

As she turned to go up the stairs, Matron moved out of the corridor to the right and stopped in the middle of the hallway, just looking at her. It was a kick in the stomach; to be caught *now*, sent home in disgrace, she probably would never get a job anywhere else – oh God, she'd have to go back to her father with her tail between her legs, and wouldn't he take his revenge! She felt sick with shame and anger.

'Miss Northey.' Not *Sister* Northey. That was bad.

'Matron.'

They stared at each other for a long moment. Any moment now . . . but there was no condemnation in Matron's eyes, just a terrible blankness.

Matron looked at her watch, and her hand was trembling.

'Since, officially, you are transferred to the *Nestor* today, I suppose you are no longer under my direct authority,' she said.

Evelyn couldn't believe it. Of all the officers who might have given her a pass, Matron was the last she'd have expected.

'I'm just going to pack and leave,' she ventured.

'Yes.' Matron nodded, and half-turned away, then stopped. Not looking back, she asked, 'Was it worth it? To abandon your principles?'

Evelyn moved closer to her. Impossible to carry on this conversation at a normal tone from across a hallway.

'I didn't abandon my principles,' she said. 'But if I had – yes, it would have been worth it.'

Matron turned back and stared fiercely into Evelyn's eyes. 'I don't understand how anyone can abandon who they are, just for – for *love*.' She said the word as if she'd said *venereal disease*.

'There's nothing better to abandon yourself to.' She spoke softly, but Matron flinched. Well, in for a penny, in for a pound. 'Dr Fanous . . .'

'He wants me to *marry* him!' As if it were an insult.

'He loves you. I've seen him look at you, with such tenderness.' She fell quiet, because Matron was crying silent, racking tears. 'He's a Christian,' she said helplessly, putting her hand on the older woman's back, feeling her tremble. 'He went to Oxford.'

With a long breath, Matron got control of herself and swiped the tears away with the back of her hand. Her spine straightened, shrugging off Evelyn's hand. Her stiff upper lip was showing. Yet there was a crack in her armour, even so. 'He's a *native*,' she said, but her voice trembled between longing and horror.

'You could have a family . . .'

'*Brown babies*?' A shudder went through her, unstoppable. 'How could I love them? Even the *thought* of it . . .' Another shudder. Evelyn had pitied her, but that bone-deep disgust was tempering the pity with anger on Dr Fanous's behalf.

'He'd make you happy.'

'Cut off from my own kind?' Matron sniffed back the remnants of tears and shook her head. 'No. No. I know my duty and I know who I am. An Englishwoman. A Briton.'

What the hell, Evelyn thought. 'A woman in love,' she said.

Matron flinched as though she'd been struck and her eyes were haunted, hunted, as though she ran from a truth she couldn't admit.

'Nonsense,' she said. 'How could I love someone coloured?'

Evelyn shook her head. She felt ill. Dr Fanous, so lovely, so cultured, to be relegated to 'coloured', as though that *mattered* next to his intelligence and caring. It was an evil word, a thing of division and hate, the legacy of conquest and slavery.

'Matron, I'm no longer under your authority, am I?'

'That's correct, Miss Northey.'

'Then I take leave to tell you, ma'am, that you're a fool.'

Matron moved away, instinctively backing a couple of steps, and then she rallied.

'And I suppose you're intending to marry that cripple?'

Anger rolled over her, that rare anger that came so seldom.

'Don't you *dare* call him that. You have the soul of a fishwife!' she snapped, and pushed past Matron to run up the stairs to her own room, pulling open the door with a huge heft and closing it again just as strongly. Just as well Hannah had an early shift today, to allow the *Nestor* girls a night's sleep. Evelyn leant against the door, barely seeing the room, and said to herself, 'Yes, but for all that guff about love, you're *not* going to marry him, are you?'

The whole incident cast her spirits down, and she sniffed back slow, hot tears the entire time she was packing. Leaving him was cutting her to the bone; stripping back her defences, flensing the flesh from around her heart to leave it open and vulnerable, all the more because they couldn't take the conventional route and get engaged, promise to be there when it was all over. What they'd had here might be all they would ever have. She still couldn't quite believe the chivalry which had caused him to draw back. If only they could have another night together, and be prepared this time!

But there was nothing she could do. War sent you where you were needed, and she was needed on the *Nestor*.

She would have to carry her unprotected heart through the duration, just like all the other lovers separated by this insanity.

•

It was a fool's errand, but he abandoned his duties for the day and went to Alexandria to see Evelyn off.

Not to talk to her, or be with her. Just to watch that bloody ship pull away slowly from the dock and steam off. He couldn't even see her at the railing. Perhaps she was on the other side of the ship.

What a fool he was.

How much he loved her.

The thought that he might never see her again was a knife in his guts.

And the next question was, he thought, as he used his cane to limp back to the nearby railway station, would he go to France?

Or would he stay here, in the forlorn hope that she would be coming back?

He'd have to find a new berth, however it worked out. The 1AGH was closing. Dr Bennett had already gone to Europe. Dr Fanous was going too. Dr Malouf, it turned out, had been transferred to a Casualty Clearing Station in the Sinai. This had been coming since the retreat from the Dardanelles, and the doctors had discussed it more than once amongst themselves. He fancied Fanous was sorry to be going to Europe – probably knew the British officers would treat him like shit.

Lewis and Kennington, the anaesthetists, were off to France and glad of it.

'If I never have to hear that bloody desert wind again, it'll be fine with me!' Kennington had said, and Lewis had nodded.

'Sparing the profanity, boyo, I have to agree.'

William didn't mind the desert. The wind, well, yes, that was horrible. But the high bright sky, the clear air . . . he had been happy here. But it was hard to sort out whether that happiness had been only about being near Evelyn.

From the railway concourse, you could just see the ocean's horizon. Was that a black speck on it, was that the *Nestor*? His heart leaped at the thought.

He was a fool.

But he thought he might just stay here anyway.

CHAPTER 20

MARCH 1916

Garden Island, the Sydney naval base, lay off Potts Point, and the Naval wharf which serviced it was at the bottom of the Point: Cowper Wharf, where the *Nestor* docked. There were big iron gates cutting off the wharf from the public, and a crowd had gathered outside them, craning to see past the wharf out to the island, where the Naval dockyards were. A line of ambulances waited on the dock, quietly foreboding. Behind them, lorries, buses, troop transport vehicles.

One by one, they ferried the patients into the waiting buses and ambulances, until there were no more patients left on the ship. Evelyn hopped into the last ambulance, which held only a young Light Horseman with a badly broken leg.

The big iron gates were open to let the ambulances and buses of ambulant patients through, and there was a throng of mostly women outside them, straining to see, trying to find out which of them had their loved ones. A heavily pregnant girl was standing, weeping noisily, by the noticeboard where they'd put up the list of those who had died on the voyage. A woman in a straw hat supported her. Poor thing. By the looks of her, she was ready to drop. To bring a child into the world already fatherless . . . She wondered which of the men she'd stood death watch over was the father of that baby.

And then her ambulance was past the gates and making its way up the hill.

•

The 4th Repatriation Hospital at Randwick was a big old sandstone building, with long balconies fronted with iron lace.

Its wards were also long; bright places with big windows and beds facing each other with a wide aisle in between. Evelyn thought of the ice rink at Luna Park, where sometimes you had to walk sideways to get between the hundreds of beds, and smiled grimly. A different kind of hospital, that was clear.

But settling the patients into their new beds and doing the paperwork was the same.

On that first afternoon, she came up behind a doctor, ready to follow him on rounds with the other ward nurses, to acquaint him with the patients they had brought so far.

He turned, hearing them approach, and she gasped. Dr Chapman! From Taree. From home. For a moment her mind whirled, but then it made perfect sense. Of course Dr Chapman would have enlisted. He was that kind of man.

'Dr Chapman!'

'Sister Northey.'

In uniform, he seemed taller and far more attractive. Younger; she'd always thought of him as much older than she was, but she realised he couldn't be more than thirty-five. His brown hair shone in the light from the big windows down the side of the ward, and he smiled at her with real pleasure.

'Welcome back,' he added.

'Thank you, Doctor.'

He nodded and swept straight into rounds. It took her back to the Manning District Hospital, where she had done the same several times. Dr Chapman had changed her life, had enabled her to be here, helping. *Doing* something in this terrible war.

And that had led to Cairo and on to here, a blue Sydney day with golden sunshine flooding through the long windows, and the matron calling them all in once rounds were over.

After rounds, Dr Chapman had smiled at her. 'Good to be working together again, Sister.'

He hadn't waited for a reply, which was good, because what could she say? 'I wish you were someone else?' She had to put every thought of William away and working with Dr Chapman would be easy. Familiar. Safe.

Matron was older, competent, and tolerated no shilly-shallying. She said so, and then smiled. 'Welcome home, Sisters,' she said. 'We're indebted to you for your care of our boys. You've got two days off and then you're on duty again.'

Those who had family in Sydney sped off to see them; most of the others slept those days away, with breaks to visit the local shops, to post the letters they'd all written to friends and family, and stock up on all the things they'd run out of – stockings and tooth powder and so much more.

She wrote to her father, not really expecting a reply, and wondered briefly if she should apply for leave to visit him. The thought made her nauseated. If he replied to her letter, then she might think about it again.

Back in the nurses' quarters she curled up for another nap, catching up on months of missed sleep. It was such luxury to lie and have nothing to do, no one waiting for you to help them. Even in the spartan quarters, the light and the soft autumn breezes made her room a haven; but all she could think about was William, and when she dozed she had fitful, frantic dreams where she was running to help a bleeding patient but never got there, or she was being drowned under a sea of stretcher cases, all of them calling for their mothers.

It was odd, she thought, that she had had very few nightmares in Egypt – as though her mind had held back until she was safely home; or perhaps it was simply that she wasn't as dead tired here, and didn't sleep as deeply.

She emerged two days later, a Wednesday, back on clock time instead of ship time, and found herself assigned to the ward where most of her charges from the *Nestor* had settled in, including Jimmy Hawkins and Arthur Freeman, both in high spirits because today was the first visiting day and Jimmy's wife would be coming.

'Ruby,' she said, remembering that dark night when they'd almost lost him. It was as if a shadow went over her, but Hawkins didn't seem to feel it.

'That's her!' he said. 'My little Ruby. She's a country girl, you know, and once I'm out of here we'll go back to Bourke and settle down. Have a family.' He was cock-a-hoop at the thought.

'But she's in Sydney?' Evelyn asked, changing the dressing on his worst wound, the one on the shoulder. He nodded and winced as the wound caught.

'Oh, she's been living here – even got herself a job! But it won't be long 'til we're back where we belong.'

It sounded wonderful; she remembered how sure he'd been that their love had crossed oceans to help him survive. God-given love. It made her wistful. To be that sure of another human being. How could anyone be that sure?

That afternoon, Hawkins had been examined thoroughly by the surgeon, and was exhausted. He drifted into sleep and was still asleep when visiting hours started.

And first through the door was a rather beautiful young woman in a blue frock, who searched the beds frantically until Annie Sanderson pointed her to – yes, to Hawkins' bed. She looked even better than she had in the wedding photo. Evelyn felt like a voyeur, but she couldn't resist watching.

Ruby stood for a moment, just watching him sleep. Her absolute stillness was striking; Evelyn couldn't interpret it. Then she walked to the bed and took his hand. Sat by him, upright as a reed. Slowly bent her head to kiss his hand. Were there tears? Her hand was shaking. He woke, gently, and said her name, and they kissed.

There was something about this slow, certain, but tremulous contact that left Evelyn fiercely hoping that Hawkins was right – that his Ruby would go off gladly with him to the bush, and have babies and keep house.

But the Ruby who'd walked in didn't look like a country girl. Not at all. She was sophisticated and sure of herself. A professional woman, even in that blue frock.

Evelyn didn't often pray, but she prayed now that it would all work out for them, even while a small voice in the back of her mind said, 'Even love's not enough when people want different things.'

•

The strangest part of being back in Australia, Evelyn decided, was having free time. She worked her shifts, and that was it. No extra time making dressing packs, or tending to a new load of casualties, or scouring the shops for those treats which made convalescence just a little easier.

Time off.

It was surprisingly hard to get used to, as was being on ward duty only, with no midnight calls to the operating theatre. The theatre sisters at the 4th Repat were entrenched in their jobs and wanted no help from her.

She had no idea what to do with her time – if it had been summer, she could have gone to the beach, but although April in Sydney was a month of clear skies and warm days, it wasn't swimming weather. She kept thinking about William. Wondering how he was. Remembering his touch. His breath on her cheek. His surgeon's hands. Although she had far more time to sleep than she'd had at 1AGH, she slept no better, lying in bed wanting him, full of frustrated desire. Full of something . . . something she didn't want to look at too closely, but which she feared resembled misery. The misery of missing him.

And she couldn't settle to anything. On the ward she was fine, but off duty her mind skipped around and she fidgeted, unable to settle to reading, to studying her Latin, her anatomy. Every diagram in *Gray's Anatomy* recalled an operation at 1AGH, or the sound of William's voice, explaining the mnemonics she could use to remember the order of bones or muscles. She jumped at sudden noises and only found calm in the middle of a patient procedure: changing dressings, massaging, taking temperatures. Then she was the person she remembered being. At other times she hardly knew herself.

After walking by the ocean on her first day off, and going to the cinema with some of the other nurses (she missed Hannah), she was at a loss for what to do when she saw that the roster was about to give her a whole weekend to herself.

She called Rebecca Quinn on the Thursday before, and was immediately invited over to stay.

Dr Chapman encountered her on her way out of the hospital, as he was getting into his car at the entrance.

'Off for the weekend?' he asked. His eyes approved the simple dark green frock she had bought only the week before. It was a relief to get out of uniform, but she had hardly any clothes and, of those, only this dress was fashionable. Clothes had changed remarkably in the small time she had been away. She couldn't quite get used to the way this dress's skirt waved above her ankles. She kept wanting to tug it down.

'Yes,' she said. 'Staying with friends.'

'Can I give you a lift?'

How odd. He didn't even know where she was going.

'I'm going to Rose Bay,' she said hesitantly. 'Probably out of your way.'

'Nonsense!' he said. 'I was just going for a drive. Rose Bay will do as well as anywhere else. I can head up to South Head afterwards and see The Gap.'

In the car, a curiously intimate setting, they talked easily about Taree people. He never mentioned her father, which she thought a kindly restraint. Many of the boys she'd grown up with had enlisted.

'And Harry?'

'He's in the Sinai, with the 4th Light Horse,' she said. She had trouble talking about Harry without crying, and her voice sounded hard even in her own ears. She tried to soften it. 'They were very glad to get out of the Dardanelles and get their Walers back.'

'I'll bet,' he said. That was a phrase he wouldn't have used in Taree, which was full of Protestant patients who didn't approve of gambling. And the thought of gambling inevitably brought thoughts of William and his SP father.

She fell silent, watching the houses of Sydney – so many kinds, so many styles! – race past the window. He didn't press her to talk. Such a kind man.

At Rose Bay, she insisted on getting out on the main road so he could continue on to South Head more easily.

'Thank you, Doctor,' she said as she got out.

'You could call me Ian,' he said, leaning over to look up at her through the passenger door. She stilled for a moment, astonished.

'To tell the truth,' she said when she had recovered her voice, 'I'd rather not – I'm afraid I'd forget to call you "Doctor", at work, and think of the scandal that would cause!'

He laughed ruefully.

'Well. Perhaps at another time, then.' She closed the door and waved a little as he drove away.

How odd. She didn't know if him thinking of her as a woman was exciting or simply confusing. If he did. Perhaps, like her, he was a bit homesick. But the light in his eyes gave that the lie. She felt, she decided, rather cross. She didn't *want* any romantic complications.

Rebecca and Jack had a small flat in a converted Victorian mansion at Rose Bay, overlooking a glimpse of the harbour. It was a small two-bedroom apartment, but it was sunny and bright, decorated with the casual flair that Rebecca brought to her own clothes, and which Evelyn had always secretly admired.

No heavy Victorian drapes or bulbous furniture – it was all Art Nouveau, slim lines and natural motifs.

Rebecca worked most Saturdays, attending Red Cross functions or fashion displays, so Evelyn arrived around five, and found Jack about to leave for an extended absence.

'He's off again with the Navy,' Rebecca said. She seemed to take it as a matter of course. Perhaps Jack did this all the time.

He was a handsome man, tall and blond and well set up, with an easy charm. Evelyn had never liked him, and had never been sure why. He didn't like her much, either, but that didn't mean he stopped trying to impress her.

'New Guinea,' he said, preening just a little. 'I've got the inside scoop on a submarine story.'

'Good for you,' she said. He gave her a sideways look which marked her lack of interest, but she didn't care; her heart was light now that she and Rebecca would have the weekend to themselves.

Rebecca and Jack kissed goodbye – a long and complex process from which Evelyn averted her eyes.

Then he was gone, with a 'Got to catch the tide!' tossed over his shoulder as he leaped down the stairs.

'Well,' said Rebecca, slightly breathless and a bit pink, 'let's get you settled.'

Rebecca was one of the few people in the world she could *talk* to. So after a scratch meal of sardines on toast and tomato soup ('Since it's just us,' Rebecca said), they settled with cups of tea and ginger biscuits on the lounge.

'Tell me everything!' Rebecca said.

'Off the record, though.'

'Of course!' Although she looked a little wistful when she said it.

'Oh, you can write up a "Gallipoli from the nurse's view-point" later if you like,' Evelyn said.

Rebecca grinned at her. 'Once a journalist . . .' she said, half-apologetically. 'Off the record. What was it like?'

So she told her. It took a long time. Evelyn was surprised she had so much to say. Perhaps William's name had come up more than she realised, because when she wound down to, 'And then I came home on the *Nestor*,' and fell into silence, Rebecca immediately asked, 'Who's this Dr Brent?'

How much to say? Rebecca had been raised by a suffragette mother, and was the most 'advanced' woman Evelyn knew. But was she advanced enough to understand a relationship which could never end in marriage?

'William,' she said. 'William Brent. We – er – we . . .'

'You're in love!'

'No. Yes. No, not the way you think.'

Rebecca looked at her with shrewd and compassionate eyes. 'You were lovers.'

'No, not really. Not . . . properly. Neither of us want to marry,' she said, cutting to the heart of the matter. 'So it was nothing serious.'

'Oh, Lynnie,' Rebecca said, gently. 'Of course it was serious, if you care about him.'

'No,' she said, as tears rose in her eyes. 'It can't be serious.'

Tactfully, Rebecca turned away for a moment, and then veered off a little.

'What's wrong with marriage? You can still have a career!'

'*You* can, maybe.' Evelyn recovered, taking Rebecca's offer of a new subject with gratitude. 'But not a doctor.'

'But you're not a doctor, yet.'

'Exactly! And I never will be, if I get married and have a parcel of kiddies before I turn thirty and get my money.'

'But if you get married, doesn't your money get released to your husband? You wouldn't have to wait until you were thirty.'

'That's the point! To my *husband*, not to me. He'd have control of everything. If he decided I wasn't to study, there'd be *nothing* I could do about it. Just like with my father.' She felt the old resentment and anger surge up in her, and let it out. 'I will *never* allow someone that kind of control over me, ever again!'

Rebecca got up and walked to the window, distressed.

'But marriage isn't *like* that, not if you marry the right person! Jack supports my career!'

'Oh really? And if you had children, do you think that young Jack-me-lad would stay home and look after them so you could keep working?'

Taken aback, Rebecca put her hand to her hair and pushed in some hairpins; maybe buying time before she answered.

'I always assumed that we'd have a nanny . . . *I* was brought up by a nanny . . .' But she looked troubled, as though that hadn't entirely been a good thing. She shook her head as if to ward off the thought. 'Anyway, what Jack would do isn't the point. What would your William do?'

'I have no idea. We've never discussed it.'

'So why doesn't *he* want to get married?'

Evelyn sighed. 'His health is uncertain. He had polio as a child . . . quite a few polio sufferers go downhill in later life. I think he doesn't see himself as fit to marry.' Which was so stupid. 'Anyway,' she said, rallying herself, 'it doesn't matter, because I'm here and he's there. I'll probably never see him again.'

'Is that what you want to happen?' Rebecca asked.

Evelyn threw a pillow at her. 'Stop with your journalist's questions, woman! Tell me about your life instead.'

Which started Rebecca off, laughing, on a long tirade about how hard it was for a woman to report *real* news and how she just couldn't get excited about hemline length.

Later, lying in Rebecca's spare bedroom on a narrow daybed, Evelyn allowed herself to think about that question. Did she want to see William again?

Oh God, yes. She did.

•

She didn't go to church with Rebecca in the morning because it turned out that she was Catholic, a thing Evelyn had never realised about her, although come to think of it she had gone to a Catholic school. There was none of the Catholic frippery she was accustomed to seeing in her father's patients' homes: no crucifixes, no statues of the Virgin Mary, no paintings of the Sacred Heart.

'Jack was raised Protestant, but he doesn't believe in much anymore,' Rebecca explained when she asked.

'But would *you* like to have them around?'

Rebecca thought about it, as though she hadn't thought about it before, pulling on her gloves slowly.

'Oh, the trappings aren't important. It's what you believe that counts. I'll be back in an hour or so. Bye.'

It seemed to Evelyn, washing up the breakfast dishes, that Mr Jack Quinn got things entirely too much his own way – but wasn't that always the way? What the man wanted, went. All of society was ranged on his side. The laws, the judiciary, public opinion. Women had to fight for every square inch of ground they gained, and then fight to keep it.

And, to tell the truth, if she let herself fall fully in love with William, as Rebecca had with Jack, she wasn't sure she could tell him 'No'. She wasn't sure if she could bring the fight into her own home. It would be too tiring and grim and dreary. She suspected that she would give in on a hundred little things without even realising it, and end up as reliant on her husband as her mother had been on her father. Much better not to risk it.

Men were wonderful; she had seen so much heroism, so much courage – and support for and, yes, tenderness to their wounded comrades. She admired them immensely, most of them. But . . . put herself under one's thumb – even William's? She just couldn't do it. Every time she thought about it, she remembered countless times her father had railed at her, scolded her, *forced* her to do as he said, because he effectively owned his children under the law and could do as he pleased with them. And the law gave husbands much the same control over their wives. Never again. Never again to bow down before someone else and obey out of fear or necessity.

Never.

CHAPTER 21

Finding another job was as easy as saying to Dr Fanous, 'Do you know where I might be needed?'

Two hours after he got back from Alexandria he was at the New Zealand General Hospital, his duffel in his hand, walking between two old brass cannons set either side of the entrance, then past rows of white tents set up in the garden, and through a drift of tulip magnolia petals and the scent of bougainvillea. It was a smaller and more homely place than Heliopolis, but thank God! it was only two levels. No more dragging himself up innumerable stairs.

Only moments after he made himself known to the orderly at reception, he was facing Major Bagly, an Egyptian Army officer who had been left in charge when the Egyptians turned the hospital over to the Kiwis.

'Sit down, sit down,' Major Bagly said. He was about fifty, a medium-height man with magnificent moustaches and dark olive skin. Intelligent eyes summed William up quickly, lingering on his leg as William limped into the room. There was something guarded in his expression. 'Dr Fanous tells me you've done sterling service at 1AGH.'

'Thank you, sir.' The term of respect seemed to reassure Bagly. He sat back in his chair and relaxed, making William wonder how hard he, as a brown man, had had to fight to gain that respect from the Caucasian doctors.

'Surgeon?'

'I've become one,' William answered honestly. 'I've been doing pretty much nothing else since last April.'

'The Dardanelles.'

'Yes.'

A shade went over the major's face; Will was pretty sure the same expression was on his own. No one who had lived through that terrible time could ever forget the dead and maimed.

'Well then, I'm sure we're delighted to have you. We may not have the New Zealand contingent here for long – there's talk of sending them to England. But in that case, the Egyptian Army will take back the hospital, and you're more than welcome to stay on.' The major surged out of his seat and escorted William to the door. 'Now, just let me know if the schedule is too fatiguing for you.'

Shame pierced him. Always, always he was judged by this bloody leg!

'I'm sure I'll be able to keep up, Major,' he said through gritted teeth.

The major slapped him on the shoulder.

'Don't get your back up, son. I say the same thing to all the young doctors. All you boys think you're indestructible.'

William managed a shamefaced smile. 'I don't, honestly. But I'm tougher than I look.'

'You'll get along fine, then, because you look pretty tough to me.'

It might have been kindness – even condescension – but it eased something in William's gut.

'Thank you, Major.'

An orderly showed him a room overlooking the flowering trees in the courtyard, and as simply as that he was on staff, alone again in a foreign land but with all the organisation and efficiency of an Army hospital buttressing him from care.

He wished Evelyn could see the flowers.

•

His first surgery was simple, an appendectomy on a unit clerk belonging to the hospital, who'd never been within earshot of a battlefield.

The next was not so simple. The boy – only eighteen, his chart said – had had half his jaw blown away. The bleeding had been stopped by emergency surgery on the hospital ship, but now they were trying to make it possible for him to chew food without it falling out of the hole that was the left side of his mouth.

He had no kind of skill in this area, but Major Bagly had, so he assisted. There was so little they could do.

'Gillies – you know, the New Zealander – is using skin from the arm to make new noses in Britain with some success, so I thought we'd give it a try with this young man's mouth,' Bagly said as they scrubbed up. 'I'll need you to close and dress the arm site as quickly as you can and then help me with the face.'

The young soldier was already unconscious when they entered the theatre – a *proper* operating theatre, complete with purpose-built lights! He'd almost forgotten what a proper theatre looked like after the last year at Luna Park and the King of Belgium's suite.

The operation was complex and fascinating. He learnt a great deal. The reconstruction was messy, and they had to put a rubber shield in the boy's mouth so he couldn't infect the stitches by eating – not that he'd be doing anything but drinking through a straw for quite a while. But when the soldier woke up and felt the side of his face, even though it was covered with bandages, he burst into tears.

'None of that,' the nurse on duty said. Her tone was sympathetic, but she meant it. 'You'll loosen your stitches, and we don't want that, do we?'

'No, Sister,' the boy mumbled, with a look of such gratitude that William's heart turned over.

As the orderlies wheeled him off, Bagly said *sotto voce*, 'We've had him on suicide watch, but I think he'll be all right now.'

How many boys and men out there were dreaming about killing themselves because of wounds like this? Missing jaws, missing noses, hideous scarring and burns . . . it wasn't enough to merely save their lives. They had to be given lives worth living.

This was the work he should be doing after the war. Putting not just bodies, but lives back together.

He reassessed his finances. He had thought he would do a postgraduate diploma in chemistry in order to work in vaccines – but now he would need postgraduate work in reconstructive surgery, and that was likely to be even more expensive.

Well. He'd just have to stop buying clothes and eating anywhere other than the hospital, no matter how boring the food was.

The look in that boy's eyes was worth going without for. To bring back life worth living to even one maimed soldier – that was a fine ambition. He imagined, as he stripped off his gloves and readied himself for the next operation, a shrapnel wound which was festering, how he would feel if some doctor said to him, 'Yes, lad, I think we can fix that leg so it looks a bit better.' It would feel like a miracle.

Every day would be a day of building something good, instead of trying to hold back a tide of blood.

When would this war end?

CHAPTER 22

She hadn't spent much time in Sydney before, and she did all the tourist things over the next few weeks, often with Rebecca. The Art Gallery, a Red Cross concert at the Town Hall, a ferry over to Manly to watch the surf riders.

It was a calmer, more even existence, and she was still helping her patients. The ones who were still in hospital, like Hawkins and Freeman, had complex wounds which needed several operations and constant care. But the sense of being on edge, the fidgeting, the lapses of concentration off duty, they were all the same.

She was bored. She lasted a couple of months before she couldn't *bear* it any longer. If she didn't have work that took her mind off William, she would go crazy.

Not knowing how to organise things, she went to Matron.

'I think I'd be of more use back at a general hospital near the front lines,' she said.

Matron sighed. 'You're the third this month,' she said. 'Once you've been in the thick of it, you girls just can't stay home, can you? Well, I suppose at your age I'd have been the same. All right. I'll put the request through.'

'Thank you, Matron.'

'And that's the first time you've really smiled since you got here. Is there a fellow over there waiting for you?' Astonishingly, her voice was indulgent rather than critical.

Evelyn could feel her face flame.

'N-not-not really,' she stuttered. 'No. No one's waiting.'

'Well, that's probably a good thing. I wouldn't like to be worrying about my young man while I was working on the wounded.'

'No, Matron,' she agreed, pulling her amour-propre back around her. 'That would be very hard.'

She went on duty, and did rounds with Dr Chapman.

At the end of rounds she contrived to be alone with him for a moment.

'I've applied to go back to the front,' she said bluntly.

His mouth compressed with some emotion (Disappointment? Anger?), but then he nodded.

'I don't blame you.' He looked over the peaceful ward, the men with good colour and better prospects. 'No, I don't blame you.' He grimaced. 'We Army types go where we're sent.'

'Well, so do we. But we can ask, apparently, to be sent overseas. Maybe you should too.'

'You don't think I haven't?' He slapped his leg impatiently, and then visibly controlled himself. 'Good luck to you, though.'

It seemed like an omen when she returned to her room to find a letter had been slipped under her door. She'd received a couple of letters from schoolfriends since she'd returned, although nothing from her father, but this one had an Egyptian stamp on it.

From William.

My dear Linnet,

I hope this letter finds you well. And happy.

I have been welcomed with open arms to the New Zealand General Hospital in Cairo, so I am set up for the duration, as they intend to keep this hospital open for the entire course of the war in Palestine and the Sinai. Very little combat is now happening along the Suez, so our patients are mostly from the desert, and suffer as often from sunstroke as from bullets or shrapnel. I'm trying to learn Arabic but with not much success so far.

Although I know I have no right to, I think of you often, with great fondness. No, that's not the right word, but I'm a duffer with words. Great affection? I dare not say more than that.

It was a wonderful gift, to have you with me even for so short a time, and I will treasure that memory to the end of my days. So brave, my Linnet, so honest and brave and beautiful as you were.

Well, I'd better stop or I'll be getting maudlin. I hope your new posting is congenial to you and that the workload is lighter than 1AGH.

I have no expectations that you will reply, but if you did it would mean a great deal to me,

Yours, always,
Will

She cried for half an hour, until Annie, who was her roommate, came in and told her to 'Buck up, dinner's ready.' Annie was a calm, comfortable girl who took other people's emotions in her stride while seeming to have few herself.

'Worse things happen at sea,' Annie said, settling her veil in front of the mirror.

'I daresay they do,' Evelyn replied. She put on her own veil and washed her face. She would write back. How could she not? But it might take her a few days to figure out what – and how much – to say.

•

Her orders came through at last, and she was assigned to a troop ship heading for France – she would be working with the 1AGH again, in Rouen! All her old friends. She went about the last few days in Sydney with a light step, and said goodbye to Dr Chapman feeling rather guilty that she was so happy.

'Goodbye, my dear,' he said, shaking her hand. 'I'll miss you, Evelyn.'

'I'll miss you too, Ian.'

He smiled at her more warmly than ever before, so much so that she regretted using his first name.

Saying she'd miss him wasn't a lie. But missing him would be an easy burden if she could get back to some real work.

•

A voyage in a ship full of healthy soldiers should have been a holiday. Evelyn straightened up from yet another bed with a kidney dish of vomit in her hands and sighed.

Seasickness was bad enough, but a strain of gastric influenza had ripped through the men and the medical staff – two doctors and four nurses – were as busy as if they were on a battlefield. At least the likelihood of patients dying was much less, although several of the men had come down with pneumonia in the wake of the flu, and possibly they might lose a few of them. Pneumonia was a killer.

She handed the dish off to an orderly, washed her hands and went up on deck for the five minutes every hour which their medical officer had mandated, to reduce the risk that they would be infected themselves.

The dark blue of a calm twilight sea soothed her; the clouds were full and low, only those on the horizon showing any signs of sunset pink and gold. She leant on the rail and breathed in the clean air. It was only in these short minutes that she had time to think of William.

She had posted a letter a week before she left, which meant he should receive it a week before she arrived in Alexandria. Possibly yesterday or today. She imagined him receiving it; opening it; reading . . . Nerves shook her stomach and made her hands quiver. What if he didn't want to see her?

What if he did?

That last night had been wonderful and yet tormenting. She had desired him so completely that, without his restraint, she would have risked everything. He was so chivalrous! Although some small part of her resented him being *able* to resist her. If they met again, at night, in a bedroom (with French letters at hand), she would make him unable to resist. She would touch and kiss him until he lost that fierce control he kept over himself every minute of the day. It was a control forged in pain, continuing pain, and she admired him for it – but she would smash it to pieces and make him mad with desire.

She laughed brokenly.

A brazen hussy. That's what her mother would have called a woman who was thinking like this. She didn't care. If she had to live the rest of her life alone, she would. But in Alexandria, she would make memories to last her through the cold years to come.

Her five minutes were up. She thrust her still-shaking hands into her pockets and headed for the companionway. Really, thinking about William shouldn't make her this unsteady.

And so warm! Oh, a woman shouldn't dwell on images of flesh on flesh. It was far too distracting.

Six more days, and she would see him!

CHAPTER 23

JULY 1916

His small bedroom was near the top of the building; in summer it was hot both day and night, but he was so rarely in it that it hadn't bothered him. As long as he had someplace private to read this letter.

My dear Will,
Thank you for your letter. It meant a great deal to me to receive it.

It's wonderful that you are settled at the NZGH. Dr Bennett thought highly of them, I know, and they are lucky to have you.

I hope you are keeping well, and are remembering to rest enough, and to have that leg massaged. That's the message from Sr Northey.

From Evelyn . . . I have a new posting – I'm afraid I'm not good at sitting neatly in a hospital at home, no matter how beautifully it's run – just think, only twenty-four beds to a ward!

So I'm off to France on the Karratha *next week. We will be berthing at Alexandria for a day and a night, so I was hoping you might get leave to see me. Even if it's only a walk along the promenade . . .*

And from Linnet . . . It would be so lovely to be able to talk over the past few months in person. I have thought of you often. Too often, I sometimes think. But I hope we can be friends and continue to write to each other.

Until Alexandria,
Yours,
Evelyn

Evelyn. Not Linnet – but not Sr Northey, either. Perhaps she felt she couldn't sign off as Linnet, even though she'd used the name in the letter itself. Perhaps she felt that signing herself as Linnet promised too much.

A day and a night in Alexandria.

If this letter was posted a week before she left, that meant it was only a week until she arrived!

Excitement churning inside him, he took a cab to the British HQ, who were most likely to know the shipping arrangements and dates for the *Karratha*.

'Due sometime this month, probably in eight or nine days,' the bored clerk told him, once he'd slipped the man a ten shilling note.

'I'm at the New Zealand hospital,' he said. 'Let me know when you know the exact date, and I'll be even more generous.'

'Right you are, sir!' the corporal said, taking down his details. 'Don't you worry sir, I'll let you know!'

Nothing like self-interest to ensure compliance, William thought.

How was he going to survive eight or nine days of this anticipation?

●

Major Bagly was sympathetic to his request for leave, but less so to his unsurety about when.

'In seven or eight days, for two days?' he repeated.

'I'm waiting on a ship arriving, Major,' he explained. 'I have to meet it at Alexandria.'

'A-hah! A lady friend?' The major twirled his moustaches with heavy innuendo.

'A friend,' William said. 'A colleague.'

'Ah, well,' the major shrugged. 'That is also good, to meet old friends. But I need at least twenty-four hours' notice, before your leave.'

'Understood.' He hoped the corporal clerk would come through for him.

●

A week later, the corporal rang the hospital and left a message for him: Karratha *docking Alexandria tomorrow morning*. It wasn't quite twenty-four hours' notice, but it would have to do. He informed Major Bagly, packed a small case and went to catch the train. On the way, he passed a chemist's. Should he? He hesitated outside, while a street vendor tried to sell him some beads and a boy offered to shine his shoes. He brushed them off and went in. Better to be prepared.

But the chemist was someone he knew from the hospital, so he ended up coming away with nothing but aspirin. Perhaps he could buy some French letters in Alexandria.

The train was uncomfortably full of uniforms, as a troop was going to the Alexandria port to ship off for France. He couldn't be bothered working out what their colours meant; sometime in the last year he'd stopped caring about the war and only cared about the wounded. As a boy he'd envied the cadets from the King's School who practised their drill in the park near his parents' lending library. He'd so wanted to be like those sturdy, upstanding young men. He suspected most of them were dead now. The King's Cadet Corps had almost unanimously volunteered early, which meant that they had probably been in the assault on Anzac. He wondered how many of the bodies he had cut into or stitched up had been the boys he had envied?

One of the sturdy, upstanding young men in the crowded train gave him a seat, and he took it with barely a blush, though inside he squirmed. To be considered an object of pity was what he hated the most. But he wasn't going to tire himself out because of false pride the day before he saw his Linnet again.

The desert outside flashed by unseen; his thoughts – dreams, fantasies – overtook him. They had only exchanged one set of letters, and both of them were conscious of the censor, so had said little. He had tried to put her out of his mind, but how could he? Every moment of work recalled her to him, even while the work itself served to banish her image. A moment of pause like this was rare, and memory overwhelmed him. One night – it seemed impossible that he was so full of memories from one night.

She had slept, briefly, and he had taken the opportunity to simply stare at her, memorising the curve of her cheek, the glorious tumbled fire of her hair, the freckles along her forearms, her strong, supple hands. That night was a gift he hadn't looked for, had never expected. That anyone could want *him*! It had never occurred to him. And nothing in his life had been harder than pulling away from her. But for her sake, he'd had to do it.

He had known she was growing fond of him, but the fact that she desired him . . . although they had not made love, it had turned his world upside down. A cripple, that's what he was, no matter how good his work. For a beautiful, vibrant woman to show her desire for him . . . Ever since he had felt that he wasn't quite sure who he was anymore.

•

Most of the big hotels had been taken over by the British Army, either as hospitals or headquarters. But he found a pension down near the docks which looked clean and neat and wasn't too close to the nearest mosque. At the hospital, he had learned to sleep through the dawn call to prayer, but he feared that in a new bed, he would start awake at the first long, quivering note.

He had most of the afternoon and the night before she arrived. Checking at the docks for the expected time was the first priority. The Harbour Master's office had a list up by the door. He was surprised – surely wartime secrecy should be kept about ship movements? But perhaps once a ship entered the Suez Canal it was considered safe.

His anticipation was getting out of hand. He sat on a low stone wall near the port and watched ratings stow cargo into a frigate while he gave himself a talking to. There was no guarantee that Evelyn would want to . . . to repeat even the limited intimacy of that last night, let alone do more. After all, no birth control was perfect – oh, damn! He'd forgotten the French letters. He sprang up, sense and self-control forgotten, and hailed a cab, then told the driver exactly what he wanted. Of course, after that he had to ward off any number of suggestions about where he could *use* the condoms, but that was easily dealt with. They found a chemist, he bought a ridiculously large box of the things – who cared, he could pass them out to the soldiers when they went on leave – and he returned to his pension in triumph.

He wouldn't *expect* anything. But he'd be ready if she wanted.

CHAPTER 24

The next morning, he was down at the dock, hat in hand, watching the *Karratha* pull in, waiting with some Army blokes with clipboards.

The first passengers off were a nursing sister accompanying two orderlies carrying a stretcher. He leapt forward, but the sister wasn't Evelyn. A flash of orange caught his eye: the woman on the stretcher had red hair.

Time seemed to stop. And then rushed past him.

'Sister!' he said, using every ounce of 'doctor's authority' he had. Automatically, the sister and the stretcher-bearers stopped and looked at him. He walked over, using his cane for the first time that day. He couldn't risk wobbling or falling down.

Yes. It was Evelyn. Pale, semi-conscious, a hectic flush on her cheeks. He couldn't quite get his breath; there seemed to be no oxygen in the air.

'Sister Northey is ill?' he asked the nurse.

'Her chest. We're afraid of pneumonia. We have to get her out of this wind.' The nurse was an older woman, who clearly thought him a fool.

'I'm Dr Brent,' he said. 'We worked together at the 1AGH. Where are you taking her?'

'To Convalescent Hospital No. 6. Then I have to leave her there and come back in time to sail for France.'

Lady de Walden's! Excellent. He could look after her there.

'I'll follow you.'

Evelyn roused at the sound of his voice.

'Will?' she whispered.

'I'm here, Evelyn.' He couldn't call her Linnet, not here, in front of these strangers. 'I'll meet you at the hospital.'

An ambulance was waiting. As they slid the stretcher in, Evelyn roused again and smiled at him. 'Not the homecoming we expected,' she said through dry lips.

Then the doors closed behind her. He ran – hop and a jump, his fastest method of travel – to grab a taxi, and told the driver to trail the ambulance. He knew the de Walden hospital, of course, but he couldn't bear to lose sight of her.

No. He wasn't going to lose her now.

Pneumonia was deadly, but with the right treatment, if the patient was strong enough, they could pull through. He would make bloody sure she got the right treatment.

Lady de Walden came out of the front door as the ambulance pulled up. He paid off the driver and jumped out as they were unloading Evelyn.

'Margherita!' he said thankfully. 'I have a chest case for you. A patient of mine, Sister Evelyn Northey.'

'William! Of course, my dear,' she said, and asked one of her nurses to show them to a private room, 'For we can't have poor Sister Northey bunking in with these rough soldiers!'

The nurse from the ship, who was leaving with the two orderlies, looked surprised, but then winked at him and left. The wink unsettled him. What gossip had he started? But she was moving on to France. With any luck, she wouldn't know anyone in Egypt to pass the gossip onto.

'She's a friend of yours, Will? I'll leave her to you, then,' Margherita said. 'Kitty will help you with anything you need.'

They put Evelyn downstairs, in a small white room with a window that looked out onto trees. He closed the shutters against the harsh sun, and sat by her bed, reading the case notes the nurse had left.

She had fallen ill after Colombo, after nursing a pneumonia case. That wasn't good. He took her pulse, listened to her chest, cursing the fact that he'd come to the docks without his medical bag. Kitty, without being asked, brought a stethoscope, an otoscope and a thermometer.

Evelyn smiled up at him woozily. She was oblivious to anyone else in the room.

'Will,' she said. 'Sweet William.'

'I'm just going to check your lungs, Linnet. Breathe for me.'

She obeyed his instructions like a good little girl, which almost broke his heart. One lung was clear, but the other had the tell-tale crackle of an infection. Her throat was red but not ulcerated. Her ears were clear.

Her temperature was high, but only one hundred degrees. His fear settled a little.

'She's going to need cool sponging,' he said. 'Aspirin, six hundred milligrams. And fluids. Do you have any orange juice? Or grape juice?'

'I'll send a nurse,' Kitty said.

The nurse, a sparky young girl with a strong Midlands accent, was clearly not going to let him help with the sponging, so he went out to find a telephone.

'I need to call my hospital,' he told Margherita. 'To tell them I won't be coming back tomorrow.'

If Bagly objected, he'd just quit. For the first time, he was glad he wasn't regular Army. He could walk out any time he chose, and there was nothing they could do about it.

'I see,' she said, her head cocked to one side. 'You and Sister Northey are engaged, then?'

What could he say which wouldn't enrage Evelyn and yet would satisfy convention?

'We . . . have an understanding.'

Her face melted into sympathy. 'Of course. You might as well have your old room back. Stay as long as you like.'

'That would be wonderful. I'll pitch in if I'm needed.'

Margherita de Walden was more than just kind. In a matter of minutes, she had sent a driver to collect his things from the pension, and had persuaded Major Bagly to 'second' him to her hospital for a couple of weeks, without mentioning Evelyn.

'He's looking very dragged down to me,' she said firmly. 'He needs a break from the pressure you put him under. When was the last time he had leave?' Her voice was accusing. '*Never?* My dear man, that's just irresponsible. You can't afford to have your doctors breaking down on you. You leave him with me for a couple of weeks. I'll put him on light duties and have him back to you as fresh as a daisy!'

And that was that. Tiny as she was, nothing stood in her way.

•

As though pulled by a lodestone, he went back to Evelyn.

And she was there. He was almost surprised. The whole atmosphere of the hospital was so much one of a British country house that he had always felt a bit like Alice in Wonderland, and it seemed unlikely that Evelyn, so straightforwardly Australian, could be here.

He sat by the bed and watched her sleep. The nurse who had sponged her down had braided her hair into two plaits. It made her look very young, like the child she must have been when her mother died and her hopes of an education vanished. He found himself angry at that. If he could meet her father and tell him what an arrogant idiot he was . . . that would be satisfying, but wouldn't help much. Evelyn had found her own way out, and in the process had learned more than most third-year medical students.

She would be a wonderful doctor.

Every croaking breath she took speared through him. It was always a terrible noise, a deep chest infection, as though the struggle to breathe spread to the listener with the sound, making everyone within earshot tense up. It hurt him to hear her breathe like that.

Her temperature was down a little, but the hectic flush on her cheeks was still there; the dark circles under her eyes were stark against her pale skin. He took her hand, and just sat. Even in sleep, her fingers curved around his.

The thought of her death curled around his heart and squeezed until his pulse beat across his forehead like a drum and his vision blurred.

She wouldn't die. He wouldn't let her die.

•

Evelyn swam up out of a dark dream where William was dying and she was empty of all ability to help him.

She blinked heavy eyes. He was *there*. Alive. Alive, and looking at her with such tenderness, such care.

Her throat was dry and sore. She tried to swallow. Quickly, Will brought water in a sipping cup and she drank. Her head ached like the devil, and she could hear the crackle in her lung with each breath.

'Pneumonia,' she said. Her voice came out cracked, so she coughed to clear her throat, but that was a mistake, because she couldn't stop. Deep, racking coughs, hard-edged, sending sharp pains into her rib cage.

Will held the sputum bowl for her; she had a flicker of embarrassment, but it was drowned by the need to cough and cough and hawk it all up. He held her, his warm arm across her back.

Afterwards, she flopped back on the pillow.

'Green?' she asked. She was so tired. Every muscle ached. She really should have been more sympathetic to her chest patients, if they'd been feeling like this.

He checked the sputum. 'I'm afraid so.' He laid it aside and gave her another drink. Orange juice this time, tart and tangy. 'But your temperature isn't too high, so there's no need to panic.'

She smiled wanly up at him. 'Not what we'd planned for this meeting, is it, Will?'

'You just rest,' he said, smoothing a stray hair back from her forehead. 'Just sleep and recover. I'm not going anywhere. We'll have our meeting, as planned, later.'

He was so dear. So *kind*. She'd seen him being kind to patients many times, and seen them relax and begin to heal almost immediately. Now she understood. Despite his physical handicap, he radiated competence and authority and intelligence. It was easy to relax into that kindness and authority as one would into the embrace of a loving father, and to hand over all responsibility to him.

Though he wasn't her father (*Heaven forbid!*). She was too tired to resist his reassurance.

'Sleep is the best thing for you,' he said softly, stroking her hair. 'Sleep, Linnet.'

As she closed her eyes, she smiled at the endearment. Right now, she wasn't worried if it were wise to care about him or not. It felt just right to hear him say that special name with such love.

'Sweet William,' she murmured, and slept.

•

That night, the crisis came. Evelyn's temperature climbed rapidly and she alternated between rasping breaths and coughing. William ordered a cool bath – the room was so hot! And then had to fill it himself, because the servants who would normally be working were off at their nightly Ramadan feast. He didn't mind. Anything he could do for her.

He put her into the not-quite-cold bath in her chemise; gave her more aspirin, which made her choke and cough; forced her to keep drinking.

As her temperature rose, she lost all sense. The febrile delirium made her mumble nonsense, and then, occasionally, a few clear words. 'No, Father!' she said, over and over and, once, 'Mother!' in such a pitying, loving voice that it turned his heart over. She didn't seem to know he was there, but she said his name a couple of times.

'I'm here, Linnet,' he said.

'Never marry Will,' she sighed, but she held his hand tight.

'I know.'

'Such a shame he's a cripple,' she said conversationally, then dropped back into mumbling. 'His poor leg . . . Awful . . . Horrible . . .' She tossed her head from side to side, coughing and coughing and coughing.

A cripple. He felt as though she had kicked him in the solar plexus. Bloody hell. Of course he was a cripple! Textbook case. Why did it feel so bad to hear her say it? He sponged her hot face and tried not to let the sharp lump in his chest turn into tears. *Awful. Horrible.* She'd been willing to come to him once, but now she knew firsthand how ugly he was, how deformed . . .

She had put on such a good face, when she'd touched his leg, he'd never suspected it had affected her like this.

He wouldn't make her say it to him. He must never approach her as a lover, ever. He pushed down a sick feeling of betrayal; he'd been lucky to have what he did. No blame to her if she couldn't stomach him.

Yet he couldn't shake his desire for her, his need for her. Numbly, almost without feeling, he realised that it was love that drove him. It was all right to admit it now, because he knew nothing could ever come of it.

But if he lost her, if he were there for her death, he wouldn't survive it. She mustn't die.

'Nurse!' he called. A young woman walked rapidly up the corridor and put her head around the door. 'Do you have ice?'

'Of course.'

They packed the bath with ice.

And he waited.

By the time it had melted, her temperature was down a little. He prayed that it would be enough.

But half an hour later, it began to climb again.

Three times they iced her down, each time fear strangling him so it was hard to breathe, hard to think.

Hours of it; hours of the ice melting too quickly because of the heat of the night and her too-hot skin. Hours of desperate prayers. He wasn't much of a praying man, but he prayed and prayed for her. His whole body was tight with fear and an insistent, trembling heartache. She couldn't die. Without her . . . for the first time, he understood those soldiers who said, 'I'd rather die than lose my leg, Doctor.' He'd rather die than lose her.

Around ten in the evening, when the ice had melted for the third time, he took her temperature, waiting for it to begin to climb again.

It had levelled off.

Half an hour later, it had dropped half a degree.

He dropped to his knees by the side of the bath and buried his face in the crook of his elbow. Shudder after shudder went through him, leaving him weak and tremulous as a baby.

Eventually, he got control of himself. Stemming the rising temperature was the first step, but there were more to come if they were going to get through this night.

He got the nurse to come in and dry her off, put her in a new nightdress. He propped her up on pillows in bed, increased the dose of aspirin and hoped nothing started to bleed internally from the violence of the coughing.

Then he sat by her bed, praying to a God he didn't quite believe in, holding her when she coughed, sponging her face and hands, spooning water into her mouth, begging God to let her live.

As the night got deeper and began to cool down, he opened the shutters to let the air in. A breeze struck him, chilling the areas of sweat on his shirt. He hadn't even realised he was hot. Outside, some of the servants had strung Ramadan lanterns from the trees. Like a fairyland of orange and blue and gold. The sound of singing in Arabic came from the back of the building.

The bed faced the window. When he turned from securing the shutter against the wall, Evelyn's eyes were wide, staring at the lights. The flush on her cheeks was dying down.

He sat quietly beside her. 'What do you see, Linnet?'

'Lanterns on the Nile,' she whispered. Then she shivered. 'It's chilly in here.'

And he knew she wouldn't die that night.

CHAPTER 25

It was three more days before he was certain that she wasn't going to die any time soon. Three days of cool baths and feeding her broth out of a sipping cup, three days of deliberately not saying anything personal to her, of being just her doctor and her colleague.

She was so exhausted by the constant coughing that she barely noticed, he thought. She would smile at him and say 'Thank you,' where appropriate, but then she would lie back and close her eyes.

Occasionally, Margherita would ask him to attend one of the other patients, but these were convalescents and his presence was more of a reassurance than anything else. He lanced a couple of boils, he restitched a wound, he gave the 'you have your whole life ahead of you' speech to a boy who had lost an arm. And then he went back to Evelyn.

When he was absolutely sure that she was going to be all right, that her tough country constitution had pulled her through, he went to Margherita and said that he was going back to Cairo.

'But my dear boy, I got you two weeks! Why not stay?'

'I appreciate it, Margherita. But your patients don't really need me. There are men in Cairo who might die because I'm not on duty.'

She glanced at him shrewdly. 'Well, of course you must do as you see fit. But you look very worn down to me. Take a couple of days leave before you go back. There are hotels still open on the beach. Bathe in the sea. Rest. Forget whatever is troubling you.'

'Thank you,' he said ambiguously, not promising anything. How could he go to the coast and swim while Evelyn was here? Much better to go back to work, where the press of daily events would keep his mind occupied.

He went to Evelyn's room. The nurse had been in to sponge-bathe her and change her linens, so she was sitting up in bed with a clean nightdress, her hair in a single plait which came down over her shoulder. Where before she had looked about eight, now she looked like a teenager – a tired but peaceful teenager.

'William!' she said with a smile, and held out a shaky hand to him.

He crossed the room and made himself take her hand. He mustn't let her suspect anything. He mustn't upset her while she was still so weak.

'You're looking better,' he said. He detached himself to check the nurse's obs. Temperature was down, although still elevated a little. Lungs beginning to clear.

'Let me have a listen,' he said, and put the stethoscope on. It took him back to their first meeting, when he'd listened to her chest as part of her physical. He had been distracted then by her vivid, lovely face and beautiful body, but he'd hidden it successfully. He could do that now, too.

'Better,' he pronounced. 'But you know what you have to do every day.'

'Tipping,' she said, and made a face. Tipping consisted of lying half off the bed with your face down and coughing phlegm up into a bowl. It was not a pleasant process, but it hastened recovery remarkably.

'Promise me you'll do it,' he said.

She looked up at him with that quickness of perception he loved. 'You're going?'

'Duty calls,' he said. 'I've outstayed my leave already.'

'Oh. Yes. Of course.' She was disappointed. Was that good? He didn't know anymore. And his preferences were at war with his professional responsibility. For his peace of mind, she should be far away. But for *her* good . . .

'Evelyn, I know you were planning to go to France . . .'

'That's where I was posted.'

'Yes.' He sat on the chair by her bed and looked down at her hand, lying so gracefully on the sheet. 'As your doctor, I don't think you should go. At least, not for some time.'

'But –'

'It's August now. By the time you're ready to travel, you'll be heading into a European winter. The conditions are fierce in the field hospitals. Evelyn, you only just survived this. You know pneumonia leaves the lungs weak. If you got another dose, I think you wouldn't come through it.'

His voice shook a little, and he could see that made more impression on her than his words.

'I'm all right,' she said. 'I'll be fine.'

'Eventually. But the dry desert air will give you a chance to really recover.'

She touched his hand gently.

'And we can work together again?'

He made his hand lie still.

'That depends on the powers that be,' he said, trying for a note of jocularity. He stood up. 'I have to go.'

'Thank you,' she said. 'I think you probably saved my life.'

'Nonsense. The nursing care here is very good.'

She seemed puzzled by his reserve. 'Well,' she said slowly, 'goodbye.' And put her face up to be kissed.

He bent to her, torn between wanting one more touch of her lips and wanting to cut the cord cleanly, to get away from the torment of being with her now he knew what she really thought of him. He closed his eyes and kissed her cheek, allowing himself just a moment of pause, there, their skin touching. Then he stood up.

'Take care of yourself,' he said, like a doctor, and went out.

He couldn't bear to be near people until he'd recovered his equanimity, so he walked down to the beach and along to the place he used to swim when he'd first come to Alexandria.

Why not swim? Maybe it would calm him down.

What a strange sea the Mediterranean was. Salty and easy to float in, but waves only happened in a storm – or at least, what *he'd* call waves. Tewfik, way back then, had cautioned him against swimming. 'Dangerous,' he'd said, 'very dangerous,' but to someone who'd surf-shot at Bondi Beach, the calmer waters of the Mediterranean didn't hold any fears.

He hobbled out into the water damning how stiff his leg was, braced himself for that moment when the cool water hit his genitals, and then dived beneath the wavelets. He swam vigorously up and down the beach for a while, and then floated, drifting aimlessly as he watched the gold- and rose-tinted clouds gather on the horizon. He'd hoped the sea would wash away the despair building in him, but it hadn't. The pain of losing Evelyn – of having lost her even before he had walked away – bit deep and hard.

Time to go back. He should get to Cairo before dark.

He flicked himself upright. Good God! He was a long way from shore! Unknowingly, he must have floated into a rip and been carried out.

It wasn't the first time – Bondi was a tricky beach at times, and rips were common. All he had to do was swim sideways to get out of the current, and then head back to shore. He could do it, although it would take a little effort.

For a moment, he stayed, treading water, being carried further out, feeling a black mood descend on him. What if he just let the sea take him? How calm it would be, how easy, to let go of this body which caused him so much pain. They said drowning was pleasant, in the end.

What did he have to go back to? Evelyn was gone from his life, and so was any hope of a future relationship with any woman. Apart from his parents, there was no one who cared whether he lived or died. No one who might mourn. That was a sad state of affairs for a man of thirty. Wouldn't it just be easier to go out with the tide?

'Nonsense!' he told himself. 'Stop thinking about yourself and think about the people you can help!' He forced himself to swim out of the rip and set off with a steady stroke. He had real work to do, and his patients deserved the very best from him.

He struck out for the shore.

In the train back to Cairo, he remembered a Michael Drayton poem he'd memorised when he was a teenager, sitting on the floor of the lending library while his father took bets for the Friday night trots.

> *Since there's no help, come let us kiss and part.*
> *Nay, I have done, you get no more of me;*
> *And I am glad, yea glad with all my heart*
> *That thus so cleanly I myself can free.*

He'd have to work at the being glad part.

•

After William walked out, without a backwards glance, Evelyn sat staring at the doorway for some time.

How cold he'd been. Except for when he was asking her not to go to France. He'd been sincerely concerned then. But everything else. How could he be so offhand? That wasn't like him at all. He'd hardly looked at her. Avoided touching her. Kissing her.

He had called her Evelyn.

Tears flowed up in her eyes and dropped down. She was so *weak*. But it felt as though her heart were breaking.

She took in a deep shuddering breath and immediately began to cough, over and over again. After it was done, she lay back on the pillows and closed her eyes. Bugger William. When she had more energy she might be angry with him. She struggled against falling asleep, but she struggled in vain.

Although she knew he'd gone back to duty, she expected to hear from him, or see him again. A telephone call, even. A postcard or letter, surely.

She wrote to him, thanking him for his care of her. She was careful to keep it formal, but she signed it 'Linnet'. He would answer, she was sure.

But there was no reply.

Gradually, she realised that he wasn't going to contact her.

She had trouble believing it. In her mind were jumbled memories of being sick and Will being there, all the time, caring for her, holding her while she coughed, stroking her hair. She was sure she remembered him saying Linnet, not Evelyn. She remembered his worried face, his gentle touch. It had felt like love.

What had happened?

Was it possible that, because he had acted as her doctor, he had decided it was unethical for them to have any other relationship?

It was possible, but it seemed so *unlikely*. It wasn't as though he was her general practitioner, with a long history of treatment behind her. This was a singular occasion, a crisis. Surely now, when she was recovered, they could leave it behind them without crossing any ethical lines?

Perhaps he was waiting until she had been discharged.

She clung to that; otherwise the mixture of annoyance and hurt she felt towards him would overwhelm her. Once she was back at work – perhaps with him – they could . . .

What?

Sleep with each other?

Even that one time of being in his room, they'd been found out.

And if they could manage the secrecy, the chances of her becoming pregnant were too great.

Perhaps William had already had this conversation with himself, and come to the conclusion that the risks were too great. That if they weren't in a position to say, 'But we're getting married!' if they were discovered, then social ruin for her and possibly for him was inevitable.

If she wanted to be a doctor, she had to have a spotless reputation. And so did he.

Restless, she got herself out of bed and wrapped in a lovely cotton robe Kitty had lent her. Her long window could be walked through; she went onto the verandah and gazed out at the sharp blue sky and palms which lay beyond the beautifully maintained European gardens around the house.

If that was the problem, why hadn't he talked to her about it?

Tears welled up again. She cried so easily now. The nurse in her knew that was as much part of convalescence as the coughing, but it *felt* real. It felt like her heart was being picked apart into little pieces, flake by flake, every time she thought about him.

There were rattan chairs on the verandah, heavily cushioned. She dropped into one and laid her head back against the wall. It was so hot that each gravel path had a mirage above it, shimmering in the sun.

He was right. They could only be friends. Colleagues. Nothing more. She turned her head so that the tears flowed sideways, off her face. She had no energy for anything else.

'Sister Northey! What are you doing out here?' Margherita de Walden rushed to her and felt her brow.

'I'm not wandering in delirium, I assure you,' Evelyn said, sitting up. How embarrassing, to be caught in such flagrant emotion.

Margherita smiled and sat down. 'There, there, my dear. No need to be coy about it. You're missing your young man.' There was an implicit offer in her tone; to explain, to gossip, to unburden herself.

'He's not *my* young man.'

Raising an eyebrow, Margherita settled back into the cushions on her chair like a sparrow into a nest.

'He *said* you had an understanding.'

An understanding. In a way, they did. They understood that marriage was not going to happen between them.

'Yes,' Evelyn said. 'I suppose we do.'

'And you miss him, naturally.'

She closed her eyes, pressing on them with her finger and thumb, but she couldn't stop the tears coming.

'Yes I do!' she said. Margherita pulled a man's handkerchief out of a pocket and gave it to her. Evelyn grabbed it thankfully. She just couldn't seem to stop crying. Every time she thought of William a piercing pain went through her, as though he were stabbing her from afar.

'Don't worry, my dear. In a week or two you'll be out of here and can go back to work, side by side.'

Evelyn nodded, unable to speak. Margherita patted her on the shoulder and rose to leave.

'Take your time. Cry it out. Get it out of your system.'

She walked away quietly. But Evelyn's tears, strangely enough, stopped almost immediately, because the image of the two of them working together caught at her breath.

No. She couldn't work with him. Not after – Not if they weren't – Everything within her revolted at the idea. She felt actually nauseated.

No.

She'd have to find another posting and make sure it wasn't the New Zealand General Hospital.

Perhaps she could get a job in Alexandria, far away from Cairo. And take up her studies again. Latin and anatomy. For the first time, that felt like a dreary prospect.

CHAPTER 26

'Hannah! You've come all this way!'

Evelyn embraced her friend with gratitude and led her to the cool shade of the verandah. The Egyptian servant, Tewfik, took them in with one intelligent glance and went off. She knew he would be back with cool drinks and pastries. He had been assiduous in looking after her.

'Well, it's not that far, and I had a day off.'

They hadn't seen each other since the day she'd left on the *Nestor*. Evelyn had sought her out and they'd had a quiet cry together then; but they'd written more than once.

Hannah was in her walking uniform, complete with jacket and hat instead of a veil. She looked very smart, but thinner than she had been, and very rosy. She shed the jacket and hat as quickly as she could.

'Oh, it's this heat! I can't eat while I'm hot. But you, you're skin and bones!'

It was so good to see her, Evelyn blinked back tears. Easy crying meant she wasn't fully recovered, but she'd got to the point where she could stop herself, at least.

'I'm getting much better,' she protested. Tewfik came back with a tray piled high and began to place the plates and glasses on the low table before them. 'See? Tewfik is feeding me up!'

Tewfik smiled at them silently and stood back, tray in hand, waiting in case they needed anything else. No matter how long she was in Egypt, Evelyn never quite got used to that. Margherita and Kitty, on the other hand, took it as a matter of course. They were probably used to footmen and maids trailing around after them in England. All a matter of what you were brought up to.

She helped Hannah to honey pastries and lemonade, and sat back contentedly. It was so good to see her.

'I'm at the 14th General now,' Hannah said. 'Mostly Camel Corps and Light Horse patients.'

'A-hah! So you're on the spot in case Linus is wounded again.'

Hannah blushed bright red. She pulled a chain out from under her blouse; it had a ring on it.

'We're engaged.'

'Oh, Hannah, that's wonderful!' More hugs and a few tears ensued.

After a big sigh, Hannah sat back and drank some more lemonade. 'He's in the Sinai, I think. Perhaps Palestine. It's terrible country.'

'Oh, you know Linus. He's a jammy sort. He'll probably stumble over a hidden oasis and be living like a sheik!'

Hannah laughed, but there was still a worried crease between her dark eyes. 'When you've seen what we've seen, you can't be too hopeful. Too sure about the future.' She fiddled with her glass, not looking at Hannah. 'Have you seen Dr Brent?'

Evelyn stilled. Of course, Hannah would ask that, but in such a manner . . .

'Is something wrong with him? Is he ill?'

'Oh, no, no!' Hannah put her glass down and raised her hand as though taking an oath. It was a schoolgirl trick, and made her look very young. 'I swear! I just . . .' She blushed, the colour rising slowly.

'What's the matter, then?' Hannah must know that William had thrown her over. Which wasn't exactly what had happened, but it might look like that to those who didn't know differently. She had never felt more embarrassed in her life. And yet, this time, she herself didn't flush, as though the embarrassment were bone deep instead of on the skin.

'I just . . .' Hannah twisted her head aside, and glanced at Tewfik meaningfully.

'Tewfik, we're fine here, thank you,' Evelyn said. He nodded with great understanding, and left. They waited until the soft sound of his footfalls had disappeared.

'Well?' Evelyn said softly.

'Well . . . it was just, I thought, before you left for Australia . . . you didn't come back to our room all night . . .' Hannah hung her head, completely unable to look Evelyn in the eye. 'I wondered if you and Doctor Brent . . . I'm sorry if I'm wrong, but I just thought . . .'

A mixture of shame and longing swept over her. That night; it had been a mad thing to do, but she'd wanted him so much . . . And suddenly she understood what Hannah was trying to say.

'You're thinking about sleeping with Linus . . .'

Hannah flicked a quick glance at her, and must have found no judgement in her face.

'I just keep thinking, what if he died? What if he died and we'd never . . . He gets leave, sometimes. Not often. We could . . . but it's wrong, isn't it? Immoral.'

Evelyn coughed a little; she was still overtaken by odd bouts of it when she tried to catch her breath. Finally, she stopped, and sighed.

'I'm not the right person to ask,' she said. 'I've never understood why it's wrong, if two people care for each other and make sure there are no children to be hurt by it. It hurts no one else.'

'Ohhhhh . . .' Hannah sat back with a satisfied expression on her face. 'That's what –'

'What Linus has been saying?' She was momentarily annoyed with Linus – he really shouldn't have been putting pressure on Hannah that way.

'Oh, no! Linus treats me like I'm . . . porcelain or something. He's never even *hinted*. No, it's just that you've said what I've been trying to work out myself. It seems to me that there are only two reasons *not* to go to him – reputation and pregnancy.'

She'd forgotten this about Hannah – the rugged commonsense which underlay the sweetness and the femininity.

'Yes,' Evelyn said. 'But you have to remember that French letters break sometimes. You're taking a risk. You're always taking a risk, every time.'

Hannah stared right into her eyes.

'You did.'

Images of that night rose before her eyes, swept through her like fire.

'No,' she said. 'William wouldn't . . . expose me to the risk.' She smiled, with difficulty. 'But I was planning to, when I saw him again.' Hesitating, she added, 'When we had . . . prophylactics.'

'French letters . . .' Hannah said thoughtfully.

Evelyn nodded. Suddenly hungry, she bit into a small honey cake and gulped it down.

'I see . . .' Hannah nodded. 'I have to pick my moment, then. It wouldn't *really* matter if I fell. We want children as soon as we can.'

Evelyn stared down at her hands, trying to put away the pang the thought of never having children always gave her. Hannah, bless her, read her mood and sat up straighter, moving on to another topic.

'But you've seen William?'

'He saved my life. He stayed here and nursed me.' She looked up into Hannah's eyes. 'But I haven't heard from him since. I think – I think he's cast me off.'

Cast me off! Could she have chosen worse words? They conjured up melodramas of women with illegitimate babies in the snow.

'I mean,' she added hastily, 'I think he believes it's better for both of us if we're not together. Risking reputation *or* pregnancy.'

She was trying to sound so reasonable, but her eyes were hot with tears.

'Oh, Lynnie!'

'He's right, I suppose. But it's hard.'

Hannah wrapped her arms around her and rocked her gently while she cried into her shoulder.

'If you'd just give up this silly idea about not getting married –'

'He doesn't want to either,' Evelyn objected, pulling back and blowing her nose. 'It's not just me!'

They left it at that, and moved on to the 'Have you seen so-and-so?' and 'What's happened to whosit?' of old friends catching up.

Hannah had heard from Alice Ross-King, busy in France, and Evelyn told her about Connie Keys, who was at the Kitchener Hospital in Brighton, and Annie Sanderson, still in Sydney. Other girls, other postings – between them they could account for most of their colleagues at Heliopolis.

When Hannah rose to go, Evelyn felt a hundred times better than she had that morning.

'I have to catch my train,' Hannah said. Evelyn stood up and hugged her.

'*Thank* you for coming.'

'Nonsense! I'll get away again in a couple of weeks, but hopefully you'll be out of here by then. My matron says, if you want a berth in Cairo for a while, she's short-handed and would welcome you with open arms.'

So her future was settled as easily as that. The 14th Australian General Hospital it was.

She should have been pleased. She had her work, and a relationship with William leading to marriage and family had always been out of her reach. But that night she dreamed of William walking away from her down a long, dusty Australian road, and woke feeling tired and bereft. She cried into her pillow for a few moments, but then Tewfik brought her breakfast in, and she had to pull herself together.

Time to face her future and be strong, no matter how weak she felt right now.

CHAPTER 27

SEPTEMBER 1916

The new matron, Rose Creal, addressed her troops. That was what it felt like to Evelyn. They were arrayed in the hall of the 14th Australian General Hospital, Abbassia, in front of the main staircase. Matron Creal stood a few steps up.

She was not, at first, an imposing sight. A middling-tall woman, with wire-framed glasses and mid-brown hair smoothed back under her veil, she was alight with enthusiasm and purpose. And discipline.

The speech she gave was stock-standard: Glad to be here, we all have a job to do, these boys depend on us. But the effect was anything but standard. All around nurses and orderlies were straightening up, raising their heads, looking proud. Evelyn was no exception. There was something about this ordinary-looking woman which was simply inspiring.

Out the front door, in the hard Egyptian sun, a train of camels went past with Australian soldiers upon them.

Many of their patients were Camel Corps men, and their squad-mates liked to walk the camels past and wave to the men on the balconies on their way to the nearby training ground.

Matron Creal looked out at the camels and smiled. 'Well!' she said. 'We're certainly in for some surprises! That will be all.'

As the nurses dispersed back to duty, Matron Creal called Evelyn over.

'Sister Northey. You're one of the more experienced women we have here, and I'd like you to take over as Senior Sister on the fever ward.'

'Oh. Thank you, Matron.' It was a shock to think of herself as 'experienced', but anyone who'd nursed through the Gallipoli campaign had a claim to that description.

'We'll have regular chats to make sure you're holding up.' Which Evelyn interpreted as meaning, 'I'll be keeping an eye on you.' But that was all right. Supervision from someone competent was never a bad thing, and as Matron Creal had been the matron of the Sydney Hospital, competence could be assumed.

'I'll appreciate that, Matron.'

Matron Creal looked her up and down. 'You seem like an intelligent girl, Northey. Don't let me down.'

'No, Matron.'

Matron walked off with a swift, tireless gait, a smooth silent rushing over the floor. She should practise walking like that. It was how matrons walked.

But, she reminded herself, she didn't want to be a matron. She wanted to be a doctor.

The fever ward was quiet this early in the day, the men exhausted by their overnight tossing and turning. She checked the charts for each of them, getting to know her charges.

One thing she had learned, through her 'experience', was that lives were as often saved by nurses as by doctors. Particularly here, in the fever ward, where constant, unswerving observation and immediate intervention if temperatures rose were often the only things that kept men alive.

No doctors around for that. She put the image of William bathing her in ice water aside. Irrelevant. She hadn't heard from him, even once, since she'd arrived in Cairo two weeks ago. They were not to be even friends, apparently. Thinking about him was a sharp, nasty twist of the knife in her heart, so she was learning not to think of him.

The afternoon shadows began to lengthen, and she called the other two nurses and the orderlies. As the evening came on, so did the fevers, always seeming to rise at night. Fortunately, although this hospital had only very primitive facilities, the Army had bought a *lot* of ice boxes, and kept them filled. Packing the beds with ice in oilcloth had proved very effective in bringing down the fevers at 1AGH, and so it was here.

As Senior Sister, it was her job to be there at shift changes, to split her shift so she could cover part of both. So at her normal knock-off time, she kept going, bringing the new shift up to date.

'Watch Mitchell, Beattie,' she told the youngest nurse they had there, barely twenty and the ink on her accreditation still wet. 'He spikes, and you have to get the ice on him straightaway.'

'Yes, Sister Northey,' the girl said with wide eyes. God help her, she'd become an authority figure! How ridiculous.

'And make sure they keep drinking.'

'Yes, Sister!'

The girl scurried off, buoyed up by the importance of her task. She was right, Evelyn thought. These men deserved the best of their care. Perhaps she would be stationed here for the rest of the war. She could deal with that. Enough time to study her Latin and anatomy, and the knowledge that she was helping, still, to save lives.

And if she never saw William again, ever in her life?

She pushed down the hard ache that brought to her chest and tried to look on the bright side. At least she wouldn't die without ever having loved someone.

JUNE 1917

For the tenth time that morning, Evelyn did up the tie of a patient. On a normal day she would do twenty or thirty. A couple of patients had wounds to their hands, and needed help with everything, but many were country men who had hardly ever worn a tie in their lives. Some of them had trouble getting the bright red strip of cloth in order.

She really wished whoever had designed the convalescent uniform had left off the tie. Blue trousers, white shirt? Fine. But why did they need a tie, and a *red* tie at that?

'It's to make sure the military and local police don't make a mistake and arrest a civilian,' Matron Creal had told her when she first arrived – God, more than nine months ago now! 'If the boys slip out and try to visit a brothel or a restaurant, the police can identify them easily and round them up.'

'Does that happen often?' Evelyn had asked, amused.

'Oh, my dear, all the time!' Matron had been half-amused, half-disapproving. 'No wonder, I suppose, all these young men . . . But really, they could at least wait until they've been released from hospital back to camp!'

They flirted, too, these convalescents. Half of them treated her like a sister, which was sweet, and the other half tried to woo her. Her life consisted of changing dressings, toting bedpans, sponging fever victims, and staving off advances.

She was so bored. Months and months of the same thing. Hannah didn't mind it so much.

'It's a holiday, really, after the Dardanelles campaign. And isn't it better to be among men who are getting better than men who are dying?'

Hannah had spent a long time on the death ward at 1AGH, Evelyn remembered. Much of the time she'd been working in the operating theatre, Hannah had been holding the hands of the suffering and dying.

Evelyn smiled at her and loaded her outstretched arms with a bundle of dirty sheets, then picked up the other linen she'd stripped off the newly vacant beds. It *was* good to know that the bed was empty because the man in it had been sent to camp, rather than the graveyard.

'Yes,' she said. 'Much better.' But repetitious.

She was on night watch this week, which was both better and worse.

Night watch in a convalescent ward was calmer than in a surgical ward, although they still had fever cases. No screams, no moans of pain. Nightmares, though, they were frequent. If one went on for longer than a few heartbeats she intervened, waking the man with a yardstick she had found at the back of a cupboard. She'd learned from experience not to lay hands on a soldier asleep. You were likely to be throttled if you were in reach.

Night duty was mostly about bringing the paperwork up to date. As Senior Sister, she had to sign off on a ridiculous number of forms. Everything from linen requests to disciplinary recommendations.

As she worked in the pool of light from the desk lamp, she wondered if this was a life she could live. Ever since her illness, her old surety about her future had withered away. Was she cut out to be a doctor? Was it worth the hard slog of so many years study, when she was already saving lives as a nurse?

At least doctors didn't carry bedpans, or wash them out either.

The best times were in the operating theatre. A single task, a pure concentration, a thing which was done and over when it was finished. That was the problem with nursing; the jobs were never-ending.

She was almost twenty-seven now. Three more years until she could get her inheritance.

Fees for Edinburgh, she had discovered, were £35 a year, plus examination costs, books, materials and laboratory charges. About £50 in total. Then she would need at least another £50 for lodgings and board. It was about that in the hall of residence for women, Dr Bennett had told her. Goodness, that seemed a long time ago. And then incidentals, clothes and ladies' necessities.

She had saved more than £130 pounds over the past two years – almost half of her pay.

Another £20 – £150 – might get her through a single year. So she could start in 1919, perhaps, or even, if she kept saving at this rate, in 1918. Unless the war wasn't over by then. It seemed to stretch on without a break. The news from France was bad and seemed to have stayed at the same level of bad for months. How long could they go on for? Either the Allies or Germany?

Evelyn contemplated a dreary future where war became normal and peace a strange, far-off memory.

A cry rang out. She started to her feet. Michaelson was tossing and turning, gargling noises coming from deep in his chest. Damn. He hadn't had one of those nightmares in a week.

She grabbed the yardstick and ran to the end of the bed, out of arm's reach, and poked him a few times. He came awake, fully awake, alert and ready to fight.

She said, 'It's all right, lad. Just a dream. Just a dream.' It took a moment or two for him to realise where he was and settle down with a sheepish, 'Sorry, Sister.' It was notable that none of the men commented, or even seemed to have their sleep disturbed. A gentlemanly tact – or the fear that next time, it might be them screaming and thrashing.

The adrenaline had her heart pumping furiously. Ridiculous. She should be used to this sort of thing by now. But the dark made it worse.

She forced herself to walk. Up one side of the ward, checking each sleeping body for signs of fever. Jones had pushed his covers off. She put her hand against his forehead. No change – still slightly elevated, but not dangerously. She left the blanket off, but covered him back up with the sheet.

Paterson was sweating, but he'd had his quinine and was packed in with ice in oilcloth bags. Ice. She would get the orderlies to bring in more ice.

And then more paperwork.

An hour and several discharge files later, she yawned uncontrollably, covering her mouth in embarrassment as Mickey the orderly came up.

'Sorry.'

'Handover's in an hour,' he said. 'I thought you might like a cuppa.'

'You're an angel.' She took the enamel mug he handed her and sipped gratefully. Hot, milky and sweet. Perfect.

'Any problems?'

'Paterson's not looking good.' Mickey's expression was grave. 'We packed him in with more ice, and it worked for a while, but . . .'

Evelyn felt her mouth tighten involuntarily. Paterson had been fighting malaria for six days now. She went to examine him. Yes, he was failing – his skin and eyes had acquired that jaundiced look, and he had lost a lot of weight.

'We'd better give him an intramuscular injection,' she said. 'He's been vomiting a lot so he may not have got the full benefit of the quinine draughts.'

Mickey was surprised. 'Don't we need a doctor for that?'

'No, no, I can do it,' she said, heading for the medicine cupboard in the scullery.

'I mean, don't we need a doctor to tell us it's all right?'

She stopped, wondering if he was right.

'All of the doctors are off-site or sleeping,' she said slowly. 'I know this is the right treatment.' Mickey was still looking very unsure. 'My father is a doctor,' she said. 'He's taught me a lot.'

That made him relax a little, but he was still frowning. 'I'd feel better if Matron said it was all right.'

'Do you know where she is? You go and ask her, and I'll prepare the treatment.'

'Righto.'

He sped off and Evelyn went on to make up the quinine and find the sterile needle pack. She was sure this was the right treatment. If she were a doctor, no one would be questioning her decisions.

She prepared what she needed. Gloves first. A tray, with iodine and lint and the syringe. Fortunately, sterile quinine solution was always kept on hand. She put a tablespoon into a 1 in 20 carbolic solution and let it rest there while she wiped the mouth of the quinine bottle with carbolic. The spoon was sterile now. She took it out and shook the excess liquid off, then laid it on the tray and poured the quinine into it. Now, the syringe. She put the tip of the syringe into the quinine and drew up 15 grains. A big dose, but that's what was recommended. She wiped the tip of the needle with carbolic, and placed it on some sterile lint. All ready.

Mickey still hadn't returned. She took the tray to Paterson and placed it on his bedside table. He'd gone downhill even in the time it had taken her to prepare the dose.

For a moment she stood there, looking out at the verandah surrounding the ward. The balconies were empty at this time of night, lit by gas mantles and whispering with a current of air. The contrast was great: out there, space and air and light, as this lovely old building used to be. Peace. In here, the heat and smell of male bodies fighting sickness, moans and snores and restless sighing. And Death, waiting in the wings.

She couldn't wait any longer. Pulling back the covers, she rolled Paterson over onto his side and gave him half the injection in one buttock, then went to the other side of the bed, rolled him to the opposite side, and did the same.

There. And if she'd broken protocol, too bad. He'd be dead by morning if they didn't do something.

Matron arrived in a quiet bustle a minute later, Mickey at her heels.

'You've *given* the injection, Sister?' she said, keeping her voice low.

'He was fading fast, Matron. I had no choice.'

In the shadowy darkness, it was hard to see Matron's eyes, but her body was stiff with disapproval.

'And who advised you on the proper dosage and administration?'

'My father,' Evelyn said. No good saying, 'I read about it in a medical journal' although that was true. It was equally true that she and her father had discussed the article. Bring in the big guns, she thought. Male authority. 'He's a doctor, and I was his practice nurse. For six years.'

Matron started back a little. Had her voice been too strong? Too insolent? But it seemed to reassure Matron.

'Very well then. I understand that you acted out of a sense of responsibility to the patient, but Sister, you are not a doctor and you may not act as though you are. A change in medication like this *must* be approved by a medical officer.' She paused. 'How long since you've had leave?'

'I'm not sure . . .' Evelyn stuttered. 'I came from Alexandria about nine months ago?'

'Hmm. Well, we'll assume this was a temporary lapse in good judgement due to fatigue. After this shift, take eight hours for sleep.'

So she wouldn't be formally disciplined for it. She should have felt relief, but found a stubborn anger in its place. She had *known* what she was doing.

Next to them, Paterson opened his eyes, dazed. That was the thing about intramuscular injections. They worked fast. Evelyn smiled down at him.

'There's water on the floor from all this ice,' Matron said. 'Clean it up. You, Sister Northey. I think you should do it before you go off duty.'

That was a breach of protocol, as the orderlies and cleaners were responsible for the floors. She was being punished, but mildly.

'Yes, Matron,' she murmured, dutifully obedient. Matron nodded sharply and walked off.

'Water,' Paterson mumbled. Smiling, Evelyn held a sipping cup to his mouth.

'You'll be all right now,' she said.

Somehow, in her automatic response to this crisis, in her annoyance at being reprimanded, she had made up her mind. She would be a doctor. Despite her father, despite the war, despite the way she'd been relegated to doing up men's ties for half the day, she could still find in herself the spark of desire to be *more*, to be useful. To heal.

And now she came to that desire with a strong appreciation of how much of that healing was accomplished by nurses. She would be a better doctor because of it.

CHAPTER 28

JULY 1917

In some lights, Hannah's beauty was more easily seen. As now, in the nurses' sitting room at breakfast time, with the early summer sun shining on her unveiled hair and picking out her delicate cheekbones and long lashes. Goodness, she was lovely! Evelyn felt a quiet pang and immediately reproached herself. What did it matter that she was red-headed and only a little pretty instead of beautiful? She wasn't planning on attracting anyone, anyway!

As though that thought had called him up, William stood in the doorway, looking desperate. Hair dishevelled, tie loose, hat crushed in his hands.

She and Hannah came to their feet immediately, staring at him.

'What is it?' Evelyn asked.

'Harry has been wounded,' he said, eyes on her face. 'At Gaza. I heard from one of the wounded they just brought in.

But not badly. Just a graze. I wanted to tell you before you read it in the lists.'

The room tilted and she put out a hand to the nearest chair. William jumped to her side, but she drew in a breath and waved him back.

'You're sure it was just a graze?'

'It was a friend of his – MacIntosh? – who saw it.'

MacIntosh. Yes, Johnny MacIntosh. Harry had mentioned him in his infrequent letters. He was Harry's subaltern. He would know.

She could feel blood coming back to her face.

'Is MacIntosh all right?'

'Broken arm. He was thrown at a redoubt.'

'Good. Good.'

She could say nothing but nonsense, now that the first shock was gone and she was face to face with him. Almost a year since they had been face to face. It seemed like only moments. Behind his back, Hannah was making shooing motions for her to go outside with him. That was a good idea. Better than having this conversation in front of all the interested eyes of the other nurses.

She led the way and they went out of the ward onto a verandah, and down the steps to the courtyard garden.

'I doubt Harry will even be sent back to Cairo,' he said. 'They'll probably just keep him in camp. But his name will be on the lists.'

Yes. She imagined reading his name there and knowing nothing else. The terror and the pain.

'It was kind of you to come and reassure me.'

'How are you?' William asked as they sat on a bench with a clear view of the door to the sitting room.

The words blurted out before she'd had a chance to think.

'What do you care? If you cared, you'd have asked before this. Sent a card, a letter . . .' She was horrified to realise that she had started to cry. No. Absolutely not. She brushed the tears away and sat up defiantly straight.

'It was better to make a clean break, I thought.'

She turned uncomprehending eyes to him. '*Why*?'

He stared at his hands, at the crushed hat.

'In your fever . . . you talked . . .'

He glanced quickly at her, perhaps to see if she had any memory of it. She had no idea what he was talking about.

'You said . . . what you said made it clear to me that you . . . found me, my leg . . . the words you used were "horrible" and "awful" . . . so I thought I was better not to, to . . . importune you again. Better for you if you never had to see me again.'

That was *ridiculous*. He had turned his back on her because of something she had said while she was *delirious*? He had condemned her to months of wondering, of missing him, of thinking she had done something wrong, that he had abandoned her, without even *speaking* to her? She could feel her temper rising, that terrible red-headed temper, and this time she let it loose.

'How does it feel to be God, then?'

He jerked upright and stared at her. 'Wha—'

'Well, you clearly think you can decide what to do with my life without asking me, don't you? Maybe all that time in the operating theatre has got you addicted to playing God with people's lives.'

'I thought – I just wanted –'

'You wanted to cause yourself the least amount of pain, so you chopped and changed my life without my consent.

Even if I *had* felt like that you should still have talked to me. Found out what *I* wanted.' Typical domineering male. And she had thought he might be different! She rose to her feet and stared down at him. He stood up, and she withered him with a glance. '*This* is why I'll never marry. No man can resist controlling the lives of the women he's involved with. Making decisions for them. Deciding what to do with their lives *without even asking*!'

She dragged her hand across her eyes where hot tears were forming.

'You want to know what I think of your leg – what I thought of it? I was *glad* about it! Because it meant you wouldn't be sent to the front and killed. I was so *glad* you were unfit for duty –'

'I didn't want to cause you disgust,' he said quietly. The shame in his eyes made her anger flare higher. He should think better of himself.

'No. Be honest. You didn't want to risk being *faced* with my disgust. That was more important to you than the possibility of us –'

He had become angry now, and cut in.

'Of us *what*? You don't want to marry me, I can't marry you, so what possibility? Better to call it off early, before either of us got hurt!'

'Without discussing it with me?'

He stood in silence. His mouth opened, but he said nothing.

'Exactly,' she said, turning on her heel. She walked up the stairs and away from him with even footsteps, as though marching, and went in to Hannah without a backward glance.

●

Hannah had, apparently, gone on duty, taking temperatures. Evelyn joined her, despite having done night duty, glad that her position as Senior Sister allowed her to inspect any shift she chose.

'He's sure Harry will be all right,' she reported.

Her veil neatly in place, her face calm, she strove to look as she always did. But there was a slight tremble in her hands when she gave the thermometer to a patient. Thoughts of William and thoughts of Harry competed with each other, neither good.

Hannah quietly did whatever had to be done. Organised orderlies to take two men to the bathroom, encouraged a third to try walking with crutches for the first time so he could take himself, changed several dressings when the orderly arrived with the dressing cart. Evelyn got back to work. It was good to keep busy, to not think. She took temperatures, smiled at jokes, wrote a letter for an ashamed young digger who had never learned to read. Beattie was on duty as well, and Evelyn kept her busy changing linen and helping those who could dress while Hannah got on with the paperwork for discharge for those men likely to be set free today.

The doctor came, and Hannah came out to do rounds.

'I'm all right,' she said to Evelyn quietly. 'Take a break.'

Better not to make a fuss. Evelyn went up to their room, suddenly aware of her weariness, and sat unseeing on the bed. Her fear for Harry was muted; she might be angry with William, but she trusted his assessment. Harry would be all right.

Her anger died away, but not her resentment. He had acted so high-handedly, without a single word of explanation. No matter how ashamed he was of his physical deformities – and he was, she had seen it in his eyes – he should have respected her enough to discuss it.

Coward.

Letting her stew over everything – ignoring her letter, because she was sure now that he'd received it – letting her break her heart over him . . .

No more of that! And best to find out now what had really happened. So she could close that book once and for all, and put it away to gather dust on a shelf. She would never get involved with a man ever again.

Sobs burst from her, unstoppable, her heart seeming to twist inside her as though wringing the tears out. She threw herself on the bed and cried. It wasn't *fair*! Why couldn't he have been the man she'd thought him?

The man she'd fallen in love with.

If love hurt like this, better never to feel it again.

CHAPTER 29

Over the next few weeks, William grabbed at anything which might be a distraction from thoughts of Evelyn. He'd berated himself non-stop ever since their meeting, images of her rotating in his head: hurt, betrayed, scornful, dismissive. It was worse because he knew he deserved her contempt.

Everything she'd said had been true.

It chafed him unbearably that she now put him in the same category as her father, but he couldn't deny the truth. He had decided her life for her as though he'd had a right to. It made him think back over all their previous encounters. He had *loved* her independence and strength. It drew him like a moth to flame. But when push came to shove, and his own feelings were on the line, he'd cut her off rather than risk her disgust.

He'd been a coward, and caused her pain. Unforgivable. Worse – he'd done it without even considering her side of things.

He brooded over his own shortcomings like a hen with a single egg. And he began to change his interactions with the

New Zealand nurses. To ask their opinions more. To respect their competence. He'd *always* respected them – but he hadn't always shown it. He might never speak to Evelyn again, but he could learn from his mistakes. He would never treat a woman like that again.

A letter from home was a wonderful distraction.

Dear Will,

I worry that you aren't leaving yourself enough money in that foreign place. It's so good of you to help us, and your father and I are grateful, but we don't need nearly as much as you send. If you needed to cut back, we'd be quite all right.

Hah. He knew what that meant – 'we'd be fine, we'll just cut out everything that makes life worth living'. Mince every second day and potatoes with bacon on the other days. No new clothes, no new books for the library, no nights out at the trots. No, thank you. Not for his parents. It wouldn't hurt him to get his shoes resoled instead of buying a new pair. These Egyptian cobblers were miracle workers.

Your letters have been few and far between, so I know you must have been busy.

Ouch! He hadn't written as often; hard to write cheerful notes when he'd been feeling so very down.

Neville Shoemaker is home again; half his left foot is gone, but he says he's one of the lucky ones, and I suppose he is, when you think of how many have died. I never thought I'd be glad of that polio, but when I think now that without it you'd be in the thick of the fighting, I can't help but give thanks.

He winced at that, but he couldn't blame her. She went on with gossip about the boys he'd been to school with: in France, in Palestine, in the Navy. They seemed so far distant. Unreal.

Outside, it was sunset, and the calls from the minarets floated out over the city. The wind was up, and the long notes were blown quickly away, along with scudding clouds. Tomorrow there was supposed to be a trip to the Barrage Gardens, up the Nile, for those patients who could be taken out in cars. A morale booster. He would have a quiet day. For a moment he thought about going to the 14th General. Not to talk to her; just to catch a glimpse of her moving through the wards. Sickly sentimentalism. What good would that do him? She was lost to him, and it was his own fault.

Your father is putting in a crop of late peas and brussel sprouts. He says that now you're not here, he might as well. He'll have to cook them in a billy in the backyard, because he's not boiling them in my kitchen!

William grinned. He hated brussel sprouts. His mother tolerated them, but disliked the smell of them cooking, so it had always been two to one against his father, who loved them. He imagined his father, crouched over his billy, waiting for his beloved sprouts – oh! It was ridiculous to cry about that. He was a grown man, not a child!

It occurred to him that there was nothing stopping him getting on the next boat and going home. The thought pierced him, sweet and sharp. *Home.* They would need doctors at home even more, with so many in the Army. He would still be doing good. He could sail far away from Evelyn, and perhaps then he would be able to forget her.

But yesterday, he had saved a man's arm from being amputated. The man wouldn't have full use of it, but he would have some, and be able to live a normal life, without being stared at wherever he went, without being a cripple.

He swiped the tears away and put the letter in his bedside drawer to finish later.

Back to work.

•

'Brent!' Major Bagly called him as he went down the stairs towards the fever ward. William went over and Bagly shepherded him into the office.

'I've had a request from the 14th General,' Bagly said, waving him to a chair. 'It's unusual.'

'Yes?' His heart beat faster. If there was something wrong at the 14th . . .

'They don't have a surgeon on staff. Just a physician. It's convalescent, you know. Mostly post-op and fever patients who've passed the crisis. Malaria, ulcers, dysentery, that kind of thing.'

He nodded, trying to look intelligent.

'But they do have some cases where shrapnel's coming to the surface and they don't like to let it fester out – you know, in this climate, how easily that leads to gangrene.'

Yes. Gangrene was an ever-present danger. He motioned for Bagly to continue.

'And there are some restitching of wounds, a few hernias. So they've asked for a part-time surgeon. Two days a week, at the most, as needed. Some weeks may not even be that. Are you interested?'

He would be working with Evelyn again. Could he bear it? Did he have the right to ask it of her? After his thoughts of going home, this seemed almost like a sign. They had been friends before they had been anything else. Maybe they could be again.

'Yes, why not?'

Bagly grunted with satisfaction.

'We'll sort out the pay situation. Don't worry about that. Mondays and Wednesdays, I think, will suit us best.'

'Fine.' He felt like a china doll, with no feelings showing, no reactions. What was he *thinking*? This was a bad idea. But it was too late to take it back.

Somewhere in his chest, a bright flag was unfurling, shining and golden. He was a fool, but he loved her so. Even seeing her two days a week would change his world.

'I'll be happy to do it,' he said to Bagly. 'We don't want the men relapsing.'

'Good man!' They both got up and Bagly shook his hand. 'It's easier with you to fiddle the books, since you're extra-to-requirements.'

He went out and headed for the fever ward again. Extra-to-requirements. It was just an Army term, meaning he wasn't an enlisted officer, and so didn't show up on the official personnel list. But it cut, nonetheless.

His work wasn't extra-to-requirements. It was vitally necessary, life-saving work. He had to remember that.

CHAPTER 30

OCTOBER 1917

One Friday night, Hannah came into their bedroom and shut the door behind her, looking unusually grim.

'What's happened?' Evelyn asked, sitting up in bed. 'Linus?'

'No. William's been asked to consult here. To operate two days a week.'

By now, of course, Hannah had been told everything, and was stoutly on Evelyn's side. 'What a fool!!' she'd said. 'High-handed idiot!' Which was just right.

'Two days a week?' Evelyn pulled her knees up and wrapped her arms around them. She was incensed to find herself shivering. Ridiculous. He was nothing to her.

'Because Dr Malouf has been sent back to the Casualty Clearing Station,' Hannah added.

Malouf had been back in Cairo after being stabbed in the arm by a delirious patient, and had stayed for a while to help them out in the operating theatre, but last month he'd

273

been transferred to 75 Casualty Clearing Station in the Sinai. They'd all been relieved to get rid of him. He'd made a bad patient and had learned no patience since 1AGH.

Her stomach was churning. 'I'm in charge of theatre,' she said numbly.

They didn't have many operations, and the ones they had were mostly corrective; rarely life or death. But she had the most theatre experience, and she was in charge. Assisting the surgeon.

'Can you work with him?' Hannah asked.

Evelyn knew she should say, 'Yes, of course I can. I can be professional.' But as she tried to form the words a wave of nausea overcame her.

The image of standing beside him, of handing him instruments, listening to his voice, obeying his instructions – everything in her rejected it.

'No. I can't.'

•

The next morning, early, after a sleepless night, she went to Matron Creal and requested a transfer to one of the Casualty Clearing Stations.

Matron Creal, much as the matron in Sydney had done, looked resigned.

'Well, I suppose we've kept you longer than I expected. Once you girls have a taste of battle medicine, it's hard to keep you settled here.'

Evelyn wanted to say, 'No, that's not it,' but questions would inevitably follow which she couldn't – wouldn't – answer.

'I'm sorry, Matron. Sister Page is more than capable . . .'

'Yes, yes. All right. I won't say I'm not disappointed, but I daresay the war effort will be helped by you being on the forward line.' She stood up and shook Evelyn's hand. 'It was nice working with you, Sister Northey.'

'And you, Matron.' She was startled. Saying goodbye already?

'You have six weeks' leave owing to you, Sister. I would suggest that you take some of it before you go forward. You'll need to be in good shape to work in a CCS.' She sent a swift, shrewd glance at Evelyn. 'Dr Brent starts here tomorrow, and I'd like him to begin with the team he'll have permanently.'

So. Even Matron knew. Evelyn wondered how many people had told her about that scene in the garden.

'Thank you, Matron. I think that's a very good idea.'

Matron came around her desk and put a hand on Evelyn's arm. 'My dear, these things happen sometimes,' she said with great compassion. 'To us all. But we go on, and we live useful lives.'

Every part of her had turned to stone. Stone couldn't be embarrassed. 'Yes, Matron. Thank you.'

She went out, head high. Useful lives. She wanted to throw something, to break something. To hit someone. *Useful lives.* What a sop to vanity! What a pale, dead, imitation of a full life! Useful.

Oh, she'd be useful, all right. And after the war she'd be a doctor, and she'd inspire others, and she'd take as many lovers as she wanted and she'd laugh at bloody Dr High-handed Brent who was making her feel like this.

God damn him for taking this job. Now she had to say goodbye to Hannah all over again.

CHAPTER 31

31 OCTOBER 1917

Just before dawn, when the desert they passed through was dark beneath a blaze of gold and red and long pink clouds, the train finally slowed and stopped.

Imara was as far as the train went. There wasn't even a proper station, just a long line of track which ended abruptly. Down one side stood a few big white tents, the same kind which had been in the grounds at Heliopolis. It made Evelyn momentarily homesick for 1AGH and her colleagues there, now all in France.

Along with several other nurses, she disembarked to find field ambulances waiting for them, as well as lorries ready to receive the supplies they had so painstakingly packed and labelled.

Captain Malouf greeted them with real relief.

'Thank God you girls are here! Off you go – remember, though, no tents until nightfall!'

276

He ran off to supervise the unloading of the freight, but paused to shout to a corporal – 'Further off! Move the nurses' tents away from the doctors'!' Still worried about propriety, Evelyn thought. Good Lord, isn't there enough else to worry about?

'What on Earth is he talking about?' Astrid Wheeler, one of the other nurses from the 14th, demanded of their ambulance driver, a dour man with a long moustache.

'You'll see,' was all the reply she got. The nurses looked at each other and shrugged. Military madness again. But there was an air of excitement in the men they passed, and there were fewer than Evelyn had expected – almost all of them wearing the colours of the ambulance brigade. Actual soldiers were in short supply, and as they bumped along a mere suggestion of a track, she realised there were even fewer horses or camels.

So there was a push on. Harry would be somewhere out there – she had so hoped to see him when she arrived, had written to him to expect her, but they were just too late. A push. She knew what that meant. Artillery barrages, shells, shrapnel. And in a cavalry regiment, like the 4th Light Horse, head injuries and paralysis from falls, crushed limbs and organs from horses rolling on their riders, broken bones and amputations.

If she imagined those things happening to Harry or Linus, she would go mad well before the day was over. Better to concentrate on getting ready in case they or their comrades needed her help.

The 75 Casualty Clearing Station seemed to be no more than a dip in the bald and barren landscape. There were people here, and ambulances, but none of the set-up they had all expected. As the captain had said, there were no tents.

Or, no tents *erected*. Because there were quite a few of the big white structures laid out on the ground, ready to be pulled up.

What in Heaven's name was going on?

'Major's over there.'

Their ambulance driver spat laconically on the ground and jerked his head to the left, then dragged their cases out of the bottom luggage compartment and set them down definitively by the side of the track before leaving.

'Well!' said Astrid. 'Let's find the major.'

The major, from the back, was a well set up man with wide shoulders and a full head of light brown hair, which they could see because he was waving his cap, giving directions to some orderlies who were laying out a groundsheet.

'A bit to the right, where the ground is flatter,' he shouted. Evelyn frowned. That voice was familiar, surely?

He turned, hearing them approach, and she gasped. Dr Chapman! For a moment her mind whirled, but then it made perfect sense. He'd got the transfer he'd wanted.

Settling his cap on his head, he smiled at them, and opened his mouth to speak. It stayed open as he caught a glimpse of her. Then he got his voice back.

'Evelyn *Northey*?'

'Hello, Doctor,' she said, ridiculously overwhelmed with shyness as all eyes were trained upon her.

'Well, I'm glad to see you,' he said, sincerity in every word. He smiled at the others. 'All of you. We'll need the very best over the next few weeks.'

Astrid gave her a little push forward. Fair enough. She should be the one to ask the questions, since she knew him.

'What's going on, Doctor? All we know is that we're here to set up a Casualty Clearing Station.'

'Yes.' He sobered. 'No harm in you knowing now. We're making a push on Beersheba today. We're hoping to have it captured by tonight. But we don't want the enemy to know we're expecting heavy casualties so soon, so we're not erecting the tents until after the attack is well underway.' He noticed Astrid looked startled. 'The villages around here are rife with Turkish spies. If they see us leisurely considering how to place our station, they won't be expecting action any time soon. But it means that we can't raise the tent poles until after 4.30.'

He let out a shout for some orderlies, and the men came running to show the nurses 'to where your quarters will be'. He gave Evelyn the high sign to wait, so she lingered until the others were out of earshot – not that she had anything to hide!

'Evelyn – sorry, Sister Northey! So this is where you've come to.' They caught up on the last year and a half quickly, a litany of postings and battles. He had been on Lemnos briefly, then mainland Greece, and now here.

'It's good to see you,' he said, and shook her hand warmly.

'And you,' she said, smiling. It was. But it made home feel all the more distant, as though they were the only two who had made it off a sinking ship. 'I'd best rejoin the others.'

'Certainly, certainly.' He raised a hand and turned to meet a subaltern who ran up, breathless, with some urgent paperwork, as the lorries trundled in from the Imara road.

A push on Beersheba. Casualties coming. Lots of them. She tried to keep herself calm as she walked to join the others. Harry and Linus were in the thick of it, then.

The background anxiety she always felt about Harry pierced her as sharp as a snakebite. He was such a harum-scarum kind of boy! With a jolt, she realised that he was twenty-five now. Hardly a boy. A man. A lieutenant, with others under his care. As she pointed out her suitcase and followed the orderly carrying it to an area where small green tents had been laid on the ground, ready to be raised, she came to the melancholy conclusion that if Harry was killed, she'd be all alone in the world. It wasn't as though she could go back to her father's house; and they had never had much in the way of other relatives.

She got her apron out of her case and put away her cape, trying to shut her worries up with it. Harry was born to be hanged, not shot. His last wound had been merely a scratch, after all. But it was a bleak picture, the one she folded away in her mind: no parents, no siblings, no husband or children. Just her alone in a cold world.

She shook herself mentally. At least it *would* be cold in Edinburgh, not like this baking, burning desert!

•

Casualties could arrive at any minute, although Dr Chapman assured the nurses they were unlikely to see any before dusk.

The most important thing was to get their instruments sterilised as soon as possible. The orderlies had set up a series of big dixies near where the operating theatre tent would be, to boil water. Evelyn unpacked the cases where rows of surgical instruments, anaesthetics and dressing packs were laid, but left the towels, masks, gloves and gowns. At least the gowns and masks had been sterilised and packed carefully before they left; and the same for the rubber gloves; they could simply use those as is when the time came. But every instrument needed to be boiled and kept sterile until they were ready to operate, which was a real challenge in the open. She decided to leave them all in their steriliser baskets in the water until the casualties arrived.

They put the tents up at 4.30 that afternoon, everyone pulling together, even some local boys. No casualties yet, and afternoon tea on the boil, so she beckoned to the tallest boy who seemed to be the leader of the kiddies and handed out biscuits from a Red Cross pack.

'If you feed them, they will become like fleas on a dog,' Captain Malouf said.

Ali, at least, could understand English, because he flushed and tried to give the biscuits back.

'Nonsense!' Evelyn said. 'They've earned these by helping with the tents.'

'I have warned you,' Malouf said, and walked away.

Ali said something in Arabic which set the four other kiddies laughing. It was better not to know what it was.

'Off you go,' she said, dusting her hands to show there was no more.

Before leaving, the boys performed some elaborate bow of thanks which made her wonder what their lives had been like before war had disrupted it. School, almost certainly, and safe homes. She wished for a moment that she was a teacher so she could gather them up and teach them and keep them safe.

'Sister!' an orderly called. 'We're ready for you to set up the theatre.'

The 'theatre' was just a big tent. Canvas on the floor, covering the sand – at least they'd cleared the ground so it was mostly level. But there was a generator and lights, an operating table and several side tables. In the end, that was what they needed.

Time to get the instruments out.

Ambulances began arriving only moments after the tents were finished, trundling in, each laden with several cases.

How familiar this felt, and how horrible that it was familiar. She was taken back to the first days of the assault at Anzac Cove; but these men hadn't seen anyone but a field medic, so now, as senior nurse, she was the one to decide who needed operating on and who could be directed to the dressings tent where Mary was waiting, soap and water and saline solution and dressing packs ready.

The first ambulance was easy – all ambulant, nothing life-threatening. Off they went to be dressed.

In the second, jam-packed with men, there were two stretcher cases – one with a bad leg wound, and the other gut-shot.

As they brought that one out, the ambulance driver looked at her meaningfully, and shook his head.

He was right. There was nothing they could do here which could save him. Gut wounds were notoriously painful. She called on Astrid to administer morphine, and tried to find an orderly to stay with him, but the whole camp was in seeming chaos, with ambulance after ambulance arriving. For a moment, she was overwhelmed by the noise, the smell, the sheer number of injured. What could one person do in all this? Once Hannah had said to her, 'We do what we can.'

The children were watching. She beckoned Ali over.

'Can you write English?' she asked.

'Yes,' he said, proudly.

'Good. Stay with this man and write for him.'

There was a clipboard on one of the tables near the major's tent entrance. She scavenged some paper and a pencil and gave them to Ali, then took him to where the gut wound had been laid, under an awning, with a sipping mug of water next to him.

'This man is dying. If he wants to write words of goodbye to his loved ones, can you do that? And give him water if he wants it?'

Ali stared at the man, his olive skin paler than normal.

'It's a hard thing,' Evelyn said. 'But it's a good thing.'

'It is a blessing,' Ali said. He took the notepaper and pencil and sat cross-legged next to the stretcher. Astrid finished giving the injection and the man sighed gently.

'This boy will write any message you have,' Evelyn said to him.

'I've bought it, haven't I?' he wheezed.

'Yes,' she said. 'I'm afraid so. Do you want a priest?'

He shook his head. 'Nah. It was a good fight. I could send a note to my girl, though . . .'

Evelyn nodded to Ali and then ran off, back to the triage, back to the noise. Perhaps she had been wrong to take that time. She might have condemned someone else to death. But Hannah had got to her, there in the dying ward, and made her realise that *how* someone died was as important to them as how they lived.

Captain Malouf had taken over triage and directed her to the theatre.

Here she was on familiar, if uneven, ground, and dived thankfully into the straightforwardly difficult processes of wound repair.

'We don't close the wounds so much here,' Dr Chapman said, as he picked pieces of shrapnel from a man's shoulder while she irrigated the wound. 'More liable to get infected if we do. Our job is to stabilise. Stop the bleeding, clean it out as best we can, give the man pain relief, and send him off to

Cairo. It's faster than you've been used to, I imagine. A bit rough and ready. But we get more through. There!'

He finished pulling the last piece out and left her to clean and bandage a still-open wound. It felt wrong to do so, but she knew he was right. They'd received too many cases at 1AGH when the wound which had been 'cleaned and closed' by an on-field medic turned out to have impurities or even more shrapnel in it. It had led to more amputations and deaths in the first month than anyone was comfortable with.

But it took getting used to, seeing a patient leave the theatre with nothing but a bandage over an unclosed wound.

'You'll be fine,' Dr Chapman said. 'Just follow orders.'

'Got a crushed leg, here, Chapman,' Captain Malouf's voice said from outside the tent.

Chapman swore. 'Sorry, Evelyn. Crushing is one of the problems we get with the cavalry units. Bring him in.'

That was an amputation, a very swift operation which sheered the whole leg through and didn't even leave a flap of skin to cover the wound.

'Less infection that way,' Dr Chapman said. But, she thought, much harder for the patient when it came time to use a prosthetic. She said as much and Dr Chapman raised his eyebrows.

'Better some trouble than be dead with gangrene.'

No argument to that.

The next was a simple bullet wound in the thigh. Almost a rest, as it had missed the arteries and gone straight through.

'In and out,' Dr Chapman said. 'Shouldn't even have come to theatre. Malouf must have handed triage to that new nurse. These cases, we just patch them and send them off.'

The pace was breathtaking. She had thought they had operated quickly at 1AGH, but it was nothing like this. They had been doing the final version, there, and had to sew up every muscle layer after cutting it open – the longest part of any serious operation. But here, it was 'cut through, find the fragment, get it out, clean and pack and move them on'.

It was exhilarating. And tiring. And horrible.

The lights were hot and glaring, and became more so as the night drew on. They had a small break while they were waiting for the ambulances to return with another load, and Evelyn went to find a privy, a cup of tea and something to eat – in that order.

As she poured herself a cuppa in the dining tent, she turned to find Ali at the doorway, still holding his notepaper.

'Ali! Come in.'

'Not allowed, miss.'

She went out to him, taking one of the sandwiches which someone had left on a tin plate. Just cheese and pickle, but he'd be able to eat it, wouldn't he? He would. He grabbed at the sandwich and thrust the notes at her.

'He died,' Ali said around a mouthful, his hand held over his mouth politely.

'I'm sorry you had to be there for that,' Evelyn said sincerely. 'But thank you. I'll make sure his people get this. It will mean a lot to them.'

Ali shrugged. 'That is good. I have seen men die before. That one was brave.' Then he took the other half of the sandwich from the plate and disappeared into the darkness.

She suspected the other half of that sandwich would go to one of his friends. A good boy, Ali. She should make sure he and the others had enough to eat.

As she went back to get another sandwich and collect her mug of tea, a familiar voice stopped her.

'I thought I might see you here or hereabouts.'

She turned, dropping the empty plate. 'Harry!'

His arm was in a sling, but he was walking. She flew to him but he put out a hand to stop her. 'No hugs, for God's sake! I dislocated my shoulder and it hurts like billy-o!'

She grabbed his free hand and held it instead. 'Are you all right?'

'I'll be fine. The doc popped it back in for me and it's getting better by the minute. A couple of days' rest in Cairo and I'll be in tip-top shape.'

'Two weeks for a dislocation, or it'll happen again,' she said sharply.

His face clouded and he led her to a table, sitting down with a heavy sigh. In the light from the sole electric bulb hanging from the ceiling of the tent, his face looked older, worried, almost distraught.

'Linus is missing.'

'Oh no.' She felt cold sweep over her. 'When?'

'S'afternoon. In the charge. He was there by my side as we went into Beersheba, then he had to swerve to miss a machine-gun emplacement, and . . . he didn't show at the rendezvous, and no one's been able to find him since.'

'It's dark . . .'

'Yes, that's the hope. When daylight comes they'll have bands out searching the battlefield – always a few missing in this kind of stoush. But most of them . . . well, sis, the truth is that most of them will be dead.'

He paled as he said it, and his good hand gripped tightly into a fist, knuckles white. His whole body was taut as a bowstring.

In the face of his anguish, she felt she didn't have the right to cry, but the tears were there, just under the surface. Linus, of all people! So *alive*. Oh, poor Hannah!

'I *hate* this war,' she said.

'Right about now I agree with you.'

He slumped in his seat.

'Let me get you a cup of tea.' She brought them both back mugs of tea and sandwiches, and they ate, knowing it was wise, but Evelyn suspected that Harry's sandwich, like hers, tasted of dust and ashes.

But she grabbed a spare bit of Ali's notepaper and wrote a quick note to Hannah, urging her to hope for the best.

Hollow words. But what else could she say? She made Harry lie down on a bed in the big transport tent and went back to the theatre, where she could do some good.

Later in the night, the procession of ambulances slowed down and they began to organise getting some of the wounded to the train and off to Cairo and Alexandria.

•

Captain Malouf was in charge of the convoy of ambulances, and he let her go to the railhead with Harry. She sat next to him, holding his hand as naturally as if they were children again, and they talked about nothing, about the heat and the dust and where he would be taken to.

'The Light Horse usually go to the 14th, where I used to be,' she said. 'Hannah will take care of you there.' She hesitated. 'You'll have to tell her about Linus.'

Harry's eyes were bleak; he looked much older than he had only a few months ago. 'I know. It's rough, the not knowing. What do I say to her?'

'Exactly what you told me. Just as you've told me. And then answer whatever questions she has. There's nothing else you can do.'

She was ashamed of the relief she felt that Harry was all right. If he had died, it would have been very hard. Very hard. She tucked the note to Hannah into his breast pocket. 'Give her this with my love, will you?'

'Will do.'

It wasn't a long journey, and soon enough they pulled up by the train. He was well enough to hop down from the ambulance, and she took his good arm to help him across to the ambulance carriage.

They embraced, holding each other tight for a long time. He released her reluctantly, and she let him go, the tears in her eyes reflected in his. He waved his right hand – the one in the sling – at her.

'Write to Dad, will you, and let him know I'm all right?'

He knew it was a lot to ask, but she could only nod. 'I will. But you send a telegram from Cairo. Don't leave him wondering after he sees you listed among the wounded in the newspaper.'

As the train pulled away, he leant out of the window and waved to her. She waved back, but at that moment the tiredness hit her and it was almost painful to keep her hand aloft.

'Sleep for you,' Captain Malouf said, 'Or you'll be of no use at all when the next load of casualties come through.'

'Yes, Doctor,' she said. What the hell, she thought as she climbed into the back of the ambulance, and lay down on the stretcher there. It was no more than a moment before she fell asleep, praying she wouldn't dream.

•

She had gone to the front rather than work with him.

Well, that was clear enough.

William worked methodically through the surgery lists on that first Monday, with Hannah as his theatre nurse. He did good work – he made sure of that. He packed away any dreams he had had of seeing Evelyn again, and went back to the life he'd planned for, hoped for, since he was a little boy. Being a good doctor.

He revised his plans to go to Edinburgh. London would be safer – he could be sure of never seeing her there.

A new batch of wounded came in from the Sinai, and he helped with the triage.

'Harry!' Hannah's voice cut through the low murmur of voices and the occasional swearword. William turned automatically.

So this was Harry. Tall and with blond hair, he was a fine upstanding young man, despite his shoulder being in a sling. That seemed to be the only thing wrong with him.

William made his way to the door of the ward, where Harry hung onto the doorjamb with his good hand, pale as a sheet. Hannah pulled him to sit down, but he resisted.

'Linus is missing.' He blurted the words out and then leant against the jamb. Hannah swayed, white in the face, and William sprang to steady her, jarring his hip as he landed. She half-fell against him, and then rallied.

'Missing?' she breathed. Even her lips were white. She needed some brandy.

'At Beersheba,' Harry said. 'I lost sight of him when I took my tumble, and later . . . we looked – I made them look . . .'

He was clearly wretched, both for Hannah and for himself. William didn't allow himself to feel too much, not now. He had to stay professional. But deep down, he felt a sharp protest at the thought of Linus dead.

'But you didn't find him. So he might still be alive . . .' A quick flash in Harry's eyes said that the likelihood was very slight.

'It's possible . . .' he said.

William slid his arm around Hannah's shoulders and pulled her away. 'Come and sit down. I'll get some brandy.' He nodded at Harry. 'I'm Brent,' he said.

'Oh. Oh. Jolly good.'

The boy's tone was forced and William wondered what Evelyn had said about him.

'I'm fine,' Hannah said. She shook off both their protective hands and straightened, adjusting her veil. Her mouth was tight and the blood was gone from her temples and cheeks; her normal rosy glow was quite gone.

'I'm his next of kin – why didn't I get a telegram?'

Harry cleared his throat. 'I told the unit clerk that I'd let you know personally.' She gave a short, sharp nod.

'I'll have to get someone else to take over so I can send a telegram to his parents.' Valiant. She was valiant. William patted her arm.

'You go. I'll explain to Matron.'

'Theatre –'

'I'll organise it all. You go.'

'I'll come with you,' Harry said. It was completely against standing orders to let him go, but what could the Army do if they found out? William, at least, couldn't be court-martialled, and he had the authority to give Harry convalescent leave.

'Yes,' he said. 'Stay with her. I'll cover things here.'

He organised a replacement, let Matron know what had happened, and then turned thankfully to surgery, allowing the case after case of shrapnel and bullet wounds to block his fears for Linus and his pity for Hannah.

But nothing blocked his fear for Evelyn, out there in the desert where even strong young men like Linus weren't safe.

•

The worst of a 'missing' report is that there is nothing you can do. No memorial service, no cleansing grief, no certainty. The fact that Linus – lively, cheeky, clever Linus – was nowhere to be found on the battlefield was bizarre, unthinkable. William couldn't quite believe it.

They had to go back to their duty as though nothing had happened.

Hannah fretted herself thin over Linus, but she managed to put that aside while she worked, as he had to with Evelyn. Being in a CCS put her frighteningly near the front line. There had been occasions where a CCS had been shelled. It could happen any time.

She would rather face potential death than work with him.

Every time he thought of it he apostrophised himself as a complete idiot. If he'd paid no attention to her delirious words; if he'd trusted her to be truthful with him and simply asked her about it; if he'd allowed *her* to make the decision . . . She was right. Men had the habit of making decisions for everyone, and too bad if not everyone agreed.

It was hard to deal with. It took him quite a while to admit the truth. But every time he thought, 'She'd rather go to the front than see me,' the lesson cut a little deeper.

He vowed, more than once, that he'd never do anything like it again, with any woman. With anyone at all. Respect, acceptance of personal autonomy – and, more than that – putting her right to control her life over his need to avoid shame and rejection.

He'd been a coward of the worst kind; the kind that dressed fear up as concern for others. If he ever saw her again, he'd admit his mistake and beg her forgiveness. Expecting nothing. Just because it was the right thing to do.

Yet his mind couldn't help but take another step – to where his genuine repentance might gain him her friendship again, at least.

CHAPTER 32

'I've never understood,' Dr Chapman said conversationally, as they dressed the wound he had just stitched, a small one which could be safely closed even here, 'why you didn't become a doctor in the first place. I didn't like to ask, back in Taree. But you inherited from your mother, didn't you?'

Evelyn concentrated on her gloved hands, moving as surely and competently as any doctor's.

'My father doesn't believe women should be doctors,' she said finally. 'He wouldn't let me use my inheritance for university.' The soldier was wheeled out and another case brought in, a trooper with a deeper wound on the thigh which needed cleaning and packing with disinfectant-soaked lint.

'Well, your father's a stubborn old bastard,' he said as they scrubbed up, and then, automatically, 'Sorry,' for his swearing.

She smiled at him forgivingly. She'd have forgiven him a great deal more than that, for the help he had given her back then.

That morning, when she had asked for his help and he had given it, had changed her life. In a very real sense, it was Dr Chapman who had made all this possible, there in his wisteria-scented room at the Manning District Hospital, when he had risked alienating her father by helping her. Forever after that, the scent of wisteria was the scent of hope.

She could almost smell it now, despite the desert air, despite the odours of sand and sweat and dung from the mules nearby. And Dr Chapman was just as kind as ever, but seemed a good deal more male and . . . and *noticeable* than he had in Australia.

'That'll do him,' he said now. 'Let's let that work for a little while, and then we'll clean him out and send him off.'

'Yes, Doctor,' Evelyn murmured.

She held out her hands to receive the gloves and mask he stripped off. As he placed them in her palms, he smiled suddenly, wryly. 'Don't think I don't know you could do my job if you put your mind to it,' he said.

She grinned back. 'Oh, no. I know how much I have to learn. But thanks for the vote of confidence.'

He put a hand on one shoulder as he passed by; a benediction, she hoped.

The trooper was coming out of the sedative. She disposed of the gloves and masks, including hers, and went to reassure him.

'Am I all together?' he asked fearfully. She smiled. This fear the men woke up with after they were wounded, that they'd been hurt in the genitals . . . it seemed to be universal.

'You're intact,' she said. 'We've had to excise some of the flesh around the wound, but all you'll have is a scar to impress the girls with.'

The relief went through his whole body and he sagged back onto the stretcher.

'Orderly!' she called. She patted the trooper on the arm. 'Let's get you on back to bed.'

•

After the first morning rush was over, Dr Chapman insisted the operating team have a break and a cup of tea.

'The others can wait fifteen minutes,' he said. 'We have to keep our strength up.'

So different from William, she thought, who pushed himself so hard that he pushed others too. She didn't know if the thought was tender or annoyed, or both.

Her mind drifted to Linus. Knowing that Harry was all right was a great relief, but Linus . . . he was so dear to so many people she cared about: Rebecca and Hannah and Harry and even William. His death would leave a gaping hole. But better knowing he was dead than the terrible 'missing', which left a constant fear fighting an inconstant hope.

She and Dr Chapman sat near the entrance to the mess tent, where a slight breeze cooled their sweat. The orderlies and two other nurses sat outside, on upturned petrol cans, looking out over the afternoon desert, a place of ochres and deep gold. A cloud of dust on the horizon showed where a column of men and horses was moving to a new position.

The tea was wonderful. Ridiculous that a hot drink could be so comforting on a scorching day.

'Your father wanted me to marry you,' Dr Chapman said, as though they were continuing a conversation.

She spilled some of her tea onto the sandy ground.

'What!'

He grinned at her. 'Oh, I know. You were only twenty, too. Ten years younger than me.'

'He – how *dare* he – oh –' She was so furious she couldn't find words. Slamming the mug onto a petrol drum, she surged to her feet and paced, instead.

'He said he didn't believe in love matches and you weren't – he didn't trust you to make the right choice.' She glared at him and he raised a hand, chuckling. 'Don't blame me. I said no. I told him you were one of the most sensible young women I'd ever met, and he should leave your future in your own hands.'

The anger left her suddenly and she felt cold all over.

'He just wanted to control my life.'

'Yes,' Dr Chapman said. 'I think that's true.' He looked up at her and something in his gaze changed. 'Ten years difference doesn't seem so great now.'

The moment stretched out, reminding her of that moment in Sydney when he had asked her to call him Ian. She should say something, but what could she say? What did she *want* to say? She didn't know.

'Well,' he said, getting to his feet and draining the last of his tea, as though it were an everyday chat they'd been having. 'Best get back to it.'

She grasped the air of normality thankfully. 'Yes, of course.'

As they went back into the operating tent, she forced her mind to concentrate only on what was before her. Blood, shock, pus, shrapnel: they were an effective antidote to personal concerns.

She considered swapping roles with Mary, the assisting nurse, but that was silly. It was only a comment, not a proposal of marriage.

But she was conscious of his hands, moving near hers, and was careful to make sure they didn't touch.

CHAPTER 33

The wounded had been held again in the transport tent overnight, until the next convoy of ambulances could take them to the railhead. Evelyn followed Dr Chapman on rounds early, before the heat could take hold.

It was a melancholy task. Severely wounded men, the smell of dried blood and gunpowder still on their clothes, tear tracks on their cheeks. The nurses did their best, but a CCS moved at such a breakneck pace when there was a push on that there was little time for giving comfort.

One man caught at Dr Chapman's hand. He was dying, and he knew it. 'Tell my wife,' he gasped. 'Tell her I love her.'

'I'll tell her,' Dr Chapman promised. 'I'll write to her.' There was some deep sympathy in his tone which reassured the man.

'Thanks, Doc.' The patient's head flopped to the side, exhausted, and Evelyn blinked back tears. It was too easy, sometimes, to block out the human, the emotional, side of their work. Too hard to remember that if they failed to save a patient, a whole family was plunged into grief.

'Get his details for me, please, Sister Northey, so I can write to his wife.'

'Yes, Doctor.'

They finished rounds and went to the operating theatre, scrubbing up side by side.

Dr Chapman was silent, soaping his hands a second time. 'I was married, once,' he said. 'She died.'

'I'm sorry.' She had wondered why he was single. Now she felt like a fool and a gossip. She could feel the blush come up over her cheeks. Dr Chapman noticed, and smiled wryly.

'My own fault for never mentioning her,' he said.

Then the first patient was carried in, and they went to work. Evelyn was anaesthetist today, as they had a spare surgeon, a new man from Lemnos, where the hospital had closed down, and Dr Rowlands was working with him in the other tent.

As always, she and Dr Chapman worked together competently enough, although not with the perfect comprehension she'd known with William.

They went through five fairly simple remove and clean jobs quickly, and then slowed down for a man with extensive shrapnel wounds, where keeping his blood pressure stable while not letting him come to consciousness used every bit of knowledge Evelyn had.

Afterwards, they both needed a break, and sat back where they had before, outside the tent, to have a very late lunch.

Evelyn had no intention of opening the discussion again, but Dr Chapman surprised her, picking up exactly from where they had left off, as though he needed to talk.

'Her name was Sylvia,' he said. 'I met her in Sydney while I was doing my residency at Sydney Hospital. A debutante. So beautiful, but flighty. She didn't know much about being a doctor's wife, but I didn't care. I was working hard, long hours, to try to make enough money to buy into a country practice. I didn't even ask myself if she would like the country.'

He fell silent, but it wasn't the silence of withdrawal.

'What happened?'

'I was at the hospital, doing a private operation – an old man's ulcer had to be excised. I hadn't even known she was pregnant, that's how removed I was from her life. She miscarried, and haemorrhaged. It was the maid's night off. If I'd been there . . .'

Guilt, thick and strong in his voice. Best not to pander to it, Evelyn thought instinctively.

'Yes. Perhaps you could have saved her,' she said, keeping her voice prosaic. 'And perhaps not. Internal haemorrhages are difficult to stop.'

His head came up and he looked at her with astonishment. He had expected another reaction. Had this whole story been to evoke compassion, sympathy, in her? Or was she being too suspicious?

Then he chuckled, darkly. 'I've never told anyone this before. It's not something you can talk about to a lady, nor to a male friend.'

'Only to a nurse, who by definition isn't a lady,' Evelyn said, lifting her eyebrows at him.

'You know I didn't mean that.' He fell silent, staring at his hands. 'I suppose I expected you to either absolve me or blame me.'

'I don't blame you,' she said.

'Huh. But you know what they say.' His tone was bitter. 'Cobblers' sons go barefoot . . .'

'. . . and doctors' wives die young.' She finished the old adage. 'Yes. But what I don't understand . . .'

'Is why I never mentioned her? After she died, they were all *at* me. So much sympathy, so much curiosity . . . I couldn't bear it. When I bought into the Manning District, I just wanted to make a clean break. So I put away my black armbands and my black hatbands and pretended I'd never been married. I didn't even mourn her for six months before I "got on with my life".' His voice was ashamed. He drank the rest of his tea as though knocking back a dram of whiskey.

'That was wrong,' she acknowledged. Again, he looked at her with surprise. Good. 'You should have mourned her. She deserved better than to be forgotten.'

'A bit late now.'

'Never too late. Give the town a fountain or a park and name it after her.' She kept her voice deliberately even. Underneath it, she was a whirl of conflicting emotions. She felt sorry for him, but more than that she was desperately sorry for Sylvia, poor young silly Sylvia, dead before her time. And that made her, perhaps unfairly, angry at Dr Chapman. It didn't seem much like love if he couldn't even mourn her.

He smiled at her grimly. 'Good idea. You know all the answers, don't you?'

'Who, me?' She got up and shook the last drops from her mug onto the sand. 'I'm only a nurse.'

She knew herself well enough to admit that she was angry because her idea of him was wrong; he'd always been so kind to her that she had built up this image of him as a paragon, and it hurt when he showed his feet of clay. Her idealism wasn't his fault; he hadn't changed. So she smiled at him as they prepared for the next operation.

'Women die in pregnancy, and childbirth,' she said softly. 'These things just happen. You know that.'

'Yes,' he said. 'Thank you.' There was real gratitude in his eyes, but part of her resented the fact that he'd got her to absolve him, after all.

•

'It would be good to work together, back in Taree,' Dr Chapman said. He sat on a log which was waiting to be split into firewood, and began to tamp his pipe with tobacco. There had been peace on the line for two days now, and they were able to take some time – and do chores, like washing, which had been building up.

The washing line was behind the tents, with nothing between them and the horizon but sand and scrub. It was exhilarating to be out under the open sky after so many, many days closeted in hot, sandy tents.

She laughed at him and flapped an apron open before pegging it to the line. 'So when I graduate from Edinburgh I should come and ask you for a job?'

'Edinburgh!'

'That's the plan. I'm saving hard. I should have enough for at least one year there by the time this is all over. And when I'm thirty I get my full inheritance and can pay for myself.'

His face was half in shadow from the washing line, the paler shadows and blocks of light chasing over it as the wet clothes swung in the breeze. It was hard to read his expression.

'I hadn't realised you were still clinging to this idea of becoming a doctor.'

Her first emotion was tiredness. Why did she have to go through this, over and over again? But she should give him the benefit of the doubt. He'd always supported her, both in Taree and here.

'Why wouldn't I?' she asked lightly, pegging a uniform dress up.

'Well . . . by the time you've graduated, and done your residency, it will probably be too late to marry and have children.'

'Yes.' Of course it would. Did he think she didn't *know* that? Know what she was giving up?

'You're a wonderful nurse, Evelyn. They're as rare as good doctors –'

'Oh, shut up, Ian!' He blinked and sat back on his haunches. 'I know all the reasons I shouldn't be a doctor, and frankly I thought better of you!'

He took a draw on his pipe, biting down hard on the stem. So she'd made him angry. Too flaming bad.

'I see,' he said finally, letting go of the smoke in a blue haze around his head. 'Yes, I see. I suppose I just hoped . . .' He gestured.

Oh, God give her patience! Was this a *marriage* proposal?

He smiled ruefully up at her. 'I rather saw us as a team, in the future. Both professionally and personally.'

It was. This was why he'd told her all about his wife. Had he thought she was angling for that information? How mortifying! She had best be as clear as she could be.

'Ian, I'm going to Edinburgh. And I'm going to be a doctor. I don't intend ever to marry.'

He was silent, simply nodding. Then he knocked the dottle of his pipe onto the ground, and got up, looking at her as though trying to decide what to say.

'Write to me when you're finished. I'll give you a reference when you need one to get a residency,' he said finally, and she was filled with gratitude and remorse that she couldn't give him what he wanted. He *was* a generous man, after all.

'*Thank* you.' He nodded and walked away, his shoulders slumped.

But she didn't think he loved her. Not really. There just hadn't been enough emotion in his eyes or his body. She would have been . . . convenient, and pleasant, and companionable. Not bad as a recipe for a happy marriage, if one wanted to marry, although not particularly exciting.

She couldn't help but compare his equanimity to William's fierce passion. Foolish of her. That ship had sailed.

But it was true that, no matter how wrong-headed William had been in their personal lives, he had never been anything but firm in his support for her medical ambitions. For a moment, she had to cling to the washing-line prop, she was so shaken by longing for him. She could tell him the story of Ian Chapman, and he would shake his head, and kiss her hand, and then her lips . . .

Oh God she missed him.

CHAPTER 34

It was a beautiful morning; the autumn desert showed no changes in its flora, but the light caught it differently. In the dawn, the sun was almost silver-bright, and the harsh ochres and yellows were tinted with soft rose reflected from the sky. Evelyn stood outside her tent, towel and bath-kit in hand, and breathed in. The air was free of dust so early in the morning, and was fresh and clean. Thank God they put the latrines downwind.

'Miss?' Ali came out cautiously from behind her tent, as though afraid of discovery. Not at all like him.

'What's the matter?' She kept her voice low – not everyone was up yet, and each moment of sleep was precious.

'Miss, I have message.' He took out a piece of cloth and unfolded it to show folded paper, kept clean. 'Another boy brought it.'

What on Earth? Perhaps it was a thank-you from one of the soldiers they'd patched up and sent back to the fray.

She took the note, a single sheet of lined paper, and opened it.

Arabic writing! How odd. Then her heart seemed to drop down through her abdomen. In the middle of the curls and flows of the Arabic, a name was written in English.

Linus Yates.

'Where did you get this?' she demanded.

Ali shrugged and pointed. Standing about a hundred yards away was another boy, a little older than Ali, fourteen perhaps, poised on the balls of his feet as though ready to run away. She beckoned him closer and he came, reluctantly, but kept the bulk of her tent between them. Her heart was racing. If Linus was alive!

'Where did you get this?' He shrugged. Probably didn't speak any English. She turned to Ali. 'Ask him where he got the message from.'

Ali asked, in Arabic, but the boy just stood silent. She showed Ali the message.

'What does it say?' He shook his head, embarrassed.

So, his Arabic reading wasn't as good as his English. No doubt the war had intervened in his education and he'd found it more useful to learn the English alphabet.

Captain Malouf!

'Stay there,' she said to the strange boy, and ran to the officers' tents. 'Captain Malouf!' she called at the entrance to his tent. 'Captain Malouf, are you there?'

He came crawling out, eyes bleary, and stood up in his nightshirt, his bare feet in the dust, clutching his uniform tunic in front of him for modesty.

'Sister Northey? Is there an emergency?'

She thrust the note at him, trying to control a quaver in her voice. 'A boy just brought me this. What does it say?'

He read it silently, and she saw him pale.

'Well?' She was too impatient to wait for him to recover his amour-propre.

'It's a ransom note, for someone called Linus Yates.'

'He's alive?'

'That's what it says. But wounded.' He paused. 'You know him?' There was a note of conjecture and reproof in his voice that she didn't like.

'He's my brother's best friend,' she said. 'A fine man. He's engaged to one of the nurses at the 14th General in Cairo.'

A minuscule relaxation of the muscles around his mouth. Oh, good, she thought, keeping the sarcasm to herself, now I won't have to deal with his judgemental piety. She was enraged that he should still be worried about morals at a time like this.

'What do they want?' she demanded.

'One hundred pounds.' He paused, looking down at his unclad feet. 'I'll get dressed. We have to tell Major Chapman about this.'

One hundred pounds. A huge amount of money. Almost a year's salary for an ordinary soldier. But the Army could find it.

•

'No,' Ian Chapman said. 'We can't pay it.' His face was sombre, and his eyes full of pity.

'But –'

'There's an iron-clad rule. No ransoms. We'll do a prisoner exchange, but if we started to pay ransoms, every little village around here would be kidnapping our men and selling them back to us. It's impossible.'

'They don't *want* a prisoner exchange. They want money.'

'And the Army can't give it to them.'

She was shaken by fury. These rules and regulations she'd lived under for so long were worthless when a man's life was at stake. The cooler part of her knew that the Army was right – it would be painting a target on the back of every man who was in the tail of a troop movement, or of every pair who went out on reconnaissance. But this was *Linus*!

'I'm not in the Army,' she said. 'And the note came to me. I can pay it.'

'Sit down, Evelyn,' he said. His office tent was tall enough to stand up in, a smaller version of the dressing tents, and he had a small table and a couple of chairs in it. He pulled one out for her, but she knew instinctively that if she sat down, it was all over. They would bring the full force of authority and strength to bear on her.

'No thank you,' she said.

'You *are* in the Army,' Ian said. 'You have a notional rank of lieutenant.'

'Notional. No one here thinks of us as being Army – certainly not the locals! And they brought the note to *me*. No one has to know that the Army even found out about it!'

Malouf and he looked at each other. Malouf nodded.

'She should take the chance,' he said. 'A man's life is at stake.'

How odd to be grateful to Malouf! Her fingers were twisted together; she was actually wringing her hands, like a heroine in a Gothic novel! She tried to relax them, but couldn't.

'But the money . . .' Ian said finally. 'I can't give it to you out of Army funds.'

'If I can get to a telegraph station, I can have the money brought here. We have to be quick! The note says he's wounded, doesn't it, Captain?'

Malouf nodded. 'It says: "The man has a leg wound", but it doesn't say how bad.'

'Anything is bad if it's not treated,' she said. 'Please.'

Her heart thumped hard against her sternum. For Hannah, for Rebecca, for Harry – and for her. It was impossible that Linus should not be rescued, now they had a chance.

'All right,' Chapman said. 'All right. But keep this between ourselves. *No one* else knows. Understood?'

Yes. For Linus's sake, it was best to keep mum.

There was a telegraph station at the railhead. One of the ambulances took her there, and she sent a telegram to Hannah. Thank God she had left those bank withdrawal slips with her! This would take the bulk of her savings, and put her entry to Edinburgh back by a year, at least, but she couldn't worry about that now.

Please withdraw one hundred pounds from bank and bring to me at Imara immediately stop urgent stop don't delay stop Evelyn

•

'What do you think it means?' Hannah asked. William shook his head.

'Nothing good,' he said. His gut was churning. Why would Evelyn need that kind of money? The only thing he could think of was blackmail, but what had she done which could be the source of a blackmail threat? 'Can you get the money?'

'Yes.' Hannah showed him Evelyn's bank book and signed withdrawal slips. 'She left these with me in case she needed me to buy her supplies and send them to her.'

She was pale and thinner than she had been. Linus's fate was still up in the air. No news of him for ten days, and with every passing day it grew less likely that he was alive. She hadn't quite given in to grief, but it had worn her away.

'Let's go see Matron, then, and get the time off.'

'You're coming too?' Hannah's voice was full of relief.

'Yes, of course,' he said. There was no question of him not going. Even if it hadn't been Evelyn in trouble, he couldn't have let Hannah go alone. She was no Linnet, confident and able to deal with anything. Hannah was a competent nurse, and a compassionate one who brought great comfort to her patients, but she wasn't a trailblazer.

He took the lead in Matron's office.

'Evelyn Northey has asked Miss Page to take some things to Imara for her. I'll act as her escort. We both need at least a week's furlough.'

Matron looked keenly at both of them. Looking for signs of an assignation. *That we're trying to get an opportunity to go off for a week of love-making*, he thought. *If only it were that simple.*

'Is Sister Northey in trouble?' she asked. There was an inflection to her voice – 'in trouble' said in that tone meant 'pregnant'. She thought they were going north to perform an abortion.

'Absolutely not, Matron!' Hannah said in a horrified tone. It was convincing; Matron relaxed and nodded.

'I want a full explanation, then.'

'If we had one, we'd give it to you,' he said. 'When we get back . . .'

'Very well. Doctor, you're your own boss. You can take leave whenever you choose. Sister Page, you have a week, and then I want you back here and on duty.'

PAMELA HART

'Thank you, Matron,' Hannah gabbled, and he just had time to nod to Matron before she grabbed his hand and pulled him out of the room.

'Hannah!' he protested.

'We *have* to hurry. I just know something dreadful's happened.'

'Pack a bag and meet me at the front door.'

•

They left the bags there and went the short distance to the Camel Corps, where the nearest bank office was. Hannah had filled in the withdrawal slip already, but when they got to the office, it was shut. William swore, and Hannah looked as though she might too.

Around them, the normal business of a Corps headquarters when the troops were away went on. Clerks crisscrossed the large parade ground with papers in their hands, a few privates were mopping the verandah which ran along the front of the offices. William approached one.

'Where's the bank chappie?'

'Still asleep,' the private said, grinning. 'Tied one on last night. He'll have a head today, for sure.' He pointed out the man's quarters, and William strode there, aware of the pull in his leg but overriding it.

He hammered on the door. 'Wake up! Bank business!'

A groan answered him. He opened the door and looked around. The man was still in bed.

It took him ten minutes to drag the bank clerk out of bed and thrust him into some clothes, ignoring his protests and the time he staggered to the washstand to vomit into the basin.

'I'm sick!' the man whined.

'I don't care what's wrong with you, you slacker, you're opening that bank today.'

Five minutes later Hannah had the money in her hand, and the bank clerk put up a sign saying 'Closed for business' and staggered back to his bunk.

The trip to Imara was easier to organise. They simply lied, and told the ticket office they were going to join the 75 Casualty Clearing Station at Imara. He didn't even ask to see their papers: Hannah's red nurse's cape was their passport – and his own black doctor's bag.

It took a long time to get there, on hospital trains which were mostly empty, taking ambulance carriages back to the battlefield after having deposited a load of wounded in Cairo.

The towns went by: Zagazig, El Saleheyah, El Qantara, where they crossed the Suez Canal and William jumped out of the carriage at the station to buy food and water. Up the coast to El Arish. By this time they were both trying to sleep as the autumn night drew deeper, but they were forced to detrain there, to switch to another, smaller train which would take them on the last stretch to Imara, and which wouldn't leave until morning.

Exhausted, they sat in the waiting room together, not talking. Every so often Hannah's hand would go to her bodice, where she had secreted Evelyn's money. Her head finally dropped on to his shoulder as she napped.

William leant his own head back against the rough boards of the wall and tried to sleep, too, but it was impossible. He'd tried so hard to put Evelyn out of his mind, but the thought that she was in trouble was a knife in his gut. He remembered his father once saying, 'Like having your family jewels in a vice!' He hadn't known what his father was talking about, but the expression was so striking he'd never forgotten it. That was what it was like, worrying about Evelyn, but being so far from her. Like having your family jewels in a vice.

CHAPTER 35

Evelyn went looking for the boy who had brought the message, but he couldn't be found, not even by Ali and his friends.

'He said he come back,' Ali reassured her. She was especially generous with lunch that day, wanting to keep the children around for when that happened. At least with Ali she had an interpreter who wouldn't frighten the other boy away.

An answer to her telegram came just after lunch.

On the way stop have what you asked for stop Hannah

The relief was enormous. She returned to the operating tent with a lighter heart. Hannah was coming and the two of them would deal with this together. And Hannah would know that Linus was alive. That was the important thing, which they had to hold onto. Linus was alive.

●

No day had ever gone so slowly. And then, in the late afternoon, word came that they were moving the camp closer to the battlefield. And worse – not towards Beersheba, to the north-west, where Linus must be hidden, but towards Gaza, in the north-east.

The whirlwind of packing and labelling which followed failed to distract her. Rather, it screwed her anxiety even tighter. What if Hannah arrived and they had already left?

At midnight, Dr Chapman called a halt and they all fell into their bunks with relief. She lay on top of hers, fully dressed except for her shoes, dozing fitfully and waking at each noise, her heart hammering.

At dawn she woke and went to the shower tent, where she found Astrid already finished and drying her hair.

'I could do without this move,' Astrid said. Evelyn assented numbly, wishing with a fierce loneliness that Hannah would arrive.

She washed and dressed and went back to work, packing up the operating theatre and its supplies, and seeing them loaded onto the mule train wagons. The whole camp was a miasma of dust and flies and mule dung, and to make it worse a wind sprang up which whipped the dust into their eyes and turned everything brown.

The motor ambulances had been loaded with men and gear and sent off ahead, so they could get the main tent and kitchen set up before the convoy arrived.

So it was odd when an ambulance pulled up beside the last tent standing, Dr Chapman's office.

Someone wounded? She hauled a duffel full of bedpans onto the wagon and went to see if she was needed.

Out of the dust, two figures emerged from the ambulance back.

A nurse, and – she would know that halting walk anywhere.

'William!' she called. William and Hannah, both looking tired and pale. She ran to them and William put his arms out.

Whatever anger she had towards him was forgotten; it was so good to feel his arms around her, his hand in her hair. The weight of responsibility lifted. It was the three of them now, and she no longer had to make decisions on her own.

A shudder ran through her at the thought, and she pulled away from William to hug Hannah.

'He's alive, Hannah!'

'Linus?' Hannah's colour came and went in her face, so that both William and she put their hands out to steady her. 'Are you *sure*?' Her voice was fierce.

'Yes. Come in here and I'll explain.'

They went into the office and Dr Chapman joined them. It was a quick explanation. William took the note and studied it. She had forgotten that he had been learning Arabic.

'Yes,' he reassured Hannah. 'It says a leg wound. So he's alive.'

'When that was written,' Hannah said. Calm now, but full of the knowledge of how quickly an infection or fever could set in.

'Which is why we need to get moving,' Evelyn said. She went out into the dust and heat, waving flies away from her face as she looked for the children. She was ready for this.

Ali saw her and ran over. She pulled a whole block of chocolate out of her pocket. His eyes widened.

'Find that boy and bring him here,' she said, waving the chocolate in front of him. 'Tell him we have the money.'

'Yes, Sister!' he saluted, and ran off, calling for his friends.

•

William and Hannah had a cup of tea and a sandwich in the mess tent while they all waited. He was glad to sit down on something that wasn't moving. To sit and look at Evelyn; to remember the feel of her coming to his arms as though they'd never quarrelled. It was a bad time to be thinking of his personal life, but he couldn't help it – hope rose inside him. If he had another chance, he promised himself, he wouldn't muck it up.

She looked tired. Worried. But calm, as she always was in a crisis. They spoke little.

There was a commotion at the mess tent entrance.

'Miss! Miss Sister!' a boy's voice shouted out.

'That's him,' Evelyn said. 'Come on.'

They rushed out to find the boy, Ali, waiting for them, dancing from foot to foot with impatience.

'He says, not here,' Ali reported. 'You come outside camp.'

'The three of us,' Hannah said.

'Yes,' Evelyn agreed.

They followed Ali to a pile of rocks not far from camp, where a stunted bush or two grew in the boulders' shade. A boy was sitting there, his robe tucked around his knees. Taller than Ali, closer up he could see that he was no more than twelve, thin and agile, his face wary under his white skullcap.

Evelyn showed him the money, and he went to take it, but she pulled it back.

'No,' she said. 'Tell him, Ali. No money until we have Lieutenant Yates back.'

Ali translated, and the boy shook his head firmly.

'Money first,' Ali said.

'Tell him we're not such fools. Tell him to take us to Lieutenant Yates. When we can see him, they can have the money.'

The boy looked at the dirt, and scuffed his sandalled foot in the dust. He kept sneaking glances at William. Of course. He wasn't prepared to take orders from a woman.

Evelyn put her hand on his arm, the boy's eyes following every movement. William looked at her, smiling wryly – it must irk her to have to ask him for help after being so independent. He turned to the boy and tried to take on authority, to stand even taller.

'Guide us to where the lieutenant is. Give us your word you'll let us all go free. We give you our oath that we will hand over the money once we have Lieutenant Yates,' William said, his voice strong, Ali translating quickly for him.

The boy looked at him for a moment and then said something, glancing quickly at Hannah and then away.

Ali said, 'He says you and your wife can come, but not the other.'

'My wife?'

The boy pointed at Evelyn and said a couple of words.

'The red-headed one,' Ali reported. 'The soldier told him to take the message to the red-headed one, so he did. She can come, and you her husband, but not the other.'

'No!' Hannah said. 'He's my fiancé!'

But the boy remained stubborn. He would only guide the two of them. Her simple touch on William's arm had convinced him, apparently, that they were married.

'No unmarried women,' he said.

In the end, Hannah had to agree, although she was in tears over it. William was half-ashamed of being male. So many restrictions placed on girls, and for what? Male pride. He felt that Evelyn had taught him to see the world in a new way.

'*I* should go,' Hannah said. 'He needs me!'

'No help for it. We won't bring him back here, because there'll be no facilities left, but you can set up a tent for him at the new camp. Take mine.' Evelyn faltered, seeing as he did the mix of hope and frustration in Hannah's eyes.

'We'll do our very best by him, Hannah,' William said.

'I know you will,' she said. They hugged, and then went back to camp to talk the logistics officer into lending them transport for the journey.

No ambulance, they were told, could be spared, but they could have a single mule. They could load it with water and some food and William's doctor's bag, which had everything a large first-aid kit had plus opiates and other drugs.

•

It was seventeen miles to Beersheba, and the track had been obliterated by horses and mules. There was no possibility, Evelyn thought, that William could make it. He simply couldn't walk that far.

She left him packing the mule and went to the Light Horse camp, to the trooper who was still there, looking after the Walers of wounded troopers until they returned to duty. Fortunately, it was Trooper Maxwell, whom she had nursed at the 14th General.

'It's for Lieutenant Yates,' she said. *'Please.'*

His face showed his conflict.

'I'll be given the boot! Dishonourably discharged!'

'Are you going to let me walk off into the desert without a horse?' she demanded.

'I have to, miss.'

Then she had a brainwave.

'How about this? I have the rank of a lieutenant, you know. How about I order you to give me the horses?'

Maxwell's face went slack as he pondered the idea, and then he slowly smiled.

'Just followin' orders . . . right you are! I'll give you a couple of steady ones.'

She borrowed a couple of slouch hats, too, to shield them against the desert sun.

•

When she returned to camp with two saddled and bridled horses, William's face was a picture.

'What the hell? Where did you get those? No, don't tell me, I don't want to know.'

She grinned at him, perched on top of a fifteen-hand bay with beautiful manners. Now that they were moving, her spirits had lifted and her optimism returned.

'Up you get, then.'

As a country girl, she had been used to long rides, but her riding muscles were long out of practice. William, she suspected, had rarely been on a horse. He sat like a sack of potatoes, but his natural kindliness kept his hands light on the reins.

She'd borrowed a pair of Ian's trousers, to wear under her skirt so she could ride astride. God alone knew what the natives would think of that.

'Bring him back to me,' Hannah said.

'We wi—' she began to say, but William cut her off.

'We'll do our very best, Hannah,' he said. 'Come on.'

They rode out of camp, the Palestinian boy meeting up with them on the other side. He scrambled on top of the mule and they set off at a steady walk, the best the mule could do.

'Sorry to interrupt back there,' William said. 'But it's better not to promise anything.'

They both knew that was wise; how many patients had they seen die, of infection or fever or sometimes simply shock? Anything might have happened to Linus since that note was written.

'I refuse to be pessimistic,' she declared. 'We're going to get him back, and he'll be fine.'

He smiled at her from under the slouch hat, a smile full of such tenderness that her heart squeezed in her chest. She hadn't expected him here, but now she knew she should have. He would never let her down. If she needed him, he would come.

She blinked away a couple of hot tears and smiled back.

CHAPTER 36

The track to Beersheba was still busy with wounded being evacuated and supplies being ferried to the occupying force.

They were forced off the road several times to let mule trains or field ambulances past, and then had to ride in choking dust for miles afterwards. The flies were a terrible annoyance. They cut switches from one of the only trees they passed, and flailed at the ones around the horses' eyes and their own faces, but it was a losing battle. She thought she would go mad at the sensation of them on her skin, and at the sweat which poured off her.

The Palestinian boy kept his hand over his mouth, but otherwise allowed the flies free rein. His attitude was certainly commonsense, but she just couldn't do it.

When it seemed that *surely* they must have gone more than seventeen miles, the boy turned the mule right off the track.

'Oy!' William called. 'Where are you going?' but he simply looked back at them and pointed to the west.

'Well,' Evelyn said. 'We'd better follow him. I suppose it was too much to hope that Linus would be in Beersheba itself.'

'The 4th Light would have found him before now if he had been,' William agreed.

The going off the track was, surprisingly, better than on the road.

Uneven ground, but mostly hard-packed. The boy led them down into a dry creek bed with high banks which had Evelyn remembering every tale of flash floods that she had ever heard. Did they have flash floods in this desert? An unexpected stab of homesickness pierced her. She wished there were gum trees surrounding them, and the blue Australian sky above.

The boy and mule disappeared around a bend in the creek and for a moment she was sharply conscious that she had no idea where she was. Her sense of direction was shocking at the best of times.

Thank God William was here.

She turned to smile at him, but the smile died. He was very pale, his face tightened against pain. Riding was better than walking, but perhaps not so much better. She let her horse drop back and they stopped together.

'Back home, on long rides bushmen ride with one leg up over the saddle,' she said. 'Like this.' She demonstrated pulling her right leg out of the saddle and bending it so that it sat across her, as though she was halfway through sitting cross-legged. 'One of them told me it takes the pressure off your spine.'

He tried it, literally pulling his leg up with his hand and dragging it across. She helped him settle it into position. A long sigh came out of him.

'That is a bit better. Thanks.'

She nodded, and they rode on.

He was so brave. He must have known what a toll this would take, but he'd never faltered.

Perhaps she had been too hard on him, before. If you lived with a deformity, as he did, it was no wonder if you were oversensitive about it. She should have explained that she didn't find him repulsive, that her comments, even in delirium, had been compassionate, not revolted. Her temper had gotten the better of her, and she had hurt him. And herself. How often had she wanted him, longed for him, since then?

He had been wrong to think he could make decisions on her behalf, but she had been wrong to undervalue the hurt her words must have caused him.

Although he had been quite right that a sexual relationship was too risky, they could have remained friends.

The thought was curiously unsatisfying.

•

Evelyn had handled his leg as though it were – normal. Not revolting at all.

Just being a nurse. That was all it was. Helping someone who needed it. But her eyes hadn't been professionally cool. They had been warm and understanding and . . . and they had held something more than friendship.

Had he misunderstood, that terrible night when she had almost died and then had sliced his hopes into shreds?

He had been wrong to make that decision for her – but had he also been entirely wrong about what she would have chosen? If he hadn't cut ties with her before *she* did so, perhaps she would never have made a farewell speech.

Had he condemned himself to more than a year of misery for nothing?

'You're a clever lad,' his father used to say to him, 'but you've got the commonsense of a day-old chick.'

He took a swig from his water bottle and brushed some flies away.

Worse than anything, had he misjudged her?

Ahead of him, she disappeared around a bend in the gully and he tried to urge the horse to go faster. It ignored him, as it had ignored him since he first mounted. He'd never ridden a horse before, only ponies at the fairground as a child. Knowing that you got a horse to go by using your heels, he'd always imagined himself atop a towering beast, going around in circles because he couldn't dig his right heel in. A ludicrous image, and one he'd never dared test.

At least this horse went straight, following its fellow, although at a pace it chose.

Around the bend, under the shade of a scrubby tree that clung to the bank, Evelyn had dismounted and was watering her horse by pouring from her canteen into her hat. He followed her example, biting back an oath at the pain as he hit the ground. He'd gone through worse than this. Much worse. It was only the heat and the flies which made it seem bad.

They ate standing up, sharing their bread and cheese with the boy, who stuffed it down hungrily and waited for more. Evelyn, of course, gave it to him. She was a sucker for kiddies. It made him sad that she'd never be a mother – but of course, on the other hand, she would save so many lives, even if she never created one.

'This area reminds me of home,' Evelyn said. 'Heat, flies, scrub. But it smells different.'

'Do you miss Taree?' Would she want to go back there, after she qualified?

'Not on your life!' she exclaimed. He kept a grin to himself. Working with soldiers for several years had introduced a lot of slang expressions into her speech. The Evelyn he had first known wouldn't have said that. It suited her.

'No?'

'A country town isn't the best place to blaze a trail,' she said. She smiled at him, waving a fly away with her damp hat. That smile was enough, tired as he was, to ignite desire. When they were on duty together, he'd tried not to look at her body. But here: the cotton summer uniform clung to her breasts and waist, flared out over the trousers she wore underneath, accentuating her hips. If the boy hadn't been watching them . . .

'Glad to hear it,' he said, not knowing quite what he was saying. She lifted an eyebrow at him, but let it go. It seemed she was still a bit shy with him, and that thought made him shy of her and of how he felt about her. Friends, that was the ticket. Just friends.

After they'd washed down the food with lukewarm water, the boy pointed ahead of them. Not far, perhaps?

William found a big flat stone to mount from, and didn't even try to look graceful as he hauled himself aboard by the saddle horn. He sneaked a look at Evelyn, expecting scorn or, at best, amusement at his clumsiness. Instead, he saw pride in her eyes, and that almost unmanned him.

They came up out of the creek bed into a narrow valley, so narrow that they could travel in shade along the western side. The sun was half down to the horizon; they had set off just before noon and it had been slow going.

There was some grass here, and he had to fight his horse who wanted to graze. The threat of being left behind by his fellows was of greater strength than William's wrists, and the bay took off after a few snatched mouthfuls, going in a back-breaking trot which sent shafts of pain up his leg at every stride. The few moments until they caught up with the others and the horse settled back into a walk were agony. He thanked God he was already so wet with perspiration that the sweat which had broken out on his forehead from the pain was unnoticeable.

The valley was long, and winding, and grew dustier and drier the further they went. Then they were out of it, and going across the dusty plain again.

Towards sunset, the boy headed down into a sudden gully to the left. By William's estimation, they had circled around Beersheba and were now to the north of it, north and a little east. If he had understood the tactical situation Major Chapman had explained to him, they were close to the Turkish lines. Possibly behind them.

It was no use to point this out to Evelyn; she wouldn't have cared.

The gully widened into another narrow valley. This one was short – at the end of it, they could just see a small village, a cluster of mudbrick houses. They looked deserted, although in the low hazy light of dusk it was hard to tell.

As they moved closer, William could see that many of them had been recently shelled; the shorn-away bricks were a brighter colour, unweathered. Artillery fire had wiped out this village. He wondered how many people had died here.

'*Emxi, emxi*,' the boy said, jumping off the mule and running towards the houses.

Come, come, that meant.

Caution returned with a vengeance. He wasn't going to let Evelyn go anywhere near that place.

Fortunately, she didn't seem to want to.

'We should wait here, for the headman or whoever to come out,' he said, dismounting.

'Yes,' she agreed, watering her horse, her skin covered in freckles which had appeared during their hours in the saddle, her bright hair uncovered. That worried him, a little, but she forestalled him, pulling her veil from her saddlebag, creased but intact, and settling it on her head with that flip and pull which was second nature to all nurses. She fumbled in her pocket for hairpins, secured it firmly, and pulled her skirts well down over her trousers, until only her boots could be seen.

'Now I'm respectable.' She smiled up at him.

'I love you.' What an idiot. What a time to pick. He was a fool.

But she smiled at him, a long slow smile that was all the reward he could have asked for. Her mouth opened to answer him and he was poised, almost on tiptoe, to hear her, when a voice cut between them.

'*Kan allah fi eawnik.*'

They turned. A man of about sixty stood there in skullcap and abaya. Thin and feverish looking.

William answered, in Arabic, 'Greetings to you and blessings on your family.'

Intense relief passed over the man's face and he began to talk quickly.

'Slowly, slowly!' William said in Arabic.

The man repeated himself, very slowly.

'The man is sick. We gave him water, but he is sick. Do you have the money?'

'Yes,' William said. 'Take us to the man.'

His Arabic had about reached its limit, and he knew he wasn't using the proper declension, but the headman understood, and gestured to them to follow.

CHAPTER 37

Evelyn tethered the horses and the mule, eyeing the boy with misgivings. But if they couldn't trust him not to steal their mounts, they were doomed, William thought.

He hoisted his doctor's bag and they walked, slowly, with him limping badly, through the rapidly dying light, to a house on the far side of the village. The place was devastated. Barely a single house was left whole. The harsh smell of cordite lingered. He hoped beyond hope that the village had been full of Turkish troops when it was shelled, but the odds were that it hadn't been. He had no illusions about how often civilians had been killed in this war.

The man led them to a doorway which had lost its door and had a brief length of cloth tied over it. He gestured them into the darkness beyond.

•

The room was lit only by a small oil lamp. William produced a flashlight from his bag and shone it at her feet so she could see where to walk. It reflected brightly off burnished tiles; this wasn't the hovel she had unconsciously expected. As the light flicked over the room, she saw rugs rolled up against the walls, and wall hangings in rich reds and browns. The furniture was a mixture of low Ottoman benches and European table and chairs. An affluent home, destroyed by war. She felt guilty that she had assumed these people to be savages, or at the best, poverty-stricken and desperate.

Which raised the question of why these apparently middle-class people were holding Linus for ransom.

A woman rose in the shadows beyond the torch's light. She was veiled, of course; a slight woman of modest bearing. She came to Evelyn and led her through to another room, where a bench bed was occupied by a sleeping man.

'Linus!'

She sprang forward and examined him, William beside her.

He was unconscious, feverish, his left leg placed outside the covers, bandaged to the knee. She began to tremble as she smelt the unmistakable gagging scent of gangrene.

'Let's have a look at him.' William's voice was flat, but there was a note of strain in it.

The woman put the oil lamp on a small table at the foot of the bed. As her eyes adjusted, Evelyn could see that they had taken the best care they could for Linus. He was clean, in clean sheets, and the bandage was a good attempt. There was water in a jug on the table. They had been trying to keep him alive. But if they'd brought him back when they first found him, that wound would not have gone bad.

If he died, it would be the fault of these people.

She and William set to work immediately, uncovering the wound and cleaning it with boiled water and disinfectant and sulphur powder. Linus was so deeply unconscious that he didn't stir. She checked him for a head injury, in case of concussion, but his head was fine. This was infection and fever.

It was bad. The foot had been crushed, and bones came through the skin in two places. Her eyes met William's, and he shook his head.

They would have to amputate.

But not here. In Beersheba, where there would be proper facilities.

'We'll have to tie him to the mule,' she said. 'How far is it to Beersheba?'

William asked the man, who stood in the doorway, silent. He shrugged and said a few words.

'Eight miles,' William reported. 'There's a track to follow, but he says we can't go at night. There are Turkish patrols.'

They both looked at Linus's foot. The red streaks of gangrene had begun to stretch evil fingers up past his ankle. If they got him to Beersheba tonight, he could keep his knee. Below-the-knee amputations were much easier on the patient and made a normal life afterwards simpler.

If they waited until tomorrow, and then took him through the heat of the day, which would stress him far more, then he might lose the knee too.

'We should go tonight,' she said.

'Yes.'

'But we'll have to rest the horses for a while. Curry them down, give them water and a feed,' she added.

She couldn't help but smile at his look of helplessness.

'I'll do it,' she said.

She headed for the door as William found a chair and set it near the bed. He picked up a glass of water, ready to feed it to Linus, but the man in the doorway put up a hand to stop her leaving. He didn't look at her, or touch her, but he was immovable.

William spoke to him and he answered, his voice betraying a dark satisfaction.

'He wants the money,' William said. 'They're going to use it to rebuild the village. He said, "Your army has destroyed us. Your money will rebuild us."'

'Fair enough.' Her emotions were topsy-turvy, fully angry and fully compassionate. She looked beyond the man to his wife, standing behind him, and offered the money to her, knowing that the man would take nothing from her hand. The woman came forward and took it with dignity, bowing her head in thanks. Then they moved out of her way, and she left them behind without a thought as she ran to the horses.

The boy had already unsaddled them and given them water. She reached into her pocket and found a coin for him, which he tucked into his skullcap with a sidelong glance at her and a slight grin. Together, they wiped the animals down with some twisted grass, and checked their hooves and their mouths. She found another coin and mimed the horses eating. He vanished and came back with a meagre ration of millet and chaff in a basket. Good enough. The horses were happy with it.

She was so tired. She was aware of the fatigue, lurking underneath a febrile excitement which was pushing her forward, a tense poise between anxiety and hope.

If she slept, she wasn't sure she'd wake up early enough, so she went back to the house and found William still dripping water into Linus's mouth. He was swallowing, which was a good sign.

'You should rest,' she said.

'I'm sorry to be a burden.' He had turned the torch off and in the light from the lamp his eyes were shadowed and deep, hard to read, but his hands were tense on his thigh.

'Oh, don't be ridiculous!' she snapped, and then, appalled at herself, put a hand out to him in apology. 'I'm sorry. But you're not a burden. You're a source of never-ending strength.'

Perhaps her voice was raw with tiredness and truth. He took her hand and stood, pulling her into his arms. Both of his hands moved to frame her face, to hold her head firmly as he looked down on her.

'I –' he started, but she was tired of all the talking. She went up on tiptoe and kissed him.

This wasn't the place for a love scene. The kiss was hard and quick, but it said what she wanted to say.

She stood back, flat-footed, and nodded decisively. 'You need to *rest*,' she insisted.

His smile bloomed like a miracle. 'Yes, Sister,' he said in mock obedience.

There was another bench on the other side of the room. He lay down there and she went to work on his leg, massaging it as she had done before, back at Heliopolis. That seemed a lifetime ago.

After a few minutes, the muscles relaxed under her hands, and she stopped. William's eyes were closed, the faint trace of a smile in the corners of his mouth. He really was handsome, when his face was without pain.

It was such a shame that he should be marred by polio. Without it, he would have grown up straight and strong, gloriously.

But then, perhaps his gentleness, his compassion, his understanding of those in pain might never have developed.

He'd been shaped by his disease and its consequences as surely as he had been shaped by his quick intellect, and she couldn't quite imagine him differently. Wouldn't *want* a William without that tacit sympathy and kindness.

Whatever it was she felt for him, love or passion or something else, something more complicated, rose up and almost choked her.

Was this what her mother had felt for her father? Almost the last words her mother had spoken to her, before she died, were, 'I loved him so much when we married.'

She thought about that, as she went back to spooning water into Linus's mouth.

Her mother had been only eighteen when she had married. It hadn't occurred to her before, but there was a large age gap between her parents; her father had been thirty-two. No wonder he thought Dr Chapman was a good match for her! What could an eighteen-year-old know about a man in his thirties? Her mother might have loved her father, but she couldn't possibly have understood him.

She hadn't realised that she had blamed her mother for marrying her father until she forgave her for it. And he? No. She couldn't forgive him for all the petty meanness he had shown to her; nor for the delight he took in controlling her life.

No forgiveness for him.

She sat for a moment, quietly, feeling a new sense of peace about her parents. Thinking about them as merely people clarified her feelings, and let the restless, worrisome resentment fade. She could condemn her father without caring what he thought of that. Maybe this was what growing up felt like.

•

At three o'clock by her watch, she went outside to saddle the horses and load up the mule, then reluctantly woke William.

He was groggy, but could put weight on his leg, which was better than she had hoped. The man and his wife appeared and helped them; they carried Linus on a rug and the man produced a litter which they strapped to the mule. William paid him extra for it, and for the water they gave to Evelyn. They covered Linus with a blanket they had brought in the mule's saddlebags and gave him morphine before they set off.

The man looked a little ashamed to take the money, but the woman spoke urgently to him and he nodded.

Ordinary people, Evelyn thought. Ordinary people pushed by war to do things they would never have done otherwise. She couldn't even be angry with them; they were just trying to survive.

Was Linus's leg a price worth paying for the survival of a whole village?

She didn't know how to begin to answer that.

CHAPTER 38

William could tell that the horses didn't like going off into the dark. Even his steady bay was nervous, scenting who knew what in the shadows. But they settled down after a while, which was just as well since he couldn't have controlled the animal in any case.

The track was clear, because here there were fields either side. They had passed into an area which got some rain, obviously. Olive groves lined the track, leaves whispering in the breeze, and paddocks with goats, pale blobs in the distance, one of which came capering up to see what was passing, and got kicked by the mule for its trouble.

Riding at night was much easier than by day. The sky was clear and a just-past-full moon was lowering in the western sky. It cast long shadows behind them and across the track, but it was bright enough to travel safely.

He and Evelyn hadn't spoken since they left the village — not a word about kisses or massages or anything else. Better that way. Of course it was. Because damned if he knew what to say.

Even if he'd been wrong about her before, everything he'd said about them not having an ongoing physical relationship still held true. It was madness to try it.

He was feeling rather like a lunatic, though.

•

His hip was burning as though it might spontaneously combust. So much pain. Well. He'd felt it as bad, before. During the Gallipoli campaign, when he was operating twenty hours a day, there had been times he'd wanted to cut the whole flaming leg off. There were ways to deal with it. Methodically, he turned his attention away from himself and out towards the world. Paid attention to Linus, who was uncomfortably strapped on the litter, his leg padded as best they could but no doubt hurting more than his own whenever he drifted into consciousness.

To Evelyn, up ahead, leading the mule, still straight in the saddle despite her weariness. Brave and wonderful.

To the scents of the night; the whispering of olive leaves, shivering under the wind; the cold night air beginning to frost the ground; an owl, somewhere, calling forlornly. In front of them, the olive groves were giving way to open, rocky ground. And in the distance, he heard something else. The jingling of harnesses, and the faint sound of hooves.

'Evelyn!' he said, speaking low. She turned: he signalled her to move off the track into the shadow of the last few trees.

She obeyed unquestioningly. They huddled the horses together in the darkness, trying to be as silent as they could. Evelyn dismounted. He didn't know why. But as the hoofbeats came closer, both horses raised their heads and opened their mouths as if to whinny. Evelyn pinched their nostrils shut, one hand on each, straining on tiptoe to reach them both as they shook their heads in protest.

Voices in the darkness – speaking something not English nor Arabic. Turkish.

They passed by, slowly – a company of twenty or so men on tired horses. The mule was grazing, uninterested, but the horses fretted against Evelyn's hold. His bay swung around and hit against Linus's leg. Linus cried out in protest, raising his head and looking around.

The men stopped and then, swift hoofbeats in their direction.

Two men, barely silhouettes against the sky, discovered them.

'Damn,' Evelyn said, and mounted her horse. Free of her hands, both horses neighed and the Turkish horses answered them. He checked on Linus, calming him. For a moment, Linus seemed to come to himself, and looked at him with comprehension.

'In a pickle?' he whispered.

'We'll come through, old man, don't you worry.'

One of the men gave an order to them. No doubt something like, 'Come out of there!'

Slowly, they emerged. The Turkish soldiers were holding rifles at the ready. At Evelyn's appearance, they broke into astonished speech. When they saw him, they came to alertness and pointed the rifles at his midsection. He found himself surprisingly calm. Either they would shoot them or they would be taken to a prison camp – either way, there was nothing he could do about it, and presumably at the camp there would be somewhere he could tend to Linus.

But loaded rifles were a bloody good distraction from pain. The men scowled at him. He realised that he was not in a uniform. Which meant that they could shoot him out of hand, as a spy, and be well within their rights.

In Arabic, he said, 'I am a doctor,' and again in English. 'A doctor.' He pointed to Evelyn. 'My nurse.' Praying she would forgive him, he added in Arabic, 'My wife.' He rode up beside Evelyn and took the mule's leading rein from her so he could turn the mule and show these men Linus strapped to the litter. 'This man is wounded.' He thanked God that he had learned all the simple Arabic words related to medicine first. Those he was sure of. Now they just had to pray that someone here spoke Arabic. Or maybe French?

'Linnet, can you say that I'm a doctor in French, that you're a nurse?'

She shot him a quick look and complied. He had no idea what she said, but there was an officer with the troop, a Turkish captain. He came closer, and raised his voice.

'*Un médecin?*' he asked.

'*Oui,*' Evelyn said. '*Un médecin et une infirmière. Avec un patient.*'

'*Bon. Venez. Voici un autre patient.*'

'Another patient, he says,' Evelyn reported. The men dismounted and took hold of their bridles, leading their horses over to the Turkish troop.

There was a man lashed to a horse. His shoulder was a mass of bandages, dark with blood. The moon was almost down now, and the light was bad. William pulled his torch out of his saddlebag and shone it on the man. The blood was flowing still. Bad.

'Right!' he said, swinging down and ignoring the nasty jolt it gave his leg. 'Get him down. Put something on the ground to lay him on.' He gestured as he spoke and they clearly understood that, if not his words.

Evelyn murmured translations as she helped him lay the man on a blanket hastily spread on the road. He gave his torch to the officer and mimed holding it so they could see. Evelyn handed him a pair of gloves from his bag and they both gloved up. No time for better precautions. They knelt beside the patient, his hip protesting with sharp jabs of pain. But he was used to ignoring that when he was working. Evelyn cut off the matted bandage.

The man had taken a rifle ball to the shoulder. He felt a surge of relief. No tiny bits of shrapnel to contend with, just a bullet to be dug out and some sewing. But he'd lost a lot of blood, and there was no guarantee that he would live.

'Tell them that he's very bad,' he murmured to Evelyn. 'That he might not live, no matter what we do.'

She relayed the message, and the only answer was the officer taking out his sidearm and cocking it. Wonderful. His stomach muscles tightened and he felt fear spike through him, making his hands shake. They would kill him first and then – a woman in the middle of a crowd of angry soldiers . . . he had best make sure this man lived, for Linnet's sake.

They worked together under the weak torchlight as they always had, with a wordless understanding based on Evelyn's sharp intelligence. When an artery started to spurt as the bandage came off, she was there, one hand pinching it closed, the other handing him suture and needle.

It was the strangest operation he could imagine, under the night sky, surrounded by a troop of horses and enemies, but working with her was still a pleasure, swift and sure. They did what they could: stopped the bleeding, dug the bullet out, knitted together the muscle over the bone, closed him up. William had no idea if he would live, but he wouldn't die just then. Not right away, which was what mattered. And then he felt ashamed of himself. It mattered anyway.

He stood up, stripping off his gloves, and staggered as the blood rushed back into his leg. Evelyn was there, steadying him.

For a moment they were close together, her scent, of sweat and balsam, bathing him, and then he found his feet and bit back the pain.

'Tell him that the man will live if they can get him back to their doctors.'

She repeated it in French.

'*Bon*,' the officer said. He gestured to Linus, and gave a couple of orders. The men undid the straps and swapped Linus's body for their comrade's, not ungently. But Linus groaned and twitched with pain.

The officer said something directly to him, not looking at Evelyn. She translated. 'I will let you live because you have saved my man.'

Then the troop wheeled and rode off, crossing the track and heading south, the mule at the back on a leading rein, the wounded man bouncing in his litter. In Linus's litter. Dragged by their mule.

Evelyn let loose with a string of swearwords he was surprised she even knew. Despite himself, he began to laugh.

'Oh, you!' she said. That temper of hers was up, but she could see the funny side of it. Or, at least, the relief from not being shot out of hand. She flicked him on the shoulder with the back of one hand as she went past to check on Linus.

There was only one way to get Linus to Beersheba. Evelyn had to ride ahead, because he couldn't control his horse well enough to get them moving; but his horse was happy to follow hers.

So he had to carry Linus. No matter how much it hurt. He prepared a syringe of morphine and kept it in his pocket in a tin which had held safety pins.

It took some doing, getting Linus up into his arms on the horse, with Linus sitting on him like a child on his nanny's lap; thank God the animal was steady and fairly tired, or they'd never have managed it. They padded around Linus's leg but every movement was going to cause him pain. After the first few steps, where Linus jerked and groaned with each movement, William gave him the morphine. It was hard on the heels of the last, but needs must.

Then they went on, as the sky lightened with the rose and gold of a desert sunrise.

The dawn wind began soon after the silver glaring sun hit their backs. At least they were travelling south-west; but the wind threw dust and debris into their faces. He was hard put to make sure Linus's mouth and nose were kept clear, and to get him to swallow any water. His condition had deteriorated while they saved the Turkish man. His fever was higher, and he was less responsive, barely realising that William was there. Even with the morphine, every step the horse took made him flinch. William sympathised. His leg and hip were one long bar of red-hot metal. It took all his strength not to moan at every movement, as Linus was doing.

Surely they'd come more than eight miles?

They were moving through the last of the rocky pastures. Up ahead, the land flattened out into the desolation of war: trenches, sandbags, abandoned wagons, barbed-wire coils.

342

Deserted, except for a couple of black rats which scurried down a long piece of timber into the safety of a trench when they saw the horses.

And up ahead, a half-mile or so away, was the town of Beersheba. It was small and, from this distance, looked more like a European town than he had expected, with steep tiled roofs shining in the early light.

The going between here and there was too rough to take Linus on. He looked around for an alternative – a track, perhaps.

'You stay here,' Evelyn said. 'Take shelter.' She pointed to the last tree standing in the field – a scrubby olive. 'I'll ride ahead and get help.'

It was sensible. Faster. So he nodded, although it made his stomach cramp to think of her riding off into who knew what danger. Their own forces had held Beersheba when they had started out, but the fortunes of war could change swiftly.

'If you see any sign that the town isn't in our hands . . .'

'I'll ride the other way immediately,' she promised, smiling at him.

'Be careful.'

She put on a long-suffering look. 'Yes, Mum.' But her eyes were warm, and she touched his hand before she left, guiding her horse in beside him with such skill that she seemed more like a goddess than a girl. Or an Amazon; some wild and efficient beauty out of legend.

Clicking her tongue at the horse, she moved off smartly, faster than they had been going. The horse, too, knew its business. It moved across the battlefield with purpose, as if it had finally worked out what was going on.

He moved into the shade of the tree and concentrated on getting Linus to swallow sip after sip of water.

CHAPTER 39

There were no dead bodies left on the field, thank the Lord. Evelyn skirted dugouts and barbed wire, and her horse surprised her by being more than ready to jump over trenches. What he'd been trained for, of course. A straight line to Beersheba was only a half-mile. And then . . . What if they were too late? That delay on the road to treat the Turk had been longer than she'd realised. Most of a night gone. They had had to rest the horses, but what if they'd left it too late? If the gangrene had spread too far, Linus wouldn't only lose his leg. He'd be as dead as if they'd never come in search of him.

Her heart seemed to clench tight at the thought, and not only for herself, or him. Linus was her friend and she'd be sad at his death, but it would hurt so many of the people she cared about.

Hannah, Rebecca, Harry, William. Back at 75 CCS, she had thought that, if Harry died, she would be completely alone, but that wasn't true. Her friends were as dear to her as family. And her comrades – Connie Keys, Lil Mackenzie, Alice Ross-King, Annie Sanderson . . . all of them would stand by her, as she would stand by them.

Mateship, she thought. That's what men mean by mateship.

The obverse was that if Linus died, many people would mourn. She must do everything she could to stop that.

'Gee up,' she said, tightening her knees, and the horse increased its pace over the rough, broken ground.

•

The town itself wasn't exactly walled, but the houses were so close together that their walls effectively barred her from entering. She followed them around until she came to a road, which had guards posted. A corporal and a couple of privates, looking sleepy at this tail-end of their shift. They straightened up fast enough as she rounded the corner, though.

The privates barred the entrance while the corporal came forward. She leant down and pulled off her hat. No Turk ever had hair this fiery.

'Corporal! We have Lieutenant Yates! He's been wounded. We need to get an ambulance out to him.' She pointed back behind her. 'I'm Sister Northey. Dr Brent is with him.'

'Laughing Linus?' the corporal said in shock. 'He's alive?' He turned to the men behind him. 'Right, you, Hunter, you run and alert the commander. 'Keddie, you have the gate. I'll take you to headquarters, Sister.'

He set off at a run and she guided the bay to follow him. There was a great relief in handing over responsibility for even a part of the rescue. The private ran ahead of them; he set a good pace, faster than the bay was capable of now. Well, the commander would be ready when she arrived, then.

Headquarters was a building beside the mosque, built of a kind of rounded brick which reminded her of cobblestones. As they approached, a small stream of local men was emerging from the mosque after dawn prayers, and they stood and watched – until they realised she was a woman, when they averted their eyes.

She couldn't raise the energy to put her veil back on. They'd just have to deal with it.

The corporal took her bridle and she almost fell off the Waler. She patted his neck. 'You're a grand old boy,' she said. 'Thanks.' The horse turned his head and nuzzled her cheek, and she almost wept, tiredness bringing emotion too close to the surface. The corporal called for a trooper to look after him, and she let him go.

Getting up the stairs was almost more than she could do, but the corporal was at her elbow.

'Thank you –'

'Gleeson, sister. Corporal Harold Gleeson.'

'Thank you, Gleeson.'

His arm was strong under hers, and they reached the top of the tall flight of stairs without her falling down.

The commander and she reached the front door at the same time, from different directions. He was still pulling on his uniform jacket, with its heavy epaulettes full of braid.

A brigadier general. A tall, lean man with a salt-and-pepper moustache and kind, intelligent eyes.

'Sister Northey?' he asked, holding out his hand to shake hers. 'I'm William Grant.'

She thought immediately of her William, and that made her voice sharper than she had wanted.

'General Grant, we have Linus Yates. He's with Dr Brent a half-mile or so away, across the battlefield. Can we get an ambulance to him?' She hesitated. 'He's in a bad way.'

He considered her for a moment, his eyes assessing. 'Best to ask no questions about how you got him, eh? Your colleague filled me in.'

'Yes,' she said, a little shakily. 'Best not.' Her fatigue was catching up with her. 'My colleague?'

'Gleeson,' he said, not answering her. 'Go and fetch Sister Page. And get that mule wagon hitched.'

Hannah was here. She was flooded with thankfulness. She forced herself to pay attention to General Grant.

'No ambulances working, I'm afraid. All of them commandeered to advance with the line of battle. I'm only here briefly myself, to make sure the wells are secured. We'll send a wagon out. Are you up to going with it?'

'Yes. No. I mean, yes I'm up to it, but there's no time. He's directly east of here, on a track towards a village, I don't know what it's called. No more than a mile. I have to get an operating theatre ready. Do you have somewhere we can use?'

'The doctors set up a clinic following the battle here. They've gone, but the facilities should be there.' His sharp gaze cut through the fog of her tiredness. 'An operation?'

'Gangrene. He'll lose at least part of his leg.'

Grant winced. 'Damn. Sorry, ma'am. But he's a dashed fine young man.'

'At least he's alive.'

'He's *alive*?' Hannah's voice, coming from behind Grant. They were still standing in the doorway. Grant moved aside and she flung herself at Evelyn, both of them holding tight to each other.

'Alive,' Evelyn confirmed. 'But his leg is bad. We'll have to operate.'

Hannah was pale and drawn, her normal healthy colour gone, but she was in full uniform, complete with red cape. She swallowed. She knew what that word 'bad' meant, as well as Evelyn did.

'I'm going to him,' Hannah said.

'Yes. There's a wagon. William is with him.'

'The wagon will go to the eastern gate, Sister Page,' Grant said.

Hannah drew a deep breath and went down the steps without another word, running as soon as she got onto flat ground.

'I think you need to rest,' Grant said.

'No time for that,' Evelyn answered. 'A few minutes might make all the difference to Linus.'

'That bad?'

She nodded. Grant harrumphed, and called into the office behind the door, 'Doherty!' A sergeant came out. 'Take Sister Northey to the clinic.'

'Yessir.'

'Thank you, General.'

'Thank *you*, Sister. It stuck in my craw, leaving Yates to the natives. But it was the only way to keep our other men safe.'

She could acknowledge the truth of that, so she nodded, then followed the sergeant down the steps and up a street leading north.

The clinic, if it could be called that, was a doctor's surgery on a side street. The 4th Light Horse had left the examination couch when they pulled out, but that was about all. But the important thing was that the place had a generator, and they could get good light onto the couch, which they could pull into the middle of the room and use as an operating table.

She got the sergeant to set a couple of privates to scrubbing the place with Lysol, and to get dixies heated for boiling water, then, at his insistence, sat down and had a cup of tea and some bread and cheese, while she thought through what they would need.

'Sergeant.'

'Yes, Sister?' She took a deep breath. There was no way to say this nicely.

'Dr Brent has a good selection of instruments in his medical bag, but we're going to need one more. A bone saw.'

He bit his lip and was silent for a moment, then nodded. 'I'll find one. Does it matter, er . . .'

'If it's been used by a butcher? No. As long as you get it here quickly, so I can sterilise it before Lieutenant Yates arrives.'

'Right you are, Sister.'

He went out at a smart clip, and she sat and drank her tea, trying not to think about bone saws or amputations or anything except that Linus was alive; and that she would see William soon, and make sure he was all right.

She'd never seen courage like his. Pain had a particular effect on a patient's face; and William's face had been eloquent of the pain he was experiencing. But not a word of complaint, not a moan or groan, not even a scowl. Smiling and kind and valiant through it all. She had admired him before this escapade, but now . . . it broke her heart that he should suffer so. It made her love him even more.

•

The noises outside stirred her from an almost-doze. They had found a proper stretcher for Linus, and two men carried him in and set him down on the operating couch, Hannah sticking close by, holding his hand, William limping along behind. His face was white. The smell of gangrene was worse; in the small room it turned her stomach, but she controlled it, as she had so many times before.

Linus was awake. Easier for anaesthetic but harder in other ways . . .

William looked terrible – almost worse than Linus. Linus's eyes focused on her and he said, 'Tell them there's another way, Evelyn.' She stood on the other side from Hannah and took his free hand.

'I'm sorry, Linus. You know, if we could . . .'

'I'd rather be dead than lose a leg!' he said. Tears of exhaustion and panic flooded his eyes and fell, washing tracks in the dust on his face. 'That's no life to have. Better to kill me now.'

Hannah slapped his face.

The sound was a thunderclap. All of them stood astonished, frozen in a kind of fear.

Hannah leant close to Linus. 'Don't you *dare*,' she hissed. 'Don't you bloody *dare* give up. You have this operation and you live and you come back to me and don't you even *think* of doing anything else.'

He stared up at her, dazed, the imprint of her hand red on his face. He nodded, a little, and she stood back and let go of his hand.

'I'll do the anaesthetic,' she announced, and went to the scullery next to the room.

'I'll try,' Linus whispered. 'But I . . .' He turned his head aside to hide the tears.

'I'll do my best for you, mate,' William said. 'But that leg has to go. Or you will be dead, and what would Hannah say then?'

A small smile trembled on Linus's lips. He nodded and let his head flop back and to the side, giving in. Evelyn hoped beyond hope that he wasn't just giving up.

Evelyn went into the scullery, where Hannah was scrubbing up, her sleeves rolled back to her upper arms.

'It will be all right,' Evelyn said. 'We've seen this before. Once it's done, they come to terms with it.'

Hannah said nothing, her face set and determined. She had so much courage. Evelyn didn't know if she'd be able to help like this, if it were William on the table. On the thought, he came in and stripped off his coat.

They scrubbed up, and began.

CHAPTER 40

They managed to save the knee. That was the main thing, always, in these cases. If the knee and enough bone beneath it to fit a tin leg could be saved, the patient's life would be far less affected. Mobility increased, morbidity decreased.

One good thing.

Hannah's plan was to stay with Linus until he was well enough to travel, and then take him back to the 14th General.

'I have to get back,' Evelyn said in distress. She hated leaving Hannah here all alone. But her leave for this exploit, while indeterminate, had clearly been intended to be as short as possible. There were other Linuses at Gaza, waiting for help.

'Of course you do!' Hannah came away from Linus's bed, where he was sleeping the sleep of exhaustion, and walked out with her. 'I'm so grateful –' Her voice broke, and Evelyn hugged her.

'Nonsense! You'd do the same for me. Besides, how could I ever look Rebecca in the eye if I'd let him down? Listen, can you send a telegram to her? She must be going crazy with worry. She's in Italy, in Brindisi, but if you telegraph her paper in London, the *Evening News*, they'll let her know, I'm sure. I'll write as soon as I get a chance.'

Hannah made a face. 'I'll sign it from you. Linus hasn't told his family about me yet.'

'Why not?'

'Because he's a terrible letter writer, that's why!' Hannah laughed.

She laughed too, a kind of release after all the tension. They embraced and then Hannah went back to Linus, leaving her on the verandah of the clinic, where they had billeted him in an empty bedroom.

William came out from the main room, brushing his coat off. His limp was noticeable, but much better than it had been the night before.

'Ready?' he asked.

'I have to get back to my unit,' she said.

'Yes, of course. I'm coming with you.'

She looked at him sharply, and he smiled. 'Do you think they'd like another doctor at your CCS?'

It was as though everything in her melted with a combination of relief and affection.

'Oh, William!' she said, trying to cover it up with levity. 'Give up your cushy berth in Cairo?'

His lips twitched, and that smile lit his eyes; the special William smile, full of hilarity.

'I don't know what I'm thinking, giving up lancing boils and salving bedsores,' he said. 'It's such a challenging job for a surgeon!'

She took his arm and pressed it, trying to say without words what his company would mean to her. He put his hand over hers. They hadn't talked about his declaration of love; perhaps they never would. But their loyalty and – yes, devotion – were real and strong, and would see them through this war.

'Let's go then,' she said lightly.

•

Brigadier General Grant had told them 75 CCS was near Gaza. They caught a ride in a supply truck over a bumpy road which had been destroyed by cavalry and artillery wagons. Crushed into the front with the driver, there was no opportunity to talk, but William could feel Evelyn's body next to his. He was too exhausted, still, to become aroused by it, but it gave him a great sense of warmth, as though he were home at last.

His leg hurt like the devil. He suspected he'd done some permanent damage, but it would take a few weeks to tell. After the localised swelling and bruising had gone down, it might be better.

If he'd been his own patient, he'd have advised himself to go back to Cairo and rest – perhaps take up his standing invitation to the de Walden hospital. Margherita and Kitty had gone to France, following their husbands, but the hospital was still there, and always open to him. It was the most sensible course.

But that would mean skipping out on Evelyn.

His hand was on his leg, little finger resting against her thigh. As she realised he was looking at her, she turned her head and smiled at him, and let her own hand slide down until her hand touched his, fingers side by side.

Not too exhausted, apparently. He put his hat over his lap.

•

At the CCS, Captain Malouf came out to meet the truck, paperwork in hand. He was momentarily astonished at the sight of them, but recovered quickly enough.

'Sister Northey! About time you were back.' He hesitated and moved closer, lowered his voice. 'I hope your mission was successful?'

Evelyn smiled at him, a full blooming smile which lit up her whole face. 'Yes,' she said. 'We got him back and he's alive.'

Malouf smiled too. The first time William had ever seen him honestly pleased. 'That's very good. Well done.' He turned to William. 'Dr Brent. Thank you for escorting Sister Northey.'

The tone was one of dismissal. He knew from Evelyn's briefing that Malouf wasn't in charge here. 'I'd like to see Major Chapman,' he said.

The smile disappeared. 'If you wish.'

Malouf ignored them after that, talking to the driver about the goods to be unloaded. William and Evelyn walked to the major's tent, but he wasn't there.

'In theatre,' his batman informed them. He nodded to Evelyn. 'He'll be glad you're back. None of the others satisfy him.'

Evelyn's pace picked up as they walked to the big theatre tent. He had some trouble keeping up, but bedamned if he'd ask her to slow down. She was concerned – the camp was full of the familiar bustle which accompanied wounded pouring into a hospital. Well, that was all to the good; he'd be more welcome if they were busy.

Evelyn stopped at the entrance to the theatre and asked the orderly waiting outside with a stretcher, 'How long?'

'Just a clean and patch,' he said. 'Should be any time now.'

They waited with him in the shade of an awning which stretched out from the main tent, until a man in operating white, cap on his head and a mask dangling around his neck, came out. Tall, good-looking, a few years older than he was, with the look of a strong man about him, William disliked him on sight for the way he greeted his Linnet.

'Evelyn!' he said. 'Thank God.' He made a move as if to hug her but then remembered either his sterile gown or the public nature of the space. 'It went well.'

She gave that smile again, and Dr Chapman blinked as it hit him.

'Yes. We got him. An amputation on the leg, but he'll be fine.'

Chapman nodded at him. 'Lucky for him you went then, Brent.'

'Very lucky,' Evelyn said. Unconsciously, she put her hand on William's arm, as she had done while talking to the Arab boy. Looking Chapman straight in the eye, he put his hand over hers and saw from Chapman's change of expression that the gesture had been understood.

'William's a fine surgeon,' she said. 'And we're lucky – he's decided to help us.'

Dr Chapman shook his head. 'Oh, no. I'm afraid we can't have any but Army medicos here. Regulations.'

'They found a way around regulations in Cairo,' William said.

'No doubt. And no doubt you did fine work there. But this is an Army base, not a hospital in a city. I'm afraid I can't possibly allow it.'

His eyes were hard. Would Chapman have answered the same way if Evelyn hadn't touched his arm? William wondered.

'I understand,' he said. 'I understand perfectly.'

Chapman's eyes flickered with suppressed anger. 'And frankly . . .' He looked William up and down, lingering on how he favoured his right leg, even standing still. 'I doubt you could stand the pace.'

It flicked him on the raw, as Chapman had intended, but before he could form a reply, Evelyn, astonishingly, was laughing.

'Oh, Ian! You think it's bad here? You have no idea what it was like during the Dardanelles campaign. We went days without sleep.' She tightened her hold on his arm. 'William operated for twenty hours straight for two weeks in a row.' Her eyes were ironic, holding a challenge he could almost feel. 'Don't you worry about William being up to *any* task.'

Chapman flushed, anger showing more clearly. 'Then I'm doubly sorry to have to refuse him. But this Station is for Army personnel only.' He turned to William. 'You can get a lift to the railhead – there are ambulances going out soon.'

'Thank you,' William said. He marvelled at how manners worked – there they were, the three of them, having had a nasty little battle where (thanks to Evelyn) William had won the moral victory, but had been repulsed by Chapman's greater firepower. And all without a blow being landed. Civilisation was a wonderful thing.

'I'll walk you to the ambulance,' Evelyn said.

Chapman nodded and disappeared back into the theatre tent.

Wounded were being transferred from ward tent to ambulance further down the road. They walked there slowly. Evelyn must be as exhausted as he was, but she didn't show it. Her pace was measured, but not dragging.

'I'm sorry,' she said.

'Don't be. I should have expected that regulations would be tighter on the front line.'

There was so much he wanted to say. To thank her for standing up for him. To thank her for being – Evelyn.

They came to a row of ambulances and a driver agreed to take him to the railhead at Imara.

'Two shakes of a lamb's tail, Doc,' he said.

He turned to say goodbye and saw, over her shoulder, Chapman standing in the entrance to the theatre, watching them.

'Can I kiss you?' he asked quietly.

'He's watching, is he?' she asked, a smile breaking out and a chuckle following it. He flushed.

'Well, yes. But I'd want to even if he wasn't.'

Still laughing, she moved into his arms, lifting her face for his kiss so naturally that for a moment he was still, just looking at her.

'I meant what I said.'

She put her hand over his heart. 'I know. We can have that discussion another time. Just kiss me goodbye.'

He slid his hand up into her hair and closed his hand around a fistful of it, pulling her head back as their mouths met.

Faintly, he could hear the ambulance drivers whistling and clapping and shouting. Part of him felt great satisfaction at the noise. Yes. Let them all see that she belonged to him, as much as she could ever belong to anyone.

He put all his longing and love into the kiss and received back everything he gave.

Reluctantly, he pulled back.

'You,' he said, giving her a very small shake, 'you look after yourself.'

'That's *my* line.' Her face was solemn. 'I'd be very upset if anything happened to you.'

Were there tears in her eyes? Even the thought of that unmanned him. He kissed her forehead gently. 'I'll be careful,' he said.

'Sorry, Doc, but we're off,' the ambulance driver said.

She let him go without a word, but she was still standing there when he craned to look back. Just standing there watching him leave.

He could feel his heart being wrenched out of his chest so it could fly back and stay with her.

CHAPTER 41

She was sick and tired of saying goodbye to William Brent.

Evelyn watched the ambulance drive away, and allowed herself, just for that little stretch of time, to imagine a world where she never said goodbye to him again.

That was what drove the need to marry, she realised: the simple desire to be near each other all the time. To never be separated.

She let herself picture it. She and William, in Edinburgh or London or Sydney, working together as medicos, coming home together to the same house, eating and laughing and living together, and then, hand in hand, retiring to the bedroom . . .

Oh, it was so tempting!

She could trust William. Of course she could. It wasn't about trust, not anymore. It was about self-determination. To make her own decisions. To have the *right* to make her own decisions. William had proven already that he would decide on her behalf if he felt it was better that way. How could she be sure that he wouldn't do so in the future? If he felt she was being wrong-headed or putting herself in danger by her choices . . .

Perhaps it was about trust, after all.

The feeling in the camp was that the battle of Beersheba was a turning point in this theatre of war. Next would be Gaza, and then the Turks would be rolled up and there would be no more young men carted in from the desert to have their limbs sawn off.

And then, what? She would be transferred, probably to France. Perhaps sent back to Australia with a hospital ship again. France was closer to Edinburgh.

She would go to Scotland and find a way to study. She didn't have enough money yet, even if Linus's family repaid her the £100, which she was sure they would. She would have to work in Britain, maybe live in the nurses' quarters of some large hospital. Save up enough to enrol.

With a jolt, she realised her twenty-seventh birthday had come and gone without her noticing. Three more years. She could survive three more years. Two, maybe. Yes, two. She would have enough for one year at Edinburgh by the time she was twenty-nine.

Two more years, and then university.

The thought didn't bring her the excitement it ought. It all sounded so . . . so *dreary*. Even learning to be a doctor felt daunting, when she had to do it alone.

She raised her chin and turned away. William's ambulance had disappeared. Let him go. Turn to the future. She parroted the bromides to herself, but all she could feel was a leaden weight in her gut. She would find her enthusiasm again sometime, but right now she just wanted to be with him, wrapped in his arms again.

•

Telegrams must have been flying between Egypt, Australia and Italy, because she received a letter from Rebecca Quinn, from Italy, in late December, expressing her thanks. There were tear marks on the paper. She curled up on her bunk to read it.

Of course I can't say enough, Rebecca wrote, *and nothing I could ever say or do could repay our debt to you. My mother wants to adopt you, so if you ever need anything – ANYTHING – we are at your disposal.*

Jack and I are essentially separated – he's gone off to Albania and who knows where to follow a story. You were right. He doesn't support my career in the way I had thought, and what we shall do after the war I don't know. If he stays in Europe I may go back to Australia, or vice versa. I'd still like to work in London. So it's goodbye to a happy marriage and to children, as I couldn't imagine having a baby with him now.

I wish you were here – I have so much to tell you which shouldn't go in a letter.

Sitting in the winter sunshine outside her tent at 75 CCS, now at Enab, she imagined Rebecca, in Brindisi, struggling to be a war correspondent all alone. It made her sad to have been right. She'd hoped so much for Rebecca's continued happiness; and if Rebecca, who was as shrewd and experienced as a city girl could be, couldn't spot a fake, why should she think she could?

But when she thought about William and Jack, there was no comparison. William was head and shoulders above him.

She wrote back immediately. *I wish we could talk too. I would welcome your advice.*

As for Linus — forget it. He's my friend as well as your brother — and about to become the husband of another good friend. Linus is our linchpin, the one who ties us all together — how could we let him go? He will be fine. So don't worry about him, or about anyone. Just look after yourself.

'Sister Northey!' That was Bradley's voice, her main orderly.

'Yes, Bradley?'

'Couple of ambulances coming in, Sister.'

'I'll be right there.'

On with the sensible shoes, the veil, the apron. Would she wear something pretty ever again? For a moment, her thoughts went to William. He had never seen her in anything other than her uniform.

That night in his room before she returned to Australia seemed a very long time ago.

Two years this February, since that impossibly wonderful night.

'How many casualties, Bradley?' she asked as she ducked out of her tent and settled her veil.

'Looks like a half-dozen, miss. But not too bad. They're mostly walking.'

An easy day, then.

•

One of them *was* bad, a fever case, and she connived to be the one in the ambulance with him, all the way to Imara, making sure he didn't dehydrate on the way. It was the first chance she'd had to go back to Imara since Beersheba — the ambulances had been going to another railhead since the camp had moved, but the road to that railhead had been shelled, and Imara was back on the roster. Finally, she had a chance to thank Ali and his family.

She saw her patient on the train and off to Alexandria, safely in the competent hands of an orderly who had as much experience as she did.

She turned from the tracks as the train picked up speed. Imara. She'd expected the village to fold up once the 75 had moved, but no, the ragtag collection of tents had grown, and some rammed-earth houses had gone up in just the few months since she was last here.

The ambulance driver had gone off to find food and drink. She should do the same. She always carried her purse with her, now that she was living in a tent which could be rifled by any passer-by. But it was more important to find her benefactor.

A scuffle in an alleyway drew her attention and a parcel of kiddies scrambled out.

'Miss! Miss!' It was Ali, followed, as usual, by his partners in crime.

She felt so happy to see him it startled her.

'Ali!' she said, smiling.

'Any chocolate, Miss?' Ali asked hopefully.

'No,' she said. 'But let's see what we can do. Where are your parents?'

'My father's fighting,' he said, shrugging. 'My mother –' He pointed to a small tent which had its sides up, exposing a small area of rugs laid over the sand. A woman was working inside, weaving a carpet.

Evelyn went to see her. She stopped outside the tent, in accordance with etiquette, and waited for the woman to acknowledge her. After a moment or two, the woman brought her needle to rest and looked up. She looked very much like Ali. She said something in Arabic.

'Hello,' Evelyn said. She looked at Ali. 'Tell your mother you were very helpful to me, and that because of you my friend lived when he would have died.'

'He lived? That is good,' Ali said, his face glowing. He spoke rapidly to his mother, who nodded. She didn't smile, but her face relaxed a little.

'My friend's family is also very grateful,' Evelyn said, making it up as she went along. She was sure Linus would back her up. 'They wish to give Ali a reward.' Ali translated as she spoke, his eyes widening.

The mother's face tightened. 'Not charity,' Evelyn said quickly. 'Other people who helped have also been rewarded. It is a thank-you only.'

Indecision was plain on the woman's face.

'Ali is a bright boy,' Evelyn prompted. 'My friend's family would like to pay for his schooling.'

The mother blinked, and then smiled.

'No!' Ali said. 'No, Miss! I don't *want* to go to school.'

His mother said something in a definite tone, and then reached to her side, where she poured a glass of something which smelt of lemons, and invited Evelyn to sit with a wave of her hands.

Evelyn sank down cross-legged and almost laughed at the expression of betrayal that Ali turned on her.

•

It soothed her, somewhat, to organise Ali's future. The soldier father had relatives in Abbassia, the mother said, who Ali could stay with. It took a ridiculously small sum to pay for the three years' schooling and board with them, barely as much as a month in Edinburgh would cost. Evelyn took the address of the school and promised to send the money to them directly, and gave the rest of the money to Ali's mother, plus a little more to pay for proper clothes for him.

All through the transaction, the woman had kept an air of aloofness, a reserve which indicated that she was allowing Evelyn to do all this from a sense of obligation. But her eyes gleamed with satisfaction when she looked at Ali, and when Evelyn rose to go, after many courtesies, the mother opened a small wooden box and took out something which she pressed into Evelyn's hands.

It was a woven ribbon with a blue bead at the end; she had seen similar ornaments worn by the Egyptian servants at the hospitals; a goodluck charm, she thought.

'Thank you,' Evelyn said. She could use some good luck.

Rising as she did, Ali's mother bowed deeply from the waist, saying something as she rose. Evelyn bowed back, slightly lower as she was younger than the woman.

'That's just a traditional way of saying goodbye,' Ali said, embarrassed.

'Tell me.'

'She said, "May all your children be sons."'

Evelyn smiled at him. 'She must be proud of her own son, then.'

For the only time in their acquaintance, Ali was lost for words.

'I s'pose I should thank you,' he said eventually. 'But –'

'You'll thank me when you're older,' she said. 'Trust me. Education is everything.'

•

On the drive back, she reflected that at least she had done something positive in this war. Something other than patching up the effects of battle. And then she thought that Ali and his family had probably been displaced by battle, and perhaps this was just another kind of patching up.

But still, it made her feel better, to have repaid her debt to him. Without him, Linus would have died.

JANUARY 1918

Another year. Evelyn carefully poured just enough water into the bowl and began to soap her stockings. They were patched and darned, but they'd have to last until the ones she'd asked Hannah to buy for her got here. If they didn't get 'lost', like the last lot had.

Another year of war. It was hard to realise. Three years and five months since it all started. And still the bodies rolled in.

Ian Chapman said they were happy with the way things were going in the Sinai and Palestine.

Better than everything, Jerusalem was in British hands, at low cost (they said low, not having had to stitch those boys up or cut off their arms or feet). It was only a matter of time, they said, before the Ottoman Empire would sue for peace.

And then what? Ordered to France, to the front there? For how long? Although the entry of the Americans into the war last year had helped, it hadn't been the decisive rout everyone had hoped. The Germans had dug in and resisted, at a terrible cost in casualties, and not all from combat. She had been guiltily glad, lately, that she was here. Dust, heat, wind, they were all better than the horrors of a French winter in the trenches, where men's feet literally rotted away, or fell off with frostbite.

Linus had written thanking her and assuring her that his family would reimburse the £100 she had expended on his behalf; but even with that she had only enough for one year at Edinburgh.

The stockings were as clean as she could make them, although they'd never lose that slight yellow tinge from the desert dust. She wrung them out and laid them aside; wash her smalls first, then rinse all of them out in one meagre bowl's worth.

She felt a lot older than twenty-seven. The desire to be a doctor sat at the back of her mind, like an old book she'd once loved, but it took too much energy to take that book down from the shelf and look at it closely.

After the war.

CHAPTER 42

'Please talk to him,' Hannah begged. William looked down at his hands and sighed.

'All right.'

He went to the large room off the verandah where the surgical cases were.

Hannah was right, of course. William accepted that he was the only one who could talk to Linus. He just wished he knew if he was there as a doctor or a friend.

Was it cowardice to fall back on being the doctor?

The surgery ward was a depressing place at best, but they'd had a new lot of casualties in the day before, and the long room was full of moans and fevered ranting. At least no one was calling for their mother; that happened at night, mostly.

Linus had had a very slow recovery, complete with all the complications: fever turning to a chest infection which had made him so weak he'd not been able to get out of bed, which had meant bedsores and dizziness and muscle wastage. Only in the last week had he been well enough to start rehabilitation.

William found a wheelchair and approached Linus's bed with the fake cheer of the professional.

'Up you get,' he said. Linus glared at him. Gaunt and still pale, his hair longer than any soldier's should be, he was barely able to sit up. The more he moved around, though, the better the prognosis for the amputation site. 'Got to get the blood moving.'

Linus swore at him. 'I'm not getting in that bloody thing. Sheer off, will you?'

'Doctor's orders. I'm taking you out into the sunshine – well, not the actual sun, but the verandah.'

Linus looked away, but a shrug of his shoulder was assent. William knew that need to look away. He'd seen it in so many men. After injury and the affront to the spirit that an amputation caused – or even a severe fever – men found themselves, for the first time since childhood, fighting back tears at the slightest upset. Sometimes he thought that was why they so often felt ashamed of being wounded, as though the emotional aftermath was proof they hadn't been manly enough.

A nurse came up and helped him hoist Linus into the chair. He was far too light for a man of his height, and his mouth compressed as he shifted, the long lines from nose to mouth deepening with the characteristic tension of pain.

William thanked the nurse and pushed the chair sedately through the lines of beds to the big double doors. Beyond, the deep shade of the verandah threw the glare of the quadrangle into sharp relief, like something out of a rather unforgiving dream. It smelt better than it had in the past. He could remember when the quad had been covered by marquees full of injured men, and the scent of blood and disinfectant. Those marquees, the doctors, the nurses, the orderlies, were all in France now. He shuddered, thinking of winter in France. It had irked him, staying in Egypt, but the reports from France had proved to him that he had made the right decision. He wasn't strong enough – his *leg* wasn't strong enough – to stand up to the rigours of field hospital work in the French mud. He could be useful here, even if it made him feel like a slacker.

Linus had covered his eyes with one hand. Too bright? Or hiding something else?

No need to hurry.

After a while, Linus sighed and sat back in his chair.

'So, are you here as my doctor or my mate?'

William twitched, to hear his own question thrown back at him.

'Whichever you'd prefer,' he said.

'Doctor, then. What are my prospects?' Linus was keeping his voice harsh. Manly. Unemotional. Fair enough. A good cobber went along with that kind of thing.

'Oh, you'll be fine,' he said. Heartily, as a doctor should. 'You've gone past the point we worry about.' Linus looked a question at him, and he smiled grimly. 'Renewal of the gangrene. No sign of it – or, rather, no smell of it.'

They both grimaced. No one who'd ever smelt that forgot it.

'So . . .' Linus prompted him. William had nothing to offer him except the truth.

'So, the stump will heal. You'll get back your strength. We'll put you on crutches, first. Once the skin is fully restored, you'll get an artificial limb.'

Linus flinched.

'Don't be like that,' William said gently. 'There's nothing to stop you having a full and normal life. No reason,' he hesitated, but he'd promised Hannah, 'no reason you can't get married and have a family.'

Linus turned his head, his blue eyes burning with contempt and anger.

'Really? Because I'll be just as good as new, eh?'

'For all intents and purposes . . .'

'How can I offer Hannah this – this travesty of a man? How could I ask her to – to *touch* me?'

'Hannah loves you. And you love her.'

'All the more reason to set her free instead of tying her to a cripple!'

That hit too close to home, and pulled an answering anger from him.

'You're a lawyer, aren't you? These days, with the work the Desoutter brothers are doing with metal legs, you'll just look like you have a slight limp. You'll halt a little. Less than I do, in fact.'

'Oh, well, that's all right then. Because you live *such* a normal, full life!'

They glared at each other.

'I do just fine.'

'*I* should marry Hannah and get on with my life, but you won't ask Evelyn. The two of you go around head over ears in love but no, you won't ask her to marry you. Why? Because you don't think you're good enough – and you've got *two* bloody legs, so don't come lecturing to me about getting on with things and having a family!'

William found himself on his feet without having decided to get up. He couldn't just walk away. He shouldn't.

'That's different,' he said.

'Oh, really?' Linus's tone was bitter. Only the truth would erase that bitterness.

'Firstly, Evelyn doesn't want to get married.'

'Hah! All girls want to get married.'

'She doesn't. She wants to be a doctor.'

Linus blinked, taken aback. William sat down again, slowly. His leg hurt from the previous sudden movement. He'd pay for that later.

'And secondly, our cases aren't the same. *You'll* get better. Every day, you'll get stronger. I won't. Many poliomyelitis cases relapse – in later life, I may well have muscle weakness, fevers, even paralysis. I can't tie Evelyn to a life like that.'

Linus rubbed his hands along the arms of the chair, as if he'd like to push himself to his feet. Then, noticing, he slapped his palms down.

'That's bullshit, and you know it!'

'It's true! I might well get to a point where I can't provide for my family.'

'Well, if she's a doctor, *she* can provide.'

'Live off my wife's money?' He was revolted by the very thought, and Linus tilted his head to show he understood.

'You're missing the point,' Linus said quietly. 'If there's one thing I've learned over the past three years, it's that *today* is what matters. Not tomorrow, not ten years or twenty years into the future. How long will you be the way you are now?'

William shrugged, the tension in his shoulders making the movement awkward. 'No one knows. I could start going downhill next week.' It was so easy to imagine, being helpless again, as he had been as a child. Not able to do a single thing for himself.

'Or never?'

'That's possible.'

'Statistically likely?' Linus was being provoking, but he was, strictly speaking, right.

'We don't really know the statistics of it. The current thinking is that about half . . .'

'*Half*? You've got a one-in-two chance of staying perfectly fine?'

'If you think *this* is perfectly fine!' William retorted, and realised his mistake immediately.

'But William,' Linus said with purring satisfaction, 'there's nothing to stop you having a full and normal life. No reason you can't get married and have a family. If I can do it, so can you.'

The number of times he'd given that speech . . . and never once had he thought how it applied to him. Never once considered that he was being a hypocrite. But he was. If he believed what he told the men – and he *did* . . . Some tight, dark stone in his gut dissolved. Linus was right. To live for now was the only sensible thing. He might get run down in the street by a camel tomorrow. Still . . .

'You've forgotten something,' he said gently. 'Reason number one. Evelyn doesn't *want* to get married. She has her reasons – and the most important is that a husband would be able to control her dowry and stop her from studying if he wanted to.'

'You wouldn't do that,' Linus objected.

William tilted his head back and looked up at the vaulted ceiling of the verandah.

'No,' he said. 'But you can't blame her for wanting independence. Would you marry Hannah if she immediately got possession of everything you owned and could force you to do what she wanted?'

Those pale hands plucked at the blanket the nurse had put over his knees. 'I've never thought about it like that.' The lawyer in him woke up. 'But surely with the right marriage settlements she could ensure her independence . . .'

'Not the way her mother's will is set up.'

'Ah.' And then, not looking at him, 'Damn shame, old man.'

'Yes,' William said. He looked down at his own hands and remembered how it felt to touch Linnet. Then he recalled why he was here. 'But don't let's get distracted. This is about you and Hannah, my lad.'

Linus flung up a hand in the fencer's salute. 'I cry Uncle!' he said. 'I'll . . . I'll think about it.'

That should be good enough for Hannah, but William himself, he realised, was equally concerned. 'Don't let the bastards take the life you should have led as well as your leg,' he said quietly.

'Play up and play the game?' Linus's glance was mocking, but then he shrugged. 'Perhaps you're right.'

They sat in silence until the sun began to wester, and then William wheeled him back to his narrow bed.

MARCH 1918

'It's going to be quiet in here, when this lot go,' Hannah said, signing the last lot of paperwork.

William nodded, and signed where he was supposed to. Releases to the hospital ship. The last one was for Linus. Hannah's hand trembled a little as she handed it to him.

Once this batch of patients had left, they were closing two of the wards; the war in the East was focused in Palestine now, and patients from there were being shipped straight to Britain for convalescence, cutting down their workload significantly.

Matron Creal came along and observed for a moment.

'I've had a request for a nurse to go on the hospital ship,' she said airily, watching Hannah out of the corner of her eye. 'I don't suppose you'd like to volunteer, Sister Page?'

Hannah actually squealed with happiness and launched herself at the matron, hugging her mightily and then letting go in a hurry. 'Oh, Matron! Oh, I'm sorry, but –'

'Yes, yes, I know,' Matron said, slightly breathless as she adjusted her veil. 'I take it you accept the transfer.'

'Yes, please, Matron!'

'Thank you, Matron!' Linus called out from the other end of the ward. 'You're a trooper!'

She smiled at both of them. 'I expect an invitation to the wedding,' she said severely, 'even if I can't come.'

'Not a trooper,' Linus said, from his wheelchair. 'An *angel*!'

All the men in the ward applauded.

Matron's face was definitely pink as she left. William leant against the wall and laughed helplessly. Recovering, he went to sit by Linus.

'You are definitely the jammiest sod I've ever known,' he said. Linus leant back and linked his hands behind his head, looking the best he had since being found.

'I am, I am at that, my lad.' But there was a trace of tears at the back of his eyes. William could only guess the relief and joy he must have felt at having Hannah go home with him.

'I want an invitation to the wedding, too, even if *I* can't come,' he said.

'You shall have one, old chap!'

The next morning, as he accompanied them to Alexandria and saw them onto the ship, along with the other patients and a bevy of nurses from the NZGH, it felt very much like the end of an era.

Perhaps he should leave for Edinburgh now, and start in the new academic year, in September. But he couldn't bring himself to leave while Evelyn was still in the Sinai. Ridiculous. Completely barmy.

But there it was. He just couldn't.

JUNE 1918

They were moving to Jerusalem, to a permanent base – ceasing to be 75 CCS and becoming 32nd Combined Clearing Hospital.

Jerusalem!

But apparently not all the nurses were needed – the combined strength was greater than requirements.

Ian Chapman spoke to her seriously, after the meeting where it had all been announced.

'If I were you, I'd get myself to England. This war will end in a matter of months, and if you're there you can get demobbed and enrol in the next intake at university straightaway.'

It was good advice. There were hospital ships leaving from Jerusalem – with Ian's help, she could get on one. And there was no need to worry that Harry might need her – the serious fighting was over and he'd come through strong as ever.

Yet . . . William was still in Cairo.

Could she leave without seeing him?

'I might take some leave,' she said. 'Visit my friends in Cairo and go from there.'

His face darkened. 'Brent, I suppose. I don't know why you're wasting your time on him, Evelyn. He's not fit to tie your shoelace.'

She stared him down until he flushed and dropped his eyes.

'They're not giving leave,' he mumbled, 'but I'll organise for you to accompany some of the wounded back to the 14th General.' He left the tent without looking directly at her.

'Thank you,' she said to the empty air.

She began to pack her things that night. Pitifully few; she should have shopped more when she was at the 14th, but she'd paid no attention to anything but her uniform. Apart from that, she had very little. One day-dress left. A pair of laddered silk stockings. A single jewellery box, with her mother's pearl brooch in it. She hadn't worn it since the day of her twenty-first birthday, feeling it had been tainted by her father's betrayal. But now, she touched it gently. Her mother had worn it often. There were three pearls, the centre one larger than the others. Perhaps she would have it reset, to a pair of earrings and a pendant. To represent a new life, without rejecting the good parts of the old.

CHAPTER 43

But it was weeks before she got on the train – since she wasn't going to Jerusalem, she had been landed with the logistics of sorting out all the pack-up and movement of not only the 75, but the remaining materials at Junction Station and Enab, which was complicated by an outbreak of malaria – the mosquitoes had been shocking after the spring rains.

The men were bad enough to keep them in situ; there was little Cairo could have done for them that they couldn't do there. She and a few of the other nurses who were extra-strength worked day and night to bring down the fevers. It was as though the war was on a loop, like those comedy films you sometimes saw before the war, where someone went through the same actions over and over and over again.

How many malaria cases had she nursed over the past four years?

They saved most of them, so she couldn't say the time hadn't been well spent; but she struggled to find any satisfaction in that.

Finally, she was on the train, still ministering to the men, making sure they drank enough, handing them the bottles to piss in when they needed it, feeding them gruel and beef tea.

She was tired, that was all. Nothing more than weariness. Nothing to do with facing a future of more drudgery until she could save enough to go to Edinburgh.

At least she would see William again.

•

She had telegraphed from Imara, and expected to see him on the platform at Cairo, but he was there at Alexandria, springing into the carriage and clasping her hands in his.

Tears ran down her cheeks. It was a wonderful surprise, but it undid her. It was so *good* to see him.

'Oh, Linnet!' he said, and folded her in his arms, to weak applause and laughter from the patients.

The train jolted into movement, sending them both rocking on their feet.

He steadied her and smiled. 'Well, how are our patients?'

For the next hour, it was like old times in the best possible way: she and William working together.

At Cairo, the familiar line of ambulances was waiting, including George and Hartley. They greeted her exuberantly. There was a general feeling of hope; as though the certainty of the war ending was creeping into people's eyes and making them shine brighter.

It wasn't *certain*, of course – but it was so much more *likely* than it had been a year ago. The end, perhaps, was in sight.

She went through the familiar process of handing over patients and settling them into their wards at the 14th. Strange to do it without Hannah.

William worked steadily by her side, and when the last of the men had been handed over, dragged her off to Matron.

'You can order some leave for Sister Northey, can't you, Matron?' he asked. 'Look at her. She's skin and bones.'

Matron Creal studied both of them, and frowned.

'I wish I could, Doctor, but Sister Northey is due to leave on a hospital ship bound for Australia the day after tomorrow. I can give her until then. That's all.'

His hand clutched hers in a fierce grip.

'I see. Thank you,' she managed.

•

Two nights and a day.

She had her duffel, mostly full of books she hadn't opened in weeks. All her other possessions had fallen away over the years, until she was stripped back to nothing but medicine.

They stood outside the 14th and William cleared his throat.

'Uh . . . Major Bagly has a house, down on the river . . . he said I could take some leave there.'

Evelyn knew what he was asking. It was like a repeat of the last time she had left for Australia; but this time, they had opportunity, and they were both older and perhaps less respectable. She knew she was going to grab at the chance to spend two nights and a day with him.

'Yes,' she said.

They caught a cab, sitting in silence together, their hands lying side by side on the seat, just touching. Swinging by the NZGH, William ran inside to pick up some clothes, and then they were off, through the flat-roofed suburbs of Cairo. It was late afternoon, sunset; the calls of the muezzins echoed across the city, and life slowed, as it always did, until there were only children and foreigners on the streets.

In two days, she would be on the ship to Australia, and probably would never see these streets again.

'What's the matter, Linnet? Are you regretting coming?'

'Oh, no! But I am disappointed.' She turned away from him to look out the window. The late summer day was fading, the swift night on its way. 'I'd hoped to get a ship to England from here, and be on the spot to be demobbed as soon as possible. Now who knows when I'll get there? Not that I have enough money to bridge the gap until I get my inheritance – but at least I'd be *there*. Ready.'

'Yes,' he said. He understood, and she was grateful for it. 'I've organised a residency with a plastic surgeon to study reconstructive surgery. In Edinburgh. It's not a paying position – the opposite. I have to pay him. But it's the best possible experience if I want to help some of these poor blighters who've had their faces and bodies torn apart.'

'That's wonderful! I'm so pleased for you. It's such important work.'

'That's what I feel.' The taxi slowed as it turned into a gravel driveway. 'It's one thing to save a fellow's life. It's another to give him back to himself so he can *live* that life.'

She took his hand and squeezed it. 'The most important work you could be doing.' She smiled with meaning. 'And perhaps we might see each other in Edinburgh.'

He squeezed her hand back in response, and suddenly they were no longer able to talk.

The dusk came down, a band of gold still at the horizon, and when they got out of the cab in front of a colonial-style house, all verandahs and columns, the evening air was soft and warm on her skin.

She took a breath of it and let it out.

'Come,' William said.

A servant let them in, and William dismissed him from duty, saying they would look after themselves. The quick look the man gave her made her flush; but it was deserved, after all. Here she was, a loose woman, about to commit fornication.

The house was a place of cool shadows and the smell of cardamom. There were three bedrooms. William put Evelyn's bag down in the master bedroom, lit by the last of the twilight slanting through the shutters, and stood there looking at her. She went to him, swift-footed, and took his own bag out of his hand, letting it drop to the floor. His hand clasped hers and she was suddenly light-headed, all the desire she had been blocking for so long surging in.

The suspense was dreadful.

But more than passion, she wanted a bath. If she were going to join with a man for the first time, she *had* to get the desert dust out of her hair, and the soot from the train off her skin.

William cupped her face. Her heart beat loud and fast.

'Don't kiss me,' she said, a finger on his lips. 'If you kiss me, we'll end up on the bed, and I *have* to bathe first.'

Bless him, his face lit up with laughter.

'Well, that's put me in my place!' She elbowed him in the side and he laughed again. 'I wouldn't mind a bath myself!'

'Me first.'

He darted in to place a swift kiss on the corner of her mouth, and led the way to the bathroom – a proper English bathroom with a cast iron tub and running water, hot and cold. And towels, laid ready. The room was otherwise bare, with ugly grey tiles on the floor and the walls rough plaster.

'Luxury,' she said, and meant it.

'I'll leave you to it.' For a moment he lingered in the doorway, and she could read the desire in his eyes. It made her flush from the toes up; she swallowed with nerves and he smiled hesitantly at her. Was he nervous too? Was it possible he was as inexperienced as she was?

Given how morbidly sensitive he was about his leg . . . more than possible.

That made her feel better. She shut the door on him with a twinkling smile. 'I'll be out soon. Go and get us something to eat.'

'Yes ma'am!'

The bath was wonderful. Hot and deep and sinking into every pore. But she couldn't relax. Even clean hair couldn't distract her from the thought of William, waiting . . .

She wrapped herself in one big linen towel and dried her hair with another. Her comb was in her duffel, in the bedroom. Well, all her inhibitions had to go, including the need to have neat hair instead of this wild red mane.

When she came out, William was in the doorway of the bedroom, leaning on the doorjamb, long and lithe and far more handsome than she remembered. He was clean too – he'd clearly washed in the kitchen and dressed in loose flannel bags and a white cotton shirt. His damp hair was black in the lamplight which shone over his shoulder and cast shadows on his face. What was he thinking? All her nerves surged up again, along with desire. Oh, she wanted him! Wanted those surgeon's hands on her, long fingered and sensitive. Wanted his mouth on hers.

'Linnet,' he said, his voice rough. She lost all caution and went to him, and he pushed off the doorjamb to meet her, one hand going around her waist, the other cradling her head, tangling in her hair. 'I love you so.'

'Kiss me first, and then tell me,' she said.

He kissed her slowly, with mounting intensity, a kind of desperation building in both of them, pushing their bodies together, flesh and bone against flesh and bone, tight.

'I've missed you so,' he muttered into her hair.

She kissed him, and there was no more hesitation or doubt, just the two of them together again, at last, after so long.

He cleared his throat and reached for his bag to produce a package of French letters.

'I didn't want you to risk . . . it wasn't like I assumed . . .' he half-stammered. She grinned at him and rummaged in her own duffel to display a handful of condoms.

'I stole them from Matron's desk drawer.'

He laughed, relieved of feeling like a cad, no doubt. 'We're a good pair.'

'Yes,' she said, tossing the condoms on the night table. She slid her hand down his chest, feeling the strong muscles underneath his shirt. 'We are.'

She fumbled with his clothes, touching each patch of bare skin as it was revealed, kissing shoulders and arms and neck as he caressed her bare shoulders, licked the last drops of water from her skin.

A shadow passed over him as he slid his trousers off and half-turned from her, to hide his bad leg, but an answering shadow of impatience that called up in her was drowned by compassion, and by desire.

'It's a perfectly good leg,' she said, as she had said once before, deliberately echoing herself.

He caught the echo, because he smiled, at last, and reached for her. She let the towel fall.

•

It was nothing like she had imagined.

She had thought, when she thought about being with William, that it would be bodies and flesh and sweat. Pleasure. Perhaps, satisfaction. Carnal.

But this . . . she hadn't understood how good it would be to be able to hold him to her; how much it mattered to have him in her arms. It wasn't only desire that overwhelmed her. It was love.

It shook her with each touch of his hand. Shattered her composure, cracked right through any doubts she still had. Opened her chest until her heart was a living, beating thing, like a bird in his hand, defenceless.

When their bodies came together, it wasn't only flesh joining. There were no thoughts, only images, only sensations: the light reflecting on his hair, the smell of his hand as she turned her face into it to kiss his palm, the sound of his indrawn breath as she touched him, a long wave of astonishment and friction as they moved together, again, and again, as one body.

Love pierced her and shook her and made her someone she didn't recognise, someone desirous and vulnerable and shameless.

He paused, at one point, side by side, and said, 'You're all I can think about, night and day.'

How could she leave him? How could she live without him? Was medicine enough to give up a lifetime of this? Was marriage so terrible a thing after all?

Of course, he hadn't asked her.

'Kiss me again,' she said. She would stick to her guns, because no other path existed, and it was a good path. But she would have her fill of him first.

'Again,' she said.

•

At dawn the next day, Evelyn wandered out into the courtyard in the middle of the house, in a loose green kimono she had found hanging behind the bedroom door. William hastily pulled on flannel bags and followed her, his chest bare under his open white shirt. What a luxury this privacy was! He would have to buy Bagly a good bottle of Scotch as a thank-you.

There was a rectangular tiled pool in the centre of the courtyard, covered with water lilies just opening in the morning light. He sat on its edge, simply watching her. Committing her to memory. Her grace, her serenity, her *aliveness*. It seemed impossible to him that she had been in his bed only moments before, no matter how vivid the memories were. In that kimono she looked like a creature out of legend.

She bent and pulled up a water lily, holding it cupped in her hands. Her hair fell around her in waves. The flower seemed to cast a light up on her face, rendering it even more beautiful.

'You look like a Rossetti stunner,' he said, his throat tight with something deeper than desire.

A shadow went over her face. 'I don't know what that means,' she said. He cursed himself for being tactless – she was so intelligent he forgot, sometimes, that she had been forced to leave school so young, that she had been immured in the country for years without access to anything other than a lending library.

'Dante Gabriel Rossetti,' he said, standing and going to her. 'An English painter. He had a passion for red-headed women. A passion I fully understand.' He put his own hands under hers, smiling down into her eyes. Her face lit with quick laughter and she let the water lily fall as his arms came around her once more.

•

Two nights and a day weren't enough, Evelyn thought.

It was all they had.

Before they fell asleep on the second night, William caught her thinking about the future. He wrapped her hair around his hand and tugged gently to get her attention.

'A penny for your thoughts.'

'I was thinking about lawyers,' she said.

Surprised, he sat up.

'Lawyers?'

'Rebecca said her family would help me with *anything*.'

'I'm sure they would. Linus said as much to me, too.'

'Linus is a lawyer. His father is a businessman – he must have a solicitor. I'm pretty sure they would help me take my father to court to break the trust.'

'That,' he said, kissing her bare shoulder, 'is a wonderful idea.' He paused. 'But if he fights it . . .'

'Yes,' she sighed, turning into his arms. She'd thought of that, too. She didn't even know exactly how much she would inherit, since it had been accumulating interest all this while. Nor how much lawyers charged. 'I might use up all my inheritance fighting him, and it might take until I'm thirty anyway. But it's worth thinking about.'

'Not now,' he said, kissing her. 'Let's think about it later.'

She smiled, pushing him down onto the bed and leaning over him, her hair a golden-red tent around them. 'Much later. Sweet William.'

•

They had no sleep, but didn't care. Evelyn was due to report at 0600. William ordered a cab for 5.30. They travelled back to the 14th in silence, and without more than polite nothings he saw her through reporting, onto an ambulance with patients to be taken to the train and then to Alexandria to the ship.

He followed: cab, train, another cab. They hadn't discussed it; it was just assumed that he would say goodbye at the last possible moment.

In the train he had to sit in a different carriage; only Army personnel in the ambulance carriages, and the orderlies in charge, men he didn't know, weren't making any allowances for doctors.

At the docks he waited, hat in hand, in the shadow of an awning stretched from the night watchman's shack, while the patients were ferried aboard. He saw her once, twice, four times, going to and from the train. Finally, all the patients were loaded. The tide was turning; sailors were working at the hawsers which moored the ship to the dock. They moved to the gangplank and he went forward, wanting to protest, needing one more goodbye.

At the very last moment she came running down, straight into him.

They kissed, careless of observers. 'It might be a couple of years before I can get to Scotland,' she said, bright tears, hot tears, reddening her eyes.

'I'll be there,' he said. It was hard to get the words out. His throat felt like glass shards had been forced down it. 'I love you.' What else was there to say?

She drew back just a little, so that she could look him full in the eyes, and laid her hands on his chest. 'I love you,' she said. Finally. At long last. 'Here.' She pressed something into his hands. 'Until we meet again.'

He was ready at that moment to brave any possible future, even one where he was an invalid and she supported him. Anything, for just a few years of this – but it would be she who paid, so that was out. Take what he was given and be thankful for it.

A sailor yelled at them, 'All aboard who's going!'

She turned and ran full pelt for the gangplank, her blue uniform kicking up around her ankles. She raced to the top and on board the ship and then turned as they took away the gangplank and slid the balustrade across the gap. She didn't wave. Just stood there, staring at him, as he was staring at her as the gap between dock and ship widened inexorably, until the ship was no longer a thing which had anything to do with the land, but was steaming away, picking up speed, towards home.

He stood and watched until he couldn't tell if the black speck on the horizon was the ship or a bird, and then let his eyes fall to his hands. She had given him a ribbon, a woven ribbon with a blue bead on the end. A goodluck charm.

Until we meet again, she had said. Years, maybe, even after this war was over.

Years without her. He didn't think he could survive that. The image of a succession of cold, grey Edinburgh days flashed across his mind: too many days, and all of them empty, without her. Years before she could achieve her goal, and be the extraordinary doctor she was meant to be. There had to be another way.

A way where *she* made the decision about how her life would go. He wouldn't make that mistake again, of making any decision for her, no matter how his heart ached, how his body yearned for her, how he longed to simply sweep her up and carry her off from wherever fate took her.

He clenched his hand around the blue bead. He was a fool. He had let her simply sail away. The worst mistake of his life. But perhaps it could be mended.

CHAPTER 44

Evelyn had sent a telegram from Colombo, and Hannah collected her at the 4th Repat. After she had settled her patients and been given leave, Hannah was there to whisk her away to the Yates house, where she had been invited to stay.

'They've been lovely to me,' Hannah confided. 'My parents are very happy.' She twisted the sapphire ring on her finger and smiled.

'That's wonderful!' It was odd to see Hannah in civvies – and what civvies! A beautifully tailored suit, the hem halfway up her calves, and soft kid shoes with matching purse. The sort of clothes Evelyn would have worn, if she hadn't enlisted. She had always known, in a vague kind of way, that Hannah's people had money and she had only trained as a nurse out of a desire to be a good mother. But the uniform had wiped away any social differences between the nurses, and this was a reminder that the old social classes were there, waiting to be slipped back into, waiting to exert their old power. She wondered, though, if they would ever be as strong again.

She felt old and dusty and grimy, her uniform creased and faded. Only the bright red of her cape still held its strength, and gave strength to her.

'I'll have to go shopping tomorrow,' she said.

'This afternoon!' Hannah exclaimed. 'I know just the shops you need.'

'No. This afternoon I want to talk to Linus and Mr Yates. About the trust.'

Hannah smiled a deep, satisfied smile. 'Good. About time you got that father of yours off your back.'

Evelyn hoped it would be as easy as that sounded.

'When will you be demobbed?' Hannah asked.

'Pretty much straightaway, they said.' Excitement and worry flared in her at the thought. To be free of the Army also meant having to earn her own living for the first time in four years. Well, people always needed nurses.

The Yates's house was on Sydney Harbour, not far, she thought, from where Jack and Rebecca had lived. Oh, Lord. Was she supposed to know about their separation? Did the family know? Best to keep her mouth shut on that topic.

As the cab drew up to the pleasant but unremarkable front door, it opened to show Linus, on one crutch, hop out to greet them, followed by a tall blonde woman – Evelyn recognised the famous suffragist from newspaper photographs, and suddenly felt shy.

Next to her was a shorter, rotund man with greying hair. His father?

They came to her eagerly, both mother and father speaking at once, over the top of Linus's, 'Ahoy, Lynnie!'

'Miss Northey, how lovely –'

'Miss Northey, I'm so glad –'

'We were so eager to meet you –'

'We can never repay you –'

Linus's face was getting pinker by the minute. Evelyn shook hands all around and smiled at them.

'It's very nice to meet you,' she said quietly.

Her composure had its effect. They quietened and ushered her into the house, Mrs Yates taking her by the arm and leading her to a lovely bedroom – and there the unimpressive front entrance was explained. This house's glory was seaward: long terraces reaching down to a sandstone wall, the harbour waves white-capped beyond. Sloops and yachts and other smaller boats she couldn't name sped across the waves and there – yes, there was a ferry, churning through the rollers towards Manly. She sighed. For the first time, she felt as though she really had come home.

'It's lovely, isn't it?' Mrs Yates said. 'I never tire of it.'

'Lovely.' Evelyn laid her cape on the brocade bedspread. 'I went to school in Sydney, and nothing says "Australia" to me quite like the harbour.'

'Welcome home, my dear.'

In person, the famous crusader for women's rights was gentler and more queenly than Evelyn had expected. And genuinely, warmly welcoming.

It was ridiculous to have tears rise in her eyes. Ridiculous to have a sudden, deep longing for William. It would be years before they met again. Unless Mr Yates could help her.

Afternoon tea was served in a light-filled room which stretched the width of the house, with big French doors opened to the sea breeze.

Silver teapots and fine china. Scones with cream and jam. Victoria sponge. Evelyn remembered enamel mugs and cans of bully beef, eaten hurriedly in the sterilisation room between operations at Heliopolis Palace, and smiled. There would be more to adjust to in civilian life than she had thought.

After the small talk and chitchat that always accompanied the pouring and serving of tea, Mr Yates hitched his trouser legs up and leant forward.

'Now, you probably don't want to hear this, but let me say it. We're in your debt. We – we would have lost Linus without you. Anything we can do for you, any time, just ask.'

Polite manners should compel her to demur, to say, 'Not at all, think nothing of it.' She couldn't afford to be polite, however; not this time.

'Good,' she said. 'Because I do need a favour.'

Only Hannah didn't look surprised. The others recovered quickly, though.

'Name it,' Mrs Yates said with intensity. 'Just name it.'

Evelyn embarked on an explanation of her situation, revealing all the embarrassing details: removed from school, working for pin money, and that being taken away when she enlisted, the terms of the will. Everything. Mr Yates tut-tutted through it all, and Mrs Yates shook her head and murmured 'Shameful!' more than once.

'So what I was hoping, Mr Yates, was that we might be able to – break the trust? Is that what it's called?'

'No, no,' he said, shaking his head. 'Judges don't like to break trusts. We'll ask for a variation in the terms of the trust, that's all.'

'A variation?'

'Yes. You're how old now?'

'Nearly twenty-eight.' God, how had she got that old? An old maid.

'We'll just ask for a variation of the terms of the trust, so that it can be wound up now.'

'Isn't that the same as breaking it?'

He looked shocked. Linus laughed. 'No fear, Lynnie. A variation is a much easier option. Then the judge can pretend he didn't really change all that much.'

Hope spiralled up her chest. 'Then you think it can be done?'

Linus and his father exchanged glances, and Mr Yates nodded. 'I'm sure of it. Easier, though, to get your father to agree.'

'No chance of that, I'm afraid.'

'Hmmm. Linus can write a letter to show him. Scare the old bas—' He cast a look at his wife. 'Sorry, m'dear. Scare the old rascal. And if he doesn't scare . . .' He rubbed his hands together. 'We'll take him apart in court.'

'Good,' Mrs Yates said. 'This will be an excellent test case for women's rights. No judge is going to say an Anzac nurse can't make her own decisions.' *There* was the reformer, full of zeal, who had been camouflaged by the loving mother. It gave Evelyn a surge of satisfaction to see it.

'You won't bolt?' Mrs Yates went on. 'You'll go through with it? It might not be pretty. We may have to play rough with his reputation.'

Evelyn could feel her mouth settling into an uncompromising line. It wasn't a pleasant sensation, but she meant it.

'Serve him right,' she said.

'Splendid!' Mrs Yates threw up her hands in delight. 'Nothing I like more than taking an old bully like him down a peg or two. I have just the barrister in mind. *And* we'll make him pay the costs!' Which relieved her of another worry. She wouldn't have wanted Mr Yates to act for her purely out of friendship – but much better for her father to pay than for her to do so!

She sat back and drank the rest of her tea while the others began to discuss Hannah and Linus's upcoming wedding. The tea was delicious. Really delicious.

'And tomorrow,' Hannah said, 'we'll go shopping.'

'And find a good jeweller,' Evelyn said. 'I have a brooch I want reset.'

•

They said that when you went back home for the first time, it seemed smaller. But home looked the way it always had to William – perhaps it had always seemed small, compared to the big church on one corner and the massive convent school on the other. He stood at the gate and looked back across the park which occupied the third corner. Alfred Square had been a training ground during the war and showed none of the greenery he remembered. It would recover, like most of them.

The garden in front of the house was in full late spring bloom – the daffs were over, but the roses were coming on full strength, and the dahlias were standing up on their sticks like soldiers on parade.

How long would it be, he wondered as he climbed the wooden steps, before our images stop being warlike?

He put his duffel down and opened the screen door which was always unlatched, ten 'til six, every day except Sunday. It was Wednesday, one of his father's busy days because of the country race meetings, and a couple of men brushed past him as he entered, rushing out, late for work. It was all so familiar – the smell of books, the shining linoleum, the botanical watercolours on the walls, painted by his Aunty Susan.

For a moment, he waited. Letting the sight and smell of home envelop him. It hardly seemed real. His throat was raw and every breath was harsh and loud. He couldn't break down now. Better make a move.

He knew what he'd find in the next room: his parents behind the library counter, his mother doing something with books and his father making notes in the betting ledger. Just like every day of his youth. What if they weren't? What if the war had changed this as it had changed so many things? He didn't think he could bear it.

One step. Another. Now he could see through to the library in the front room. One more step to the doorway. Relief flooded through him. There they were, a little older but still the same. It was like a blessing.

'Cooee,' he said, as he'd said every afternoon when he came home from school.

Both heads snapped up, and his mother gave a wordless cry, her hand to her mouth. Then they surged around the end of the counter, and there was a welter of hugs and kisses and back slaps and more hugs and yes, a few tears because why not? Why not? He was home.

He brought his duffel inside and for the first time ever in business hours, his father closed and locked the front door.

'Let 'em wait, the bastards,' he said with satisfaction, one hand on William's shoulder, guiding him to the kitchen. 'The gee-gees'll still be there tomorrow.'

'I can't believe you didn't tell us you were coming!' His mother put the kettle on and pulled down the biscuit tin.

'Hope it's not Anzac biscuits in there,' William joked, and her face crumpled a little. He went as fast as he could and hugged her. 'It was only a joke, Mum. Anzacs'll be fine.'

She pulled herself away and gave herself a shake. 'Well, it's shortbread, you'll be pleased to know. I just. I just don't like imagining what you went through, that's all.'

'What *I* went through?' He laughed. 'I was in a cushy hospital job the whole time, miles away from the front line! I told you!'

They sat at the old kitchen table, so familiar under his hands. His father cleared his throat and looked embarrassed.

'We thought you might have gilded the lily a bit, for our sakes.'

For a moment, the horrors of the Gallipoli time flashed before him. He *had* gilded the lily during those months, more because he couldn't bear to write about it than because he was protecting them. Afterwards, he was glad he had.

'Not for the past couple of years,' he said. His father nodded as though he understood. Perhaps he did – he'd been in the Boer War.

His mother had taken hold of his hand, as though he were three years old again, and he didn't mind at all.

His parents exchanged a glance, and his mother nodded.

'About that dosh you sent home,' his father began.

William waved his free hand. 'Nothing to be said about that. No need to mention it. I'm just glad it came in handy.'

'Very handy.' His father's mouth pressed together in that way that meant he was holding back emotion. 'We, ah – we appreciated it.'

'We certainly did! Your father was breaking his back at that greengrocer's. It made all the difference.'

'Things all right now?' He held his breath. If they needed him, still, that would change everything. He couldn't let them down.

'Oh my word, yes! Once the news hit that the Armistice was coming, every man and his dog was back to their old tricks. The Sat'dee two-up is going like nobody's business. And the boys in khaki'll be coming home soon enough, and the races will be back on full strength. No, we're well suited, lad. No need to prop up the old folks anymore.' He slapped William on the shoulder; both their eyes were a little moist. William tried not to let his relief show.

'And now you're home,' his mother said happily. 'What are your plans? Where are you going to work?'

'I don't know.' The whole complex relationship with Evelyn was there, waiting to be explained. But where to start?

'What about that nice nurse, Sister Northey? Is she home too?'

He laughed. As if he could keep anything from his mother. Perhaps he'd written a bit too much about Evelyn.

'She's on her way to Taree, her friend Hannah said. She came home to – look, it's a long story . . .'

'Have a cuppa first then,' his father said. 'All that can wait.'

The kettle whistled, as if confirming that was a good idea, and they all got up to perform their accustomed tasks: his mother to make the tea, his father to get the cups, and he himself to lay out the biscuits on a plate. For a brief second, it was as though he were an actor performing a part in a play, but then he opened the tin and the smell of the shortbread hit him. Aunty Carol's shortbread, sure as he lived. Abruptly, he was himself again, fighting back tears. He put the biscuits on the plate with the yellow roses – his mother's favourite – and sat down.

'It *is* a long story,' he said, putting sugar in his tea. 'But I'd like you to know about it.'

He thanked God that he had parents he could talk to. Parents he could rely on. Poor Linnet, with her horrible father.

'So, it's like this . . .' he said.

•

It took two kettles' worth of tea before it was all told (or almost all; he left out Major Bagly's house).

'So, if I understand you right, you might be going to Edinburgh and you might not, depending on what this Evelyn girl decides?' his father said.

'Yes.'

His mother blinked a tear away and got up to clear the dishes. Automatically, the two men helped.

'I'm not sure what to hope for,' she said.

Guilt washed over him. It had been so hard for them, without him these past years, and before that even, when he'd lived in at Sydney Hospital. He'd been gone a long time.

'Grandchildren would be nice,' she said. 'But none of those red-headed Scottish girls from Edinburgh, thank you! I don't want that temper in the family.'

'Um . . .' he said. She looked at him, astonished, her own blue eyes wide.

'Don't tell me that Northey girl is . . .'

He shrugged. 'Carrot red. Titian red.'

'Oh my Lord!' She started to laugh, leaning against the sink. 'That would be typical of you, Will! You would choose yourself someone contrary! I'll bet she's stubborn!'

He couldn't say she was wrong.

CHAPTER 45

NOVEMBER 1918

'You wouldn't dare,' her father said. 'It would ruin your reputation.'

'No. It would ruin yours.' She stared him down. What had she been afraid of, for all those years? He was a caricature of a man, like someone out of Dickens, mean and grasping and petty. 'I've spent the last four years saving men's lives, Father, running wards and operating theatres in the worst of conditions, and doing it well. There isn't a judge alive who would declare me incapable of handling my own affairs.'

They were in his study, as they had been the last time they spoke. It was hotter, a November day so bright that it hurt the eyes to look at it, but in here it was shadowy, the shutters half-closed, the windows shut. She went to the window and opened it wide, pushing the shutter back with it.

'What are you doing that for?' her father grumbled, but in a desultory way. She ignored him.

'I want my money,' she said. Her bag was on the small table by the door. She took the letter Linus had written for her and handed it to him. 'If you don't comply, I *will* take you to court, and we'll see whose reputation suffers the most.'

'No judge will give you money so you can be a doctor.' He brushed the letter aside.

Evelyn laughed. 'Times have changed, Father. I have the woman who was in charge of hospital services for the entire Serbian theatre of war as a reference.' Dear Dr Bennett – when Evelyn had telegraphed her to ask for her support, she had immediately replied with her happiness to make a statutory declaration on Evelyn's behalf.

Her father looked shocked. 'A *woman* was in charge?'

'Captain Bennett,' she said. 'The first woman captain in the British Army. You're behind the times, Father.'

'There's a difference between keeping up with times and abandoning your principles! You'll have to take me to court!' he said viciously.

It was like a kick in the stomach, familiar from so many conversations with him. But this time she wouldn't back down. She slapped the letter down on his desk.

'You'll hear from my solicitors, then.'

He flinched away from her, clearly astonished that she would go through with it.

In the silence that followed, someone knocked on the front door. Her father looked relieved at the interruption. It wasn't surgery hours, but any country doctor was used to being called upon out of hours.

Their housekeeper showed him in.

'William!' Evelyn could feel her face flush bright red. A mixture of joy and astonishment, of embarrassment that William would see, now, how her father really was.

But she went to him because she couldn't not go. They clasped hands and he smiled slightly, just that warming of the mouth and eyes he used to do, back when they had pretended to themselves that they were just friends.

'What are you doing here?'

Her father said at the same moment, 'Who is this, Evelyn?'

'I came to bring you something.' He took an envelope out of his pocket and handed it to her, then went across the room to her father and held out his hand. 'William Brent,' he said. 'Dr William Brent.'

Her father unthawed a little, and shook hands. But he didn't ask William to sit down.

Evelyn looked away from him unwillingly and opened the envelope, which hadn't been stuck down. Inside was a bank cheque for £400 made out to her.

She looked up, not understanding, and found William staring at her with so much love that her breath caught in her throat.

'It's important that you enrol in the next intake,' he said. 'I can get your Latin up to speed on the ship to Scotland.'

'But – but your residency.' She couldn't take this money. It was ridiculous. It was so, so – so *lovely* of him. To give up his ambitions for her. To put his needs second. What other man would do the same?

He shrugged. 'I can take that up later.' He laughed. 'You can pay me back, if you want to, after you get your inheritance. But you really shouldn't have to wait two more years before you enrol. The world needs you as a doctor.'

'Are you offering to *pay for my daughter*?' Her father was spluttering with outrage. 'What do you think she is, some slut off the streets?'

'Be quiet, Father.' Evelyn went to William and laid her hands on his chest, as she had once before, when they said goodbye at Imara. 'And you? What will you do?'

'If it's all right with *you*, I'll get some job in a hospital in Edinburgh,' he said seriously. 'And we can be friends.'

Lightness invaded her, as though she were pumped full of some buoyancy gas. Not just the money. It was *her* decision. He understood at last. And his acceptance that they would, could, simply be friends if she wanted, that was the last thing she needed to dispel any doubts she had about the future. She touched the pearl pendant on her chest, for luck, and hoped her mother was watching.

'No,' she said, shaking him gently. She tucked his cheque back into his pocket. His face was full of disappointment and a little anger. 'No need for that.'

'I know you can take your father to court, but who knows how long that might take, or how much it will cost?' he began, but she put her finger across his lips.

'No. We don't need to take him to court to get the money. All we need to do is get married.'

'*What*!?' her father roared, but it was a background sound. William's eyes were locked on hers, and the tension had fallen away from his mouth, leaving his face open and vulnerable.

'Are you sure?' he asked.

'If you'll take the risk, I will,' she said.

'Seems to me that you're taking all the risk.' He touched her cheek, her hair, lightly, with love. 'What if I become a decrepit old man?'

'Well then, it'll be just as well I'm a professional woman who can support us both.'

Her father understood only a fraction of this. 'You're going to *live off my daughter's money*?' he yelled.

William turned to face him without flinching. 'I'm going to marry your daughter. And then the future will take care of itself.'

'I forbid you to marry a cripple!' her father said.

Evelyn simply ignored him. She tucked her hand in William's arm, that lightness and joy lifting her up even higher.

'Come on,' she said to William. 'I'll show you to the hotel. We should get married in Sydney, I think, so Linus and Hannah can come.'

'Good idea.'

They went lightly out the front door into the main street and walked down towards the centre of town, where there were a surprising number of people out and about for a Monday morning.

'You know what day it is?' William asked her. 'And what time?'

'Almost eleven,' she said, checking her watch. 'I've lost track of the days . . .' And then she realised. 'Oh, William, is it the eleventh?'

Answering her, the church bells in every church broke suddenly into peal, a joyous jubilation of sound. Around them, men threw their hats in the air and women hitched up their skirts and danced.

'The eleventh hour of the eleventh day of the eleventh month,' William said.

A newspaper boy yelled, 'Armistice! Armistice! War ends in Europe!' but he was drowned out by the cheering and yelling and bicycle bells ringing and car horns tooting.

'It's over,' Evelyn said breathlessly, not quite believing it.

'Over,' William echoed. He looked as dazed as she felt. 'Over. And we're together.'

She turned into his embrace and slid her arms around his neck. A small voice, her mother's voice, warned her against displaying so much partiality in public in front of people who knew her. What damage was she doing to her reputation? that voice asked. She ignored it, as she had ignored her father.

'Together forever,' she said.

They kissed, and kissed again, while all around them the world went mad with peace.

LIST OF ABBREVIATIONS

1AGH	Heliopolis Palace, the 1st Australian General Hospital
NZGH	New Zealand General Hospital
75 CCS	75 Casualty Clearing Station ('Clearing' meant that patients passed through but did not stay)
32 CCH	32nd Combined Clearing Hospital

ACKNOWLEDGEMENTS AND AUTHOR'S NOTE

As always, my thanks go to the fantastic editorial team at Hachette Australia – a joy to work with.

I would also like to thank Professor (Emeritus) Robert Anderson, of the School of History, Classics and Archaeology at The University of Edinburgh, for very kindly finding out for me how much it would have cost Evelyn to study there in 1919.

Thanks are also due to historian Kirsty Harris, whose book, *More Than Bombs and Bandages – Australian Army nurses at work in World War I*, was my chief resource for the actual, day-to-day nursing and operating procedures *The Desert Nurse* describes. It's a fascinating book based on contemporary accounts and interviews with WWI nurses, and I highly recommend it to anyone interested in further information about this era.

A posthumous thanks should also go to Sister Selina (Lil) Mackenzie, whose photographs of Heliopolis Palace and her fellow nurses added so much to my understanding, and description of, life there. You can find them at collections.museumvictoria.com.au/articles/3586 and the Australian War Memorial website. For those interested in knowing more about the women who nursed with the AANS, look at http://ww1nurses.gravesecrets.net

For those who are interested, the Arthur Freeman who appears in one section of this book was my grandfather (known always as Freemie) – it was his experiences which sparked my interest in WWI in the first place, and led to my first historical novel, *The Soldier's Wife* (where you can find out what happened to Jimmy and his Ruby when he went home).